I0553786

The Bones Dance Foxtrot

Second Skeleton Series Mystery

Donan Berg

Published by DOTDON Books

ISBN 13: 978-1-941244-07-4
ISBN 10: 1-941244-07-6

DOTDON Books are published by

DOTDON Personalized Services
514 17th Street
PO Box 1302
Moline IL 61266-1302

Order: http://www.abodytobones.com
E-mail: bergdonan@gmail.com
Author e-mail: mystery@abodytobones.com

Copyright © Donan B. McAuley 2009, 2015

Produced and/or printed in United States of America

Original Library of Congress Control Number: 2009903500

ISBN: 978-1-941244-07-4 (paperback)
ISBN: 978-1-941244-06-7 (e-book)

Second Printing: Revision January 2015
10 9 8 7 6 5 4 3 2

For ballroom dancers and community theater actors.

We all share life with special people be they grandparents, parents, spouses, brothers, sisters, sons, daughters, godchildren, cousins, nieces, nephews or friends.

In meaningful little ways, remember to say thank you to each of them. If you find my fictional story triggers a warm feeling, a happy heartbeat or a joyful recollection, I dedicate all the blissful moments to you and yours.

What others say:

The Bones Dance Foxtrot

"Five Stars. If you enjoy a good mystery with twists, turns, false leads, a little gambling, betrayal, clues left in the unlikeliest of places and a hidden stash of bank loot, then pick up a copy of The Bones Dance Foxtrot."

--Featheredquill Book Review

"Clues eventually fit together in clever and significant ways . . . dramatic tension builds around which woman Jake will pursue."

--National reviewer

Novels by Donan Berg

A Body To Bones
First Skeleton Series Mystery

The Bones Dance Foxtrot
Second Skeleton Series Mystery

Baby Bones
Third Skeleton Series Mystery

Abbey Burning Love

Adolph's Gold

Short Stories by Donan Berg

Bubbling Conflict and Other Stories

Amanda

Prologue

Jake Brown's big rig chrome rain cap popped and dropped. The cemetery's black wrought iron gate in his side mirror shrunk until he descended a West Virginia hill and it disappeared. With wife Athena's remains buried beneath fresh sod, her Bible lay rubber-banded on his Kenworth's passenger seat.

He loosened his knotted blue tie and undid the top button of his white shirt, its purchase receipt jammed yesterday into his wallet. Even though freed from the shirt collar's constraint, Jake's chafed neck continued to ache. He stretched its muscles left and right to no avail, needle pricks of pain merengued on reddened skin. His right hand smoothed his cherished tie across his insidious paunch. When worn fifteen years ago, it hung straight in front of his toned abs as he waited at the altar for the love of his life.

In Central Pennsylvania, a dark-haired stranger answered the door at Jake's brother's last address. With a child crying in the background, she said she didn't know a Wayne Brown.

As Jake piled up the westward miles on I-90, he counted himself a family of one. At a truck stop, he locked Athena's Bible into his cab and carried his strapped brown suitcase into a trucker's lounge. After a skimpy maroon towel wiped away the shower water that didn't splash at his feet, he hurled it into a canvas laundry cart. Comfortable in an open-necked blue plaid shirt and relaxed-fit blue jeans, he carried his funeral garb to a table facing a lounge wall. His hands trembled as he layered into his suitcase his black suit, white shirt, blue tie and spit-shined black oxfords, soles up.

"Perhaps you could escort me."

Jake whirled to his left. The woman's sparkling blue eyes outshined her sequined black ankle-length formal gown. He racked his brain until he succumbed to the conclusion he hadn't met the woman at any dance. The lounge, empty when he'd entered, had but a "truckers only" sign to enforce the rule. He slid his suitcase's two brass clasps closed and grabbed it to flee this beguiling truck-stop Lolita.

"Didn't mean to startle you." Jake struggled to decipher her plaintive words. "I'm at my wits' end. My Red Wing Trucking dispatcher ran out of options and my family answers no texts."

"You're putting me on?"

Her left hand reached for a black clutch purse. "Want me to show you a company ID or my CDL?"

Jake raised his suitcase, a shield to his burdened heart. "Red Wing, you say."

Her head, with its short-cropped black hair, bobbed twice.

"Ran into Red Wing driving twins south along the Blue Ridge last year. Recall last name Thompson. Know them?"

"Ray and Ryan. They're shooting the Rockies this week."

While Jake didn't cotton to peak climbing, as to Ray and Ryan, she was dead on. Jake's shoulders slumped and he let his left hand relax and release its suitcase grip. "Pleased to have met your acquaintance." He pivoted toward the exit. His suitcase swung and bumped his right hip without damage before he twisted his shoulders and head left. "When you see them, give them a shout out from Jake . . . Jake Brown."

"Nancy. Wait a minute, please."

She scurried around him and her nylon-covered feet skidded to a stop. Jake allowed his heels to stick to the linoleum.

She extended her hands, palms up. "I wasn't teasing. You could be my escort. That suit you packed would be perfect. My sister's getting married tonight and my International water pump busted a gasket. None available until tomorrow."

Jake lifted his gaze and chin to the ceiling's flickering fluorescent light. He suspected the harsh light, together with his droopy eyelids and matted brown hair, cast him as a zombie.

"Please, I won't bother you for a ride back."

Jake pondered being a Good Samaritan. His dispatcher didn't expect Jake's contact until the morning. "Only if you're going west with no gravel road detours." Jake's shoulders mimicked the Tower of Pisa when he thought she readied to hug him, or worse yet, plant a kiss. She didn't.

"Cleveland, Ohio."

"One condition."

"What?"

Jake shifted his body's weight to his left foot. "My offer's for a hitch; that's all. Ain't putting on no suit. Ain't sitting at no fancy family gathering."

"Deal. Want to shake on it?"

"No. Your word's good."

Three minutes later, Jake latched their travel bags into his empty fifty-three-foot trailer. Before he let Nancy hike her skirt and climb past the passenger door, he snatched Athena's Bible and tossed it onto his sleeper bunk's down-filled sleeping bag.

Small talk evaded him as he delighted in jammed gears and passed RVs. In his big rig's wake, a smorgasbord world of cities crawling up valley walls, roads circling mountains and flashing lights signaling tolls, accidents and speeding ambulances never acknowledged his existence, almost the same with Nancy. Their companionable silence broken, by his count, but thrice in two hundred miles.

One exit past Dead Man's Curve on the AMVETS Highway, Nancy alerted him to follow Cleveland's East Shoreway and pull off I-90 near Euclid where it and Ohio's co-signed State Route 2 separated. Parked on the shoulder next to rain-puddled asphalt, he and Nancy bade farewell. His fingers tapped his steering wheel as Nancy, overnight case in hand, tiptoed into the mist.

Dispatched first to central Indiana, Jake used the drone of his tires being ground into particle sized pollution to allay his grief. From the Midwest to the East Coast and south on I-95 to the Southeast, he zigzagged and backtracked with an abandon that numbed his mind and belied his trip log. He blasted his horn through thunderstorms, snow blizzards and steadied his front bumper against howling wind without precipitation. Fueling next to the Thompson twins's Red Wing semi, he forgot to ask about Nancy. Two truck stop Christmas meatloaf dinners had intervened since he had dropped her near a red Taurus.

No idle thought existed without Athena. On the road, his life's happiest memories featured Athena. They fluttered and waved through his mind like triangular pennants strung on unending roadside telephone lines along interstates and two-lane state highways.

Isolated from his emotional and spiritual anchor—Athena—Jake longed to jettison his heart's gloom and recapture what he had lost. The dark threatening clouds beyond his windshield forecast a bleak day in Paradise he needed to speed through.

A flashing red light and traffic to his right required he brake. It was then he noticed the new hand-painted, double-posted, four-foot wide sign. He stared at its top line: "Welcome to Paradise, Minnesota" before he dropped his gaze to the second line promise: "Where Fulfilled Dreams Begin."

Chapter One

"Excuse me." Jake throttled his impatience when the barkeep didn't jump to attention. "Where might I find Miss Hutchins?

The door poster said actors should apply inside." The young Afro-American male pointed his right hand to a woman seated near a stage, thirty feet to Jake's left.

Jake raised his eyebrows when the expected gray-haired theatrical matron lifted her younger than thirty-year-old brown eyes. Her faltering smile deflated his enthusiasm more than it crushed his stereotype of a playwright. Yet, after his admission of no prior stage credits, his laden eyes and weary heart must have triggered Director Emily Hutchins's sympathy.

Propelled by his desire to discover how his life should be reconstructed, he cast aside all doubt to say "yes." His commitment to be the fifth member of a Paradise, Minnesota, community theater ensemble wasn't open-ended. "I'll give it my best," he promised with the expectation he'd be on the road in six weeks.

Miss Hutchins displayed a re-energized smile. "I'm counting on you."

Jake inhaled twice to calm his trepidation.

"Be here tomorrow, five p.m. Since I own this place, The George Street Ballroom and Bar doubles as our rehearsal site."

On his third rehearsal day, the warmth of cast member handclaps gladdened Jake's heart as he lay prone on the stage floor. His left foot had tripped his right during his first scripted fall attempt, but five weeks remained to untangle his footwork. Above his head, painted flats awaited final brush strokes to fashion a frontier saloon. Jake's right hand fingers rubbed the contours of his left knee bruise, positive it would bloom purple. No broom pusher sweep of the unpadded, polished maple floor would discern the impact spot of his awkward spill.

"Bravo, Jake," Emily said. Her projected voice filled the ballroom. "Bob, Reverend, Patricia, Jacob, great job all. We'll resume same time tomorrow."

Dressed in an open-necked white shirt and black slacks, Actor Robert "Bob" Hunter, a.k.a, Tycoon, the gunslinger, offered Jake his right hand. Jake marveled at the speed in which Bob had packed his black Stetson, cowboy vest and string tie with the pearl clasp into a blue sports bag.

"You've convinced me you've faced a gun's barrel end before. Is that true?"

"I have." Aided by Bob's hand tug, Jake stood. "Fortunate for me, never met a straight shooter." Jake laughed. "How about you? Same question."

"Never have and don't want to either. Must go. My wife expects me home for supper on time tonight. I've been late all week. See you, Jake, same time tomorrow."

"Bye, Bob," Emily called out.

Bob waved and pivoted toward the ballroom's exit. He hastened to catch or pass Reverend Olson and Jacob.

Patricia's frilly rainbow-patterned blouse caught Jake's fancy. Its blues, reds and yellows hidden the entire rehearsal by a tailored gray pantsuit jacket. The colors, imprinted on his retinas, teased his brain as she hustled to catch Bob at the ballroom's Main Street exit.

"What are you thinking, Jake?" Emily asked. Her words uttered from behind him. "Worth the risk?"

"More captivating than yesterday," Jake murmured. He felt his cheeks warm. Emily, young enough to be a daughter he never had, had caught him immersed in a daydream about a departed Patricia. Lest his cheeks' redness expose his embarrassment, he counted to ten before he faced Emily. "Sorry. What did you say?"

Her dialogue dissection tone drilled into him. "Asked if you believed our theatrical play was worth the risk to join?"

His right hand tousled his brown hair. "I've struggled daily to make wise personal decisions. So far, it's great."

"A zillion miles off Broadway, the Spring Daisy Theatre ranks as my greatest passion, although the bar and dance income keeps the bank happy and gives me a place to live. If it weren't for the ballroom dancers that gather here Tuesday and Saturday nights, we'd have to close." As she sat on the stage's edge, Emily gazed wistfully at the roof that sheltered the bar, raised stage and maple ballroom dance floor. "Why choose Paradise?"

"To be honest . . . don't know." Jake plopped into Emily's canvas-backed director's chair opposite her, blanketed in comfort by her energetic smile. "Needed to ease my foot off the gas pedal. Been balling-the-jack night and day nonstop for two years." His gaze rested on the floor. His brain shifted into a mental idle. Until he forced a swallow, a lump in his throat throttled his lips from uttering any word. "Athena and I would've celebrated our seventeenth wedding anniversary last week, if she had not died two years ago." He bowed his head and indented his upper teeth into his lower lip as the image of Athena in a coffin paralyzed his brain. He raised his chin to force his lower right eyelid to keep the tear welling behind it trapped.

Emily reached out her right hand. When halfway to him, she retracted it. "I'm truly sorry to hear that." Her sympathetic gaze steady. "If you mentioned that the first day, it didn't register."

His lifted gaze locked onto hers. "Thanks. For the most part, I'm past the traumatic heartbreak and have learned to live with her . . . her memories." His left eye twitched. "Since February, I've wrestled with where to park my truck. To choose to keep my feet planted on the ground scared me."

Emily leaned forward until an arm's length separated them. Jake pushed his shirt's right sleeve past his elbow. His left-hand fingers then rubbed his left kneecap. He winced when his fingertips kneaded the adjacent exterior muscle.

"For three, maybe four, years after her breast cancer diagnosis, I cared the best I could for Athena. Blocked out the doctor's words that losing her would be inevitable. Disguised my tears with shower spray and saved a brave dry face for the woman I loved." He yanked a handkerchief from his rear jeans pocket, wiped his moist lower eyelids and dabbed the unfolded handkerchief to his cheeks. "After her funeral, I volunteered for every interstate haul. Drove until interchange lights, highway centerlines, diners, rest areas and truck-stop showers blurred into desperation. Grief ravaged my insides, still attacks."

When Emily's eyes glistened with unshed tears, he feared he'd prodded her to conjure up an unwarranted guilt. With her lip corners tugged by gravity, she leaned her stiff shoulders and erect head forward, her palms flush to her knees.

Jake balled his soiled handkerchief in his right hand and rested both on his right knee. His conscience's clarion call dared him not to sully Emily's pure mind to salve his own. "Over the years, Athena and I had been to the Paradise flourmill and Hofensteger's Brewery. A week ago, I revved my engine from Baltimore to your flourmill. Then completed a Hofensteger delivery to Minneapolis with a Wisconsin stop for a full trailer of preprinted flour sacks." Emily sighed. He bypassed the "Welcome to Paradise" as too gauche. "After unloading the sacks at the Paradise flourmill, I began to walk around. Direction didn't matter. Had no clue of what to do next."

"People who waggle their tongues at both ends say I wander aimlessly." Emily radiated kind empathy, not subtle mockery.

Jake cut short his failed smile attempt. "My dispatcher requested I hang loose a day while he worked through delayed and missed deliveries from a severe Kansas thunderstorm. I checked into the Mayflower Motel to shut out the world. After my first full night's sleep in three days, I called my dispatcher with the motel's switchboard number and lied that the flu demanded he not assign me a trip ticket until I called him." When a nervous fidget struck his fingers, Jake interlaced them.

A patient Emily crossed her legs at the ankle and let her folded hands rest in her lap. If she napped, she had him fooled.

"Many misinterpret an on-the-road life to be glamorous and high adventure, not so. Regardless, I entertain visions of being off the road, a regular family guy." Jake sighed. "Emily, I'm sorry to heap this on you. You're the first person I've told."

Emily pressed her lips together. Jake regretted he couldn't decipher if her mannerism bespoke good or disdain.

"Obviously, I'm glad you joined our acting group. And . . . I believe your fellow actors share my opinion."

Jake understood she evaded his implied question if she would help with or promote his goal to settle down. He stood and shifted his weight from left foot to right. If he circled around play questions, Emily might be stuck giving him an answer on his choice to keep his feet grounded. "Acting has been fun, except for today's awkward fall."

"I see you massage it. Maybe you need a doctor?"

"I'm positive I don't." Last thing he wanted was for Emily to feel sorry for him. No Wild West hero or desperado in a duel steadied his body with crutches. What he missed was a confidante like Athena. "Your listening provides the best cure."

Emily's hands weren't large enough to hide the overpopulation of red blood cells under her cheek skin. She did the next best thing by rising, stepping onto the stage and hiding her blush in stage cleanup. Jake tried to locate fifty-two scattered playing cards.

"All actors have been very nice," Jake said. "A mixture of contrasting personalities if you ask me." He eased onto all fours to sequence a clubs royal flush.

"Yes. Each actor's unique." Red blood cells drained from Emily's face and her skin reverted to its natural creamy coloration as she folded a round tablecloth. "Each one very skilled in their everyday occupation coupled with a willingness to experiment, to challenge their personal comfort zones or to portray a lifestyle not their own. For example, take Patricia." Jake's ears perked up. "On a normal day at work or home, she's a shy, unassuming person."

Jake stood in spurts. "You kid. Patricia walks in as a natural flirty frontier belle. Never in my wildest dreams would I believe she's shy and unassuming." Jake shuffled his gathered cards, set the deck on the stage bar and cut to a heart queen. Where's a draw like this when he holds an ace in real blackjack? Or is it an omen? The heart queen held a flower in her hand.

Emily's voice ended Jake's meandering dream. "She is, no lie. Here she wears contacts and unbraids her hair. As the Paradise librarian, she winds it up and fastens it tight with a clasp. She claims she needs her black-rimmed eyeglasses to read through stacks of book reviews and title summaries. I don't know. . . " Emily tossed toy six-shooters and holsters into a props box.

"I must be the oddball." He buried the queen in the deck. "I match both my character's physical characteristics and his script occupation because the overland stagecoach evolved into a truck. Can't carry my comparison to the foxtrot because it wasn't created, however, we both enjoy drinking beer."

Emily chuckled. "Jake, you have an interesting way of unfairly putting yourself down. You're not an oddball, at least not as far as I can tell in three days." Her right eye winked.

Jake's spirits soared with Emily's smile. He sauntered close enough to inhale a whiff of the grapefruit fragrance perched on her shoulders as the top of her head paralleled his chin. Whoa. He hadn't anticipated Emily's crossed arms, a nonverbal stop sign. That her hands rubbed the bare skin at her elbows, he attributed to his boldness. Perhaps her DNA nourished a shyness gene identical to Patricia's.

If he hadn't yet violated a town custom nobody had informed him of or irritated Emily beyond redemption, he needed to test the waters. "With no acting experience, you must have given me a chance because I can portray myself."

"Yes, all directors consider that." He slid his right foot rearward, followed by his left. Emily's shoulders slumped. "So far you've come across the footlights as honest." She clasped her hands in front of her well-defined waist. "That's the best clue to a successful actor. You might not be honest." Jake's eyebrows arched. "You could possess a hidden and dastardly background . . . or a secret motive. Three days is too short to know." Emily's eyes scanned Jake's face. "You may have searched for an unsuspecting and out-of-the-way town big enough to lie low in until the bloodhounds lost your scent."

Jake averted Emily's gaze. What had he started? If Emily thought he projected himself as Al Capone, what chance did he have of friendship with any woman, for example, Patricia? Jake, his hands at his sides, fisted both and then relaxed his fingers. "Have you written any plays yourself?"

"I'll admit I once wrote the required screenplay logline. And I received a polite, fancy-written literary agent rejection slip. I never knew if anyone even read it." Jake became puzzled when Emily again grabbed hold of her elbows. He hadn't inched nearer. "I gave up and contacted a publishing house to send me published plays suitable for three to six characters without dancing or singing. Audiences won't watch dancing chorus lines or singing quartets at the Spring Daisy Theatre."

Since Emily had endured his soul's unburdening, Jake subdued his dislike for small talk "While you may not recognize it, I bet a successful play lurks in your mind, and its words wait to flow onto paper and be discovered to light up Broadway."

Emily's cheeks radiated a light pink color, the corners of her mouth rose and her lips parted the width of a playing card. "Oh, I don't know." Her arms dropped to her sides and she gazed up into Jake's eyes. "You do flatter me though. With all the traveling you've done, I'd bet you've lived an interesting story yourself." Emily hesitated. Jake stood motionless. "If you'd hear me out, I have an idea for you."

"What?" Caught off guard, Jake scratched his left wrist to gain time. His mind alerted his muscles to be ready for flight. He'd never made two personal decisions in a three-day span.

"I'm a part-time school teacher." Emily's pride piggybacked on her words. "Sixth grade. If you gave me an hour's time, you could visit my class and answer student questions about what truck drivers do and maybe tell an amusing travel tale or two. We'll serve punch and cookies."

Jake shrugged. "Let me think about that some."

"Well, you can't think too long. School's out for summer vacation in six weeks, the Friday before Memorial Day."

Jake slid the cards into their box and tossed them into the props box. He couldn't offend Emily or shrug off her request. "I'll give you an answer soon, maybe tomorrow. Right now, I'd better follow Bob's lead and depart for supper." He ambled to the George Street exit, successful in his resolve not to glance back to determine if Emily watched him leave.

Patricia Swanson's right forefinger pushed her black-rimmed eyeglasses to the skin between her brows for a clearer focus on the catalog picture. The black lace strip atop the red brasserie cup with its black polka dots mimicked an emerging spring ladybug in all aspects but one. A ladybug's center didn't plunge to expose cleavage as wide as a high school boy's dream.

She tried to envision how either the tiny narrow over-the-shoulder straps or the string-like elastic straps, attached at the cup's bottom and fastened between her shoulder blades, would enhance her unpadded B-cup breasts. It could work, if not flimsy lingerie, but a demure bodice top. The colors fit in with a saloon belle costume for *Cowboy Boots Right Side Up.*

"Pardon me."

The male voice jarred her. She jerked her head right, toward the library's card catalog. She peered straight ahead and recognized the man introduced to her as Jake, the new-in-town cast member in *Cowboy.*

"In what aisle or under what reference number would I find the book you're reading?"

Embarrassment-warmed blood flamed from her cheeks to her forehead and stimulated all blood vessels in between. She maneuvered her left hand to cover the bra illustration until her right hand flipped the catalog closed. She fought off her urge to ask him to leave. In her library whisper, she asked "I'm sorry, what was that?"

"Came here to find a book."

What book? Why didn't he elevate his eyes? She always kept her pantsuit jacket buttoned while at work. Fear of the unknown circled the reference desk panels that protected her and her chair. A sly smile crept onto his lips.

Patricia glanced at where she expected his gaze landed. Her inhale congealed across her tongue to starve her lungs. She plastered her forearms to the catalog's back cover where a bra-and-panty-clad model, busty and leggy, graced the back cover no more modest than the inside black bra. *Aren't I a hypocrite.* Her friend Sarah last year had teased her with a similar gift of tiger-striped lingerie for her thirty-fifth birthday. *No, I'm not.* Haven't worn Sarah's gift and it'll stay hidden in the bedroom dresser's bottom drawer.

Patricia sat erect to reclaim her dignity. While her forearms slipped off the catalog, she left her left palm at the model's waist. Her right hand tugged make-believe wrinkles out of her favorite tailored gray pantsuit jacket with its high-buttoned blouse she'd worn earlier to rehearsal.

"Didn't . . . didn't intend to tease. I'm sorry. My name's Jake, Jake Brown. Emily introduced us at play rehearsal." Jake scratched his left wrist. "Didn't know until I saw you sit behind this desk that you were the reference librarian."

"That's okay." The warmth in Patricia's cheeks died out.

"You work every night after rehearsal?"

"Do on Thursdays to allow the reference employee time for supper. We're open extended hours until eight p.m. during the school year." Patricia chided herself for being too chatty. The catalog paper beneath her left palm stuck to her sweaty skin.

With his right hand, Jake pointed to the far side of the computer row. "I was over there. After I summoned up enough courage—" Jake gazed to where he pointed.

Patricia slid the lingerie catalog right, under a large atlas. Jake mumbled, "Again, I'm sorry."

The thud of a book to her left broke their silence. Patricia uttered a hushed: "Is there a book I can help you find?" Her shoulders tensed when he placed his right hand on the reference desk counter. Her eyes flitted to his face.

"Yes . . . yes, there is." He drummed his right hand fingers.

Patricia forced herself not to call out: "What book?" Politeness coaxed her to ask softly: "Does it have a name?" To lessen her edginess, she hitched her chair a foot from the desktop. Her gaze lingered, fixed on his callused hand.

"Do you . . . I mean, does this library have any history books on Paradise or biographies of original settlers?"

"Only one. Two years ago the city celebrated its centennial. A committee comprised of townspeople interviewed or collected articles written by prominent individuals. The stories detailed recollections of either town settlement or homesteading in Paradise County. Our reference—"

Jake's fingernails struck the desk's mahogany to increase the timber of his prior rhythmic finger taps.

Her concentration lost, Patricia started again. "Our reference section has a copy. When behind the computer cubicles, you were standing near it. Find a long wooden plank table with eight chairs and you're in the right place. Search the wall shelf for the book entitled *Welcome to Paradise.*"

"Thank you." Jake's right hand paused twelve inches above the desk. "Would it be possible for us to sit and talk sometime?"

Her desk telephone rang. Patricia raised her right hand's index finger. She answered the caller's question and returned her attention to Jake. "Here's not—" Patricia's lips, stung by her right hand palm smack, refused to let her street voice disturb library patrons. She slid her hand to her throat. Her Adam's apple bobbed when she whispered, "Here's not good now."

"Understand. I'll see you tomorrow at rehearsal."

Patricia exhaled to a measured andante musical count. At the count of eight, confident Jake had reached the reference section, she rose from her chair and glanced left and right. Convinced the coast clear, she dashed, with the lingerie catalog tucked inside the atlas, to her library director's office.

Relaxed, she carried the atlas, sans catalog, to the reference desk.

Unable to find *Welcome to Paradise,* Jake flipped pages in a cancer reference book until frustrated by the medical words he couldn't pronounce or define. Unable to add new information, his mind dwelled on a mental visual of Patricia's frilly, multi-colored blouse he'd seen at rehearsal, not the monochromatic color slice above a buttoned pant suit jacket worn at a library desk. For hair style, Jake preferred Patricia's sexier saloon belle style to the tight bun on the top of her head. Her black eyeglass frames or contacts were inconsequential as long as her blue eyes provided him a glimpse into her soul.

Footfalls of a tall lanky sedate man in a khaki uniform interrupted Jake's daydream. His eye roll stopped by a shiny Paradise Police badge pinned to the man's left breast pocket. A right pocket nametag read: Sergeant Roger Smyth.

The officer's curt voice asked, "You Mr. Jake Brown?"

"Yes, sir." Without rising from his chair, Jake squared his shoulders. He trusted his instinct to be polite. "What can I do for you?" The officer's right hand fingers patted the butt of his

18

holstered revolver.

"Is that your semi-trailer truck parked at the Mayflower?"

"Yes." Jake slipped a paper scrap into the cancer book.

"Let's go. There are a few questions about you and your truck." His right forefinger pointed at the door. "Now."

Jake rose. "I'll follow you."

"No. I'll follow you."

"Okay." Jake gulped when, on the library steps, the officer's handcuffs rattled. "Can you tell me what this is about?"

"Keep walking. Stop at my squad's rear door."

Jake did. No other vehicle was parked on the street he knew as George Street. He stared through the mesh that separated him from Sgt. Smyth nestled in the driver's seat. Was their real destination to be the Mayflower Motel?

Patricia's gaze skittered past the top of the computer cubicles. Sgt. Smyth's library entrance unleashed a gastrointestinal queasiness she controlled with closed eyes and five seconds of willed concentration. She disliked her choices: risk a headache or play a game of hide and seek in the stacks. When he hesitated a step inside the entry, she kneeled behind the reference desk counter before his eyeballs rotated her way. Patricia constricted her breathing until her lungs hurt. Aisle footfalls faded.

Without a force field to divert him, Patricia dreaded standing. She did and a glimmer of hope surfaced. She exhaled into her cupped hands as Roger strutted to the reference section table where Jake sat with his head bowed and his finger tracing a book's page. Neither Sgt. Smyth's words, nor Jake's reply, were loud enough for her to discern. She executed her plan to circle the reference desk, not bold enough to stride to the card catalog or sit in a computer cubicle. *Why did Roger's hand grip his revolver?*

Patricia retreated two steps without the slightest inkling why Roger abandoned his routine to seek her out and marched Jake out the library's front door. Jake's wrists weren't cuffed.

A left shoulder tap from behind spooked her. She whirled. Kate Newark in a Sadie's Friendly Home Town Diner cook's uniform unleashed a transparent playful smile. Patricia's breath escaped in a long, slow whoosh.

"What was that all about?" Kate asked.

"Have no clue." Patricia pressed her right forefinger along both eyebrows before her right hand's second finger pushed her eyeglasses closer to her eyes.

Kate tucked a book under her left arm. "When I came to the end of the cookbook aisle, Roger was at the reference table speaking to a guy I didn't recognize."

With her emotions unanchored, Patricia glanced over her right shoulder with the unexpressed hope Sgt. Smyth hadn't reappeared. "Did you hear any of what was said?"

"Something about a truck. I couldn't stomp into the conversation or appear nosey. You know how Roger can be."

Patricia raised her upper eyelids and snapped, "Unfortunately only too well."

"You and Roger going out socially, yet?"

Patricia suppressed her sarcastic retort to Kate's incredulous comment. *How could Kate, an intelligent woman, ignore her facial disapproval of Roger?*

"Told him long ago he should stop asking." Patricia crossed her right hand fingers that her snippy tone, coupled with renewed facial muscle tenseness, drove home to Kate her strongest wish: stop asking.

"I hear lots of diner gossip." Kate's right hand grabbed the recipe book clamped to her left side by a bent elbow and laid it on the reference desk. "You shouldn't listen to backbiters who claim I've loose lips. I don't wag my tongue at both ends nor spread tall tales about friends. What, may I ask, has he done?"

Before it tumbled from her lips, Patricia tried to coat her lie with sincerity. "Oh, nothing. Let's only say he's eight years younger than me. That's too big a difference."

"Maybe not. He looks virile."

Patricia shook her head at Kate's inconceivable lack of ability to grab hold of her expressed reality.

As Kate stood poised to contemplate additional words, the intensity in Kate's eyes softened. "While menopause awaits me, beware, your body's maternal clock is ticking."

Patricia shrugged. With a polite nod now and then, she listened to Kate prattle on for she understood her friend would shut up quicker if left uninterrupted.

"He has a decent job. I understand from diner conversation he became a police sergeant in record time. He's good looking, never married. If he wants, he may well own his parents' farm south of town in a few years." Kate didn't seem to notice Patricia's right hand cover her yawn. "His two sisters, one older, one younger, have left home, never returning after college. Heard the younger one eloped with a fella last year to live in a California commune. You know, you could do worse."

"I'll not be doing with him." Patricia's sharp reply surprised even herself. "Thank you very much."

"Forget I ever mentioned Roger." Kate snatched her book from the reference desk. "For myself, I'd be happy to find any man who loved dancing to big band music." Kate waved to one of three ladies in the checkout line.

"Have a great evening." Patricia attempted a smile. She understood that Kate, when flitting between her diner's breakfast customers tomorrow morning, would pry loose the nitty-gritty of any dramatic happening within Paradise or with Sgt. Smyth. Kate always did.

A Mayflower Motel sign cast a shadow across the hood of Sgt. Roger Smyth's Paradise Police patrol car. Jake questioned why park here. The silence broken by the click of his rear door. Jake breathed in the humid evening air. Where could he run to? No onlookers gathered to aid his escape.

Jake strode to the motel's rear parking lot escorted by Sgt. Smyth. At least the officer hadn't pulled his revolver.

Sgt. Smyth commanded, "Unlatch the trailer."

"No problem. The trailer's empty. See for yourself." Jake swung the rear double-latched doors of his fifty-three foot trailer wide and stood to the right.

"Stand farther back," Smyth ordered. "Is that your white tarp spread out at the front?"

Jake shielded his eyes with his cupped left hand. With the sun's final rays blocked, he crouched and gazed into his trailer's dim interior. "Never saw it before."

Smyth grabbed Jake's right arm. "Step this way, Mr. Brown. Now nice and easy, put your hands behind your back." Jake complied. "Shuffle this way so your back's flush against this trailer door and hold still. I'm placing your right wrist in one handcuff and will thread the other through the trailer's locking rod. No funny business. Raise your hands so I can secure your left wrist."

Unexpected by Jake, Smyth yanked Jake's arms. A sharp right shoulder pain caused him to wince. Forced to face his cab, Jake's clothed shoulder blades rubbed against the outside of the now swung open rear trailer door. Jake visualized rodeo calves' legs tied in a natural, extended position. He muttered, "Roped calves obtain more humane treatment."

"What's that?" Jake's right shoulder absorbed the slight pressure of the sergeant's forward lean. "When I told you to stay put, that meant for you to keep your mouth shut."

Jake glared straight ahead. *Bastard.*

He listened to Smyth rattle the trailer's opposite door before footsteps, he assumed were the sergeant's, creak the trailer's plywood floor.

Smyth called out. "Mr. Brown, did you say you never left a painter's tarp in here?"

"Never." Jake shouted in reply. *Idiotic morons lived lives with better sense.* His covered, four-sided box trailer, like all others, needed to neither haul nor strap down cargo tarps.

Sgt. Smyth tugged tan leather driving gloves from his khaki uniform's rear pocket. Three steps from the headwall, he donned his gloves and crouched so as allow light entering the trailer streak across the tarp. His extended right hand lifted the nearest end of the paint-splattered, heavy-grade tarp.

Smyth jerked his right hand away and toppled backward. A swarm of dipteran flies targeted his horizontal neck and unguarded face. He clamped his lips tight. While his right palm aided his scramble to his feet, his left hand swatted blow-flies.

The anonymous tipster had been right. The Mayflower Motel truck trailer hauled a person—a dead person.

His left hand swats continued to protect his face as he lowered his body and steadied himself on his right knee. His right hand slow motion tarp lift gave him a glimpse of the corpse's bloated and bluish face.

His elongated calf and thigh muscles pushed him erect as he lifted the tarp higher. While gold chains were commonplace, he thought he recognized the victim's necklace.

He gasped for breath and swallowed a gulp of the trailer's putrid stench. The clammy air seeped through the weave of his clothes. With the calculation he could with ease secure the scene, he dropped the tarp onto the battered victim. A trace of white powder adhered to his glove's tan fingertips.

When he reached the trailer's open doors, he heard Jake Brown call out, "So what's with that tarp?"

Smyth jumped out of the trailer and stared at his suspect. "Don't play me for a fool. You know damn well what's under that tarp. We caught you red-handed. Lucky we investigated before you left town or drove to the river."

"Officer, I own no tarp and haven't opened my trailer box since my unloading at the flourmill three days ago. And that's the truth."

"You're under arrest, suspicion of murder. Don't wiggle." Smyth savored the euphoria that would be forthcoming, especially from The Chief and influential Paradise citizens.

"Why don't you listen? I didn't do anything. I'm innocent."

Smyth reached behind his suspect's back to test the holding power of his applied handcuffs.

"Where do you think I'm going? I ain't Houdini."

Smyth shook his head. "You wise guys are all the same. Step back slow and easy before I close this trailer door and you won't be hurt. Also, shut your smart mouth."

When his suspect hesitated, Smyth shouted a repeat of his step-back order. For encouragement, he added a left shoulder hand shove. He latched the semi's trailer door with this Mr. Brown still handcuffed to it.

By use of the mike clipped to his shoulder, Sgt. Smyth radioed the police dispatcher for assistance and to record of his moment of glory. In the fading daylight, he paced the length of the trailer ten, fifteen, then twenty minutes before he heard tires brake on asphalt. When a vehicle door slammed, Smyth stepped away from the trailer. His pulse quickened when he recognized the squad car door with the word "Chief" painted above "Paradise Police."

When Jake, both arms aching from shoulders to wrists, heard "how-dee," he groaned after a futile attempt to catch a glimpse of the speaker.

Sharp gray eyes devoid of emotion stared at him. "New in town, are we?" asked the elder gentleman in a white tailored shirt that bulged at the abdomen. His deep-blue trousers sported a crease sharp enough to slice butter.

"Yes, sir. Why treat me like this? The flourmill dockworker closed my trailer when he finished unloading their pallets." Jake squinted, unable to see an officer's nametag. His voice trailed off. "Haven't unlatched it since."

"What's the name of the individual in your trailer?"

"Don't know of any person in my trailer." Jake strained to remember the dockworker's name. When he couldn't, he struggled to recall the mill foreman's name. He came up empty and exhausted. Now his mind ached.

"Don't you lock your trailer?" The elder officer's right hand stroked his chin.

Jake didn't know if the chin gesture signaled Sgt. Smyth. Regardless, Jake vowed to himself he would, sooner or later, rub the smirk directed at him off the sergeant's face. "Always when loaded. But never empty. Why lose a lock or have someone damage the trailer doors when there's nothing to steal?" Jake watched two male spectators, twenty yards away, edge along a cyclone fence on the parking lot's perimeter.

The unintroduced officer extended his right hand, palm up. "I'm impounding your truck as evidence. Be cooperative and

24

hand me all your truck keys."

"You need to release me. They're in my jeans pocket."

The elder officer nodded to Sgt. Smyth. While Jake moaned and squirmed, the sergeant dug deep into Jake's right front jeans pocket to pull out a key ring.

"And, my name's Chief Coltraine. You'll be occupying one of my vacant cells. In case you have an accomplice, the sergeant here will add our departmental locks to your trailer. We'll also detail a patrol car to drive by regularly."

Again in Smyth's squad, Jake's right hand fingers tried to scratch his left wrist and failed. *Athena, I'm following your advice. What have I done wrong?*

Chapter Two

When Jake's handcuffs jingled the next morning in front of his stomach, he praised his jailer for the kindness. His downcast eyes found little cheer in the leg shackles. They restricted his jail corridor stride to a duck waddle.

At the end of his fifty-foot cell-to-courtroom journey. Jake complained to his escort bailiff.

"It's what the law requires," the jailer said gruffly.

Jake wasn't surprised that beyond the courtroom door existed a room cramped and stuffy. It, like his cell, existed in the basement underbelly of the Paradise police station. Uncertain of what he should do, Jake waited until the bailiff's arms wedged a separation between two men in a line. He then shuffled forward, pulled by his handcuffs, to fill the created space. After the man to his left jostled him, Jake retaliated with a left shoulder nudge. The bailiff cautioned all to stand straight and be quiet. He then disappeared beyond the door Jake entered.

To his left, Jake counted three men in orange jumpsuits and a ramrod straight man in a charcoal-gray suit. The man, square-jawed and not restrained in steel, held a list. Jake clenched and unclenched his fists. He squared his shoulders, not as an affront to society, but to project his dignity. He refused to stare at the courtroom's painted-gray concrete, chilly to his soles.

A stiff, stern-faced, black-robed judge seated behind an elevated judicial bench nodded to the gray-suited man. "Take Jones, Anderson and Stevens to the prison van," the judge said. With a stolid expression, the square-jawed man escorted, one-by-one, all three orange-clad men to Jake's left out of the courtroom. Jake didn't want to go to prison. Yet, he was next.

"Next," shouted a gray-haired woman seated below and to the right of the judge. In a staccato voice, she intoned, "State of Minnesota versus Jake no-middle-name Brown, felony case number 09-431. First appearance." The list-man touched Jake's left elbow and urged Jake forward. Jake twisted his neck left to read the wall clock: nine twenty-three a.m.

"Here he is, Judge." The list-man this time tugged Jake's left elbow. Jake waddled four short steps and tilted his face upward to permit his eyes to focus on the judge.

"Good morning, Mr. Brown," welcomed the judge, his voice sonorous. "Let's see why you're here." Jake pressed his lips and his knees together as he watched the judge flip white paper pages and then continue. "Says here you're charged with the multiple felonies of assault, assault with a deadly weapon, battery and concealing a felony or felonies." The judge recited several sections of what he referred to as the state criminal code, none of which Jake's memory retained. "These are very serious charges against you." The judge's stare weighed on Jake. "Do you understand what the state is saying?"

"Somewhat, Your Honor." His voice sounded nasal. "I did nothing wrong." A cold shiver rasped his nerves. His psyche struggled to grab the nonexistent safety bar in this unfamiliar world of legal jargon and physical restraint. His heart raced.

Both knees wobbled like jelled cranberries.

Alone, without a steel-cab world to protect him, he feared collapse. Strange pale faces with black eye sockets and heinous grins gawked at him from every direction. The identical images, no matter the speed or duration of his squirms or rollovers on the jail's thin mattress, had filled his last night's dreams. He shuddered. Today the people were real.

The judge glanced at the list-man and then returned his gaze to Jake. "Later, but not this morning, you'll be asked to plead guilty or not guilty. Have you hired a lawyer?"

"No, sir." Jake closed his eyes. His attempt to excise the demons from his mind failed.

The judge waited while a crowd murmur rose and died. "Since you're being charged with crimes that could imprison you in the Department of Corrections for more than a year, you're entitled to a public defender if you can't afford to hire private counsel. You employed, Mr. Brown?"

"I drive an independent, over-the-road, tractor-trailer rig. Dispatched by Magnum Trucking out of Cincinnati."

"You own any property?"

"Just my truck, sir." The judge wrote a note. "The police confiscated my truck keys yesterday." Jake's voice wavered.

"Any checking, savings or other money account?"

"No, I use a company account check or credit voucher when I need to fill up. To pay other expenses, I get cash advances at company terminals." He fought tears when he remembered Athena. "One bank holds trust money from when my wife passed away two years ago."

"The clerk will give you a form to fill out to verify what you're now saying. A public defender may visit you today or tomorrow." The judge closed Jake's file. "Do you have any questions?"

Jake coughed to clear his throat. "What's my bail?" Perspiration he couldn't wipe chilled his forehead. His heart pounded ribs at the force and cadence of a jackhammer. "If I can call the bank or a friend, how much money do I need?"

The judge reopened Jake's file. "Weighing the pending charges, that the police department impounded your truck and there's listed no prior criminal record, your bail's set at $250,000.00 with ten percent bond. Next."

The escort bailiff stepped forward and clasped Jake's left forearm. Warm breath invaded Jake's left ear. The bailiff whispered, "You're lucky the young prosecutor over there didn't object to the judge's bail." Jake resisted the first tug of his left arm by the unseen hand. A "Let's go." order by the bailiff propelled his waddle toward the courtroom's jail exit.

"Don't feel lucky. Can I make a phone call?"

Jake's eyes caught the bailiff's right head rotation without a verbal response. Jake let his shoulders slump as he slid his jail-issued flip-flops across the jail corridor's concrete floor. His chin rub against his right shoulder dried a tear caught by his unshaven stubble. He again thought of Athena, A tear freed itself from his lower left eyelid and trickled across his cheek.

Halfway to his cell, the bailiff said, "You can make collect calls from the interview room at the end of this hall. If no one's there, you can do it now."

Jake nodded. The unoccupied interview room raised a sliver of hope his luck had changed. He utilized directory assistance to contact Third Bank in Riverdale, Connecticut. After Jake explained what the judge said, he learned he needed ten percent of $250,000.00 or $25,000.00 cash with all $250,000.00 owed should he skip any scheduled future court date. He pressed the earpiece to his right ear as the bank official outlined that he was authorizing a one-time emergency withdrawal. To show his gratitude to Athena's spirit for the financial lifeline, he mouthed a "thank you" to the gray ceiling tile.

While the bailiff gave the bank officer the court's address to wire $25,000.00 via Western Union, Jake prayed that no impediment but processing time blocked his freedom.

Chief Robert Peter (R.P.) Coltraine, in his second floor police station office, two floors above the temporary arraignment courtroom, skimmed Sgt. Smyth's laudatory Thursday night patrol log entry recounting his Mayflower Motel arrest.

The Chief fidgeted with Doc Beck's skimpy medical report,

troubled that the coroner had pronounced death without affixing a cause. Where the truck had been parked also unsettled him for investigative reasons. The Mayflower Motel wing between it and the well-traveled east-to-west Main Street limited direct observation. The opposite problem existed with the adjacent machine shop visitor lot to the south. A three-foot high wire mesh fence allowed no privacy and precious little motel parking lot security. Thursday he had shooed six or seven curiosity seekers. Two, with officers in the trailer, had jumped the wire fence and had raised the cab's hood to steal pawnable parts.

While convinced the state crime lab would confirm his unexpressed conclusion of a homicide, his decades of experience cautioned him to take nothing for granted. At the scene, he had agreed with Sgt. Smyth the victim's head and throat lacerations and stomach contusions appeared not to have been inflicted postmortem.

His glance through a street-side window spotted the white state CID van. The Chief closed the file and hustled downstairs. When he arrived at the sidewalk, the van was parked. "Len, Bob, how are you two this morning? My knee predicts rain."

The athletic and matter-of-fact Len asked, "Where's this tractor-trailer?"

Bob shrugged. The Chief preferred to share a beer with the gap-toothed and pudgy Bob, but ten a.m. and Len's sour face said he shouldn't suggest it. "Parked behind the Mayflower on Main." His right hand extended a key ring. "Here's the keys."

Len nodded, pocketed the keys and led cohort Bob to the white Criminal Investigation Division van with its official state license plates.

The Chief called after them, "Report as quick as you can."

At the Mayflower's rear parking lot, the cab door with "JB Trucking" printed in white surrounded by red identified for Len the truck they sought. A second positive sign was that he could unlock the cab for Bob before he began a systemic examination of the big rig's exterior.

Within ten minutes, Len had reached the trailer's rear doors and grabbed his pen and notepad to record Bob's findings. "Cab and sleeping compartment gave up but a cell phone, which I've bagged. Lifted a few prints when spot-dusting the steering wheel and the interior door handles. Do the wheels and undercarriage hint at where this truck's been?"

"Nothing except dirt accumulation, and very little of that. Either the driver washed the trailer nearby or it's been driven on paved highways. No sign it's been moved in three or four days." Len asked a gawker with a suitcase to move on.

Bob's crime kit clasps rattled until he set it on the asphalt. "Found no possible weapon, nor blood stains or contraband in the cab. What need I do to help you with the box?" He popped a mint into his mouth.

"Check those fastening straps on its inside right. I've already taken the wide-angle evidence pictures." Len, accustomed to Bob's race-ahead speed, refused to abandon his measured style, fearful he'd miss something important.

Len unclipped a spray bottle from his right hip. He sprayed Luminol at the half dozen dark stains he suspected to be human blood. Those on the trailer's plywood floor near the tarp intrigued him. Two spots, each four to six inches in diameter, earned his undivided attention. The rest, from a miniscule drop to a dime-sized spot, he logged with professional, if not enthusiastic, interest.

He rolled clean evidence-vial swabs into each large blood site. His intuition categorized his collected samples to be from passive blood stains caused by gravity. He cursed under his breath that some idiot had double-folded the tarp and laid it next to the headwall. For the time being, he left it undisturbed.

With tweezers he picked up small wood splinters, a one-centimeter strip of paper caught and lost from the wire spiral of a notebook and other small papers including a gum wrapper. He placed all items in separate three-by-four inch evidence sleeves obtained from his kit.

Uneasy about the disturbed tarp, he backpedaled three steps to click supplemental photos, each angled to avoid the flash's reflective glare or created shadow. Bob joined him.

"Not much blood, is there?" Bob mumbled. "Anyone tell you if our victim was male or female?"

"Dispatch didn't. One short dark hair strand I found without its root wouldn't tell us a blessed thing." Len stacked his sealed evidence envelopes into his kit. "You find any blood on the sidewall, straps or any non-floor surface?"

"None." Bob reached into his front pocket, but his right hand emerged empty. "What's that chalky dust on the tarp?"

"Your guess better than mine. I'll swab it and the forensic tech can graph its characteristics. Suspect it's cement or dried paint pigment."

Len glanced at his wristwatch, picked up his kit and motioned Bob to the trailer doors. "Watch out for drag marks."

Bob gazed at the floor as he strolled. "This entire trailer sports multiple and varied nicks and gouges. Shifting cargo or inattentive forklift drivers could account for any or all."

Len caught Bob's arm. "Wasn't looking for a nick or a gouge, but a long scratch, scrape or black rubber heel mark."

Bob crouched to scan the trailer's floor with a penlight. "Can't isolate anything even close to drag marks."

"Neither do I. The lack of drag evidence points to the victim being wrapped in that tarp and carried the trailer's length."

"Would you agree that the victim's wounds had to have been fresh to seep or ooze blood?" Len nodded. "That's my conclusion, too. Also, no blunt force trauma blow struck inside the trailer or else we'd have splattered, not pooled, blood."

"But if the body's wrapped, isn't it strange to have blood outside a moisture-resistant tarp?"

Bob's right hand scratched his ear. "Either the coroner allowed blood to drip or whoever carried the body dropped the tarp and the body rolled out. Either way, the victim's toted forty to fifty feet." Bob's right eye twinkled. "Suggests a muscular killer or maybe a killer with two or more helpers."

"Excellent points. Keep me on my toes and I might approve your raise." Len flashed his full set of teeth.

Bob gave Len a two-thumbs up.

"You notice usable shoe treads?" Bob shook his head no. "I

didn't either. Hardened asphalt creates dead ends. Let's leave our kits and bring out that tarp. We'll do the microscopic exam in the lab while we wait for the blood and print sample results."

Len led Bob into the trailer where they wrapped the tarp in plastic and loaded it into their van. When finished, Len turned to Bob. "Let me radio Chief Coltraine."

"Chief, Len here. Bob and I have finished the initial semi collection, both cab and trailer. So far, nothing earth-shattering. We're transporting the white tarp to the lab along with several blood and trace samples. You can expect our report by normal channels. We've locked the vehicle."

The Chief tamped fresh tobacco into the pipe bowl his left hand cradled. He struck and blew out a lit wooden match, annoyed by Minnesota's six-month-old public building anti-smoking law. Nevertheless, he sat pleased, surrounded by his prized office furnishings, with the exception of a corner cabinet and his old desk. It couldn't fit in a Paradise office one-third the square footage of his prior Ohio office. After thirty years and six moving van transports, he expected his professional law enforcement career to end in Paradise.

His private line rang. "Yes, dear. I'll remember we're having neighbors for dinner tonight. My love, too."

He loved to tease Roberta, his second wife, that, if he stayed home as much as she craved, he'd lose his tan. He lost his point and had to admit she was right when she countered his workaholic office hours weren't under a sunlamp.

More than Roberta's wishes motivated him, he had to assuage twenty years of guilt. When his first wife, Helen, and their daughter, Catherine, died in a fiery auto collision with an escaping felon in 1989, he sobbed until an IV was required to hydrate him. Yet, his sobs didn't cleanse his chagrin that his work mania cheated them and him. While his passion to bring criminals to justice intensified, his empathy for innocent crime victims blossomed.

After Helen's and Catherine's tragic deaths, he forced himself to spend more time with family and friends. Part of his life never changed. He still abhorred planting spring flowers, pulling summer dandelions and shoveling winter snow, and, in all seasons, washing dishes. He, without shame or hesitation, bored his neighbors with his not-to-do list. However, without protest, he escorted Roberta to Sunday church services at Paradise's First Lutheran Church.

A second telephone ring interrupted his reverie.

"Councilman, thanks for your support. I'm game to recast our crime figures to convince your colleagues this department needs one more patrol officer."

Despite the caller's enthusiasm for him to try again, The Chief wasn't inclined to ignite additional criticism of his "spendthrift" ideas. After his 4-to-1 defeat, the representatives of the city's 5,029 residents had voted to remodel the station's basement storeroom to create one cell for an arrested female. This cell to supplement the three existing cells, which, when fully occupied, housed five males. The city auditor had convinced the council of the new cell's payback by its elimination of the present expense to transport each female arrestee to the county jail. At the same time, the city built the small basement courtroom, also to pinch pennies. As a result, the council majority reasoned that the no longer needed prisoner transport duty increased the patrol time of the existing three officers: a lieutenant, a sergeant and a patrolman.

The Chief tried to find a folder and shook his head in frustration. He bemoaned the fact his present desk lacked a clear spot for one additional report stack when his old, larger-than-normal desk collected dust in offsite storage. While his favorite dark oak chair didn't match the Paradise-provided blonde-oak desk, he swiveled in his beloved desk chair. Its beefed up leather cushion, chosen by Helen, made him appear taller.

An additional officer remained his goal. With his distrust of computers, he started a fresh notebook to record the facts that would eventually close his Mayflower Motel murder. In the process, he'd succeed in hiring an additional officer.

Jake paced and sat alone in his two-person cell. Able to choose his desired upper bunk, he rated the benefit—whoop-dee-do.

"Mr. Brown," called out the jail guard. Jake jumped off his high bunk ecstatic that his bail money arrived.

A baritone voice echoed. "How's the Mrs., James, James?"

Jake hadn't summoned a minister. He tried to recall the name of the one who was a fellow play actor and his mind went blank.

The guard, who had served as his court bailiff, motioned him away from the bars. Jake hopped onto his top bunk and the guard unlocked Jake's cell door. Shame seized Jake for he recognized the face above the entering black suit and clerical collar. The guard relocked Jake's cell door. Jake racked his brain while he apologized: "Wish I could offer you a chair."

"No problem." The minister's shoulder blades leaned against the door's bars. "In case you don't remember, I'm Reverend John Olson of First Presbyterian Church."

Jake extended his right hand. "Do admit your name escaped me." His legs dangled from the upper bunk.

After two steps forward, the minister's firm grip pumped Jake's hand twice. "Please don't be concerned with names. Jails fog and erase memories. Earlier today, when speaking with Jacob Cummings, he said you'd been arrested. He's also in the play along with Bob Hunter and Patricia Swanson."

Jake, pleased the reverend triggered his memory, asked, "Is Jacob the guy who works at the refrigerator plant and talks about dancing at the B&B?"

"Correct."

Pleased he had recalled a local slang term for the George Street Ballroom and Bar, Jake noticed Rev. Olson's left hand clutched a Bible. He drew in a deep breath as his eyelids drooped. How could he explain, without sounding insincere, that he had joined the acting troupe on a whim and by his second day elated to be welcomed as a full-time cast member.

"I don't know your religious preference, or if you'd ever consider First Presbyterian, yet, with you being new in town, I hoped a visit could comfort. Every cast member has expressed concern about your welfare."

"Not been much of a church-goer." Nostalgia saddened him.

Athena had laughed when he, reading Bible passages to her as she drove, mispronounced Old Testament names. "But humbled you created time to visit. Even if not Presbyterian, I'll join you in a prayer."

Rev. Olson spread his Bible pages to a marked passage. Jake bowed his head and listened to the minister's deep baritone extolled the virtues of forgiveness and love. Rev. Olson, his left index finger pressed to a Bible page, raised his eyes to Jake. "Keep your spirits high. I'll be expecting you soon at rehearsal and don't forget our church door is open for you, too." He rattled the cell door and called out, "James, I'm ready to go." He gazed at Jake and whispered, "He attends my church."

Jake had never been in a situation where the lives of others intertwined so. Athena had longed for it, but they had sacrificed the outside community for each other and their dream of a financially secure retirement. He knuckled under to share her excitement to live near her Arkansas son and enjoy her expected grandkids, ones to substitute for theirs. Jake jumped off his bunk. Behind bars, he couldn't allow his fondness for a grandfather's life, at least twenty years away, to add agony to his subconscious depression.

A noisy key jangle escalating in volume apprised Jake that James responded by deed, not word.

From the corridor, the guard said, "Mr. Brown, the court has verified the bank wired your bail." Rev. Olson pivoted his body toward Jake and smiled. James paused with a key in the cell lock. "Pastor John, you'll have to depart first. You can wait for Mr. Brown upstairs in the lobby." The minister nodded.

"Certainly." The reverend closed his Bible. "I'll go now." He twisted his face to Jake. "I'll meet you where James said."

With that, the guard unlocked the cell door and escorted Rev. Olson, in an unhurried gait, toward the cell block door.

Jake, sprung from his cell, resisted his urge to sprint to freedom. James led him to an upstairs office where Jake skimmed and set on the table his copy of a form advising him of his next court date. He pawed through the items James poured from an envelope. His truck keys weren't among his wallet, belt, shoelaces, socks, coins, comb, pocketknife and motel key. He asked about his truck keys and his cell phone.

James shrugged. "Anything not here remains as evidence."

Jake's euphoria slipped two notches. Freedom without his truck wasn't freedom. Deficient in courage and caught by the force of authority, he retired behind a screen to toss his orange jail uniform into the provided basket. He slipped on his blue shirt and jeans, tightened his belt and laced his work boots, anxious to breathe freedom's air after one nightmarish night behind bars.

He folded and pocketed the court date form as the heavy entry door to the cells clanged shut. With James gone, Jake doubted the reverend would've waited fifteen minutes. He expanded his lungs until pain forced his exhale. He needed a telephone to reach the dealership that sold him his truck and ask if he could order a spare ignition and door key.

In the lobby, his eyes widened. Emily sat on a visitor bench an arm's length inside the police station's front entrance. With her legs crossed at the knee, her tan skirt hem split her lower kneecap. Secured by her toes, one fringed, calfskin moccasin dangled an inch from her left heel.

When Jake advanced, Rev. Olson curtailed his gaze out the station's glass front door, pocketed a cell phone and strode straight to where Emily sat. He extended his right hand to Jake. "If you'll excuse me, I'll leave you with our director."

Jake shook the offered hand. "Of course. I'll see you at rehearsal. You truly were a messenger sent by God."

The reverend waved good-bye to both of them.

Jake turned on his boot heel. "Emily, why are you here?"

She unfolded her arms. "Concern, I guess." She tugged a wrinkle from her collared, white blouse. "I was rethinking what you shared with me yesterday. It must be totally scary to be in an unfamiliar town and end up behind bars accused of murder."

Jake bristled at the word. "I'm not charged with murder." When the impact of Emily's flattened brows and stretched lips struck him, he softened his tone. "Not yet, at least."

His taut nerves re-amplified his voice. "Have no idea who

they found in my truck trailer." He exhaled a deep breath, glanced left and right to verify they could talk privately and resumed in a lower, normal volume. "Really blessed to have complete strangers concerned about what happens to me."

"Yeah, the town's big gossip today was a body found last night at the Mayflower. I heard it on the radio early this a.m." Emily squirmed until she placed her two palms on the bench aside her hips.

Jake struggled to make heads or tails of why Emily wore a skirt. At rehearsals she wore blue jeans.

Emily uncrossed her knees. "When I stopped by Sadie's Diner, Kate mentioned it involved the new guy in town with the big rig. Her brief description told me it had to be you."

"Really appreciate you came. Yet, without my truck, don't see what you can do for me." While his extra team-hauls with Athena had paid off the Kenworth loan early, if idled, he lived between a rock and hard place to pay his motel and food bills.

"Well, maybe I can help," Emily replied. "You can tell me everything at Sadie's. It's close. Four blocks at most." Her coy smile broadened until it lit up her face. "You said yesterday I excelled as a listener."

They descended the police station steps one by one until they reached the sidewalk. Jake savored the glee of joining three people walking in the late morning air and watching four cars pass. He fantasized his sunshine-filled lungs floated him six feet above Emily, who had been at his left side. She said not a word.

Jake's joyful memory circuits overflowed. His first face-to-face encounter with Athena the most vivid. Employed by a small West Virginia regional trucking company, he parked his rig every Friday night next to a local dance hall. Athena, a graceful ballroom dancer, had been unlike the many aggressive females who filled his ears with their needs. Amenable and willing to listen, she asked him about his dreams, his goals.

Emily's willingness to listen struck a cord in Jake that she could be as trusting as Athena had been. Her question broke their companionable silence. "Soooo, what's next?"

"Don't know and definitely don't want to go through what I

did two years ago. When Athena died, I lost control. Felt totally sorry for myself, I guess. After dropping off fifty-pound cement bags in Los Angeles, I detoured to Lake Tahoe for two, almost three weeks. Drank a little, well, a lot."

Jake lifted his gaze from the sidewalk to Emily. From her calm facial features, he judged Emily wasn't shocked. Encouraged she hadn't crossed her arms as she had the day before, he continued. "At first my luck at the craps table soared. Then I stacked $25.00 chips on losing bets and failed to realize multiple snake eyes had swallowed my pass line luck whole. The odds dealt an unrecoverable blow to my euphoria. Squandered the three thousand dollars we'd saved for a house payment." Jake swallowed hard. "After two years of dark clouds, hope began to reappear in my life. Now, the police confiscate my truck."

They started walking. "How will you live not working?"

"Magnum owes me nearly a grand in haul fees I can't get to unless I hitch to Cincinnati and leaving the state breaks my bail conditions." Jake chided himself for wallowing in self-pity. "Shouldn't be dumping my troubles on you."

"I was hoping you'd stay around for a while." Emily didn't cock her head to meet Jake's gaze. "We must finish our play."

Jake restricted his stride to match Emily's slowdown. His right hand rubbed where the jail uniform collar had chafed.

Emily fixed her gaze on him. "You ever live in Mississippi?"

"No." Her question prickled his nape. Strikers who banished sticks had chased his truck ten years ago after he crossed their Biloxi, Mississippi, picket line. Lucky for him, Athena remained asleep in their cab's bunk. "Why do you ask?"

"Clem, my bartender, hails from Mississippi. After you left yesterday, he said that you appeared very similar to a man he'd seen in his hometown." Jake halted his advance. Emily averted her gaze for what seemed like half an hour to Jake, but wasn't. She turned to face him. "He recalled the man's name as Braun. And, the Mississippi police had questioned Clem about this man once when he was eighteen or nineteen."

Jake flicked his head. "Clem can't be much older than that today." He pressed his dry lips together.

"He's twenty-three, four years younger than me." She blushed. Her right hand dropped to her hip.

"Emily, prior to this week at the B&B, I've never even seen, let alone met Clem." Jake guessed the hint of a frown at the very edge of Emily's lightly glossed lips meant he hadn't convinced her. "Driven through Mississippi on Interstate 10. Had frequent in-and-out runs to Biloxi years ago. That's it. I've concentrated east of Cincinnati, up and down the Atlantic Coast and west as far as Kansas and Colorado."

"Another rumor has it you're from the South, like Louisiana."

"Who started that stupid rumor?" He scuffed his left boot sole across the concrete. "Not Clem again? Do I sound Cajun?"

Emily retreated a step and shook her head.

Jake rocked back and forth. His brain counted one, two, rock step. His feet mimicked the swing rhythm again and again until Emily spoke.

"I've an idea. Care to listen?"

Jake didn't desire to think of anything but how to get his truck. He blurted out, "Say, aren't you supposed to be teaching school today?"

"No, today's a day off for me."

Her wearing a skirt had been the impetus for his question. "Just thought . . ."

"Besides, elementary should have let out minutes ago, fifteen minutes earlier than high school's regular three thirty."

Side-by-side, they resumed their walk to finish the final two blocks to Sadie's. Emily's blonde hair, natural or from a bottle, he couldn't tell, had been cut short. A gold belt end dangled to her front. Her grapefruit scent stronger with a breeze change. She reminded him of a stirring, soulful television model.

"So how long have you lived here?" Jake asked.

"All my life. My parents farmed outside of town. The country drafted my late grandfather after Pearl Harbor, which inspired my father to enlist for Desert Storm. Father came back to the farm after one enlistment with my brother born in 1994. Then, after the 2004 harvest, my father sold the homestead and bought a wheat farm in Kansas."

Jake understood farmers planted crops, but the intricacies of what produced the most income eluded him. When they reached the curb at Willow and East Main, Jake hadn't figured out a polite way to redirect the conversation.

"For the third time, I rebelled against my father's wishes. I rented the one-bedroom apartment above the B&B and worked three years at Sadie's, substitute taught and filled in as a B&B server. When the B&B owner, Bob's wife's cousin, died two years ago, I convinced my dad to loan me the upfront money to buy the business on contract. My father never believed me that with a Bachelor of Arts degree specializing in elementary education I could teach in Minnesota, but would have had to fulfill a residency period and pass a skills test to qualify for a Kansas teaching certificate. Now, instead of B&B apartment rent, my father requires I send him a check each month to repay his loan. I try to visit each Christmas. That's about it. My life story in a nutshell."

"Sounds like quite a challenge to stay in Paradise."

"It is. Hiring Clem helped. Best thing I did."

"Why? Never before seen a Black in Paradise." After his words, Jake noticed a hurt in Emily's eyes.

"Character's important," Emily said. The guarded tone in her voice baffled Jake. "Clem's a decent person who overcame a broken home to earn a scholarship for one year of college." Her inflection sharpened. "He may not be conversant in automobile engines or duck hunting, but he's unequaled in his knowledge of European and American literature and can carry on an intelligent conversation."

"Whoa there! I believe you." Jake didn't have to imagine he spilled water on a hot rock. "Shouldn't we walk?"

"Good idea. Sadie's should be quiet. Lunch crowd's eaten, and the early supper crowd hasn't yet arrived."

"Guess you know what you're talking about," Jake replied, happy for the restored calm. He shortened his stride. The horizontal sign with red letters across the one-story roof in front of him seemed to sprout a foreboding he'd never recognized.

When Emily opened the door to Sadie's Diner, a woman in a swirling skirt rushed to give her a big hug. The woman loosened her grip of Emily's shoulders when she saw Jake. His lips twitched as he attempted to smile. His mind counted one, two, rock step. He buried his trembling right hand in his front jeans pocket.

"Have you met Jake, Jake Brown?" Emily asked.

"Can't say I've had the pleasure. Hello, Mr. Brown. I'm Kate. Welcome to Sadie's Friendly Home Town Diner." She wiped the palm of her right hand across her apron and extended her hand to Jake. He extracted his hand and shook hers.

"Thank you, ma'am. Pleased to meet you. Emily says you have the best food in town." Emily blushed. Still, Jake expected his white lie wouldn't be remembered or cause any harm.

"Kate, can we have a seat against the far wall where it's more private?" Emily asked.

Jake perceived that with but two counter patrons any table would give Emily her desired privacy.

"Take Table 12. Coffee's on the house." Emily turned to Jake, pointed to a table and marched toward it. Jake, as he kept his eyeballs on Kate, ambled in Emily's wake. He quickened his last two strides to catch up to Emily, confident that neither she nor Kate had noticed his extended Kate observation. He shuffled plastic menu sleeves until Kate approached his table.

"You a veteran?" Kate asked. Her right hand held a glass carafe of steaming coffee. Two ceramic centennial mugs touting the city's founding hung from her left forefinger.

"Served on the USS Midway." The animation in Kate's eyes uplifted him and brought out the truck stop comic in him. "Galley rat, first class. The Navy issued me a paring knife to attack fifty-pound bags of No. 2 Idaho potatoes. If they would have awarded medals for dishpan hands, peeling curlicues and potato hole marksmanship, I would've had a chest full."

He lurched his upper body forward to position his hands beneath the carafe should it slip from the grip of a laughing

Kate. From out of the corner of his right eye, his glimpse took in the shrugs of the two people at the counter.

His left ear caught Emily in a giggle until she said, "Kate has always given special attention to town veterans. She can tell you about her special room. However, I caution you." Her left eyelid blinked. "Do not repeat you have potato peeling skills. Kate may put you to work."

Jake glanced sideways at Kate. With the hem of her apron, she wiped coffee drops from the carafe's lip. Her eyes radiated genuine warmth. If he continued to stare, she'd be convinced he truly was an old salt or a common day lecher.

"You better let me help," Emily said. She slipped the cups from Kate's fingers and placed one in front of her and Jake. Kate filled both cups and set the carafe on the table.

"Either of you need cream?" Kate asked. Jake shook his head, and Emily said no. "Sugar's on the table. Enjoy."

With Kate out of earshot, Emily explained, "Kate, and she only wants you to refer to her as Kate, always asks a new male customer if he served. She's a widow of a veteran." Emily suggested Jake visit the diner's memorial room and pay special attention to a framed Purple Heart and photograph shrouded in black silk. She excused herself to visit the ladies room.

Unsettled by the miasma generated by a counter patron's stare, Jake rose and strolled into the memorial room. He wasn't sure what he'd gain or why, except to be free of the indiscreet piercing eyes. His head swiveled left and right. Three walls plastered with pictures of soldiers, airmen, Red Cross nurses and sailors joined by bond recruitment posters and memorabilia numbed his mind. He almost saluted an American flag hanging in the corner to his right, next to an American Legion flag. A brass bald eagle replica topped each flag's staff. He bent forward to read a plaque attestation by a United States Senator that the American flag had flown over the U.S. Capitol Building in Washington, D.C.

The picture Emily referred to was centered on the far wall. A brass plate identified an American sailor named Hans Newark, husband to Kate. The year 1991 inscribed on the photo's lower left corner. A lump rose in Jake's throat. While Paradise remembered its fallen, no village, town or city recorded his presence long enough to immortalize his likeness or name in metal or stone.

His gaze flitted past unknown faces. A dented and dulled bugle, hung on the wall, caused him to hum the classic swing tune about the boogie-woogie bugle boy of Company B.

Emily lifted her soaped hands from the sudsy women's restroom sink when Kate entered.

"Say, Emily, don't you think you're really out on a limb with Jake? Wasn't he arrested for the Mayflower murder?"

"He's been released from jail, which tells me good points exist in his background. It's true I've only known him this week, but I spoke to Robert Brand at the flourmill when I first considered him for my play." Emily grabbed a paper towel.

"So what did our mill manager have to say?"

"He spoke all positives. Robert especially remembered one incident where the shipper either had an inventory error or a forklift driver put on an extra pallet. He said Jake could've easily sold the molasses and pocketed the money, but he pointed out the manifest error to the supervisor on duty."

"I'm concerned for you, that's all." Kate exhaled a motherly sigh.

Emily couldn't resist tweaking Kate's over-protective nature. "Why? I thought you always gave every benefit of the doubt to a military veteran?"

"I do. Henry Warner served on the Midway in the 90s. I realize it's a big ship, but, if Jake had galley duty, Henry could have run across him since the entire crew had to eat."

"You're right." Emily balled up and discarded her towel. "I'll be okay. It's not like we're traveling together into the morning's wee hours."

Emily closed the bathroom door with Kate inside.

Jake sipped from his second cup of coffee.

Emily slid into her chair. "Sorry I took so long."

"Never ask. Learned that valuable lesson long ago." Her brief frown didn't strike him as playful. "Viewed the memorial room while you were gone. Very striking and fitting."

Emily's hands encircled her cup, but she didn't drink. "I don't know how to approach this." She bit her lower lip. "Best way I guess . . . just start and let you ask questions. Cottonwood State Park, right outside town, seeks to hire a caretaker. I thought of it after you replied to my how-are-you-going-to-live question. One advantage, the caretaker lives in a house or lodge within the park. Bob knows more about the position than me."

"Is that the Bob Hunter who's Tycoon in the play?"

"Yes."

His too-sharp awareness of her delicate features scared him as he rubbed his chin to delay a response. "Don't know nothing about caring for a state park. Yet, I do need a place to live. Don't know when, or if, the police chief will give me back my truck. Do know The Mayflower won't let me stay free."

A faint glow crept onto her face. "So you'd be interested?"

"Guess so. Can we speak with Mr. Hunter first?"

"If we hurry, he might still be in his Hancock Boulevard office."

"Should we walk?" When Jake realized his question's stupidity, he shrugged and cast his gaze to the diner door.

Emily arose and smiled. "Bob's office sits between Sadie's and the B&B. If we hustle, we'll have time to speak to Bob and make play rehearsal. Drink up."

"Yes, ma'am."

Halfway to the door, Emily waved to Kate. "See you later."

"Thanks for stopping." Kate stepped from behind the counter. "Say, Emily, when are you putting on a play I can star in?" Kate lifted her left heel to spin on the ball of her foot.

"I'm always looking. Any old play won't do. We need a very special story to showcase your talent." The diner door closed behind Emily before Jake could hear any reply from Kate. He started walking before Emily reached the sidewalk.

"Jake! Jake!" Emily cried out.

Jake completed a one-eighty pivot, slapped his hands to his hips and stared at Emily. "What?"

"You're headed in the wrong direction. We need to go west on Main Street."

At Hunter Realty, the receptionist offered to inform Mr. Hunter of Emily's arrival. Jake, seated in front of a bay window, plotted his next move. A door's mournful creak sapped Jake's courage to jog to the diner, ask Kate for a bolt cutter and rescue his truck. If he swapped it for cash at an auction house, he could team up with a none-the-wiser driver until police lost his trail.

"Hi, Emily."

Jake's gaze scanned Bob Hunter's ice-cold, dark eye sockets and his grim, stone-carved-like stationary lips that translated well into the archetypical Old West gunslinger named Tycoon in Emily's play. He clasped his large, steady hands in front of his lanky six-foot frame.

"What brings you here today?" Bob asked. "Oh, hi, Jake, nice to see you too." Bob escorted them into what he explained to be his realty office's closing room. With a right hand waist-high wave he offered Emily and Jake adjoining seats at a table with four chairs on each side. Bob sat across from them.

Emily spoke first. "Please tell Jake about the caretaker position at Cottonwood. He's interested."

"This is difficult." Bob focused his attention on Emily. His velvety soothing tone at variance with his stoic mien. "All I know is that the police yesterday arrested him in a murder."

Jake squared his shoulders. "That's true, but I'm innocent." He unfolded his arms and rested his forearms and palms on the table. "And, the judge didn't charge me with murder."

The week's events flowed past Jake's lips faster than beer from a tapped keg. "Only thing I'm guilty of is parking my truck at the Mayflower on Monday. Someone, not me, confused my truck trailer for a burial vault. Could have been Thursday when we were rehearsing Emily's play or the day before."

Bob's raised eyebrows failed to act as train-crossing gates to Jake's full head of steam.

"Never been arrested before. You have my permission to ask the police chief. I'm sure he's checked if there's a warrant out for my arrest or if I'm an ex-con." With deliberate clarity, Jake enunciated, "He won't find what doesn't exist."

He scanned Emily's expressionless face without a clue as to whether he'd said too much. He filled in the room's silence. "Since The Chief impounded my truck, I need a place to live and earn money. Emily's only trying to help."

Jake twisted his head left in an attempt to eyeball Bob and Emily. Emily hadn't moved or lifted a finger until she raised her gaze from the wooden tabletop to Bob.

Emily's soft voice pleaded. "Just tell us what the job entails. Maybe Jake will decide he needs something else. Five minutes can't hurt, can it?"

She sighed when Bob replied, "You're right. I can get the official job description, but, Jake, here it is, simply put."

Jake clasped his hands and tried to smile.

"Cottonwood State Park has a park ranger and a deputy, and neither resides at the park. A hired third person, called the park caretaker, lives in a park residence and performs varied duties. Think janitor or maintenance man."

Emily's smile encouraged Jake to think positive.

Bob cleared his throat. "There's grass around the lodge and RV and tent campsites to be mowed, brush trimmed, trash barrels emptied, lodge bathrooms cleaned and lodge flower gardens weeded. Since the lodge is rented to the public, primarily during the summer months, this is a busy time to be without a caretaker. In addition, the ranger expects the caretaker to be alert for unauthorized persons in the park after closing."

"Did you say clean campground toilets?" Jake asked.

"No, lodge bathrooms. Park hires a private firm to clean park port-a-potties. At most, you might refill toilet paper."

"What besides free rent?" Emily asked. Jake's forefinger rubbed his left eye.

"Six hundred dollars a month. If a lodge renter requests extra services or leaves a tip, that would be yours to keep."

Jake accidentally touched Emily's left elbow when he again

expanded his hands. She pulled her arm closer to her body. "What about linens, pots, pans, household stuff?" she asked.

"Recall that prior caretakers left linen and a hodgepodge of kitchen items. Nothing fancy. You're free to use or bring your own. For laundry, you'll need to use the town laundromat or its out-of-town dry cleaning delivery arrangement."

"What do I do to be given consideration?" Jake asked.

Jake detected no encouragement in Bob's facial features. His scan right noticed Emily nod once.

"Wait here and I'll get you an application. You can fill it out here or give it to me later at rehearsal. It'll be at least Monday or Tuesday before I can follow-up. The park expects a commitment to stay until mid-September."

"Thanks, Bob. I do appreciate your help." Jake waited as Bob slid his chair from the table and stood.

At the door before he departed, Bob turned toward Jake. "I'll see you both at rehearsal."

Jake twisted toward Emily. "Don't know how I can thank you," he whispered. Emily fixed her gaze at the open door. The receptionist appeared to give Jake two copies of a one page, two-sided form that included a medical questionnaire section.

Outside the realty office, Jake gazed past the form at Emily. "This appears to require extensive personal detail, less on custodian skills. Hope Mr. Hunter is being more than nice."

"Bob will give you every fair consideration and then some." Emily stepped within a foot of Jake. "It's his job to find bona fide renters for his realty clients, and, in this case, capable employment candidates." Emily lowered her voice. "Rumor has it a caretaker two summers ago lost his job because of a personality feud with the ranger. Bob wouldn't wish for that to happen again." Her speech volume rose to normal. "I'm sure you can do a good job. If you need a reference, put me down."

Jake wrapped his arms around Emily's shoulders and, before his hug impulse subsided, he released them from her rigid muscles. When she rotated her head, he couldn't read her eyes, the expectant anger hidden by her sidestep to safety.

How could he explain? His feelings vacuum-packed inside a

heart strapped by a hurt he ran away from. Afraid she might rein in her help, he said, "Must check my truck and change clothes. See you later at the B&B for rehearsal."

"I'll accompany you to the B&B."

Jake's taut nerves relaxed. All relationships carved out boundaries. His joining her play had been his entry into Emily's life. Superficial friendships marked his road life after Athena. He kept his hands in his front pockets, unwilling to trust himself to understand or say what Emily expected.

"Or more theatrically correct: the Spring Daisy Theatre."

They walked in companionable silence until Jake prepared for their separation. "Here's the B&B, see you later." He paused until Emily disappeared into the B&B's Main Street Entrance.

A block later, a Paradise squad car, its wheels revolving slower than maple syrup in January, rumbled through an intersection. When it caught Jake mid-block, Sgt. Smyth lowered the driver's window, glared at him and then sped off. Jake hurried west toward the Mayflower Motel.

Early Friday afternoon, Chief Coltraine perused his draft patrol schedule for the upcoming week. The ring of his office's private line interrupted his switch of Sgt. Smyth's off nights.

"Doc, what can you tell me about the Mayflower body?"

The Chief opened a folder and clicked his pen, ready for Coroner Beck's report.

"I completed a preliminary exam, no full autopsy. Subject to full lab results, the person, I should say victim, had been dead less than fifteen hours. Cause of death narrowed to blunt force trauma to the skull's crown or strangulation. Body had signs of both. The most serious blow left a one-inch open wound on the skull's rear, top left. It fractured and caved in the parietal bone, which caused underlying vessels to bleed. Three brown glass shards in the wound indicate the weapon to be a glass bottle such as a Hofensteger."

The Chief scribbled: weapon/beer bottle?

"Wouldn't rule out a combination. For example, a blow to the head to stun followed by thumbs pressed hard on the throat to cut off air to the lungs. Additional head and face lacerations and bruises likely caused by closed hand blows. Older bruises in the stomach area indicate the victim suffered up to five prior midsection punches. These blows not life threatening."

Doc Beck paused and The Chief's pen drew concentric circles while he waited for additional information.

"Ruling will be homicide. Wish to have me explain anything else?"

The Chief jumped in. "Identity information?"

"Female, expect DNA will confirm victim as one of the daughters of Adolph Krump, a local businessman."

"Roger said he recognized a necklace he'd seen worn by Kathie Krump in a store where she worked."

"He may be correct. A recovered gold necklace had no fingerprints other than the victim's. To finish, Caucasian; age about thirty; well-nourished; no identification on her person; brunette; five feet, three inches; brown eyes; one hundred and twenty pounds; small sunflower tattoo on the nape of her neck, no other discernible birthmarks or scars, except from the assaults mentioned earlier. Anything else?"

The Chief cursed a full page and reached into a drawer for a sheet of paper to finish the victim's description. "Assume you'll copy me on the lab results, especially if they show any illegal substances or blood alcohol concentrations." He paged back to his folder-form line reserved for a victim's name and inserted a question mark. "Call me, please, if you verify the name."

"Will do. I've faxed the victim's prints to the crime lab."

The Chief's shuffle through missing person reports disclosed no females that matched the victim's description. His homicide experience categorized the death as either a bar fight or domestic violence. Yet, his beat experience warned him to be suspicious of the obvious. The time of death troubled him. Fights occurred most often on Friday and Saturday nights, not midweek or early Thursday a.m. hours.

The Chief puffed on his Fifty-one brand e-cigarette. Doc Beck had added little to what he'd observed at the scene. The Chief assured himself he still possessed the wherewithal to solve a murder despite the paucity of information. There would be no blunder as when he was a rookie cop. He remembered vividly the written reprimand he had received on his first murder case when he had the suspected murder weapon stolen from his unlocked patrol cruiser. No Paradise resident, he suspected, had any inkling of his awkward and forced Deputy Chief resignation in 2006 from the Kannaville, Ohio, Police Department.

While he'd jailed criminals caught acting stupid, he found it hard to believe Jake Brown would leave a corpse rot in his trailer. The Magnum Trucking dispatcher on the telephone explained that experienced truckers often left empty trailers unlocked to avoid break-in damage. Thus, at least, one portion of Jake's story rested on factual support.

If the murder occurred away from the motel, Jake ostensibly had no transport vehicle other than his truck. And, by all appearances, it had remained parked in its Thursday spot for at least two days prior. If not Jake, the circumstances implied the victim dumped for expediency, or to frame Jake.

The Chief telephoned the Krump men's store.

"No sir, no customer by that name."

"You sure? It's B-R-O-W-N, like the color."

"Positive."

Stymied, he reviewed the logged assistance calls for the prior Wednesday or Thursday. None appeared to be even remotely related. Since experience reminded him it could take three or four days for an officer to record his activity, he wrote himself a note to query each officer.

"Chief." Isabella, a dispatcher and his unofficial secretary, stood in his office doorway. Her hands carried no message slip.

"Yes, Bell, what is it?" He set down his e-cigarette.

She frowned. "Telephone call from reporter Josh Miles."

"Okay. Transfer it to my public line." Isabella departed.

"Josh Miles, *Herald-Gazette*. How are you this afternoon?"

"Great until you called." The Chief paused and shrugged. He preferred face-to-face conversations to observe the other person's reaction, especially when he tried to tease. "I'm kidding, Josh. You're my favorite reporter."

"As the only *Herald-Gazette* police beat reporter, I'll translate your compliment to mean you're in a good mood today. I'm calling to ask about the Mayflower body. I know you arrested a suspect. I attended the arraignment."

"You're right. We arrested a Mr. Jake Brown at the scene." The Chief peered at a folder on his desk. The computer-printed Paradise Police blue sheet summarized all arrest details.

"Any reason why no murder charge?"

"No comment. That's the prosecutor's discretion."

"What can you tell me about the victim? Coroner Beck refused comment and said I'd have to speak with you."

"Why don't we leave it be for today?" The Chief's mind struggled to articulate a reason until he saw the folded local newspaper on his office sofa. "*Herald-Gazette* doesn't publish a Saturday edition." The receiver in his left palm slipped.

"True. I'm working on our Sunday morning edition." That The Chief heard no anger surprised him. "I couldn't find a funeral home scheduling a service."

"Let's proceed this way. Call tomorrow after lunch and by then I might have releasable information. I'm not planning a news conference. Your out-of-town competition won't get a scoop from me if you wait. We're still investigating and I don't want to piecemeal information to jumpstart the gossip mill."

"We don't have a long track record, but I'll be friendly and do it your way. I'll still dig for the facts elsewhere."

The Chief set the handset in its cradle. His sigh of relief filled his office. He gazed out his office window for a minute before he pressed his intercom button.

"Bell, I'll be back in a few minutes. I won't be in my car."

Chief Coltraine's stroll to Hancock Boulevard ended at Larry's Tattoos where he interrupted Bill Jones, the current owner of Paradise's exclusive tattoo parlor. After a quick glance at a wall cluttered with multi-color swirls and black-and-white barbed wire designs, a floor-to-ceiling beaded curtain hindered The Chief's visual inspection.

"Need to ask about sunflower tattoos."

"Was popular with sophisticated ladies," Jones said.

"Haven't inked one since buying out Larry two years ago."

"You have records?"

"Only the two years since I bought the place."

The Chief read Jones as credible and requested he contact him should he run across any sunflower tattoo records. Presented with another brick wall, The Chief lamented that he couldn't muster in Paradise the tactical squads he did in Ohio.

I'm retrogressing to a baton-swinging patrolman, chatting with citizens I meet, learning who to trust and who not to believe. I'll stop by the B&B tomorrow night to observe this visiting truck driver. This murder I'll crack myself.

Jake was willing to tolerate a shower's hot spray to soak his mind with life's present positives and cleanse his memory of yesterday's gloom. Refreshed, he'd be ready to tackle his caretaker application and find his script. He twisted his Mayflower Motel room key and pushed the door inward.

Whoa, what the—

He retreated, losing his door handle grip.

The door slammed shut. He scanned rows of doors left and right, the parking lot behind. No one. No vehicle movement.

The room's drawn window drapes forced him to reinsert his key, unaware of whether anyone lurked inside. He stood square, turned the key with his right hand, the doorknob with his left.

His right foot kicked the wooden door. Freed from his grip, the door crashed flat against the interior wall. He straddled the threshold. His clothes lay everywhere—on the floor, on the bed, on the room's single chair. Two overturned dresser drawers lay on the floor in the middle of the room.

He shouted, "Anyone here?" No answer. His fears gathered in strength. Had he been heard behind the closed bathroom door? He doubled his yell's volume and readied to be rushed by an intruder. When it didn't happen, he exhaled, uncertain if he should check the bathroom to make sure.

After ten seconds passed, Jake suppressed his nerve ping with the salve the motel manager had utilized a master key for a police search. Still cautious, he left the outside door ajar for his escape as his extended right arm backhanded the bathroom door. He retreated and held his breath. When he exhaled to the sibilant sound of his own breath, he checked under the bed to prove he was alone and to verify no threat hid there.

The hangover smell of flat beer invaded his nostrils. He halted his steps at the bathroom door. Foamless beer filled the sink. Two stale bread slices dotted with greenish mold in a twist-tied, plastic loaf bag floated atop the beer alongside a plastic sandwich box containing a packet of shriveled, half-eaten luncheon meat.

When Jake discovered his last Hofensteger Beer bottle in a corner, uncapped and empty, he doubted a police search. He pressed his left palm against the sink drain stopper to permit what could've been a refreshing thirst quencher swirl away.

Jake set the shower spray to blast hot and, without a bathroom exhaust fan, he cracked the frosted window. After he tiptoed through the floor clutter, he shut and chained his room's door, undressed, grabbed a bar of soap and eased his shoulder blades behind the shower curtain. The pulsating spray joined with his *Cowboy* rehearsal anticipation to buoy his spirits.

Refreshed, he shrugged off his room's upheaval. Anger should be his servant, not a master. Athena, in not so subtle words, had preached this. Since he packed nothing a fence would buy, Jake focused on the positives of employment and his membership in a play cast that welcomed his friendship.

Familiar with many a dance venue, Jake considered the George Street Ballroom and Bar's Quonset-type building unique. Ever since his first truck delivery, he'd always concentrated on remembering addresses, distances, directions and street layouts. What had begun as a driver necessity, quadrupled into a quirk of how he lived his life.

East and south of the West Main and George Street intersection, the George Street entrance allowed a patron to enter a small lobby. On the left, a door led the visitor to stand in front of the ballroom's bar. Straight ahead, the eighteen-by-twenty-four inch sign on a second door screamed: Private and Do Not Enter. Emily had told him a flight of stairs to her apartment existed behind this locked door.

His ten paces east from George Street added up to twenty-five feet between the George Street and the B&B's Main Street entry. A six-foot wide corridor greeted the patron. A right-side paneled wall extended ten feet before it allowed the visitor to turn right and stand in front of the B&B's one main bar.

While the entire floor consisted of two-inch, tongue and groove, hard maple, a rectangular piece of square-patterned sheet linoleum eight-feet wide fronted the bar's entire length. A decorative one-inch brass strip transitioned linoleum to maple. Steel columns, girdled with a wood facade, supported the building's roof. At the end opposite the bar, a raised sixteen-foot wide by twelve-foot deep bandstand eighteen inches in height filled the space between two columns.

Two days previous, while prone on the bandstand, Jake had viewed a suspended metal track, parallel to the bar. It supported an expandable, accordion-type panel to wall off the Spring Daisy Theatre. Cotton curtain panels affixed to the ceiling and colored lights mounted on two vertical support columns transformed the ballroom bandstand into a theater stage.

Jake paused to stare at a poster picture on the Main Street entrance wall showing ballroom tables clumped together on stage for a little-girl afternoon tea party. A lump formed in his throat. He bet the girl's parents relished the excitement experienced by their daughters. He knew he would have, if he had been a father.

Above the bar area, his eye traced a level ten-foot high ceiling. Elsewhere the ceiling arched Quonset-style. He assumed the lowered ceiling doubled as the floor of Emily's apartment above. He counted two high, small, curtained windows visible from below. Jake estimated the 6,000 square foot building provided a 2,000 square foot dance floor, including the Spring Daisy Theatre space.

A sixteen-by-twenty-four inch poster taped to a column caught his attention. It advertised Saturday's dance featuring the Dale Beaver trio. Although the band was new to him, he'd danced to the trio's repertoire of 1940s-style swing, big band ballroom and '60s rock 'n' roll.

The exterior door hinges squeaked and Jake pivoted.

"Hi, Jake. Reverend Olson, but call me Pastor John."

"Thanks. I'm both pleased you visited me in jail and glad to be out for play rehearsal."

Pastor John's right hand fingers loosened his cleric's collar. "You're welcome Sunday at First Presbyterian Church. For good or bad, people remember me easier once they've experienced one of my sermons. I'm told it's the baritone voice." He chuckled. For what reason, Jake didn't know.

Jake jammed his right hand into his rear jeans pocket. "Have you been preaching in this town long?"

"Four years this July. We're a small nine-hundred registered congregation. Considering Paradise's eight churches among its five thousand residents, give or take, we're blessed." Pastor John winked. "Could always use one more."

"Don't know." Jake hesitated. "As I told you in jail, believe in God the Almighty while missing the opportunity to belong to a church. Attended Sunday services Athena found and paid no heed to what Bible the preacher read from. Of late, can't say that God has seen me much."

Pastor John gazed into Jake's eyes as if they were windows to his soul. "You'd be surprised what God sees. Unanswered prayers are sometimes the best." Before Pastor John could utter another word, the Main Street entrance door squeaked again.

"Whatcha doing, Preacher, bringing in the lost lamb?"

Jake recognized the speaker as Jacob, a play cast member and an inch or two taller than himself. While Jake understood Jacob kidded, Jacob's verbal innuendo struck close to the bulls-eye of where Jake's faith lay. *Could God be watching?*

"That's always my mission, Jacob," Rev. Olson replied.

"Hello, Jacob," Jake said. He promised himself he'd attempt to remember Jacob's last name later.

Rev. Olson and Jacob ambled off, their heads bobbing in conversation. Jake, visible to bar patrons, edged past a column.

"Stop right where you are, you pervert," shouted a burley man in a red plaid shirt, blue jeans and work boots.

Jake ignored the shout as not applicable to him and continued toward the stage.

The man jumped off his bar stool. "I said stop." The man brandished his right-hand fist within inches of Jake's chin. Chest-to-chest, the man's breath reeked of alcohol. "I know you killed my son and put him in that there truck of yours. He hasn't been home since I left for work midnight Wednesday."

"Slow down, mister. I didn't kill your son." Jake shifted his left foot six inches forward to solidify his balance.

"Don't lie. I saw Doc Beck zip that body bag taken from your truck." The man's torso wobbled with each pant. "My boy told me he was going to get out of this town. You . . . you found him in your truck . . . and . . . you killed him. Now . . . I'm going to get just— . . . justice, right here, and now." The man cocked his right arm and swung. Jake ducked his head to avoid the right, then gasped. The man's left jab landed below Jake's right side rib, square on his external abdominal oblique.

Before the assailant launched a recoiled right fist, Clem, his feet planted shoulder-width apart, grabbed the man from behind. His bear hug pinned the man's arms against the red plaid. The man spit at Clem's clasped hands.

"Let me go, you black swine," the man shouted as he struggled against Clem's grasp.

When Clem's unforgiving biceps tightened, Jake feared for the man as a flush crept up his neck.

"Let's hold on there," the Reverend's deep voice commanded. "Stand back." His extended fingers and crossed thumbs became the leading edge of arms designed to separate the combatants. "There's no reason to fight."

Jake angled his backpedal to give Rev. Olson space.

"He," the man pointed at Jake, "killed my boy." The man's saliva joined his words spat into space. "I feel it."

"Ed, you've been drinking," Rev. Olson said. "You need to go home. I think everyone here will leave it at that."

Jake, his side aching, couldn't see the man's face. This Ed deserved to sober up in the cell Jake vacated.

"Why you Blacks protect this outsider, I don't know. Things

a lot better before this country elected Obama."

Jake slid his soles left until half of Rev. Olson's body protected his right side. The sparks of rage in his attacker's eyes signaled no truce. Red splotches encircled the man's pupils.

"Ed, Mr. Brown here can press charges against you if he wants to call the police." Rev. Olson's calm voice added: "I'd ask him not to do that. Whiskey doesn't mix with grief. Please tell me you'll go home."

Jake felt the bar and ballroom's collective gaze focus on the unscheduled drama.

"Ed, give me your arm," coaxed Rev. Olson. He waited until Ed tilted his gaze to the floor. "We'll go outside and I'll give you a ride home. You can collect your pickup tomorrow."

Jake circled Rev. Olson to stand behind Clem.

"I don't like it." The back of Ed's right hand wiped his twisted mouth. "You've got me outnumbered. Okay."

Jake remained silent while his clenched teeth fought the pain of his right-side oblique spasm. Pastor John led Ed out the Main Street door. Jake offered his thanks to Clem, who stood with hands raised, ready to again intervene.

Emily's voice echoed across the room. "Actors, front and center . . . announcement time."

Jake sauntered after Jacob, who had crept up behind Pastor John after Jake had shifted to be nearer Clem. They joined Emily and Patricia at the foot of the stage. Jake guessed Patricia, since he hadn't seen her enter, had come in the George Street entrance. Bob Hunter accompanied Rev. Olson's return.

Emily glanced left and right as if she counted noses. "Glad everyone's here. While we left off with the poker table scramble last time, I'm skipping two scenes to begin in the cemetery." She flipped script pages. "Okay. Bob, Reverend and Jacob on stage. We'll pretend a man hangs in the big cottonwood tree at stage right, a noose around his neck. I didn't cast the part because it's the only scene the person would be in. Expect either a mannequin or a dressed up Red Cross dummy to play this dramatic leading role." A light smattering of laugher followed Emily's quip.

Jacob tapped Jake's arm. "What a nice part," he whispered. "No dialogue to memorize, no costume changes." Jake nodded once. He didn't wish spoken words to distract Emily.

"Okay, places everyone," directed Emily.

Jake's eyes failed to locate a nearby chair not on the stage. He winced as he stretched his torso to lift a small table before he carried it to a position near stage left. When he returned with two chairs, Patricia, watching the three actors on stage, stood adjacent to the table. Jake set a chair behind her and then sat and leaned his right elbow on the table between them. In an undertone to Patricia, Jake said, "Please have a seat."

"Thanks," Patricia answered and seated herself without a glance at Jake. Despite his attempt to visualize the strung up dummy, the cemetery scene failed to affect him with the unblinking intensity Patricia displayed.

"Excuse me, Patricia." Jake lifted his buttocks off his chair and leverage his torso toward her using his right elbow as a fulcrum. "May I borrow your script? Forgot mine."

Without a word, Patricia extended her left hand to lay her script copy on the table within his reach.

"Thanks," Jake murmured, and then picked it up. She didn't react. He thumbed to the poker table scene and started to read. When he heard footfalls, he spied Clem stride past the stacked ballroom stage partition and Patricia's chair empty.

Patricia, her footsteps angled to intercept Clem, glanced over her right shoulder to be sure Emily hadn't changed the scene.

"Clem, the library today received the copy of *The Anthology of 19th Century Literature* you expressed an interest in."

"Thanks, Miss Swanson."

"Why, may I ask, are you interested in such heavy reading?"

Clem lifted his unfastened green bar-apron top that hung below its tied waist strings and wiped both hands. "My humanities correspondence course suggested it as a reference." Clem's eyes flitted left to the three bar patrons. "Thought it might also be useful for my next literature class."

"You planning to enroll at the community college this

summer?" Patricia catalogued her collegiate undergraduate days under the bold heading of distant memory.

"No. I've got to save some money first." She nodded. "I'm trying to earn credits for a teacher's aide certificate."

"That's wonderful." Patricia beamed. "Give me your feedback on the book. I always try to please dedicated readers."

"I sure will."

Patricia twisted toward Clem after Emily's call for actors. "One quick question, do you know where Jake hails from?"

"Not really sure. I thought he looked like a guy I saw years ago in Mississippi, but Emily said Jake denied he ever lived there. Why do you ask?"

"No reason. Must go." Patricia scurried off to the stage.

Jake, unsettled and puzzled, shielded his intense stare of Patricia with his left hand, its fingers separated. While it wasn't unusual for Patricia to converse with Clem, tonight's timing accented Patricia's aloofness. Stuck in no-man's land, he let his jealousy of his outsider status fester unspoken.

Jake, to protect his side, abandoned his habit of hopping onto the stage and availed himself of the stage's two side steps. It was all for naught as Emily reversed herself and directed a sixth cemetery scene run through.

After the actors, given three additional tries, flubbed their dialogue and bumped elbows not called for by the stage chorography, Emily decreed time for a break. She joined a silent Jake and Patricia at the table. "Sorry that lasted so long."

"No problem," Patricia said.

Emily, her annotated script grasped and pinned to her side by her left hand, refused Jake's seat offer.

Emily dog-eared a script page and asked Bob and Jacob to corral three tables and eight chairs. Jake refused to be coddled and grabbed his and Patricia's chairs.

On stage, Emily called out, "We'll rehearse the scene where the angry out-of-town gunslinger busts into the saloon. Patricia, before Tycoon arrives, I want you to bat your eyelashes with wide goo-goo eyes. Pretend Jacob needs to be enticed. When he responds too hands-on, splash a glass of beer in his face to drive home the idea he's outta line."

Emily stared at a grinning Jacob. "Jacob, remember this is pretend hands-on." She pointed to an empty stein. "We'll save beer today. Use an empty glass."

A prepared Jake stood behind the bar.

"Jake," Emily said, "you're hiding behind the bar until Jacob gives you the cue to appear. Bob, remember you must look menacing. You think one of the scheming poker players hightailed it out of the saloon, but you couldn't find him outside, so you slam the saloon's swinging doors against the walls with fire in your eyes, six-shooter drawn."

Emily swiveled her body and her attention. "Reverend, you must use your peacemaking skill to persuade quick-draw Tycoon not to shoot. Let's all give it your best. Now action."

Dialogue stumbles caused Emily to call frequent stops. At each occurrence, Patricia gravitated to actors other than Jake. While he owed her a heap of thanks for her script loan, he feared Jacob would exaggerate his mention into a teasing quip or soap opera melodrama.

Minutes short of the two-hour rehearsal mark, Emily announced, "Good job, all. We're progressing. See everyone here Monday, same time."

Only Patricia lingered on stage when Jake limped across it toward the side steps. As he passed her, he handed Patricia her script. "Thanks again. I'll try to remember mine next time."

"Happy to help out." She gazed at the floor. "You'd do the same for me." Patricia tucked the script under her right arm.

"Look forward to seeing you Monday."

"I'll be here." Patricia's monotone voice loitered in Jake's subconscious. Not forgotten when Bob doubled back to tap Jake on the left shoulder and exchange good nights. Patricia circled tables and chairs to the stage steps and strolled after Bob. Jacob waited at the George Street door to be Sir Galahad and hold the exit door for both.

Jake hollered and waved good-bye to Rev. Olson. To his left, Emily bent forward at the waist to right an upended chair.

"Let me help you with that," Jake offered.

"Everything's good."

Jake plopped himself into a chair near Emily. "You were easy on me, switching scenes like that."

"Well, it served two purposes. I figured you probably hadn't rehearsed your lines last night or this morning and didn't need to be put on the spot. Pastor John needed extra rehearsal time and the cemetery scene accomplished both goals."

Emily, her eyes streaked with fatigue, slumped into a chair adjacent to Jake's and rubbed her drooped eyelids.

"You're a great director," slipped out of Jake's mouth.

"You're too kind." Her eyes closed, and then opened.

"I'd better head out. I promised myself that I'd give Sadie's Diner a chance to stuff me to the gills. By the time I leave this town, I'll have every Main Street sidewalk crack from Sadie's to the Mayflower burned into memory." Jake stifled a laugh when the pain in his side flared. "Would you like to guess the number paces between your Main Street entrance and the Mayflower?"

"No, no, that's okay." She pushed herself erect. "Did you get the park application filled out?"

"Yes, handed it to Bob at the first break. I wrote your name down as a reference."

"Good." She collapsed into her chair.

Her shallow breaths alarmed Jake. "You okay, Emily?"

"Fine. Just tired. You don't need my troubles."

Jake interlaced his fingers. "Patricia's mad at me." Emily cocked an eyebrow. "She acted very standoffish at rehearsal. Probably spoke out of turn at the library yesterday and I don't want my mistake to bring strife undercurrents to your play."

"I've heard no tongues waggle about a library incident. I told you she's reserved."

Jake, with both hands slid into his front jeans pockets, summarized his library encounter with Patricia and her sexy lingerie catalog. Emily interrupted to ask if it was a Victoria's Secret catalog. He said he didn't know and then recounted his chilly rehearsal interaction with Patricia.

"I wouldn't consider her actions today, as you described them, to mean she's upset. You were probably more outgoing for someone she's just met than normally makes Patricia comfortable." Emily stretched her shoulders rearward. "Be patient, less judgmental. Like I told you before, Patricia in the play and in real life can be perceived as two different women."

"Hope you're right. Someday I expect to repay all your kindness." Jake jerked both hands from his pockets.

"Don't fret any about paying me back. For the time being just stay out of our police chief's public accommodations."

"Good night now."

En route to the Main Street door, Jake flashed a left hand thumbs up to Clem behind the bar.

Outside the B&B, Jake turned right toward Sadie's Diner. To double-check if anyone tracked his Main Street trek, he paused at the first Main Street intersection to inspect his wallet's bill compartment and to re-enact a Boy Scout's look-both-ways traffic caution. Satisfied no one followed, he continued.

"Hello again," Kate said as he entered Sadie's. "Pretty full tonight. There's a spot at the counter, second stool from the end. Take a look at the menu. I'll be there in short order."

He gawked at Kate who dipped and swirled from table to table with a theatrical flourish.

"Thanks for waiting. Anything of interest?"

"Yes. Took a peek. Gorgeous." The sight of Kate's firm calves had replayed Jake's memories of drivers flirting with servers they'd never see again. His double-entendre of a peek with a reference to gorgeous sparked an embarrassment that warmed his two cheeks. He chastised himself for he desired to regain his life, not recreate a gauche lifestyle glorified by others.

"Chicken dumplings are gone. I'd suggest the hot German potato salad with two sausages and rye bread." Kate's left hand adjusted a hairnet to recapture her freed black curls.

"I'll try it. Please add a piece of meringue pie and black coffee."

With a full plate before him, and not feeling rushed, he

savored each bite, even crushing meringue pie crumbs between his fork tines.

"So how was everything?" a chirpy Kate asked.

"Just great." Jake remembered his luncheon meat before its mold. "It's the first tasty meal I've had in this town."

Kate turned her head at the sound of dishes shattering in the kitchen.

Jake utilized the diner's fortuitous misfortune to burn the allure of her hazel eyes into his memory along with her black curly hair, cut short; ears exposed. He expected no man missed her buxom silhouette, yet, when she rotated her smile to him, her teeth's white gleam drew his gaze upward.

Her exaggerated gestures didn't fit a strict German heritage suggested by the menu, but her playfulness diverted attention from her short stature. Jake surmised she couldn't be taller than five-foot, two-inches and recalled the swing song: girl, five-foot-two, eyes of blue, but the lyrics didn't fit Kate. He mentally assigned her non-work personality to a rumba—slow, sensual and romantic.

"I hesitated to suggest potatoes after what you told me about your Navy duty." Kate's smile captivated him. "I'm glad you ate slow, past the supper rush. Gives us a minute to talk."

Jake's thumbs tapped a rumba beat on the counter. "Everyone has been exceptionally friendly, except for the jerk causing me all this trouble."

Kate swiveled on the counter stool next to Jake. "I was in the library last evening when Sgt. Smyth came to you, but not close enough to hear your conversation. Outside, from a distance, I saw a police car turn into the Mayflower."

Jake tried shallow breaths to counteract her perfume, strong to his nostrils. He daydreamed about a touch of her bare skin, beginning with her hands.

"However, not 'til this morning did I learn of a dead person found in a truck trailer. The *Herald-Gazette* reported an arrest. Then when I first met you with Emily this afternoon, your presence confused me."

"Had punches thrown at me today by a B&B drunk who

shouted I killed his son."

"Oh no." Kate's hands trembled. "That's despicable."

"Pastor John called him Ed."

Kate stiffened. "I believe I know him. Son claims his father beats him." Kate dropped a menu into a condiment holder.

"Can understand part of that. Athena, my wife . . ."

In the nano second, before Jake's constricted vocal chords relaxed, Kate's sweet cherub expression contorted into that of a gargoyle. "I never had to deal with raising kids." Kate's voice tinted with sadness. "From time to time I regret that." Her smile exploded. "Then, this diner can be as demanding and finicky as any rebellious teenager."

Jake winced when he touched his right side. He'd never strike a child. "I'm praying this whole ordeal will end soon."

Kate and her stool swiveled one revolution. "There's a special place in my heart for veterans and Emily. She's still a best friend, even though she doesn't work here anymore."

Jake wasn't aware of Kate's relationship to Emily other than their former employer/employee link. He sensed she protected Emily, and Kate's grouping Emily with veterans solidified his impression.

"At Emily's suggestion, peeked into your memorial room earlier today. It's impressive." Kate's radiance engulfed him. "You must be proud."

"Very much so. I was widowed eighteen years ago at age thirty-five. Oops—" Kate's blush spread beyond the two hands she slapped to both cheeks.

Jake jumped in to belie his *aha* moment and promised, "Won't add or subtract and what you said already forgotten."

"Glad you understand jerks don't eat well in Paradise." Kate's grin stretched ear-to-ear. "My husband, Hans, after our marriage in 1988, purchased this diner in 1990 from a woman in her eighties named Sadie." Jake nodded. "We retained her name for its reputation and enhanced goodwill. In 1991, Uncle Sam activated Hans's reserve unit." Kate's lips quivered. "Shrapnel killed Hans while on duty south of Baghdad. My pain double-sized because we had decided not to start a family until his unit shipped home."

Jake waited until he was sure Kate had finished. "Athena and I married late in life. With our life on the road, children weren't an option."

"Were you and your wife separated or divorced?"

"Neither, she died two years ago . . ." He forced the C word past his lips. "Cancer."

"I'm so very sorry. Every day I feed parents with children in the military. Tension is etched into their facial features. Fathers, who defended this country, now worry about their sons trudging with M-16 rifles or riding machine-gun-armed patrols on dusty desert roads with life-threatening danger around each bend." She inhaled an audible breath. "Hanging a picture pales in comparison to how those who have made life's supreme sacrifice have honored us. The American Legion meets in the room rent free. When there's a veteran's funeral, the diner offers the family a free after-the-service luncheon."

"That's more than commendable."

Kate's lips trembled. "It's the least I can do in Hans's memory."

Jake's right eye released a single tear. With the back of her right hand, Kate wiped away his tear and ignored her own.

"That's Sadie's and my military background. While on the USS Midway, did you know a sailor by the name of Henry Warner?"

"Really don't remember." Jake waited while Kate patted her cheeks with her apron's hem to revert to her diner owner exuberance. "Did he by chance have a nickname?"

"Not to my knowledge." She paused a moment. Her right hand wave acknowledged the arrival of two jabbering couples. "As a veteran, you have my prayers for all the best."

"Appreciate that. If you have my bill, I must be leaving."

Jake paid at the register, echoed Kate's thanks and began his tedious, boring journey along Main Street to the Mayflower. When he passed the B&B, jukebox music blared into the street. Tempted to venture inside for a beer, he didn't. He speculated that, while Clem would be there, so might others, like Ed, emboldened by booze into fuzzy thinking with their fists.

Jake arrived at the motel to find his room upheaval unchanged. He picked up a Gideon Bible from the floor and held it for ten seconds before he placed it, unopened, into the desk drawer from whence he believed it came. A found ice bucket he filled at the motel's ice machine. His room phone rang upon his return. His hello answered by silence and a disconnect click.

In pajamas, he cleared his bed of strewn clothes by a two-handed bedspread lift. Although a drapery peek confirmed the sun had not set, he slid under the top sheet, punched the pillow twice, pressed ice cubes wrapped in a washcloth on his oblique bruise and laid his head to rest.

The telephone rang. A second hang up. Jake retrieved his makeshift ice pack from between the sheets. He chilled his purple skin as he sat in the room's chair, his buttocks pressing new wrinkles into crumpled clothes. He stared at the phone.

Chapter Three

Delicate morning sun rays sliced through the vertical gap between the motel window drapes and the wall. Jake debated whether to lounge in bed or make coffee. Coffee won. He kicked aside a pile of his clothes, found his portable coffee pot and carried it into the bathroom.

Tugged free of its magnetic latch, Jake's left wrist flick banged the medicine cabinet door against the wall. "Well, I'll be damned!" he said aloud, his gaze transfixed.

On the door's white porcelain interior, two three-inch elongated ovals in brilliant red lipstick, each with a filled in dot the size of a dime, stared at him. Above each oval arched a red line with small marks, slightly curved and angled outward.

Eyes! A pair of eyes! What in the blazes for? I haven't been in this town long enough to be the butt of someone's joke.

Bewildered, Jake closed the cabinet door.

He muttered to himself: "It's not even seven a.m. and I'm awake without having driven all night." Wild, galloping thoughts whirled as he sipped his room-brewed coffee. Without the highway's adrenaline-infused diversion, the pain of missing Athena gnawed at his heart and soul. His recurring emptiness enfeebled his spirit.

Like a caterpillar's cocoon, his big rig cab functioned as a sanctuary from life's hurts. The criminal charges had locked his escape hatch to mental calmness. Even if he could compare himself to a pupa, he had to jettison his caterpillar analogy. Nature gave a pupa who enters a cocoon two choices—either transform into a butterfly or die. Jake desired to resume a self-supporting life, not transform.

After two years and multiple women who had shunned him, and he them, he accepted he couldn't resurrect a life patterned on Athena. With different negatives, he'd met three women in Paradise. The first, Emily, had been kind and her youthful age fostered his belated desire to be a father he'd never been. However, he desired a partner, not an adult daughter. Patricia's physical beauty and personality contrasts attracted him from the get-go. Regardless, he'd rubbed her the wrong way, and he estimated his chances to be nil. And now, Kate. Intrigued, he could foresee his interest in her growing, but he'd have to sacrifice his parental desires. Nevertheless, while she flirted with him, he doubted her life's vision included the possibility of a remarriage.

Jake tucked a red-striped shirt into his jeans before he pulled on gray crew socks. A knock at his door disrupted his room cleanup. He left the safety chain fastened and cracked the door.

"Mr. Brown, my name's Josh Miles. I'm a *Herald-Gazette* city reporter. I'd like to talk with you. Ask you for your side."

"Have nothing to say."

"Everyone says that at first. I'm just trying to learn the truth, let you tell the whole story." Miles spread his arms apart.

"There's nothing to tell." Jake unleashed his sharpest tone of indignation. "The Paradise Police arrested an innocent man."

Miles inched closer to the door. "Can I quote you on that?"

"Well, yes. And that's all. This conversation is finished."

Miles beseeched Jake, "Do me a favor please. Take my card." The reporter fished a business card from his shirt's top pocket and inserted its edge into the motel door crack.

With his right hand fingers, Jake grasped the card without a millimeter of door movement.

"Call me when you change your mind, even if it's off-the-record. You'll find me easier to get along with than the swarm of out-of-town reporters bound to hound you when the victim's name hits the Associated Press. I've written my home telephone number on the card. Call any time."

"Thanks, but no thanks. Said all I'm willing to say. Closing this door now." Jake waited sixty seconds before pressing his right eye to the closed-door peephole. No reporter. However, he hadn't heard a vehicle engine start.

He tossed his unsorted underwear and socks in the bottom dresser drawer to bring his belongings to pre-invasion status.

Bored with his *Cowboy* script, he retrieved the Gideon Bible and cradled its double-cracked spine. It fell open to Numbers. A line had been underlined: "Whoever touches the dead body of any human being shall be unclean for seven days . . ." Jake, longing to dwell within the living, skipped ahead to search for shreds of hope, trying to spot any passage Athena had quoted.

Past numerous dog-eared pages, he found, as expected, the Lord's uplifting promise of a home and a future in Jeremiah 29:11. With his curiosity refreshed, Jake paged slow through Jeremiah, skimming unfamiliar names and places. His mood grew heavier as each chapter forecast doom. His spirit sunk the deepest at Jeremiah 48 where the same ink that underlined the line in Numbers had circled, with no apparent rationale, nine words. His right forefinger lingered beneath: "Bethel," "men," "brick," "wall," "waters," "beard," "shaven," "hands," and "tied." He recognized Bethel as a biblical place, but his brain tired in his exhaustive word rearrangement to fathom a meaning or decode a coherent message beneath the nine words.

The Bible slipped off his right knee and bounced when it hit the floor. When Jake shifted his right leg, it tingled. Rubs to his right thigh reawakened his leg. The Bible's cracked spine had let it lie open, face down. He picked up the book, flipped it and read a beginning line of Psalm 13: "The fool says in his heart, 'There is no God.'"

From there he began a search until he came upon a margin entry next to Psalm 23. It read: "Repent before thee be saved." While he'd heard the words in many a radio preacher's sermon, Jake dismissed its relevance and attached little significance to the multitude of scribbles, random lines, arrows and circles within circles he found inside the back cover. He deciphered words. "Joni loves Chachie," "Emily craves Roger," "Jake is a double-crosser," "Clem likes boys," "Roger did Kate," "Tonto loves the Ranger," "Kitty runs more than a saloon," "Patricia will love Roger," and a second Jake reference: "Jake should repent." Jake rotated the page to make sure he'd read every word written.

A knock on his door preceded a woman's voice: "Housekeeping." Fearful the reporter still lurked nearby, Jake said "Good morning" with the safety chain engaged. A youthful Hispanic woman stood outside his door. Her white collar hid her name badge.

"Would you hold off until tomorrow?"

"Si` senor. Yes."

He waited until she rolled her cart out of his peripheral vision to close the door. Relieved he was alone, Jake fanned his Gideon without finding additional writings before he stowed it beneath two shirts in his top dresser drawer.

Stripped naked to enjoy the invigorating warmth of a second shower within twenty-four hours, he challenged the pulsating spray to dispel his sluggish, restless muscle tension. He shaved while shirtless and noted his oblique bruise had blossomed into a bluish-purple.

Chief Coltraine cut short his lunch at Sadie's to return to his office at thirty minutes past noon. He hadn't eaten a bite without a diner customer pestering him about the Mayflower homicide. His repeated comment: "We're still investigating." satisfied no citizen. Even he chafed at mouthing the only response he could utter to safeguard the investigation.

With a patrol officer called-in sick, he wished a councilman would stop by to learn how an under-manned police force threatened public safety. If he patrolled the streets today, there'd be no officer to answer the station's telephone.

The Chief's public phone rang.

He picked up to repeat to Josh Miles, in staccato verbatim fashion, the verifiable Mayflower victim facts Doc Beck had relayed. The Chief, his throat raspy, coughed twice. While he mentioned blunt force trauma, The Chief withheld that the Doc had found glass shards in the head wound.

"Any name?" Miles asked.

"No. Identity not yet verified. Off-the-record, coroner inked fingerprints to run through FBI's AFIS database. If we're lucky, we'll match the victim's fingerprints."

"Any idea or timeline on when you'll know?"

"None." The Chief twice inhaled e-cigarette vapor.

"Any identifying marks or tattoos?"

"Can't answer. It's a critical part of the ongoing investigation. Your story shouldn't speculate." The Chief realized Miles would read between the lines of his admonition.

"I hear you. You still securing the truck at the motel?"

"Yes . . . and I want citizens to stay away. Truck holds no souvenirs and any messing with the semi could interfere with our investigation and let the suspected killer go free."

"You referring to Mr. Jake Brown?"

"No, no." The Chief's yell irritated his larynx. His left hand fingertips stroked his throat. He struggled to project his normal volume. "I spoke in general. Mr. Brown is out on bail. Further charges against him will be the prosecutor's call."

"Source told me he dined last night at Sadie's."

"Every man has a right to eat. I hope he didn't have to endure constant interruptions." The Chief puffed his e-cigarette to avoid venting his lunchtime aggravation. "Any other question I can repeat no comment to?"

"No. Expect me to poke my head in Monday when I review your released weekend police reports."

Pleased Miles hadn't been as obnoxious as diner patrons, The Chief turned his attention to regular duties. He discarded Sgt. Smyth's note that stated no Wednesday or Thursday patrol or citizen reports to add to those logged in the computer.

The Chief fleshed out his scribbled notes of his morning visit to the Mayflower manager's office.

While Manager Aleck Werner told The Chief he witnessed nothing, a desk clerk had told Werner he'd seen a woman wander around the motel parking lot Wednesday night. The description had been vague: short, jeans, wore a nondescript head covering and looked old, which to the desk clerk meant past age thirty. The clerk remembered she paced back and forth several times and then disappeared. He recollected no vehicle nor did he see the woman enter any room.

Werner's response to The Chief's question said the clerk's observation had occurred during a five-minute smoke break around ten p.m., on the step outside the office's rear door. The Chief's Thursday observations verified the clerk's view would have been limited to the south parking lot and room doors on the motel's off-street side. His inquiry failed to uncover any employee who saw either vehicle parking or room entrances that faced Main Street. Werner was instructed to have Aaron, the desk clerk, call The Chief within twenty-four hours.

The Chief pondered the mysterious woman. Might be the victim, a few similarities, but nothing definitive. Polar opposite theories logical: a hooker waiting to meet a john or a vacationing, all-American mother and housewife, locked out by a spouse. To fit the pieces together, he needed concrete facts, not conjecture. He would poll his officers if the victim matched any working girls known to frequent the motel.

The Chief's private line rang.

"Chief, Dr. Beck. I received additional victim findings."

"Hope you got a name?" The Chief re-opened his case file.

"Sure do, but first a test result. Van Urk color test confirmed lysergic acid diethylamide-25, better known as LSD."

The Chief's pen dropped. "LSD! Did the woman overdose?"

"My experience says no. LSD is rarely fatal. Most deaths are indirect as users harm themselves or others because of their altered perceptions while on an 'acid' high."

"Take off your coroner hat and speculate with me." The Chief swallowed to buffer his throat pain. "Could the victim's attacker have been on LSD? Hit her with a beer bottle?"

"Possible. LSD's a party drug. Rather than speculate, I'm trying to isolate the wound's glass fragments. Shards had characteristics of a Hofensteger beer bottle. Even if identified, glass trace evidence, as you know, is not individualizing. It can only exclude, not include, a suspect."

"With the victim likely moved, finding the bottle weapon creates an impossible task. What about other illegal drugs?"

"Lab ran Scott test for cocaine. Came back negative. That means her bladder urine didn't indicate ingestion within four days prior to death. However, and the main reason I called, fingerprints identify victim as Kathie Krump of Paradise. She's the youngest daughter of Adolph Krump, the late retailer."

The Chief wrote "Krump, Kathie/Mayflower." Her name resounded in his memory. Bank robbery, Halloween, 2007. The crime, biggest in Paradise history, had occurred nine months after he signed on as Police Chief. Others suspected her; he lacked evidence. "Anything else, Doc? Name of killer?"

"You always want me to do your job, don't you?"

The Chief now had to piece together whether an over-the-road driver hauled illegal drugs. Marijuana, hidden in and harvested from Midwest cornfields, prospered in epidemic proportions. Mexican drug runners trucked in harder drugs via the interstate system.

He meditated on how he would handle the public revelation of LSD in the victim, notably a female descendent of a wealthy, respected businessman. He rifled through his file cabinet for his

Halloween caper file. Two bags of gold coins, bonds and money stolen by a gang of daring robbers not recovered. He recalled a chilly fall day, the closest Saturday to October 31. He had stood on Main Street, near Sadie's for a two p.m. Halloween parade. Young and old citizens alike reveled in purchased and homemade costumes. He hadn't seen the veiled bride or the masked groom. The parade and the fake wedding party had given the crooks cover to strike before the bank's automatic timer locked its vault at three.

His notes of two years previous said the bank that afternoon had operated with a skeleton crew. He chuckled to himself. While he had meant a reduced staff, he must have been in the spirit of the holiday. A connection overlooked in 2007 jumped out at him. The get-away car had been sighted near the flourmill after two-thirty. A trailer empty eighteen-wheeler parked at the mill's loading dock could have swallowed both robbers and car.

He had no doubt the semi wasn't Jake's. The burned-out big rig had been found a week later south of Paradise near Silverton. When he visited the scene, nitroglycerine's faint banana smell and scrap metal hurtled a quarter mile left no doubt that multiple TNT sticks had exploded. A three-inch piece of generic wedding veil on a farmer's field fence, snagged by barbed wire, remained a vivid visual memory.

"Hey, Chief. Anything to report?"

The Chief lifted his gaze to Lt. Samuel T. Sigourney dressed in khaki beneath a Kevlar vest. Paradise's second in command, ten years younger than The Chief, stood thick through the chest and arms. The Chief withheld his criticism of Sigourney's longish brown hair.

"Been quiet. Remember it's you against the world. Call Sgt. Smyth if you need backup."

The Chief closed his Halloween file. His unfilled stomach would welcome Roberta's lasagna without guest interruption.

Minutes before seven, Jake completed his Mayflower to B&B trek for his first dance. Inside the Main Street entrance, he combed his wind-blown hair and decided not to pinch his neck with the top button of his yellow-striped dress shirt. He felt light on his feet as his leather-soled black slip-ons and thin cotton socks replaced his everyday sweat socks and work boots.

He handed Emily a crisp five-dollar bill. She smiled, stamped his hand with a W, and wished him well.

Jake planted his elbow on the bar's end and tried to act inconspicuous. Emily greeted Jacob Z. Cummings and Patricia Swanson. Neither spotted him before they parted for different tables. Four couples entered before Emily said, "Hello, Kate. I didn't expect to see you here this evening. Must be the band!"

"I felt bored. Sadie's emptied out, so I thought I'd follow my diners and attend the dance. Never heard this band before."

While Kate searched her purse, Emily hurled a flinty expression in Jake's direction. He jerked his head and shoulders sideways to allow the gentleman next to him to shield his face from Emily. When ticket sales required Emily's attention, he peeked right to spot a vacant chair next to Jacob. He hurried to it and rested his palms on the chair's back. "Is this seat taken?"

"It's yours on one condition," Jacob replied.

Jake rose to the bait. "What's that?"

"If you see a gorgeous woman looking for a seat, you must say something like 'I'm going to the bar for a beer, please take my seat next to the handsome Mr. Cummings.'" Jacob winked to the other two gentlemen at his table.

Jake rolled his eyes.

"You can shorten and forget the beer part if it's too much."

"No problem," Jake said. "But let me warn you that no woman will be interested in leaving the dance floor while I'm out there." Jake punctuated his boast with a soft laugh.

Jacob's emerging smile told Jake that Jacob relished the verbal jousting.

"Fellows," Jacob said, "this here's Jake. He's a member of the Spring Daisy Theatre cast. Jake, this is Rick and Joe. Both co-workers at 3N Refrigerator. We all do parts assembly." Before Jacob added details, the band began their first song—a medium tempo foxtrot. "Okay, gentlemen, the ladies are ready to dance. Lace up those shoes."

While Jacob and his two friends strode across the floor, Jake hesitated. As the music played, he ambled halfway around the dance floor perimeter. Thirty-five couples danced. He saw Kate with a gentleman in a suit. Jake gazed at his black dress slacks and moved on. When he saw a seated Patricia engaged in conversation with a woman at her table, he widened his circle.

When the band switched to Glenn Miller's theme song, Jake, his butterflies calmed and his toes energized, bee-lined it straight to Patricia. He perceived her lips formed a "no" to his dance request until the woman seated with her spoke up to say their chat could wait.

Patricia sparkled in a knee-length, pink, silk-chiffon pencil dress with a portrait collar. Sexy, long strapped, low-heeled dance shoes graced her feet. Since three strings of pearls draped Patricia's throat, Jake judged pearls were the in thing for he had seen a strand accentuate Emily's high black collar.

Jake started with multiple basic foxtrot steps, each a set of slow, slow, quick, quick. At the floor's corner, he rotated his closed-position dance frame to lead a promenade step and a partner's arch turn. He relaxed his left-hand fingers so as not to crush Patricia's right hand. With flawless precision, Patricia executed additional basic steps and a set of two parallel breaks. With a quarter-left pivot, Jake avoided a collision with a back-stepping couple in front of them. Two additional quarter turns rotated he and Patricia clear of potential body bumps and into the proper counterclockwise line of dance. While Patricia smiled, neither of them spoke. When the music stopped, Jake escorted Patricia to her seat and thanked her. She nodded.

Jake overheard the lady Patricia had been seated with say, "You two looked elegant out there." In his mind, Jake agreed.

With his gaze still on Patricia, he stepped sideways and crashed into a woman he didn't know. The band picked up the tempo with a '50s rock 'n' roll tune that alluded to Beethoven. Jake uttered a quick apology and, without deliberation, asked the woman if she cared to dance. With a yes, Jake and she were amid two dozen dancers. His initial awkward arm jerks told Jake his swing footwork wasn't in sync. To enhance his body's rhythm, he kept his moves simple with single loop and arch turns, a man's back-pass and the basic swing step. When the unexpected swing became a medley to salute Memphis, the repetition of two-count triple steps and single-count rock steps revitalized his antidote to frazzled nerves.

The woman introduced herself as Mary. He replied, "Jake, and thank you for the dance." After the bandleader announced a short break with a waltz set upcoming, Jake strode to the bar.

"Diet cola in a beer glass," requested Jake.

"Coming up," Clem said.

Jake sipped his drink while he watched a woman in his chair converse with Jacob. Without a good reason to interrupt, he chose to be a friend and stay where he was.

He spied Kate twenty feet away. She stood resplendent in a kelly green, scoop-neck top with cap sleeves and white slacks creased to visually lengthen her legs until green pumps peeked out from a miniature flare. A gold chain adorned her neck, no pearls. Jake believed every other male with a pulse, even if married, would be transfixed by her stylish beauty.

Jake meandered in Kate's direction. She said yes to his waltz dance request and to the open floor they went. After two basic rotating box steps devoid of clashing toes, Jake raised his left hand on the second half of the third box. After a left foot rotation to the one-two-three rhythm, he shortened his right step to face her when she completed the underarm turn.

He whispered, "Are you comfortable leaving the box step?"

She grinned and nodded. He completed three progressive waltz steps before his pivot into a counter-step to dance backward. He rotated his dance frame so they could resume basic progressive steps before the music ended.

Jake held Kate's right hand to lead her from the floor and she didn't move. "Jake, I like to waltz and most bands play two in a row. So, let's wait and dance another."

"That's fine by me. You're an excellent dancer."

"Thank you. Easy to tell you've been on a ballroom dance floor yourself."

They continued to chitchat about the B&B and the weather.

Jake noticed Patricia eyed them without a physical movement in their direction. When a German waltz with its quicker tempo began, Jake attempted to duplicate the identical waltz pattern from their first dance. He succeeded until he forgot to raise Kate's right hand for the lady's second promenade turn. However, before he could recover, the music stopped.

Jake walked Kate to her table. After a polite thank you, he wove through milling couples toward Jacob's table.

Patricia met him en route. "I've requested a polka and the band said they'd play it after two waltzes. Do you polka?" Patricia's right foot tapped the floor.

"Have, maybe a little rusty. If you're asking, I'm ready."

"I'm asking." Jake welcomed her generous smile.

With the first downbeat, Jake and Patricia led the pack's triple step to a state-inspired late 1940's polka. Jake stumbled twice, but caught himself to avoid a barrel roll into Patricia's legs. Patricia's unbounded energy encouraged twirls and spins until his arms ached. The whirl of tighter and tighter floor circles left Jake, not Patricia, winded.

Between two gasps for air, Jake said, "I'm glad you're here and willing to dance with me. I hoped you weren't holding Thursday's smart-aleck library remark against me."

Patricia met his gaze. "That's behind me." She glanced around to perceive if anyone eavesdropped and then leaned closer. "I shouldn't have been so sensitive. It was only a picture. Here's Emily."

"What are you two doing? Practicing your lines for *Cowboy*?"

"Don't you wish," Jake kidded. "We were commenting how nice a dance this is, the band and all."

Emily, a grin on her face, stood by Patricia. "So you like the band. That's great. The crowd seems to have responded to them. I must check a cooler. You both have a good time."

Jake watched a gentleman's arm wave at Emily as she sashayed across the dance floor. The blood in his facial capillaries warmed when Patricia's eyes rotated from a distant Emily and intersected his riveted gaze at Emily's hip sway.

Patricia smiled at Jake. "Thank you for the dance. Would you dance the next foxtrot with the woman in red at my table? She's been here often and of late doesn't dance. She needs a strong leader such as yourself."

Jake placed his right forearm in front of his stomach and his left behind his back and formally bowed to acknowledge her compliment. Her right hand stifled what Jake perceived to be a coquettish giggle.

"Be happy to," Jake said. "Expect a foxtrot real soon."

As Patricia departed, Jacob approached. "You weren't kidding me when you said the ladies stay on the dance floor when you're there." His hands carried three empty mugs.

"Not all. Saw a pretty woman sitting at your table a few minutes ago." Jake tried to spot this woman again, but couldn't. "Stayed away to give you an opportunity to try your best line."

Jacob set the mugs on a table. "I'm thinking that, if we play our cards right, together we'd have every single woman here fighting to dance with us." Jacob imitated a boxer's stance.

"Think I'll pass. Seek a good time, that's all."

"Well, you better watch out," Jacob warned. "I've observed both Patricia and Kate keeping their eyes on you, and each spying the other." Jake shrugged. "Before that polka, I've never seen Patricia approach a guy with a dance proposition like she did you. And Kate saw her."

"You're overanalyzing a simple dance."

"Don't think so. I've known both women for years. Danced with each a time or two. They're friendly, but I've never perceived either had a romantic crush on me."

Behind Jacob, Jake heard the clink of music stands and the click of drumsticks. To Jacob, he uttered a talk-to-you-later. True to his promise, Jake strode direct to the lady dressed in red who sat opposite Patricia. The woman consented to his dance request and Patricia's smile broadened.

When the foxtrot ended, Jake brought Sarah to the table where Patricia still sipped a cola. He ignored the feminine jealousy Jacob had spoke of and asked Patricia to dance the expected foxtrot. Jake fancied the groove Patricia's graceful movements induced in him. Not since tripping-the-light-fantastic with Athena had his feet glided across the buffed maple without hesitation or deliberate thought.

The band's intermission allowed Jake to excuse himself from Patricia's presence before his emotions exploded. He required no restroom water to cleanse hands never in contact with a poisonous nightshade, yet, bittersweet feelings sprouted within his heart and pulsed through his veins.

Jake crumpled a paper towel when he stood at the bar. Before he ordered, an out-of-uniform Chief Coltraine halted his advance a step past the Main Street entry corridor. The Chief's serious gaze surveyed the ballroom tables and then the bar.

"Mr. Brown, I didn't know you danced."

"A little, it's good exercise." Jake followed The Chief's eyes to the bar's beer glass with dried foam to Jake's right.

"I've come to enjoy the music." The Chief greeted Clem and said, "Maybe later." He turned to Jake. "Enjoy dancing."

Jake nodded and dallied at the bar to watch The Chief greet others with pats and handshakes as he strolled toward the George Street exit.

Encouraged that his leg muscles hadn't stiffened, Jake danced with four or five different ladies to start the second half. He confused himself by trying to memorize names with faces.

When the band leader announced an upcoming waltz, he sought and found Kate chatting with a middle-aged couple. "Kate, excuse me, may I have this next dance?"

"Of course. Why attend if one doesn't dance?"

On the floor, Kate commented that he was fast developing an eager following of female dancers. Jake desired to shrug off Kate's expressed observation without a comment. Kate's expectant stare didn't ebb.

"It's a dance. Everyone should enjoy themselves." Kate nodded. "You appear to be having fun." Jake led a promenade. "You're a good dancer."

"Thank you." Kate squeezed his hand as the waltz ended.

Before the band packed their instruments, Jake danced with nine ladies, four where he initiated the request. He didn't dance with either Patricia or Kate again, but did say good night to both before they left. Jake sat on an empty bar stool.

"Another usual?" Clem asked, a diet cola in his right hand.

"No. Give me a Hofensteger bottle and a glass."

Jake savored the coldness of two sips. He responded to a tap on his left shoulder with an upper torso twist in that direction.

"You really impressed the ladies tonight with your footwork and willingness to switch partners," Emily said. Jake's hips and legs completed his body's rotation. "Alert me next time. I might post your attendance on the bulletin board under the name of the band to give the ladies fair notice."

Clem extended his right hand, its thumb up, toward Jake.

"It was fun, a fine band and the ladies all dance well."

"You better be careful," Emily advised. Her facial muscles tightened. "One of the ladies here tonight might have designs on you becoming their exclusive dance partner. In fact, I think I could name two candidates already."

Jake, on guard that Emily may have been conspiring with Jacob, also readied himself to ferret out any subtle sign of jealousy. "Keep speaking that way and I'll be embarrassed."

"You just mark my words." Emily fingered her pearls.

"And I predict we men will join forces and persuade or coax you onto your own dance floor."

"I'll think about it." A coy smile danced on Emily's lips.

Clem eased closer to his boss and Jake. He had what Jake interpreted to be the perplexed expression of one who thought he'd missed something important, but remained too scared to admit it. Clem asked, "Ever haul to the chemical plant in Moss Point, Mississippi?"

"Not that I remember. Why there?"

"My mother raised me in Moss Point. You look familiar and I recall, as a teenager, the police questioned me about a man with a name like yours. I don't mean no harm."

"None taken." Emily rotated her left ear toward Jake. "Not the man to fit your recollection. Would you sell me another beer and leave the cap on? Want to take it with me."

Clem's right hand, dripping water, plunked a capped beer

bottle on the bar. He wiped it dry and collected Jake's money.

"Good night, Emily, Clem."

Jake guided his feet to the Main Street door and began his long, dimly lit, crack-counting trek to his Mayflower room. He tried not to anticipate what he might discover. A westbound Paradise police car, speed reduced to a crawl, rolled past him.

He sensed more than the squad car tailed him. A half block after George Street, Jake's abrupt pivot had him face an unpopulated street.

A block further on, a rag-tag man, facial features obscured by shadow, waved from a bench seat across the street. Jake hesitated. When convinced the man would not disrupt his motel journey, Jake waved once and hustled onward.

Chapter Four

No early morning sun bombarded Jake's eyes or warmed his whiskered cheeks this Sunday morning. The unopened, contents-warm bottle of Hofensteger beer, ready for his breakfast, stood next to the TV. Jake refused to pounce on it. While its presence and his sleeping in a motel room constituted physical freedom, his locked truck together with the court's travel restriction presented a larger geographical cell.

He threw back the covers, and his right-hand fingertips stroked both calves. Early a.m. calf-muscle cramps had woken him twice. Even so, he counted himself lucky. Neither his knees nor his side ached after his two-year-delayed return to the ballroom. He squeezed an abdomen skin fold with the belief, if he had a scale to verify, he'd lost two pounds.

He showered, but didn't open the medicine cabinet doors. No eyes, not even drawn lipstick ones, he chuckled, soft and low, would see his naked body. The forced walks, his self-made promise to substitute diet cola for beer and Paradise's exquisite dance ladies would keep him limber and sober. While he longed to jump into his big rig and outrun his fear, last week's choice no longer existed. As the white towel fluffed his wet hair, he envisioned himself to be a solitary figurine captured inside a snow globe.

For fifteen years, Athena, his emotional support pillar, had encompassed his entire family. Without regret, he had given up kids for her companionship. Not only had her death showered him with grief, it resurrected the middle age reality that mortality permitted no redo. Within a week, his fellow actors had, in differing ways, been there for him. While they could cushion his future, he alone faced the stark inner reality of uncertainty in a ticking, uncompromising world.

His room's 2007 telephone book displayed the address of First Presbyterian Church as near the intersection of Chestnut Street and Hancock Boulevard. It's street map showed Hancock Boulevard even farther east than Sadie's. His inner voice urged: *Better to know one preacher than none.*

Jake eased a curtain from the window, scanned the clouds and searched the bottom dresser drawer for his trusty green poncho. He donned a clean blue shirt and his black slacks and his leather slip-ons worn the night before.

While he enjoyed the distraction of a new Paradise route, he cringed when his map's gaze encountered Willow Street. The jail existed on Willow. His unexplained wonderment of not locating a cottonwood street, boulevard or avenue dissipated with the more practical concern if it would rain before noon. He tossed the phone book aside, locked his motel door and set out to arrive at the church for the ten-thirty service. As his left hand clutched his poncho, he walked east on Main Street, ready to protect himself should the gathering clouds spit out raindrops.

At the B&B, he turned right to stroll south on George Street. After a block, the wind gust soughed through the trees that lined both street sides. Left and right of him were old, stately, front-porch style homes of wood and brick, no huge estates. Redone sidewalk concrete thwarted his crack count for there were none.

At the intersection of George and Chestnut Streets, he turned left. Chestnut's serene character parroted his George Street observations. In its second block a classic Dutch colonial with its distinctive roofline reminded him of his parents's home. Two upended tricycles and a sandbox aside the house spoke of a family with small kids. Next-door, a neat two-story brick bungalow beckoned visitors with its classic front porch. Well-mulched flower boxes nurtured sturdy stems populated with buds ready to burst. Red and white flowering tulips, flanked by spaded soil, predicted additional annuals. Six ascending steps led to the porch. The breeze ruffled the canopy of a wooden porch swing hung to the left of the home's front door.

Jake could envision a real life Dennis the Menace and Mr. Wilson scenario between these two neighbors if the brick house residents didn't adore children. His brother had been nicknamed Dennis. His childhood past faded when he saw ahead a sign for Hancock Boulevard.

He turned right on Hancock. In the middle of the block on his left loomed the simplified gothic-styled steeple of a dark-red brick church. Concrete steps ascended to double oaken doors. Steps on both sides of the main upward path accessed descended to lower level entrances Jake didn't have time to explore. Cars filled street spaces. Jake skirted eight people in conversation clumped together on the sidewalk.

He climbed the steps with the air of a veteran churchgoer. An usher extended an open palm and welcomed him. "Go straight ahead. Find any vacant seat." Jake slid into a left side sanctuary pew to unfold and refold the dry, unworn poncho he deposited on the pew. His gaze found Reverend John Olson, in multi-colored vestments dominated by green, lead the liturgist to the altar via the sanctuary's center aisle. With the service begun, Jake stood and sat, guided by those in front of him. The

Bible readings sounded familiar.

Rev. Olson's baritone voice didn't require amplification. While Jake listened to the sermon's main theme of justice within the world, his mind wandered and the reverend's voice inflections did little to keep his attention. His subconscious heretic voice told him that the world lacked justice.

The voice asked why, if Jesus had embraced justice, didn't He select the biblical person with the name translated as justice to replace Judas, the disgraced disciple? Why hadn't the Gospel explained that? Did the person named Justice represent evil, the opposite of Jesus's love? Jake shuddered to think Paradise "justice" had determined he represented evil? How in scripture could "justice," a positive earthly trait, be negative and be forsaken by God? On the road he never entertained doubts. If he had a question, Athena had an answer. Living outside his cab's door without her ripped at his heart and soul.

At the oaken doors, now an exit, Pastor John, radiating a broad smile, welcomed him. "What a definite pleasure to see you in our midst."

"Engaging sermon. Had me thinking."

"Please stay for lunch?" Pastor John adjusted his vestment. "It's a long story, but we have a few families of Greek ancestry. Once a year they challenge our taste buds to abandon bland Midwest food for authentic Greek specialties. And today you're in luck. Please stay and give us time to talk later."

"Will do that. Thanks."

Jake hesitated at the bottom of the church's front steps and joined a line headed down the steps to his left. His breakfast-denied stomach grumbled. When a young boy ahead of him turned to face him, Jake raised his hands to flap his ears. The boy buried his face in his mother's skirt. Moments later the boy snuck a peek behind and Jake smiled. At the end of the line, Jake paid and six food servers each added a specialty from an aluminum pan to a tray before the last offered it to him.

Seated, he gazed at a full chicken quarter prepared from a Greek oregano recipe, gyros, spanakopita, rice pilaf and Greek bean salad. He gave thanks and the chicken, closest to the fork, won the first-item-to-be-eaten honor. In the fellowship hall background, a CD played up-tempo Greek folk dance music. Hot black coffee satiated his caffeine deficiency.

Halfway through his plate's mountain of food, he heard a man's voice ask: "Is this seat taken?" Jake looked up, surprised to gaze at cast member Bob Hunter.

"Why no. Please have a seat. Didn't expect to see anyone I knew, except for the reverend."

"While not a Presbyterian, I do enjoy their food festivals. And today's a double blessing when my wife and brother-in-law visit her mother."

Jake flashed back to remembrances of eating tasty morsels served by Athena's mother. On the road, Athena scoured ad flyers for Greek restaurants. His memories temporarily paralyzed his vocal cords. He fought his left eye's release of a small tear. "This morning I decided to visit God for an hour with the expectation of walking to Sadie's for lunch." Bob nodded. "After the service, Pastor John tipped me off about this spread." Jake wiped a paper napkin across his chin.

"I'm glad I found you." Bob's gaze flitted left and right. "I had planned to find you last night at the B&B. However, my wife, who isn't a dancer, distracted me from my trip downtown. I've good news about your application. Would you come to my office tomorrow, say about eleven?"

"Sure. Be happy too. Since you mentioned dancing, I'd be willing to help you and your wife learn simple ballroom steps."

"Oh, I don't know. Rita doesn't want to stand out. She'd get flustered with other people watching." Bob closed his teeth and lips on a bite of chicken.

"No pressure. Made the same offer to Emily when she said she couldn't dance, and she owns a ballroom. Sure you and your wife's presence would help Emily. We could close the Spring Daisy Theatre panels to give us privacy. One Frank Sinatra CD would provide all the foxtrot tempos necessary."

"Oh, I don't know. Let me think about it. I do own an Ol' Blue Eyes CD." Bob smiled and ate another forkful of chicken.

"Like I said, no pressure."

"Now who called this thespian meeting?" Jake, without the tilt of his head, recognized Pastor John's voice.

"He did," Bob said, pointing a fork with impaled green beans at Jake. Jake nodded in the affirmative.

"Bob, nice to see you here again. We're always willing to take a handful of Lutheran dollars out of your billfold."

"I savor this Greek food." Bob slid his chair back. "And last week I helped one of your kitchen cooks sell one house and buy another. He told me he expected me to taste the spanakopita he prepares. Besides, I'll count Presbyterian faces at our church's summer festival in July." Bob winked at Jake.

"No doubt you will. I might lead our group. Say, Jake, I see you're about done. Can I pull you away for a moment?" Pastor John waved to another table en route to an exit.

Jake bent his shoulder and head in Bob's direction. "Thank you," he whispered. "Trust me to be at your office tomorrow."

Bob bid Jake good-bye.

"How was the food?" asked Pastor John as he and Jake stood on the church's front, empty sidewalk.

"Great. Fully stuffed." Jake's right hand patted his stomach. "Want to thank you for my rescue at the B&B Friday. Was between a rock and hard place. Take a beating or fight and be in more trouble." Jake's right forefinger rubbed his right ear.

"You should thank Clem more." Pastor John clasped his hands. "He pinned Ed's arms with that bear hug. I only tried to make peace, a character trait of the role Emily gave me. This morning's paper showed Ed's accusations were unfounded." Jake's jaw dropped. "The *Herald-Gazette*'s front-page story said a woman, not a boy, was found in your semi."

"Haven't read a paper. Everyone's more informed than me."

"Can I assume you can't leave town?"

"Right."

"Then I'd surmise a truck driver with no truck would put a severe dent in your finances."

"Right again." Jake shifted his weight to his right foot. "But I'm hopeful."

"Glad to hear that. Here's what's on my mind." Pastor John

extended both hands. "Summer's fast approaching and this year the church plans to replace the roof. We have a roofer member who needs help. Not with shingling, but unloading bundles from a delivery truck, carrying them up the scaffold and picking up the old shingles tossed off the roof." The reverend paused. "Likewise, a member painter will spruce up the interior. He also needs help. Both have given the elders a reasonable work bid. I may be wrong, but I would estimate a helper to be paid the minimum wage of $6.50 an hour. Would you be interested?"

Jake stretched his gaze past the Chestnut intersection. He expressed his worry to Pastor John. "Don't you have church members that would want these jobs?"

"Both craftsmen told me they passed the word with no takers. Thus, if you agree to help us, it would benefit the church and, I hope, you as well."

Jake tried to determine how to save this opportunity if his interview with Bob tanked. "Could I have time to think it over? Perhaps give you my decision Tuesday at play rehearsal?"

Jake observed Pastor John's slow exhale and the relaxation of his shoulders. "That would be fine. If you became a member of our church, then that would eliminate your concern about offending another by taking the job or jobs."

"Beginning to get an inkling of how you maintain such a large congregation."

"We pray and try to do the Lord's work." Pastor John drifted into his sermon voice. "That includes not only consoling souls and preaching, but keeping the altar dry from the Lord's welcome rain and having a bright, uplifting sanctuary in which to worship Him. No one during our services should need to use the poncho I see in your hand."

Jake felt a sheepish grin spread across his face.

"God speed." Pastor John pivoted.

Jake stood in place while Pastor John descended the church steps. Then he marched right toward Sadie's Diner.

"**H**i, twinkle toes!"

Surprised by Kate's remark, Jake froze. "Oh, hi, Kate. Do

you work every day, including Sundays?"

"Cook's sick. I'm the substitute."

Jake's memory dwelled on Kate's white slacks of the night before and her affectionate hand on his right shoulder. Today, a full-length, grease-splattered apron hid her multi-colored, swirling skirt. Her white cook hat failed to flatter.

"Only interested in a cup of coffee."

"Oh, is that all?"

Jake sensed the flirtation. He tightened his lips into a straight line as he watched Kate's face for a telltale coquettish smile that never appeared. "Need . . . need a ham sandwich and a slice of meringue pie to go." Jake's facial muscles lost their rigidity and a low, soft chuckle escaped through his parted lips.

Kate blushed. "Coffee's coming right up. How about Table 12?" Jake nodded. In addition to Kate, he counted three diner patrons and one server.

"One coffee, black, no sugar. Do I remember right?"

"Yes, you do." He poured a cup from the carafe as Kate vanished into the kitchen.

She returned to sink into a chair across from him. "You made quite an impression with the ladies last night at the B&B."

"How so?" He tipped hot coffee to his lips.

"By the way you danced. More important, that you were a gentleman willing to dance with everyone. Two female customers this morning asked to know more about you." Kate realigned the salt and pepper shakers. "I told them you were a dirty rotten scoundrel. An out-of-town playboy passing through."

Jake swallowed hard.

"Just kidding."

It was then Jake saw the flirtatious gleam in Kate's hazel eyes, reminiscent of his earlier visit. "Really enjoyed our waltzes. Guess we'll have no encore chance until Saturday?"

"For a ballroom waltz, yes. But if you're ready for a fast, down-home, rockabilly waltz with a rambunctious crowd, then you only have to wait two days until Tuesday."

"What's Tuesday?" Jake's chest expanded with an

unexplained surge of expectation.

"Didn't Emily tell you? Tuesdays are heavy into rock 'n' roll. Most attendees dance solo, gyrating wild to the musical beat, lights and strobes."

Jake lowered his cup to the table. "Not much into this partner-less rockabilly stuff. For certain foxtrots, an upbeat tempo can match be-bop's swing. Might be, like last night, a little rusty and uncoordinated." He reached for his cup.

"Let me tell you from personal experience, you weren't uncoordinated last night. I didn't feel any rust." Kate smiled.

Jake didn't interrupt her glance toward the server at the counter. "You're too kind." Jake gazed across the room to the diner's front window. "The clouds appear to be darkening, brewing up a storm. If I can't dance like a cowboy, must hustle to the Mayflower to learn their lingo."

"The server has your order. How about a travel cup?"

"Not necessary." Jake rose from his chair.

"I'd love to give you a ride, but I can't leave until seven." Kate stood. "The cook should recover by tomorrow and the weatherman predicts sun. What say tomorrow I fancy up leftovers and we can enjoy an afternoon picnic?" Kate's eyes pleaded for a yes. "There's one western swing I can show you."

Jake, now caught off-guard twice by Kate, pushed his chair under Table 12 to give his brain thinking time. "How's half past one?"

"Great. If the lunch rush has slowed, we'll be off. If not, I'll fill you with coffee until I can leave. Okay?"

"Look forward to the sun's bright return, a picnic lunch and your smile." Kate's face glowed. "Until tomorrow."

Jake spotted a folded *Herald-Gazette* on the counter. When he paused, Kate offered to let him take it with. He discovered no new sidewalk cracks on Main Street and aborted his attempt to whistle after one pitiful try.

Kate's dance appearance re-entered his mind. Patricia, in her pink silk-chiffon dress and sexy, strapped shoes, had pushed Kate off his frontal lobe. As he quickened his pace, memories of sparkling pearls that had adorned Patricia, Emily and others glinted out of brain cells crowded with tactile remembrances of soft shoulders and delicate hands. Pleasured by memory cells working overtime, he arrived at his Mayflower room in less than fifteen minutes.

While his prepaid stay expired Tuesday, Jake shunted aside whether to add a day and ambled to the ice machine outside the motel's office to fill his room's plastic bucket. He iced his unopened Hofensteger bottle, the ham sandwich and the meringue pie in his room's bathroom sink before he sat in the bedroom's only chair to unfold the *Herald-Gazette*.

A top-of-the-fold headline screamed: "**Female Body Found in Truck at Mayflower.**" When Jake read the coroner had ruled the death a homicide, he dropped the paper, clasped his hands to his cheeks and recited the Our Father. He re-read the entire article three times to find only the victim's basic height, weight, hair color and age—no name or other identification.

In a daze, he yanked open the dresser drawer to bury his fears in the hopeful words of Jeremiah 29. When he read further, he grappled with the nine circled words. His frazzled mind wove them into the details of his present life. His *Cowboy* character was unshaven. He found "beard" and "unshaven" in the Bible's circled words.

Jake trembled when he linked the words "hands" and "tied" as a reference to Sgt. Smyth's cuffing him to his own truck. The word "waters" he envisioned to be anything from a lake, stream or river to a symbol of baptism or initiation. "Men," "brick," "hands," "tied," and "waters" could be combined to signify or forecast a mob execution by drowning. His *Cowboy* character faced a pistol pointed at his forehead.

Jake tossed the Gideon Bible and the newspaper into a dresser drawer and slammed it shut.

Come on, mind, shift it into reverse, and revert to white slacks, pink chiffon, pearls, foxtrot, waltz and pretty women . . .

Jake slumped into his chair and buried his head in his hands.

The fact I'm alone doesn't give you unlimited opportunity to torment me. After Athena, I shed enough tears to last a lifetime. I couldn't control she had breast cancer. Don't drive me crazy.

I decided a week ago not to continue running away from life.

He wiped the tears from his cheeks and gazed at the ceiling. "Lord, it's too early for me to quit. I owe Athena."

He shivered when a clap of thunder portended the rain and potential violent winds he had avoided all day. While the closed drapes simulated a shroud, he feared life's protections eluded him. The diffident recesses of his mind into which he had locked Athena's love would be flooded with grief. Just as the drapery crack would diffract lightning, the oracles of evil awaited to decree his fate.

His heart battled his inner voice's plea to bolt Paradise.

Chapter Five

Josh Miles, *Herald-Gazette* reporter, knocked twice on Chief Coltraine's office doorjamb.

Seated in his desk chair, The Chief, annoyed by the interruption, grumbled, "I'm not in." After a second knock, he tilted his gaze upward. "You again?"

Miles edged into The Chief's office. "Yes, sir. I bet you're busting with joy to make my Monday."

The Chief refused to let Miles's sarcasm faze him. With courtesy, he waited until Miles opened his notebook.

"I can tell you the state lab fingerprint analysis identified the victim as Kathie Krump of Paradise. Age thirty, she's the daughter of the late Adolph Krump." The Chief flipped a page in the open folder on his desk. "Not for publication, but my ID comes from state fingerprints after her arrest five years ago."

Without invitation, Miles plopped into a chair in front of

The Chief's desk. "Café source told me that Ms. Krump was supposedly seen alive at the Mayflower a day or two before her corpse appeared. The motel denied me register proof, but when I asked, the reaction told me she wasn't a signed-in guest."

"Can't confirm or deny." The Chief rubbed his chin with a left-hand knuckle. "Again, not for publication, I heard about a suspicious woman at the Mayflower. However, I'm not ready to run traces on every registered guest since that would be an extraordinary waste of time."

Miles shifted his gaze from his notebook to The Chief. "Any official determination on cause of death?"

"No, just the preliminary stuff I told you Saturday." He stiffened his posture. "We're still trying to identify or verify all the substances in her body." The Chief relaxed his muscles.

"Holding to a conclusion she was killed in the truck trailer?"

"It's the most logical. We're also exploring the possibility the killer murdered her elsewhere and then left her in the truck trailer until a better place could be found. The Cottonwood and Minnesota Rivers have been suggested. In Ohio, with which I'm more familiar, the expanse of woods in a neighboring state park would be a prime disposal location."

Miles glanced up at The Chief. "Police find or identify the blunt force trauma instrument?"

"Still looking." The Chief remained convinced his decision not to mention the head wound's glass fragments was sound, but he offered a hint. "We're searching for something with an edge breakable upon contact."

"Thanks." Miles rose to leave. "I'll stay in touch."

"Hold on a sec. Since I'm new, curious if anything like this has ever happen in Paradise?"

Miles adjusted his cap. "Can recollect a murder or two. Husband shooting wife or vice versa. To waggle tongues, the town's never seen anything like this." He tugged at his cap's visor. "I guess no town is immune these days."

"Appreciate your sharing." The Chief arched his back. "Trust me, this killer will face justice."

Chief Coltraine tipped his hat to the Needles and Pins Tailors counter clerk. He had telephoned ahead to meet with Herman Krump, Kathie's older brother.

With his hat in his lap, The Chief sat opposite Herman in the store's manager's office. "My sincere sympathies on the death of your sister." Herman remained stoic. "I understand two things. First, this is awkward. Second, I'm not on your personal holiday card list. Nevertheless, I'm hoping we can set differences aside and expose the truth."

Herman's clasped hands rested on the cherry desk The Chief's knees almost touched. "We of the Krump family have no respect for the way you trashed Kathleen two years ago. She's been working in this store since 2002." The Chief shifted his knees and glanced away to avoid a constant stare. "She may have had difficulties in the past, but we rallied around Kathleen and made sure she received the best medical treatment. Now you're planting those vicious stories again."

Herman pounded his left fist on the desk.

The Chief fixed his eyes on the exquisite threads of Herman's suit lapels. "Mr. Krump, no stories have been planted or released by my department. I know how hurtful the media can be so I control all media contact."

The Chief refused to vent an anger still bottled up after thirty months. The Ohio media had misquoted his statement about coddling criminals. His political adversary, the Kannaville Mayor-elect, pounced on the controversy. When sworn into office, the mayor cited a lack of trust in Deputy Chief Coltraine and replaced him with a favored son of the mayor's largest campaign contributor.

"Herman, if I may call you that, my only concern is solving crimes to keep this city safe."

"Those are platitudes I don't trust."

The Chief cringed at Herman's last word. "Let me explain what the coroner found. Lab tests showed clear medical evidence of illegal drugs in your sister's system. While I won't dispute your statement she had undergone treatment, I can only restate the facts. However, let me also tell you that I have asked

93

the coroner to postpone an inquest. That's so I can find Kathleen's killer without inflaming the public with the incorrect image we live in a drug cesspool."

Herman touched his forehead to the desk before he straightened his shoulders to gaze at The Chief. "Other community leaders I've polled said you're a man of integrity. I won't rest until Kathleen's killer pays the highest price justice can deliver."

"Agreed. If I may ask a question, did your store handle wedding dresses or Halloween costumes in 2007?"

"No way. My father prided himself on men's tailoring. We've continued that except for the 2008 addition of a limited line of men's Western apparel."

"Thanks." Chief Coltraine stood.

Herman lifted his gaze. "With Kathleen, if you promise me right here and now, no equivocation, and don't pester or harass my family, that you'll seek justice for her, I'll be available to aid you. Otherwise my door is closed."

"I offer you my hand and my word. If you stop by my office, I'll share what I know about your sister."

The men shook.

Jake arose, his eyes crusted at their inner edges. While his coffee perked and the shower spray temperature climbed to hot, he squeezed his calf muscles unable to find the typical post-dance ache. He wrote a note to buy coffee, to locate a laundromat and not to forget his court date in two weeks.

For his eleven a.m. appointment with Bob, Jake opted for dressy casual with his last clean cotton/polyester-blend blue shirt, black slacks and black oxfords. At ten, ready to leave the Mayflower, he decided to take his *Cowboy* script on the oft chance he wouldn't return to the motel before play rehearsal. As he closed his door, he discerned the housekeeper three doors away. He approached her, and today he could read her nametag.

"Carlita, you can do my room anytime."

"Si´, senor, gracias."

He strolled at leisure along Main Street. A bearded stranger asked him for a match he didn't have.

Outside Hunter Realty, Jake vacillated between a walk around the block or an early arrival. He chose the latter. The tinkle of the door's overhead bell alerted the receptionist he recognized from his visit with Emily.

"Good morning. Can I sit and wait?"

"That's fine. Mr. Hunter's with someone until eleven. When he's free, I'll tell him you're here. Are you Mr. Brown?"

"Why yes." Jake, in a wooden visitor chair, sat upright.

"I overheard two ladies this morning at the Sunrise Restaurant. You made quite an impression Saturday night at the B&B dance."

"Been making an impression ever since Thursday," Jake mumbled. He then adjusted his attitude and spoke louder. "Hope the dance comments were positive?"

"They were. I wish I could dance. Bob does a little."

Jake's eyebrows arched. "Is that Bob, Bob Hunter? Can I ask if you are related to him?"

"He's my husband."

Jake balanced the script on his lap. "What's your name?"

"Rita."

"Nice to make your acquaintance." Jake tucked the script under his left elbow. "Sat next to Bob, ah, Mr. Hunter yesterday at the First Presbyterian Church Greek dinner."

"He told me he intended to eat and visit a client there before he chased bugs at the state park for his collection."

A bemused Jake said, "That's an interesting hobby."

Rita frowned. "Icky if you ask me."

"My hobby's ballroom dancing. Told Mr. Hunter I'd be willing to give him and his wife—that would be you, now that I know you're his wife—beginner ballroom lessons. Made the same offer to Emily at the B&B. So far, no takers."

"I'd not want to take a class at the B&B, too many onlookers." Her right hand covered her lower lip.

"What if we found a more private, less public venue?"

"I'll think about it. Have to talk to Bob."

"Great. We can work on it together. Anywhere that has a

wood floor works." Jake heard a door open behind Rita.

Bob Hunter in a white shirt and red rep tie appeared to Rita's left. "Good morning, Jake. Please follow me to my office. There's someone I would like you to meet."

Jake's stomach fluttered. He hadn't mentally prepared himself for a group interview.

Bob stopped at an open door and ushered Jake into an office filled with framed and hung pictures of homes. Two red leather chairs faced a mahogany desk cluttered with folders.

"Jake, I'd like you to meet Ranger Jon Scott."

As Jake said, "How do you do?" the ranger stood. With a firm grip, he shook the right hand Jake offered. Above the wrist, Scott impressed Jake with his bulging biceps left exposed by the tan short-sleeve uniform shirt that matched his wrinkle-free pressed pants. His shoulder patch stated in stitched letters: State Park Service Ranger. Jake estimated Scott stood six feet and weighed one hundred-seventy pounds. A face bronzed by the sun set off Scott's black hair and dark eyes.

When Jake's glance encountered Scott's spit-shined black engineer-style boots with nary a scuff mark, he lifted his gaze so as not to highlight his dusty oxfords.

Bob, the last of the three to settle in, spoke first to Jake. "I've discussed your application with Ranger Scott. If hired as caretaker, he would be your boss. A concern is your background indicates you've never performed this work. However, you have a stable work history and your Cincinnati trucking supervisor gives you high marks. Minutes ago, Ranger Scott and I agreed it takes dedication to sustain a living as an independent trucker, which you've done for fifteen years."

When Bob read the backside of the paper in front of him, Jake gazed at Ranger Scott. The ramrod-straight ranger sat with his palms pressed to his knees. When Bob again spoke, Jake shifted his attention to Bob.

"Although you didn't list him, I also called the flourmill manager, Robert Brand. He said you're honest, dependable and straightforward—a no excuse kind of guy were the words he used. Emily also had praiseworthy comments. Ranger Scott?"

Jake's gaze met the ranger's as both twisted toward the other without arising from their chairs.

"Mr. Brown, my only concern would be how long you'd stay."

"If the question concerns my arrest, expect that to be straighten out. Wish the Mayflower Motel had invested in either parking lot surveillance or a night watchman. Then there would be proof that after I parked my tractor-trailer I was nowhere near it. On Thursday afternoon, as Mr. Hunter can tell you, I was at play rehearsal for at least two hours and then visited the library where the police found me an hour later."

Jake let his *Cowboy* script slip into the gap between his left hip and the chair's leather arm.

"In hindsight, should have locked the cab plus the trailer. But for years, common sense told me that with no load to protect I would avoid vandals damaging my trailer if I left it unlocked at truck stops or while sleeping at highway rest areas. If I'd had a dead body in my truck, wouldn't you think I'd be smarter than to let it decompose all day and create a stink."

Jake construed the ranger's austere glance at Bob as a sign he had irritated the ranger with his off-question ramble.

"I'm not going anywhere," Jake promised. "If there's a trial, it won't be until early next year, maybe later. Never renege on my word and I'll do whatever is required and more. You can be guaranteed I'm not going anywhere without my truck, and the police now have it."

Jake waited for the ranger's second question, relieved he again commanded Ranger Scott's attention.

"Jake, we've relied on Mr. Hunter to help us make judgments on those we hire, except summer temporary help. He's put his reputation on the line for you. I'm willing to offer you a thirty day probationary trial. I've had youths in legal trouble hired into temporary positions. All but one succeeded."

When Bob shuffled papers, Jake caught his hint the ranger had finished. "Mr. Scott, thank you. Won't let you down."

"Mr. Hunter brought up to me earlier that you may have a transportation problem in that the state park is three miles out of town. I don't know if he told you, but the caretaker is allowed use of a park pickup. It's not the latest model, but it runs."

Jake's insides leaped. Bob hadn't mentioned the pickup perk. The ranger's additional words didn't sink in until Jake heard the word "police." "What was that?"

"It's a legal thing," Scott said. "The Paradise Police have no jurisdiction over state lands, but they are the nearest facility and we, as a state park, have a cooperative agreement."

"Oh." Jake interlaced his fingers.

"As caretaker, you can use the pickup for personal errands if you document each trip and pay for gasoline consumed plus ten cents per gallon to defray related maintenance. As a self-employed trucker, I'm sure you know about vehicle operating expenses." Jake nodded. "If you're at the state park tomorrow morning, say nine a.m., you can start work and learn in greater detail what's expected."

Jake gazed first at the ranger and then at Bob. "Yes, sir." A home picture glass to Bob's left rear bounced Jake's smile into his eyes. "Will be there by nine sharp—even if I have to walk. Anything else you need?"

"Not at the moment. Tomorrow, bring two IDs and be prepared to complete forms. The bureaucracy loves forms."

Jake stood and extended his right hand to Ranger Scott. After a thank you to each, a buoyant Jake breezed past Rita to leave Mr. Hunter's office, fifty minutes after his arrival.

Since Jake doubted he could eat, he bypassed Sadie's and zigzagged north with the library as his final destination. After a block on Ash Street, he noticed the Sunrise Restaurant Rita had mentioned. The library's rear facade towered above the trees in the next block. When a familiar street named George greeted him, he veered right to the library's main entrance.

In the reference section, he grabbed Patricia's recommended volume on Paradise history, set his *Cowboy* script on the table and pulled out a chair. He read the history introduction first.

After several minutes, a *Cowboy* reference snaked through Jake's engrossed mind. "So, you've memorized all your lines to make a lucky saloon belle swoon?" He dismissed the line as his mind playing tricks. Someone tapped his left shoulder.

"So cowboy, you need a gun pointed to your face before you'll speak?" His head twist saw Patricia's right hand forefinger finger pointed at him. "Is that how you want it?"

"Sorry. Your voice didn't register." It wasn't a lie. Lying to her would be shameful. "Guess my sorry echoes in this place."

Patricia, who wore her large, black glasses, smiled. She lowered her make-believe gun. "I thought after Saturday we were past sorry. If I hadn't forgotten my sandwich in the refrigerator this morning, I wouldn't have seen you sitting here. Had lunch yet? The Sunrise's close."

Jake tried to think fast. He couldn't blab to Patricia about Kate's picnic lunch in an hour. Moreover, he decided to hold off on his job news. He feared each woman would offer to drive him to the state park tomorrow and he didn't wish to offend either with a rejection. No, he had to be smart.

Why did he decide the library was a good idea? Rita's comments should have alerted him that others in Paradise tracked his activities and whereabouts.

"Not very hungry. Made a wrong turn on my way here and ran across the Sunrise Restaurant." While each fact was technically true, the overall implication he ate there registered false on his guilt meter. "Ready to have a cup of coffee."

"Good. As you found out, it's close. Let me hide your book until we return." Jake watched as Patricia stowed his script and the history book behind the reference desk. "Library rules give me only thirty minutes, same as every other city employee."

"Yes, ma'am, my horse is saddled and ready at the hitching post. Giddy-up." Jake's right hand covered his mouth.

Patricia truncated her soft giggle. "Go on, git. Patrons will think you're eating Old West loco weed. And I can't waste an hour explaining you've read one of your *Cowboy* lines."

Jake believed he'd dodged a relationship bullet when Patricia hadn't suggested Sadie's. Best of all, with her short lunch break, he had time to keep his date, ah, appointment with Kate. He prayed Emily wasn't eating lunch at the Sunrise for its location existed closer to the B&B than Sadie's.

On entering the Sunrise, Jake's furtive glances landed on no familiar face. God smiled on him. He followed Patricia to a window booth where both slid in, on opposite bench seats.

Without writing a note, the server, a plump woman, listened to Patricia order the tuna salad sandwich special and iced tea. She left after Jake limited himself to black coffee.

"You come here often?" Jake asked.

"Not really. I usually eat at my desk. That way I can continue to browse my catalogs."

Jake pursed his lips. He lifted his menu without reading it.

Patricia's blush peaked, then faded. "I should be more specific—books-available-for-purchase catalogs."

"That was my understanding. Not saying anything else." Jake's stationary head hadn't prevent his eyes from peeking at Patricia through his eyelashes.

"What's new with you since Saturday night?"

"Not much." He paused for the server's order delivery clatter to fade. "Yesterday I heard Pastor John preach, and he invited me to a Greek feast in their fellowship hall. Bob came to sit at my table."

"Was his wife at her mother's?" Patricia bit into her tuna fish sandwich.

"That's what he said. How did you know?"

Patricia paused to chew. "Just a guess. Bob has said he always eats at home on weekends unless Rita is away and I know she visits her mother on certain Sundays."

Jake's cup rattled his saucer. "Neighbors or friends track what others do, right?"

Patricia sipped her iced tea. "It's a small town. Concerned citizens help each other."

Jake, until that moment, never pieced Rita into his puzzle. Rita may have eaten breakfast in the same booth Jake now sat in to overhear the dance conversation she related to him.

"The menu lists eggs and toast. Do you eat breakfast here?"

"I have, but not in weeks."

Jake struggled to maintain a neutral visage. It appeared he dodged a second potential embarrassment. *Yay, today's good luck is waltzing strong.*

Over Jake's protest, Patricia paid for his coffee and left the tip. With the proverbial skip, hop and a jump, they entered the library. Jake counted twenty-five minutes until he had to meet Kate at Sadie's, and he expected he could be a little late.

Patricia handed Jake the script stacked on top of the Paradise history, wished him a good day and said she would see him later at play rehearsal.

"Can't wait." His hands squeezed the books as an energized Patricia, in a navy blue pantsuit, vanished beyond the card catalog and left him in an aroused state. Seated at the reference table, Jake tapped his right toe as he tried to read dry history for fifteen minutes. Since the words read didn't stick, he rose, script in hand, tilted his head to the floor and exited through the library's front door.

With each sidewalk step, he wondered who watched. If snow had been falling, he'd be the snow globe figurine. His jitters subsided when he entered Sadie's. He erupted with a soft laugh when he observed a reserved sign on Table 12. Kate darted in multiple directions and her swirling skirt mesmerized Jake into thinking she simultaneously traveled in opposite directions. In Jake's mind, a dark-haired enchanting princess who twirled to the melodic violin strings of a Vienna waltz.

On the first of Kate's passes past Table 12, she left him a mug and a full coffee carafe. On the second, in hushed tones, she said, "One packed basket in the cooler ready for a picnic in ten." Jake nodded. He scanned for, but didn't notice, an available newspaper. At one-twenty, Jake perceived the diner lunch rush had ended and an attentive Kate confirmed.

"Meet me outside in three minutes," she told Jake as she picked up his carafe and mug. Jake executed forty swing steps in place while he waited. A uniformed schoolgirl scampered past him. Her angled right step avoided their collision. *Will she tell her mother I'm at Sadie's?* He shrugged off his paranoia.

"Ready?" Kate appeared in a pair of light-blue jeans, the bottoms rolled up to form a cuff, a dark-blue blouse and a white kerchief tied under her chin. Four to six black hair wisps dangled in front of her forehead.

"Wow, that was a quick change. You look nice . . . not that you don't look nice every day."

"This is personal time." If he'd swallowed his foot, Kate ignored it. "No uniform required. Ready for a picnic? I am."

Jake caught a whiff of her waltz dance perfume. "All yours. Where we going?"

"Come 'round back. Put the picnic basket in my truck."

When Jake reached the delivery side of Sadie's, he approached a reddish-brown 2007 Chevrolet S10. A ten-pound bag of charcoal lay on the rubberized truck bed. He saw a golden-brown wood picnic basket on the S10's bench seat.

"Thought we'd take a short ride to the river overlook. There's a picnic table with a grill. Fantastic river view."

Jake's left elbow anchored the basket's lid. If he'd had any romantic intentions, which he didn't, the basket's placement created the perfect deterrent for their five-minute ride.

When they arrived at the overlook, one car occupied the gravel area meant to serve three vehicles. A man of average build and a nondescript white shirt leaned against the sedan's farthest front fender. He toyed with a camera. When Jake exited Kate's S10, the man scurried from the car toward, and disappeared past, a green outhouse.

Kate grabbed the basket and led Jake, with the charcoal, to a picnic table to their left, as far from the outhouse to their right as was possible.

"Looks like we have healthy, mature Cottonwood trees to give us shade," Jake said.

"Can you pour the charcoal?" Jake let briquettes tumble until Kate told him to stop. She doused them with lighter fluid and struck a wooden match.

Jake and the flames jumped. When the flames flickered yellowish blue, Jake inquired, "What's the charcoal for?"

"Steaks. I rescued two top sirloin steaks left over from a backroom party." Kate folded foil from eight-ounce strips.

Jake walked around the grill. "Steaks aren't leftovers."

"Can be." Kate's right hand grabbed metal tongs. "How do

you want yours? I prefer seared with a warm pink center."

"Same here." Jake waited, anxious for the coals to gray.

"I'll tend the steaks if you set the table. Check the basket." Kate pointed to it on the table.

"Wow. There's a feast for a king . . . or a queen in this basket." Jake noted Kate smiled at his royalty correction. "Anybody ever tell you that you should own a restaurant?" Kate's hearty laugh pleased Jake.

With an already moistened cloth he extracted from clear plastic, he wiped the picnic table and benches before he spread the red-and-white-checkered tablecloth. On it he stacked food containers, rye bread and a thermos of pink lemonade.

Kate requested two paper plates. Jake complied and sat at the table while Kate served both steaks and slid onto the opposite bench. "How is it?"

Jake mumbled, "Great, really great." Between bites Jake added, "Won't need to eat for two days after this lunch."

"I'm glad you enjoy. It's not often one finds a man who can waltz and has a sense of humor. Can't have you leave town without wearing a hole in your dance shoes. Now can we?"

When Jake continued to chew and didn't respond, Kate's eyes relaxed. At each outside corner, tiny crow's feet appeared.

"Love to dance a hole in my shoes. It's someone leaving a corpse in my trailer I don't like."

Kate's eyelids slumped.

"Sorry. Shouldn't throw a wet blanket on such a nice, beautiful picnic. Disregard what I just said about my truck. Opened my mouth and inserted one large, size-ten foot." He bent sideways for his right hand to grab his right ankle.

"Save the demonstration before you hurt yourself. I get the picture and there's no apology necessary. Normal you'd be anxious and all." Her gaze drifted to the upper tree branches. "It'll probably be more upsetting to the entire town once the authorities disclose the woman's identity."

"Then maybe that will spark a clue to get my truck back."

"One has to admire your spirit, Jake. Many a man would've holed up and become invisible. You seem resilient, going out and enjoying life. What's the old saying? If life gives you lemons, make lemonade?"

"Neither of us really knows much about the other. Don't believe in fate per se. Athena instilled in me to trust in a God who grants humans a free will, which must mean our lives have choices. Lately, my choices are blurred." Jake caterpillared his thighs to the end of his bench, but didn't stand.

Kate didn't move except to arrange the steak knife on her plate. "I can agree with what you're saying." She gazed upward into the tree branches. "Life's not shown to us in a crystal ball. We have only the present. That's what we have to live in."

"In the present we've both lost spouses." Beneath the table, Jake clenched his right fist. "Surprised you're still single."

"It's personal. I've my passion to help veterans and keep alive Paradise's patriotic spirit." Kate enunciated her words in a funeral march cadence. "At first, the goals kept my mind busy performing acts the community regarded as positive, crowded out self-pity and made me too tired at night to lie in bed and fret. Later, I realized I had to make a living and the diner provided that."

Her eyes twinkled when she mentioned her diner and veterans. His gaze intercepted Kate's. Emboldened, he sharpened his underlying question. "Surely you must have met eligible single men. To borrow an analogy, you're not the ugly stepsister, you're Cinderella at the ball."

"Oh sure." The pale blush on Kate's cheeks receded into her natural glow. "Don't carry that analogy too far or you'll be changed at the stroke of midnight."

"Isn't it the wrong season for pumpkins?"

Kate shook her head. "But to answer your first question. After I burned my black veil, I ventured out to dances. Was asked out to dinner a few times. Didn't enjoy the smoking or the drinking to excess. Not that I'm a prude, but a roll in the hay with a drunk for the price of a dinner isn't my idea of a relationship. The whole process embittered me."

"Can't believe philanderers populated the whole local adult male community." His right fingertips tapped the table.

"Maybe not, but I convinced myself that it wasn't worth the pain, humiliation, anger and gossip to find the one needle in the haystack." Kate's lips stretched into a coy smile. "This country's changed. The 1950s ideal of a man as sole breadwinner and a woman at home no longer exists." Kate reached to flip open the basket top. "I'm fortunate the diner has no glass ceiling."

Jake's lips parted, but Kate continued. "Folks in this town realized circumstances forced me to operate Sadie's when the Navy called Hans and not much changed when he wasn't shipped home alive. Now, if I were Emily's age, expectations would be different."

"How so?" Jake handed Kate two condiment bottles.

"Emily's younger. Even if she works, this town expects she will marry and raise kids. Nobody will say anything about me that has not already been said."

"She seems to have chosen just a career. And I don't get the sense she's unhappy." Jake added their soiled plates and Styrofoam trash to a plastic bag.

"Four years ago, when she worked for me, Paradise saw a different Emily—wilder, less inhibited, with a strong devil-may-care attitude. I think her parents decided to sell the farm to take her away from the negative influence of her friends, which included one Kathie Krump. Emily refused to be uprooted."

"Interesting. Who exactly was this Kathie?"

"She was a daughter of the Paradise tailor. The baby of the family, Kathie exhibited no discipline as she grew up."

"Heard that about last born kids." Jake wiped his chin with a napkin. "No disrespect, but I can't envision the goal-driven Emily I've met to run wild or let friends dictate her life."

"Kathie knew people who could supply marijuana for parties Emily attended. You saw Emily at the dance?"

"Yeah, of course." Jake tapped his two thumbs together.

"Remember the high collar around her neck?"

"Okay." Jake's forehead twitched.

"Emily always wears a high collar to hide her neck's sunflower tattoo. I was told that Kathie, during a weekend party, persuaded Emily to get a tattoo identical to hers."

"Emily doesn't smoke weed now, right?"

Kate's hands fluttered in front of her chest. "No. Absolutely not. She's outgrown what I'd call her teenage rebellion. In fact, she has stayed to herself inside the B&B so much this past year that malicious gossipers speculate she and Clem are engaged in an affair."

"Haven't noticed that."

"Me neither." Kate snapped lids onto food containers and hissed in low tones. "Ugly gossip makes my blood boil."

When Kate finished her cleanup, Jake lifted his side of the tablecloth, relieved to see her expression lightened.

"I'm convinced women should be individuals," said Kate. "Be treated as equals, and be more than a brood mare and a diaper changer. What about you? Have I scared you yet?"

Jake withstood the pierce of Kate's eyes. His upward gaze into the branches Kate had surveyed allowed him to relax for two seconds. "That's powerful. When Athena died I highballed it all over this nation, that is drove, not consumed the alcoholic drink. Most ashamed of one instance of uncontrolled gambling, although there were bouts of drunkenness."

While he didn't observe disapproval in Kate's expression, his reversion to his life's negative sent a shiver up his spine. "Hopefully it's out of my system without any lasting damage except for a healed nick or scar on my soul. My reaction to the grief inside me caused me to abuse myself, not someone else. I avoided people . . . told myself no one else knows my hurt. For two years, ignored Athena's deathbed wish telling me to rejoin society. Finally, her advice motivated me to join Emily's play."

Jake caught flickers of grief intersperse the backdrop of sadness that clouded Kate's eyes. It was as if she ached inside the same way as he. His inner voice cautioned him not to push Kate to relive a forgotten war and spark the pain she seemed to have conquered.

"The play, my baby steps into reality, has provided me a group's common cause within a playwright's funny make-believe world. I'm determined to live better. Dance constitutes my new drinking and gambling. If I have one regret, it's that Athena and I decided to have no children."

Jake tried not to stare as Kate began in a soft voice. "In days gone by I often felt sorry for myself when walking past a playground. Then I'm heartbroken when I hold my neighbor's Down syndrome grandson. I know if he were mine, I'd love him deeply, but the thought always resurfaces that the risk to wait having children probably was best, then and now."

"From the outside, I've watched families, wondering."

"If I conjured the future . . ." Kate's palms moved to and fro until they hovered above the thermos as if it were a crystal ball and she a fortune-teller. "The present is all that any of us have in life. Since Hans, I live with no expectation I will find another life partner. If I do, it will be someone to stand beside, not walk three steps behind. I don't fashion myself to be the zombie Betty Friedan wrote about decades ago. But I'm determined to be myself first and a woman second. And for any third, it's still yet to be determined."

Her hazel eyes were translucent. Wide. Thoughtful. He was still working out how to proceed with Kate. Should he pursue her. Her invitation, although not explicit, seemed near to the surface. He thanked his good luck for Kate's picnic invitation. If he had only known her from the diner, he would say she possessed qualities of graciousness, efficiency and, of course, attractiveness. Now he began to unravel her deeper qualities—personal strength, conviction and direction. "Not to be trite or condescending, you're really impressive. Have I told you how great this lunch, ah, feast was?"

"Well, thank you again. A lady can definitely enjoy honest, sincere flattery. Cooking can be an oppressive burden or a creative expression and, if the latter, more than the cook should be there to eat and enjoy it."

Jake pondered her words. "Agree both with what you said and your expression of what I've been discovering of late. That is, the same action or word can be either positive or negative depending on one's perspective." Kate's cheery facial expression enlivened Jake. If she had donned her diner mask, he didn't care.

She tapped the basket lid. "I think we've devoured every morsel except the pie. Let's save it. A walk can keep our waltz legs in shape."

Both rose. Jake arched his shoulders as they strolled toward the bluff that overlooked the river.

"This view's fine now," Jake said, "but it must be gorgeous in the fall when the cottonwoods turn a golden yellow."

"The river valley does overwhelm come fall. That's why they built this rest area for travelers. Today's extra quiet. The songbirds must be resting or on retreat."

"Can I give you a hug?" Jake didn't wait for a verbal answer. He acted on the "yes" in Kate's hazel eyes and surrounded her with his arms. Both uttered not a word. Their worlds suspended for delicious seconds until a breeze clattered the long-stemmed the leaves. Jake's nostrils filled with Kate's body scent and the hint of honey in her fragrance.

"Time for pie?" Kate ducked Jake's arms and grabbed his left wrist to lead the way to their picnic table. "You're not easily categorized."

"Can't categorize myself," Jake replied. He avoided the table's support as they, legs within an inch of each other, crowded onto the bench. "Probably similar to a quilt you have in your diner display case before it was sewn."

"What about quilts?"

"An analogy. Quilts are made up of discarded cloth remnants where each by itself would be useless, but when sewn together create a prized item of beauty or a utilitarian blanket that keeps one warm. Periodically, I think the pieces of my life represent my choices, and then I try to visualize how they fit."

"If I believe, as I do," Kate began, "that I determine my own life, I can't be consistent if I try to force another person to abide by my choices. With that said, you and I have shared at least one experience by the loss of a spouse. If there are pieces in life, those pieces change. The past evolves into the present, which is all we have. From your analogy, we either choose the remnants of life or weave a new quilt."

Jake, overpowered by Kate's incisive eloquence, offered no immediate words. "You're right." He added softly, "I guess."

"What you may need to consider is the sewer's work done between a pile of pieces and the finished quilt."

Jake swallowed hard. Was his agreement with Athena to forego fatherhood one of the pieces or was it his pre-Athena goal? Could he revive his desire for children without ripping the threads out of his happy memory of Athena? Jake welcomed the distraction of trying to chose if he should reach for the meringue pie in Kate's left or right hand. "What a great choice."

Kate's smile buried Jake's brooding. In companionable silence, they ate until all crumbs disappeared.

He carried the picnic basket, and Kate toted the lightened charcoal bag. At her vehicle, Kate lowered the charcoal onto the cargo bed and pointed for Jake to add the picnic basket.

Within twelve minutes, Kate's S10 idled in front of the B&B. With a gentle touch, she grasped Jake's left hand. "Thank you for a wonderful time."

Jake's lips longed to lean sideways to taste the richness of her red lip gloss and he cocked his head toward her. Her wide eyes cautioned him and he squeezed her fingers with the gentleness of a baby's grasp. His right hand unlatched the passenger door and he slipped his left hand free.

"Propose we call that picnic table No. 13."

"Now you take care. I'm sure life will be okay."

Jake believed she read his dilemma. He waved as her S10 gathered speed. Its taillights headed east on Main Street.

Inside the B&B, Jake asked Clem, "Can I ask a favor?"

Clem closed a box of potato chip packages. "Yes, if it's not dance related or being your fight second."

"Asking to hire you to drive me to Cottonwood State Park tomorrow morning." Jake's right hand swiveled a barstool before he hoisted his buttocks onto it. "Must be at Ranger Headquarters by nine to fill out papers for a caretaker job."

"No problem. You must understand that without a taxi license there's no meter in my truck so I can't charge you. If

I'm at the Mayflower by eight forty, how's that?"

"Great. Since you're working, I'll prepay two Hofenstegers for your home refrigerator." Jake pulled a ten from his billfold. "My treat."

"**H**i, Jake," said Emily. "You're early."

Jake, his slip-ons propped on a chair by the stage, didn't stir. It troubled him he couldn't decipher what Kate had meant by saying her reason for staying single was personal.

"You angry? I thought you should be happy."

"Oh, hi, Emily." With Kate's sunflower tattoo revelation fresh in his mind, he bypassed his compliment that her cardinal red high-collared blouse layered a glow to her supple throat and cheeks. "How's the world's top play director today? Ready to crack the whip and keep us actors on cue?"

"Hardly."

Jake expected a livelier response from Emily. His house of funk thrived with a population of one and he had no intent to share any gloom with Emily. Kate's impressive remarks about living in the present drove Jake to act without heeding her caution that one should not try to change another person.

"If you were younger, I'd buy you a lollipop."

A smile fluttered on Emily's lips. "That good ship sailed years ago."

"That's better. Since you're unlikely to be tossed an orange inmate uniform, no use for us both to act crushed by fate."

"It's you who should be happy." She yanked the chair beneath Jake's heels for her own use. "I heard the good news from Bob. What time do you want me to pick you up tomorrow morning? I called the motel at least twice since noon and, on the second, the desk clerk let it slip you hadn't answered any of several calls this afternoon."

Jake stood to give his lungs length to breathe. "Thanks, but Clem's agreed to give me a ride."

Emily frowned.

"After my meeting with Bob, I hiked to the library with my script to delve into Paradise history. Please believe me that you've been a Godsend." To break his stare, Jake tilted his eyes above the perfect symmetry of Emily's face. "Consider I've been given a trial . . . that is, a chance to demonstrate I'm able to be a park caretaker. Not that I'm on trial like the arrest hanging over my head. Same word "trial," two different meanings." He snapped his mind away from its diversion. "You've been so kind already. Hated to ask another favor."

"What favor?" Emily arose to retrieve her director's chair.

Rather than shout, Jake waited, seated on the stage's outer lip. He stretched his knees horizontal and crossed his ankles. "Told Clem that my job isn't certain, which is true to a degree. There's still papers to fill out, plus probation."

"Those don't impress as big problems."

"Yesterday, Pastor John offered me church construction work. Since I haven't said yes or no, I'd like to keep this caretaker job under my hat for a day or two." Two right hand fingers rubbed his chin. "Might be able to do both jobs."

"I won't make any grand announcement."

"Great. And I'd like to really thank you for being a reference. That helped convince Bob to go to bat for me. You've both gone out on a limb for me and I promise to be forever grateful and not to embarrass either of you."

"You're welcome." Emily's left palm smoothed her jeans as she elevated her gaze to the apartment windows. "Something's nagging at me . . . may have left my stove burner turned on." Emily's lips blossomed into an impish smile. "I need to clear my mind before we start. I'll be back in a few."

"I'll be here." He refrained from even peeking at her march away. After she had been blasé in Bob's disclosure of Jake's caretaker news, panic engulfed him that his picnic with Kate would be grist for the gossip mill. For seventeen years he'd never worried about what he said or who he jabbered with. Truck stop conversations were forgotten or participants never again seen. The insipid, bland dialogue seldom advanced beyond loads, roads, weather and sports. He feared Paradise represented a transparent world where camouflaged grudges or envy flared to teach him he couldn't hide, nor run.

He crossed both his forefingers with second fingers. Since daybreak, he'd dodged many figurative bullets. No reason he couldn't duck one or two more before sunset.

One by one the *Cowboy* cast and its director assembled next to the stage. Jake's nerves remained calm as Emily stayed focused on the play. Patricia hid a smile with her left hand when Jake flubbed his saloon line directed to her character. Not until his fourth repetition did Jake garner Emily's approval, Patricia's smile and Jacob's pat on his left shoulder.

Before the rehearsal ended, Jake privately asked Pastor John for, and received, one additional week to accept the church jobs.

"**S**ay, Clem." Jake leaned his shoulders and head forward, his elbows on the bar. "Any reason why Kate at Sadie's is single twenty years after her husband was killed in Desert Storm?"

"Only gossip," Clem whispered. "I heard that years ago she spent time with a married military recruiter and his wife found out. Nothing happened to Kate, but the enraged woman was said to have started an argument with her husband and a rifle in her hands accidentally went off. He died two days later."

A startled Jake held his breath for four counts. "Anybody mention the guy's name?"

"Think Harris, ah, Harris Dalton. Guy had been on the USS Midway in the Persian Gulf and re-upped to be a recruiter."

"Don't recall that name."

Hundreds of stars twinkled in Paradise's night canopy. Jake forgot Main Street's cracks. While vehicles drove past, a green van slowed before he reached an intersection, and then gunned its engine. Before it zoomed into the night, Jake couldn't recall if he had seen the van in the motel's parking lot.

At the Mayflower, Jake entered the motel office. He spoke to a slim, bushy-haired young man seated behind a counter nameplate that read: "Aaron." "Excuse me, name's Jake Brown." The clerk glanced up. "What time's checkout?"

"Eleven a.m.," Aaron replied.

"While tonight's paid for, have a morning meeting at nine and don't know if I'll be back in two hours. Could leave my packed bags inside the door and not get charged another day?"

"Since you've been here a week, I can have housekeeping shift you to the end of the clean list. Can you return by one?"

"Will telephone if I can't. Thanks." Jake pivoted to the door.

"Say, Mr. Brown." Jake halted his departure, his right palm pressed to an exit doorknob. "Are you taking the truck?"

"Don't know that I can. Police hold my truck keys."

Aaron's eyes flicked left and right. "Do you know Joseph DeCamp? Sometimes he's called Big Joey?"

"No. Why do you ask?" Jake released his doorknob grip.

"Since I saw him near your truck at three a.m. Thursday, you may have been hauling a special load for him."

"You see him in or open my truck trailer?"

Aaron frowned. "No. He paced back and forth in front of your trailer doors like he expected to meet someone."

"Did he?"

"Only saw him. Since he's not one to mess with, I stayed out of the light to finish my twenty cigarette puffs."

Jake nodded, turned and exited the office for his room. Not ready to sleep, he searched Jeremiah 44 for circled or hopeful words. He discovered neither as Jeremiah prophesized the Lord's destruction of the wicked by fire, disease and famine.

Jake bolted upright. His bed, an unmoored craps table, floated as his feet pedaled. Gambling chips and upside down beer glasses drifted in the motel room's nightmarish blackness. He trembled with the realization his startling dream visions depicted his past, not Emily's play. His numb hands slid off the craps table as the casino floor failed to cushion his fall. His body lay prone and he struggled to stand. Three pairs of female eyes watched from a smoky distance. The faces appeared to be of various ages, yet he couldn't fix a name to any face, although none resembled Athena.

When his flailing left hand grasped a chair's arm, the reality and confines of a Paradise motel room struck him. The front of his white T-shirt, wet with sweat, clung to his chest. He clambered out of bed. His mind's images stayed, even after he'd plucked the Gideon off the floor and slammed a dresser drawer with it inside. He paced, executed a dozen swing steps to a ragged rhythm and fought to stay awake. Fear of the agony that sleep would bring nipped at his bare heels. Faded joyous memories of Athena were a porous shield to his mental torment.

Chapter Six

Jake propped his two packed bags against the inside motel room wall, next to the door. He balanced the folded *Herald-Gazette* article, saved from Sadie's, and the Gideon Bible atop the taller bag. Since he had no word the police had inspected the bathroom's lipstick eyes, he wished the eyes and his nighttime demons an extended stay. He locked his room's door and, after long strides, patted his truck's front fender. While all appeared well with his truck, his wistful glance beyond the parking lot reminded him the town's promised fulfilled-dream dawdled.

At eight thirty-five, he paraded behind a line of parked vehicles in the Mayflower's front parking lot. He waved to Carlita. On time, Jake discerned Clem lean out his driver's window and wiggle his fingers in Carlita's direction.

"Good morning, Clem. Carlita appears happy to see you."

"We're friends, that's all. Any luggage? There's room."

"No." Jake hopped into Clem's 2004 F-150 pickup. "Mayflower will let me leave them in the room until one. This way you can drop me off at Ranger Headquarters and not have to stick around. You're doing me a big enough favor."

Clem nodded and drove. Within thirteen minutes, Clem announced, "We're here, Ranger Headquarters directly ahead." Clem coasted to a stop. "I can wait in this visitor space."

"Thanks, but no need. I'll see you at the B&B this afternoon." Jake stepped off the running board, waved to Clem and followed a flagstone pathway to three stone steps leading up to a brown door with "Entrance" painted in white. He tried the knob. Locked. Jake pressed a doorframe buzzer, careful not to telegraph his nervousness with repeated punches.

When the door swung inward, it exposed a dark, chocolate-brown corridor behind Ranger Scott. "Come this way, Jake."

Escorted straight ahead, Jake counted fifteen paces to a spacious office. Blue drapes that pooled on the floor vertically framed the room's two windows adorned with scalloped fabric valances. A raised sash allowed the wind outside to whip and snap the lowered plastic blinds until Jake closed the room's door. Surrounded by cream-colored walls, Jake gazed at a multi-colored braided oval rug that warmed the floor's gray tile. He guessed the humongous mahogany desk to his right, with its ten-foot width, was the Ranger's.

Scott directed Jake to have a seat at a second desk to the left, less than half the size of its room's counterpart. "As I mentioned yesterday, I have forms."

Jake flexed his right hand fingers twice before he completed six multi-section forms. He sat silent to await Scott's return.

"Let's walk to the caretaker's house," Scott said.

As his soles crunched two hundred yards of park road shoulder gravel, Jake hustled to be no more than two steps behind Ranger Scott when they approached a flagstone walkway to a one story, brick, raised cottage. The concrete front stoop led Jake to a solid, windowed, dark-walnut door that opened into a great room with two doors along its right wall.

Ranger Scott's shoulder nudge maneuvered Jake past the great room's second door and into a bedroom. Scott explained it was the largest of the two bedrooms and accessed the home's one bathroom.

Again in the great room, Jake saw a kitchen stove beyond an archway. Jake passed through the kitchen to find three descending steps. At the lower landing, one wood door to the right provided access to the basement stairs and a second windowed door to the left provided a backyard view.

Similar to the rest of the house, the rear outside door had roller shades, no curtains. When Jake gazed through its windowpane, his eyes widened. A blue pickup, parked at the far end of a gravel driveway, faced the unattached single garage.

"What do you think?" Scott asked.

Inwardly elated, Jake replied, "This will work just fine."

The two worked through a house checklist. They turned on taps that ran rusty water for the first fifteen seconds. Dark rust stains circled the porcelain toilet bowl's bottom. The locks worked, as did the forced-air furnace. After Scott plugged in the refrigerator, its compressor banged twice before it settled into a constant hum. All electric stove burners glowed red and radiated heat. The telephone handset emitted no dial tone.

When Jake moved the only furniture, a double bed with mattress and box spring, the ripped bath towels and stained linens he found piled beneath it disgusted him.

At ten forty-five, Jake sat with Ranger Scott on the caretaker's residence front steps.

"Drive the pickup into town to purchase whatever supplies you may need and spend the afternoon walking the grounds. It's far better to experience the park than to listen to a boring explanation. The caretaker's duty list will offer a good guide. I'll requisition four uniforms. Until Minneapolis ships them next week, any shirt and blue jeans are fine."

Ranger Scott stood and Jake did likewise. "Thank you, Mr. Scott. The Mayflower has my clothes and I'll hustle back."

"Welcome aboard. And, Jake, please call me Jon."

The men shook and Ranger Scott left.

Jake started his list of needed items with soap, linens, towels, laundry detergent and bleach. As his list grew, he canceled his plans for the Tuesday B&B dance. After play rehearsal, he had to locate the nearest laundromat.

Reminded by a stomach growl he hadn't eaten lunch, Jake delayed a conflicted choice between Kate at Sadie's or to take a chance Patricia ate at the Sunrise Restaurant. When the pickup's engine purred, he longed to blast an air horn it didn't have. An upper left corner windshield mileage sticker listing last week's oil change at 93,000 miles left maintenance off his to-do list.

He drove three miles to Paradise, plus added a mile as he circled the Mayflower's south parking lot. Jake wished he could tow his big rig away. That he couldn't, left him with tossing his luggage into the pickup's box and driving from store to store. While shopping depleted his cash reserve, Jake appreciated how wheels helped accomplish striking items off his list.

His expectation to meet Patricia at the Sunrise went unmet. He ate in solitude until he heard, "Hello, Mr. Braun, nice to meet you again."

Jake's head rotated to the voice and he recognized Sarah from Saturday's dance. At his booth, her lithe body stood relaxed, contrasted with her quiet facial tension.

"Nice to see you, but I think someone gave you the wrong pronunciation. My name's Brown, like the color, not Braun."

"I'm so sorry," Sarah mumbled. She elevated her gaze to avoid prolonged eye contact with Jake. "It's been such a long time since Robert, my old dance partner, introduced me to a gentleman I would swear could be your twin."

"Please don't be embarrassed. You're Sarah, right?" She nodded. "I'm Jake, Jake Brown."

"Though I enjoyed our dance, I bet Patricia put you up to it. You two impressed like '*Dancing With the Stars*' contestants."

"Patricia and you deserve the credit if I look good." By design, he sidestepped and hoped Sarah wouldn't re-ask about Patricia's dance prompt. He calculated Patricia had desired to be nice for a reason not apparent to him.

"Nice meeting you. Enjoy your lunch and I hope to see you at an upcoming dance." Sarah executed a foxtrot pivot step, departed and left Jake without time say "Likewise."

After lunch, Jake decided to challenge fate and visit the Paradise Police Chief. His left hand squeezed his trembling right hand as he forced out his inquiry to the dispatcher on the availability of Chief Coltraine. She ushered him into a conference room and requested he sit on the table's far side.

"**M**r. Brown, what can we do for you?"

The Chief sat, his hands on the table, next to Sgt. Smyth. As if to block Jake's escape route, their chairs were nearer the door.

"Chief, this might be unusual, however, I must, if at all possible, help myself. It's about the woman at my truck—"

Sgt. Smyth interrupted. "Your conscience now bothers you and you want to confess, is that it? Despite your charade at the truck," his voice rose to a crescendo, "I could tell from day one you were guilty."

The somber Chief relaxed his grim, straight lips.

"I'm innocent." Jake scowled at Smyth. "Want to tell you that the Mayflower's night desk clerk will tell you he saw a fellow named Joseph DeCamp near my truck trailer around three a.m. last Thursday."

Long wrinkles emerged across The Chief's brow. "Who?"

"Told it was Joseph DeCamp, nicknamed Big Joey."

"Why would he hang around your truck?"

"Told he was waiting for someone."

Jake ignored Sgt. Smyth's head shake at his every word.

"Who?" The Chief asked. He peered intently at Jake.

"Don't know. I'd question those arrested with illegal drugs."

While The Chief's eyebrows arched at the mention of illegal drugs, he said nothing. Jake rested his hands on the table.

Sgt. Smyth chimed in, "Sounds farfetched if you ask me, Chief. Story's made up to save his hide, nothing more."

His right hand clenched, Jake glared at the sergeant. "You probably tossed my room. Painted those red lipstick eyes."

"Wait a minute." The Chief's right hand slapped the table. "Tossed your room? Lipstick eyes?" The Chief steadied his sideways glance at Sgt. Smyth.

The sergeant stood and pursed his lips as deep vertical lines emerged between his brows. "Look, Chief." Hostility permeated Smyth's voice. "After you left Thursday evening, I admit I searched Mr. Brown's room for the murder weapon . . . other evidence. No one would have been able to discern my effort. Aaron, the desk clerk, let me in. He was there. He'll verify." His voice oscillated between pleading and anger. "I know nothing about any lipstick eyes."

Jake ignored Smyth. "Somebody tossed my room. Then Friday I discovered two eyes drawn in red lipstick inside my medicine cabinet, behind the mirror door."

"You still in your room?" The Chief asked.

"No. Checked out this morning. Had until one to remove my belongings." Jake, his palms on the table's edge, extended both arms to push his chair away.

Smyth's head jerked toward Jake. "You leaving town?"

Jake bristled. "Staying at the state park."

Urgency percolated The Chief's investigative genes. At his vision's fringe, the wall clock's big hand had dropped past the smaller to indicate one-fifteen. "Sgt. Smyth, call the Mayflower. Tell them it's imperative that no one enter Mr. Brown's room and that I'll explain when I arrive."

"Right, Chief." Sgt. Smyth stomped out.

A docile Jake rose. "Don't know if I should say thanks or not. You can think what you will. Will be leaving now."

Unwilling to delay his investigation, The Chief hurried Jake to the lobby and backpedaled until certain that Jake had exited the station's front door. After climbing one flight of stairs two steps at a time to his office, The Chief rousted a lounging Sgt. Smyth from his tawny vinyl sofa.

"Let's go, Roger. I want to verify, if I can, what we were just told. I questioned Aaron at the Mayflower the other day and he didn't reveal Big Joey hung around."

When The Chief heard Sgt. Smyth click his car's passenger seat buckle, The Chief asked, "What do you think? In the conference room you were very condemning of Mr. Brown."

"Don't see much there. I wouldn't envision a crafty, slick character like Big Joey lollygagging in the Mayflower's parking lot at three a.m. He'd have an underling do the dirty work and be somewhere else for an alibi." The Chief nodded. "We're seeing one criminal rat out another. Brown being an over-the-road driver provides good cover for illegal drug distribution. We know Big Joey has his hand deep into drug profits."

"From what I witnessed Saturday night at the B&B, I'd discount your criminal conspiracy theory to include Brown. His truck may have indeed carried illegal drugs, but my gut says he was unaware they rode with him. Then there's nothing to tie together the death of Kathie Krump and any illegal drug shipment." The Chief slowed for a car turning left.

"From street information, she was a user, an addict."

"She may have been. But no drug ring surfaced five years ago when she was arrested in Silverton. When I telephoned a police contact there this past week, he confirmed. No, I have to believe the odds are she would score, not deal. Snort cocaine in addition to popping LSD."

"LSD?" The Chief's front passenger seat groaned as Sgt. Smyth pressed his left shoulder into the backrest.

"Oh, I'm sorry. I'm behind in my updates. Doc Beck discovered LSD traces in her body."

Smyth straightened his body to the front and let ten seconds elapse. "I can interview the motel clerk tonight."

"No. I'll talk with Aaron myself. After our room check, I want you to find Big Joey. He travels a lot, that I know." The Chief glanced at Smyth. "And, one more thing, keep both the drugs and Big Joey's possible connection to yourself and Lt. Sigourney. If there's a sighting of Big Joey, no need to add it to your patrol report. Just inform me direct."

"Yes, Chief. Will do."

The Chief angled his squad car across two parking stalls in front of the Mayflower's office. The Chief marched in first.

"Good afternoon, Chief. Mr. Brown's room is as he left it," said Aleck Werner, motel manager. He reached for a key that hung inside a wall-mounted key box. In the manager's hand, the key jangled against a metal ID tag. "You have a warrant?"

"There's no expectation of privacy if Mr. Brown checked out. We'll enter pretending we're the maid."

"Let's meet outside then. I need to lock this office if I'm

going to lead you to the room."

Werner knocked and opened the room Jake had vacated. The Chief entered first. As he walked to the bathroom, the unmade bed and the towel crumpled on the carpet didn't stir suspicion in his gut. His pen behind the medicine cabinet door bottom eased it open. Two red lipstick eyes stared at him.

He poked his head into the bedroom and shouted, "Roger, check the dresser."

Sgt. Smyth donned latex gloves. "All six are empty."

"Guess I'll have to replace the Bible," Werner said.

The Chief asked, "What needs replacing?" He rejoined the other two near the bed.

"Gideon Bible," Werner repeated.

Sgt. Smyth peeked under the bed and reported no Bible.

While he judged the detail to be unimportant, The Chief, nevertheless, asked, "You sure?"

"We place one in all the rooms," Werner replied. "If the drawers are empty, it's missing. Of course, guests may take them. Very few do."

"Aleck, let's forget the Bible for today. We mustn't disturb this room. I'll call the state criminal lab, but can't guarantee when they'll get here." The Chief calculated that if the carpet hid glass slivers, Len would find them.

"I'll tell Carlita not to clean and we'll take it off the reservation list."

Sgt. Smyth had inched to the doorjamb's public side. The Chief failed to decipher if his sergeant's blank expression meant boredom or an anxiety to leave.

Seated with Roger in his car, The Chief spotted Carlita outside a room. He made a u-turn, drove toward her and leaned out his driver-side window to call to her. "Good afternoon, Carlita. I've a question maybe you can answer."

She grasped a vacuum cleaner cord. "Si´, senor."

"In room nine, Mr. Brown's room, did you vacuum or see a red lipstick drawing behind the bathroom sink mirror?"

"No, senor. Not open mirror until guest checks out. Clean inside before Mr. Brown come. See no lipstick."

"What about vacuuming?" The Chief noticed a silent Roger skipped watching Carlita to scan the parking lot.

"Vacuum yesterday. Carlita does a good job."

"Gracias, Carlita."

While he drove to the station, The Chief's thoughts explored the drug connection. LSD, a 1960s craze, had captivated the young and the old. The acronym also existed as an abbreviation for Lake Shore Drive, the premier highway route around Chicago's downtown lakefront. He doubted any national truck driver to be unfamiliar with this route through the Windy City. His intuition cautioned him to keep it in mind, however, Big Joey's activities dwarfed any Chicago route shorthand.

After he reiterated to Sgt. Smyth his instruction to track Big Joey, The Chief settled in at his desk. Absentmindedly, he lifted his telephone handset before he realized he must speak to Aaron, the Mayflower desk clerk, in person to observe facial expressions and other body language. He called the state crime lab and left Len a voice message for a new investigative task.

After he divulged his clue to the Chief, Jake, at his new residence, unloaded his household purchases that included food for a cooled refrigerator. He gripped his new key ring, locked the house and garage and started to walk to the pavilion area.

Tall, stately cottonwoods lined the road and a hiking trail parallel to its asphalt. Near a pavilion, one of his keys unlocked a barn-like shed. Alongside a green riding mower hung an array of shovels, hoes and rakes plus garden hand tools. Enough seen, Jake clicked the shed's padlock and wandered past stumps sawed flush to the grass and lance-shaped dandelion leaves.

A pebbly sand strip hemmed the river's edge. *Beautiful*. He mentally visualized he and Kate the day before gazing from the overlook. He sighed, content to stand there all afternoon, yet he shouldn't. His right foot swivel left a depression in the sand.

Near a second pavilion he discovered a scaled drawing of the park protected by clear, hard plastic. To either side were pictures of foliage, animals and several descriptive paragraphs. He read the one centered on the left:

The Cottonwood tree is one of several North
American poplar trees related to many species of
poplars and aspens. It has shiny leaves that
shimmer and shake in the wind. The Cottonwood
tree may grow to heights of 30 meters or 100 feet.
It likes wet soil, which means it can be found
along riverbanks, lakes, and irrigation ditches.
Cottonwoods have been known to live 100 years.
The bark of the Cottonwood tree is gray, thick,
rough, and deeply furrowed. See picture above.

While the cottonwood tree information failed to excite him,
a paragraph on the cottonwood borer fascinated Jake. He traced
the words with his right index finger.

Cottonwood Borer. A large black and white
insect that can be up to 40mm long and 12mm
wide. It is a type of beetle. One of the largest
insects in North America. The larvae burrow
into the tree, especially the roots and may take
up to two years to mature. It usually appears in
summer to eat leaf stems and small twigs.

Jake chuckled. *I'll have to check that tool shed for a
baseball bat.* He skipped paragraphs to read about the
cottonwood's seed. The concluding paragraph said the female
tree launched its well-known fluffy white seeds in early
summer. Jake noted the sign didn't describe the male tree. He
chuckled a second time. He doubted he'd be able to tell the sex
of any cottonwood. At most, if he ever came across a little,
puffy, reddish-looking cottonwood growth, he'd remember the
ugly picture of Eriophyid mite galls.

When a cloud released the sun, he strolled from the
informational displays to enjoy the riverbank's quiet
peacefulness. Where the river meandered to the right, Jake
spotted a well-trodden upward trail. He weaved between
exposed limestone to ascend the trail's small hill to a clearing
with a wooden bench. He chose to tackle a steeper branching
path. Twice his lungs labored for breath and halted his advance.
His inner voice whispered that a summer hiking these paths will

make his dancing swing for three straight hours a snap.

When his right sole slipped off an exposed tree root, he averted a tumble, but not a branch recoil, which stung his right shoulder blade. Unable to rub the shoulder pain's site, Jake inhaled deep to infuse his nostrils with the sweetness of spring wildflower fragrances caught in the breeze. White, purple and yellow colors waved before his eyes. He thought he discerned a deer nibble a low leaf amongst the foliage.

Exhilaration filled his veins as the downhill grade propelled his jog into the pavilion area. Jake skidded to a stop when he saw Ranger Scott between vehicles he hadn't remembered.

"Find the home of our pesky raccoons?" he asked Jake.

"Can't say I did, but I think I saw a doe."

"There's plenty. Well, the raccoons like to emerge at night and rummage through the trashcans for food." The ranger pointed to his left. "You might want to carry the trash liners from those two pavilion receptacles to the dumpster beyond the far tree line or you'll see the raccoon's handiwork. New liners are on a barn shed shelf. Have any questions?"

The task seemed simple enough so Jake nodded his head.

"Warner from the Mayflower grabbed me at Sadie's. You might want to give him your telephone number once your line's activated. He said you've been getting numerous calls."

"Consider it done." Jake poked his right hand into his front jeans pocket for his key ring.

"Also, please check the lodge. Tomorrow morning you'll need to clean it for a Friday meeting. I'll leave our completed renter's form in the kitchen." Jake again nodded. "A locked closet in the kitchen's northwest corner should have all the required supplies. A running inventory list, posted inside the closet door, needs to be updated as you use and replenish supplies. Requisition forms are taped next to the inventory list. Supply requisitions are due at Headquarters by the fourteenth."

Jake shifted his body weight to his right foot. "Understand."

"Bright and early tomorrow morning I must drive to the marina upstream to approve the retrofit of our dry-docked water rescue boat. I'm counting on you to ready the lodge and keep an eye pealed for suspicious activity until my afternoon return."

"Will be here."

Ranger Scott hopped into a pickup with a state emblem and "Park Ranger" painted on the door. It's modified design told Jake it was a newer 2008 model, although his older pickup had been painted an identical blue.

His keys unlocked the lodge and its supply closet where he found the lists and supplies his boss had described.

The Chief skimmed his case file notes of his face-to-face with Aaron, the motel clerk. He entertained no second thoughts to include a veiled reference of his not-so-subtle threat that loosened the clerk's lips to admit he saw Big Joey in the motel parking lot early Thursday. Aaron also verified he had let Sgt. Smyth into Jake's room Thursday. However, when pressed, Aaron swore he hadn't stuck around for fear a guest would complain of a vacant office or unanswered phone.

Sgt. Smyth reported he had tracked Big Joey to Jack's, a local bar, ala pool emporium. According to his sergeant, the following occurred: While Big Joey said he knew of the Mayflower Motel, he told Smyth he didn't remember his last time there. Big Joey's two bar friends profusely vowed Big Joey had been at their house for a Wednesday night party that lasted until Thursday noon. When Sgt. Smyth suggested a high stakes poker game, blank expressions and shrugs abounded, especially from Big Joey.

The Chief deleted Sgt. Smyth's hand roll of a cue ball toward the eight ball, which ricocheted the black and white eight into a side pocket. Likewise, his edit left out that Sgt. Smyth stared Big Joey square in the eyes and threatened: "If I find out you're lying to me, you'll be behind an eight-ball rammed into a pocket with no table ball return." He also refused to humiliate his officer by leaving in that Big Joey laughed loud. Or that Big Joey's friends smirked as Big Joey said, "See you later sa–sarrr–gent. Be careful out there."

When his private line rang, The Chief flipped his folder closed. "Thanks for returning my call, Len. New developments have arisen regarding the woman, Ms. Krump, found in the Mayflower Motel truck." He detailed his need for trace evidence from Jake's motel room, especially the carpet.

The Chief listened to Len's update that the paper pieces, splinters and other small trailer bits and pieces had no forensic value. The Chief remembered the 2007 bridal veil remnant had also been worthless because the rest of the veil couldn't be recovered for a comparison.

Len reported the blood results to date had only matched the victim except for one small spot identified to belong to an unidentified male.

When The Chief's handset touched its cradle, it rang. Upon answering, The Chief squashed his real emotions to be polite to FBI Agent Redburn. He'd once met the agent, a tall, thin, WASP elegantly dressed in an expensive gray three-piece. *He and Big Joey likely patronize the same tailor.*

"Need to request you pull back from Joseph DeCamp. I was advised Sgt. Smyth created a scene at Jack's."

"Do I dare ask how you know?"

"Don't." The Chief scratched his left ear. "You should keep confidential there's reliable information DeCamp was at the Mayflower Motel in Thursday's wee hours. We're twisting the prosecutor's arm to recommend dismissal of all charges against Mr. Brown. I'd request you notify him to be in the courtroom after the prosecutor gives you a date and time."

"Is throwing out the charges a good idea?"

"It's a tactical move. The charges can be dismissed without prejudice and then re-filed after corroboration of what I expect to be stronger evidence."

The Chief switched the handset to his left ear. "Did you know the coroner's lab results showed Kathie Krump had LSD in her system?"

"No. Please send a copy of his report to me in Minneapolis." The Chief waited for Redburn to resume. "If the prosecutor gets the charges dismissed, delay the truck release a week."

"Will do. And we'll not molest Mr. DeCamp."

The Chief clunked the receiver into its cradle. *Wow, we*

must have stepped into a hornet's nest. When Chief Coltraine had first arrived in Paradise, Redburn wanted him to ignore, almost trash, the state police. He refused. Ever since, Redburn had been cold and distant, in contact only when absolutely necessary. The Chief ruminated he may not be right all the time, but he didn't backstab a fellow officer for personal glory.

He pressed the intercom and asked Bell to summon Sgt. Smyth. Fifteen minutes past four, the sergeant knocked on The Chief's office door.

"Come in. That glory hound, Agent Redburn, called. We're to stay away from Mr. DeCamp. He told me reliable intel had Big Joey at the Mayflower early Thursday. He's also getting the charges against Mr. Brown dismissed."

Smyth plopped into a visitor chair. "No one had to tell me that scumbag and his cronies lied. You told who saw him?"

"Redburn's withholding that juicy tidbit."

"I'd lay odds there was a party with women, drugs and high-stakes poker and that Big Joey wasn't present all night. I'd give even higher odds Ms. Krump attended this same party."

"You definitely may be on the right track." The Chief lifted and sealed a tobacco pouch that had lain on his desk.

"Why toss out the charges against Brown?" Smyth pressed his palms against the khaki fabric that covered his knees. "We should be pitching his butt into jail for murder."

"First off, I suspect the FBI wants to follow him well past Paradise's city limits. Gather information the same way they know you caught up with Big Joey today." Smyth glared. "Second, they don't want us peons messing up their operation, whatever it is. I suspect interstate drug trafficking to give them jurisdiction. Our murder may be but one small puzzle piece."

The Chief puffed his e-cigarette. Through the vapor, he fixed his gaze on Smyth. He enunciated his intense final instruction very slow. "Stay away from Big Joey."

"Understand," Smyth replied, his boastful voice weak. "I'll tell the other two."

"Not required. I'll do it. You just forget you ever had today's conversation with Big Joey . . . How's the city?"

"Pretty quiet, except complaints have mushroomed that cars speed where school children play. I'm creating a speed trap along Chestnut near Hancock." Smyth pushed himself upright and nodded to The Chief's farewell wave.

For the afternoon's third time, The Chief's private line rang.

"Hello. Yes, sir. I understood you were dropping the charges against Mr. Brown. To repeat, you want me to have him in the downstairs courtroom tomorrow between nine and ten a.m. I'll notify him at the B&B on my way home tonight."

Jake pocketed his pickup keys and waited at the B&B bar until Clem approached. "Thanks for this morning. See any other actor go past the partition to the stage?"

"Just Emily. She was here like fifteen past five."

"She said five-thirty." Jake glanced at the bar clock. "So I'm still five minutes early."

"You know a Kathie Krump? Morning paper said she was the woman in your truck."

"Never." And while Jake didn't, he also didn't wish his joyful mind to be draped in black cloth. "Thanks."

"Hi, Jake."

Before Jake could rotate and respond, Patricia, with an opaque drycleaner's bag, ducked through the Spring Daisy Theatre partition gap. Jake hurried to join her.

At the stage, Patricia pulled off the black protective cover to reveal a dress with a fluffy, billowy, solid scarlet silk skirt with an attached nylon petticoat. Black polka dots accented a bright, vibrant red bodice. Jake let out a guffaw. Patricia's hands scrambled to cover the dress with the bag. Jacob, Bob and Pastor John stood slack-jawed.

"Patricia, will you be the ladybug star?" Jacob asked.

Patricia pouted at Jacob's comment. Jake boomed a laugh.

"Don't mind them, Patricia," consoled Emily. "Your costume's design is very creative. The audience will adore it."

A hush descended when a uniformed Chief Coltraine parted the theatre partition and strode straight for the *Cowboy* cast.

"Jake, Mr. Brown, could I have a private word with you?"

128

"Sure."

The silent cast members exchanged puzzled glances.

Jake followed The Chief to the George Street door lobby.

The Chief spoke first. "Mr. Brown, I'm directed to inform you that you should be in our police station courtroom at nine a.m. tomorrow morning."

Jake lowered his eyes. "Am I . . . am I going to jail?"

"I'll let the judge explain everything." The Chief placed his left hand on Jake's right shoulder. "You'll not be locked up. Trust me. You're not getting hoodwinked." Jake nodded. "You can rejoin the others. I didn't want to speak to you in front of them. I'm sure they'll have questions. I'm leaving it up to you as to what you tell them. Be there tomorrow, nine a.m."

Jake inhaled deep twice, and each time he let the exhale find its own way out. He reckoned he had no choice but to obey The Chief. All eyes were on him as he neared the stage with his shoulders square and his facial muscles tensed.

Before anyone could ask a question, Emily spoke. "Okay cast, let's begin where we left off. Jake, your scene begins with 'Yes ma'am, my horse is saddled and ready at the hitching post. Giddy-up.'"

Although he tried his best to clear his mind of The Chief's instruction, Jake plodded through rehearsal. He led the cast in flubbed lines. Emily interrupted frequently to appeal for more zest until six-thirty when she dismissed Jake and Pastor John and asked to speak with the remaining three.

Jake sought out Rev. Olson and the two faced each other on Main Street. "Pastor John, I've started a job today at the state park. It's not a glamorous job, but it gives me a place to live. I fear I won't have time for the church jobs."

The reverend grasped Jake's right hand. "I'm saddened you can't help us out. I'll pray you have God's blessing. We'd welcome your attending our services Sunday and thereafter."

"Thank you. If you're curious why The Chief came to see me, all I know is I'm to be in court tomorrow at nine a.m. and I'm not returning to jail. Can I ask you a question?"

"Absolutely." Pastor John released Jake's right hand.

"Found a Bible in my motel room that had circled words."
Pastor John squinted as he waited for Jake to continue.
"One of the words was Bethel. Is that an important place?"
"Joshua renamed Bethel from Luz."

Jake swallowed hard. "That doesn't mean much to me." His
mind whirled. "Is there any other biblical significance?"

"Let me think. Rebekah's nurse named Deborah was buried
under an oak below Bethel. King Jeroboam built two golden
calves as gods for his people and one he set up in Bethel, the
other in Dan. God, for a reason I forget, shriveled up King
Jeroboam's hand when he stretched it out before an altar. Then,
when Elisha went up to Bethel, youths jeered at him because his
head had no hair. Sorry, Jake, without my Bible for assistance
that's all I remember."

"The word Bethel have any significance to Paradise?"

"Once knew a Bethel-named church nearby. That's all."

Jake ran his right hand through his hair. "You said King
Jeroboam. An old Jewish trucker I'd meet near Indianapolis
referred to a large wine bottle as his 'Jerry boam.' Strange."

"Not really. A jeroboam in biblical times held three liters of
wine. What's so important about these words, if I may ask?"

"Really don't know. Maybe nothing. Sorry to have troubled
you. Best let you be on your way."

The reverend again grasped Jake's hand. "Maybe you'll find
the answers elsewhere in Jeremiah?"

Jake shrugged. "Should've known you'd recognize Jeremiah
without my quotation."

He assumed his B&B flight disappointed the others, but
he'd explain tomorrow. A suitcase filled with his dirty clothes
rested on the pickup seat next to him. Seven blocks north of the
Mayflower Motel, he parked at the EZ-Wash Laundromat.

Jake plinked quarters into one washer and waited for
another. A dozen loud young adults teased and joked while their
laundry rinsed and spun. He wondered if they attended the local
liberal arts college Emily had. He leaned against his washer and
buried his eyes into his script.

"Say, cowboy, would you buy this little lady a drink?"

"Patricia?" Jake's voice echoed his surprise. Patricia in black culottes, a yellow blouse and sneakers had spoken one of her *Cowboy* lines. "What are you doing here? Would've thought you'd have your own washer/dryer."

"Unfortunately, not big enough."

For the first time, Jake, with no sexy dance shoes to distract him, noticed her pale legs and her thick ankles.

Patricia reached for a white plastic bag on the floor. "Mine can't fit this bulky winter comforter. Need a larger commercial-sized washer and thought tonight would miss the crowd."

"For me, it's either visit a laundromat or buy new clothes I can't afford." Jake steadied his gaze on Patricia as she pushed a hair strand behind her right ear and noticed that, since rehearsal, her librarian bun had re-emerged.

"You'll have time to rush back to the B&B tonight and dance at least the last set?"

"Won't happen." Jake twisted a quarter between his fingers. "Thought about attending before realizing Emily would frown if I, having no clean clothes, showed up naked."

Patricia's cheeks blazed red.

"You're imagining my naked hips swaying to a rumba or cha-cha, aren't you?" Patricia covered her mouth with her right hand and giggled. "Or, switching partners at a nudist colony cotillion. You can be honest. It won't hurt my feelings."

"No, no, no. I'll be right back." Patricia grabbed her comforter and hurried to a washer six machines away. Jake heard her quarters clunk into the washer's coin box.

Jake tossed washed whites into a dryer before she returned.

"We're happy to have you back." Patricia gazed at the ceiling. "We were all concerned . . . Emily said jail hadn't been kind to you."

"Let's say it wasn't a vacation."

Patricia's right forefinger traced a washer dial and Jake counted her washer being five machines away.

"While you're kind enough not to ask, you must have a question about why the police chief called me out at tonight's rehearsal. Feared it was my last."

Patricia's lips tensed. "Why?" she whispered. She clasped her hands in front of her waist.

"When the sheriff, I . . . I mean the police chief, came by he told me to show up to court tomorrow, nine a.m." Patricia's lips parted. Her white teeth showed without the hint of a smile. "Although he said I wouldn't be returning to jail, he didn't say much else. The judge has to explain everything."

"Sounds strange. What are you going to do?" Unclasped, her right hand fingertips rubbed her left forearm.

"Going to show up as ordered. If I don't, then expect I'd be in real trouble." He pocketed his quarter.

"To paraphrase author John Milton, you've had more Paradise lost than Paradise gained." Patricia rolled her eyes to the ceiling. "Need a ride to the Mayflower?"

"Thanks, but I don't stay at the Mayflower any more. Started work today at Cottonwood State Park. As the caretaker, the park provides a residence and a state pickup."

"That's really great." Patricia clapped. When six nearby students clapped to follow her lead, she smiled sheepishly at him and he bowed to her.

"In addition, if I want to throw a picnic, suspect I patrol the largest covered pavilion in this area."

"After a while, you'll notice most families use red-and-white checkered tablecloths. High school marches under red and white colors. I plant red and white tulip bulbs."

"When I figure out my future picnic plans, I'll try not to forget red and white. Can I put you on my invitee list?"

"Jake . . ." Patricia's mien and mood dived to somber. "It's nothing against you, but I don't do picnics. Let's leave it there."

"You've dialed up my curiosity. Assume you've had a bad past experience to now shun picnics. All of Paradise has probably been told I lost my wife Athena to breast cancer two years ago." Jake sighed. "Gradually learning you can't shut out life because you couldn't control the past."

"I'm sorry for your loss." Her eyes rolled upward. "The particulars are news to me. I should eat more often at Sadie's."

"So what's wrong with picnics? They're patriotic, raise

money for churches and charities and a boy can steal a sweetheart kiss, if he's bold or extra lucky." Jake spied a Paradise Police squad car coast past the laundromat's large plate-glass front window. Patricia's eyes locked into Jake's.

"Looks like Sgt. Smyth's on patrol," she explained.

"He's a jerk."

Patricia covered her mouth and whispered between her right hand fingers. "Now that's something we can both agree on."

"Can you tell me how he became sergeant when so young."

"Short version?" Jake nodded. "The former chief's youngest son impregnated Roger's older sister at college. Since they weren't married, Roger exploited the embarrassment to fast track his way to sergeant. His sister avoids Paradise with a passion. Roger has been, and is, only interested in Roger."

"Would've thought he'd have been married by now."

"Not Roger. He enjoys chases and trophies, not commitment. Go out with Roger, even an innocent dinner at a public restaurant, and he's telling stories of conquest, even if it's nothing but his fantasy. Ask Emily. Rumor has it she slapped him when he pulled . . . oh, you know, the protection guys carry in their wallets that makes rings in the leather. I don't believe a word Roger says."

Jake sensed an ice crust girdled her words.

"I have to be civil to him in public, but that, for me, is as far as it goes."

"He must have invited you to a picnic." Jake's inner voice lambasted him: *wrong sarcastic ice-breaker.* He had crossed the line to earn an official jerkdom ribbon.

"Pretty close." Patricia's eyelids didn't even twitch. The cloudiness in her downcast eyes disguised any revelation that fiercer emotion smoldered within her soul. "That's all I'll say. It's not ladylike or Christian to gossip."

"Truth's not gossip per se."

Jake's rock step calmed his, if not Patricia's, unease. Their heads jerked right when chiming end-of-load-timers invaded their silence. Jake didn't repeat his unanswered comment. With her laundry task completed, Jake was surprised Patricia paused at the chair he occupied.

"Was it hard on you to leave your ill wife at home?"

Jake wiped his moist brow. "She didn't stay home. Athena wanted us to spend as much time together as possible. We kept motoring between the white lines and did, however, rest longer or shorten a workday here and there."

"I had to take care of my ill mother for six years and that totally exhausted me at times, but she didn't leave her house."

Jake wished to be empathic. "Bet that still restricted you from having friends over, going out when invited or being able to have time to call your own."

"Sometimes. But children have a responsibility to parents. There'll always be time later for personal enjoyment."

Jake jumped in quick. "Wouldn't be so sure about that."

Patricia's eyes flashed with irritation. "Jake! Are you deliberately provoking my anger?"

Since he didn't sense an escalating argument, just an establishment of boundaries, he shook his clenched his jaw to prevent further utterances with unintended consequences.

"I've mentioned circumstances in my life and you're probing my inner self like what I've decided to do wasn't right. Why? Because I won't tell you why I won't come to your picnic?" Jake squirmed on his chair. "I'll not attend any picnic."

Tears, visible at the corners of Patricia's eyes, quivered, posed to dampen her cheeks. While Jake realized he'd pushed too far, he didn't understand why. He had never thought about kids caring for aging parents.

With the belief it provided a neutral, common ground for he and Patricia without camouflaged emotional trapdoors, Jake suggested: "We could practice the play if you have time."

Patricia nodded and pulled a tissue from her blouse pocket. She sat next to Jake and dabbed at her eyes before they turned their attention to the *Cowboy* script. Patricia dramatized her part. Jake recited all the male cowboy parts, except for the mannequin. No laundry patron interrupted them as they creaked rickety wood folding chairs reenacting an Old West fantasy.

When his last dryer cycle ended, Patricia wished Jake good

luck in the morning and said she'd look forward to his later Spring Daisy Theatre attendance.

A physical chill prickled Jake's skin when he entered the dark caretaker house. He dialed the furnace thermostat to seventy-two degrees and lugged in his laundered clothes. With no hangers and no dresser, he stacked socks and underwear in a kitchen drawer. He left his shirts and jeans in his suitcase, tossed a new sheet onto the mattress, fluffed his new pillow and sat on the edge of his unmade bed. Shivers generated by emotion racked his body and he had no Athena to be a sounding board.

A diffident Sarah had mistaken him for an acquaintance from her past. *Okay, possible. Recollections can trick.*

Kathie Krump's name had been brought up by Kate the day before he learned Miss Krump had been his truck's victim. *Not too weird.* If Kathie not close to Kate, it would explain why she harbored no suspicions about Kathie missing. Same for Emily.

Jake closed his ruminations when it dawned on him that a hole could exist in Kate's knowledge. Not everyone ate at Sadie's. He hadn't, and that was why Sarah found him.

Jake arose to peer out the kitchen window. Nothing stirred. He began to pace, front door to kitchen stove. Patricia conflicted him. It was obvious she had mentally locked away a past trauma. She did, however, exhibit an interest in how he handled emotional events, like illness. She also joined him in his new-job joy and his hatred of Sgt. Smyth.

Jake refused to believe her past doomed their future.

The Mayflower's Gideon lay on his kitchen counter. Fate's three sisters had worked overtime. Nevertheless, his mortal grip resembled a butterfingered juggler unwilling to let even one ball strike the ground.

Patricia's comment that children have a responsibility to care for their parents pierced through his mental fog. He wasn't ready for a rocking chair, but would rearing a child spin the cocoon that replaced his cab? Athena had always advised him to think positive. She left no clue if he would survive his sea of turmoil to be washed safe upon an island's shore.

Jake collapsed on his bed. He slept little. He dreamed Chief Coltraine died and his promise of no jail vanished when Sgt. Smyth grabbed the reins of acting Chief. The ghoulish courtroom spectators shrieked as he danced naked.

He arose a third time to snap his bedroom window's roller shade. Excess furnace heat stifled his ability to breathe until he raised the sash. Interlocked cottonwood canopies allowed only the strongest rising sun rays to cast beams across his bedroom floor. Jake's wristwatch read two minutes after six.

His trusty coffee pot gurgled behind him as he stood in the kitchen spooning honey-flavored oat bits and milk into his mouth. A quick stir of instant coffee with his shaky right hand prepared one-half of his daily caffeine ration, enough to stave off an afternoon headache.

His heart raced. He had forgotten to notify Jon of his morning's absence. He penciled a note to explain an hour's absence on a blank page ripped from the Bible. When he failed to find a mail slot at Ranger Headquarters, he forced his folded note into a crack between the entrance door and its doorjamb, six-inches above the door's handle.

To distract his mind, Jake strolled to the lodge for his first extensive interior look-see. Its kitchen contained six-foot cabinet runs on each side of two commercial ranges and two double-doored refrigeration units. An eight-foot steel preparation counter dominated the kitchen's center. On it Jake found an event form that said to expect 125 Rotarians. The adjacent green-carpeted banquet room had a second door exit to the north front-entrance vestibule.

Wood stairs ascended from the vestibule to a second floor hallway with two rectangular rooms, one on each side, entered through opposite doors. Jake peeked into one room filled with large, overstuffed sofas and three large oaken cabinets with glass-paneled doors. Individual cabinets displayed stuffed birds, tree exhibits and Indian artifacts. The second room was empty, except for two neat corner stacks of beige folding chairs.

Jake retraced his steps. In the kitchen he hunted for stairs to the basement his exterior observation said existed. Unable to locate any, he ventured outside. On the building's south side, two slanted metal doors with a lock affixed aroused youthful memories of his grandfather's storm cellar.

He unlocked the doors and, with caution, proceeded down concrete steps into a space of intensifying darkness. He pulled a cord strung through an eyehook. A bare light bulb glowed to illuminate his last step before he ducked his head. With his right palm raised to fourteen-inch wood beams, he estimated seven feet between a poured concrete floor and the beams that spanned the building's width. Eight posts supported the beams at their midpoint. Adjustable, screened ventilation vents, three to a side, substituted for windows.

Jake surveyed the basement. Six paint cans and an eight-foot wooden ladder lay alongside two visible paint-stained white tarps in a heap, ten feet to his left. Jake didn't count, nor measure, the expanse of cobwebs, not as scary to him this day as were his grandfather's cellar spiders.

Without a breeze, the webs hung in Jake's vision with the infinite patience of the dead. He shuddered at an image he couldn't explain and, undisturbed, locked it in the basement.

Upstairs in the kitchen, Jake removed a duster and a vacuum from the supply closet. He retrieved a vacuum dust bag from a closet shelf and reduced its supply list quantity by one. The form listed three tarps. As the third may have been hidden in the tarp pile, he dismissed his need to account for any discrepancy.

Ninety minutes until due in court, he applied duster repetitive swishes to the banquet room perimeter without reducing his anxiety. He switched to count wall-to-wall steps as his vacuum crisscrossed the carpet. The mundane distraction of pushing and counting eased, but didn't eliminate, the gnawing apprehension that coursed his veins and tingled his extremities.

No available Willow Street visitor parking spot awaited Jake. To find a space, he navigated two side streets behind the Paradise Police Station. With the town's church bells posed to toll nine a.m., he crossed his fingers for luck. His heart beat against his ribs, in rhythm with the imagined war-cry drum tempo of native 19th Century Sioux Indians.

Without prior instruction, Jake chose to sit in the half-filled courtroom spectator section. He recognized the judge, James, the bailiff, and the young prosecutor. He craned his neck unable to find The Chief.

Jake refocused his full attention on the judge when he saw the bailiff whisper into the prosecutor's ear. The latter handed the judge a file folder. The judge, his eyes downcast to a folder page, called out, "Case No. 09-431, State of Minnesota v. Jake Brown. Is there a Mr. Brown present?"

"Here, judge." Jake, in the second row, stood. A handcuffed woman to his front and left stared at him.

"Please come forward, Mr. Brown. Do you have an attorney to represent you?" The judge's bushy eyebrows twitched.

"No, not yet." Jake edged forward, first with the help of a railing, and then he grabbed the edge of a shelf built into the courtroom's dark oaken bench. Even standing, Jake was required to elevate his eyes to gaze upon the judge seated eighteen inches above him.

"Mr. Brown, I'm able to inform you that the state has moved to dismiss all charges against you without prejudice. I'm assuming you don't object."

Jake's jaw dropped. His head shook sideways. His racing heart braked so suddenly his mind registered *heart attack!* The war cries in his head dissolved into silence. Jake observed the judge write.

"Mr. Brown, I must explain that while the charges against you have been dismissed, they can be re-filed by the prosecutor without advance notice to you."

Jake's knees wobbled. His thumbs failed to crush the wood between them and his fingers, but they tried.

"That's what 'without prejudice' means. You're free to go. If you've posted bail, which I assume you must have, talk to the clerk about a refund. There'll be court fees subtracted, which will be explained to you. Any questions?"

"Yes, sir." Jake stretched his neck muscles to jut his chin

upward. "Do I get my truck?"

"That's determined by whether or not the police have completed their evidence collection. You must speak with them. I'll order it returned to you within forty-eight hours of the completion of all evidence processing." The judge waited for the clerk to finish writing. "Anything else?"

"Thank you. No, sir." Jake stood immobilized by emotion.

"Mr. Brown, you're free to go," the judge said. "Return to your seat. The clerk will talk to you in about fifteen minutes."

Jake kept his right hand on the shelf edge as he slid his angled left foot forward to test his steadiness. He waved James off and willed his legs to reach his prior seat. With each step, his legs wobbled less, his heart beat stronger and his breathing deepened.

Twenty minutes later, James, the bailiff, introduced Jake to the clerk. She explained $300.00 in clerk and court fees would be deducted from his $25,000.00 bond deposit, netting him $24,700.00. Jake agreed to pick up the refund check from the police dispatcher after ten a.m. Friday.

Outside the police station, Jake inhaled each breath with a slow intensity. The trees struck him as greener than yesterday. A songbird's tweet warbled more melodious. His eyes squinted into a brighter sun. The gardenias and daffodils at his feet filled his nostrils with a fragrance sweet enough to convince him life blossomed on his path ahead.

Jake, at Ranger Headquarters, extracted his wedged-in note and jammed its crumpled form into his front jeans pocket.

Unburdened, he attacked his lodge cleaning task like he'd been given a head start on the devil. He dusted, washed, shined, polished and vacuumed. His assumption the kitchen would be the most difficult proved to be wrong. Refinished cabinet exteriors sparkled with a damp cloth wipe. His pots and pans inspection showed they didn't need to be touched. Trays of polished silverware had been protected with plastic wrap.

He returned all tools and unused supplies and, as a last task, completed the inventory list. He sipped water as his right shoulder rested against the kitchen's exterior doorjamb. When his left hand rubbed his scraped right knuckle, he wondered if his task required a spotless basement.

Without an expectation of any change, he retrieved a flashlight from his pickup and carried a broom and a wet cloth with him. From the lowest concrete step, Jake's right wrist movements swung beams of light left to right and up and down.

Something's not right. Something's not right. Nine circled Bible words, especially "wall," "brick" and "waters," floated between his memory cells.

Jake started at the basement's west side and paced parallel to the ceiling beams to end at the east wall. His counted steps equaled, within a double-width of the vacuum's head, the number of steps he'd counted in the upstairs banquet room before court. He adjusted his starting spot to be fifteen feet north and counted an equal number of west-to-east paces.

His elevated adrenaline levels boosted his awareness despite his prior night's disrupted sleep. He altered his direction to north/south and paced off the distance perpendicular to the overhead beams. While he counted a greater number of steps north/south than east/west, two parallel north/south routes consisted of an equal number of steps.

Intuition told him the main floor length and width should equal the basement. He ascended to the banquet room and paced off its width. No difference there.

He retreated to the rear door sill and counted his paces through the kitchen, banquet room and vestibule to the front door sill. He didn't believe he counted two extra paces. His recheck both ways verified a two step or a five-foot difference.

If the basement had a bookcase wall he could search for the switch to open the hidden room. But it didn't. Each wall had been constructed of concrete block.

He set aside his discovery to commandeer twenty-four wire coat hangers from an upstairs closet for residential temporary duty. After he hung his suitcase clothes, he ate a self-prepared sandwich and napped until almost three p.m. Since he expected Jon had returned, he walked to park headquarters.

"Come in," Jon said.

Jake tried to contain his smile and failed. "Two things. First, the Paradise court today dropped all charges against me. I'm a free man."

"That's great to hear, Jake. I'm happy for you. And, second?" Jon slid three folders across his expansive desktop.

"While cleaning the lodge, found it odd the basement length turns out to be five feet shorter than the first floor. Was it built that way?"

"You sure?"

"Paced it off twice."

"I would've never done that. Why did you?"

"Part nerves, part testing my intuition." Jake didn't have a better reason. Nor, did he wish to expand on how frazzled his nerves had been prior to court.

"Let's check the blueprints. Have a seat and I'll be back." Jake tried to whistle a tune. Defeated, he gave up.

Jon spread out a blueprint on the small desk and read aloud the basement's outer foundation dimensions. These dimensions, with identical square footage, equaled the upper two floors. Jake peered over Jon's shoulder while Jon's right index finger flipped large blue pages with white lines to the basement detail.

"What's this second basement wall?" Jake asked. "Didn't see it when I explored the basement. Posts, not interior walls, hold up the floor beams."

"This blueprint shows a fifty-four inch space or room the entire width of the basement's north end. There's no similar space at the south end where the entry doors are." His right forefinger pointed. "One interior entrance door here. And the blueprint doesn't explain why it's built that way. Maybe the interior wall adds first floor support."

"Could the first to second floor staircase be the reason?"

"Maybe," Jon replied. "It's below the vestibule. Also could have been designed for locked-door paint or chemical storage or as a makeshift tornado bunker. I can only guess."

Jake shrugged. "There's no interior door at the basement's far north end. It's a solid concrete block wall."

"I'll meet you at the lodge basement doors in ten minutes.

There's a phone call I must return before close of business."

Jake waited with the lodge basement doors unlocked.

Jon shined his flashlight into the basement and descended first. Jake yanked the light cord.

The ranger confirmed a cement block wall with no door. "I'd say somebody removed the doorjambs and blocked the door in. That the seams here aren't staggered is further proof. The blueprints must be outdated."

"The straight joints escaped me. What now?"

"Masonry work requires higher approval. I need to make an inquiry. Please lock up."

"Yes, sir." Jon frowned. "If it's okay, I'd like to take off in a few minutes for play rehearsal. I finished the lodge cleanup."

"No problem, except "sir" not required when we're alone. We're unlikely to have a cement work response until tomorrow anyway. When is this play going to be performed?"

"Three weeks or so. I can get you the exact dates and times." Jake completed locking the basement door.

"Great. Plan we'll meet at eight a.m. tomorrow."

"**S**ay, Jacob." Jake paused to let a B&B patron pass he and Jacob near the bar's Main Street end. "Did you go to the dance last night?"

"Sure did. The ladies looked for you, lucky dog. So what's up with you and the police chief? Pastor John evaded questions after you high-tailed it without a word."

"I'm sorry about that. Chief Coltraine told me to be in court this morning. I'm free." Jake stretched his lips into a full-face grin. "All charges dropped. I'm waiting to get my truck back."

"Fantastic." Jacob rotated his head and shoulders to shout across the room. "Hey, Bob, Patricia, Jake's a free man."

While Patricia and Bob paraded single-file toward Jacob and Jake, Pastor John approached from the Main Street door. "I see I'm the tardy one."

"Reverend, Jake here is a free man," Jacob repeated.

"Tell us what happened," said Bob, buttoning a vest.

Jake outlined the events from the time the police chief

visited rehearsal to his appearance in court. He skipped his biblical conversation with Pastor John, his laundromat meeting with Patricia and the clerk's bail return explanation.

Emily joined the group at the point where Jake stood before the judge. She smiled and clasped a clipboard to her chest. "Looks like we have an old-fashioned sunset western ending where the good guy wins. Sorry, Bob, every play must have a villain who bites the dust. Everyone reassemble near the stage and I'll check my notes to see if I have any announcements."

Bob gave Jake a pat on the shoulder.

Patricia interjected. "Jake, you didn't mention your new job." All movement and conversation came to a halt. Five pairs of cast member eyes stared at Jake.

"Oh yeah. Started work as the Cottonwood State Park caretaker. All of your vehicles will be personally checked by me to make sure you have an up-to-date entry permit."

Jake laughed until a lump formed in his throat. He realized Bob had told Emily he had a park job, and presumably not Patricia. While he was pleased Emily had kept his confidence, he'd explain it all later if Emily asked.

As the others headed for the stage, Jake dawdled and circled past the bar. "Clem, can you do me a favor?"

A smiling Clem whispered, "Sure."

"Could you loan me a few bucks so I can buy beers later to celebrate my release to freedom?"

"No problem. Just order and I'll make sure the B&B's not shorted. That's great about the new job. You can pay me back when you cash your first check." Clem flashed a thumbs up.

"Thanks. Once I roundup two chairs for my park residence, you're invited to my first official barbeque."

"That's very hospitable. You better scamper. My boss's evil eye looked this way and she might blame me for your lateness."

"Coming, Emily," Jake shouted. He half-jogged to the stage.

Actor energy coursed through play rehearsal. Jake invited all to stay late and have a beer to celebrate his good fortune. Four ordered Hofensteger. Pastor John and Emily passed on the beer and toasted with diet cola.

Patricia surprised Jake by her out-of-character request for a beer, although she used her play line: "*Say, cowboy, would you buy this little lady a drink?*"

Fellow cast members, except Bob, chuckled. He frowned at Patricia. "Miss Kitty, rehearsal's over." And then he laughed.

One by one, the cast members finished their toasts and departed until only Jake and Emily remained.

"Jake, I'm ecstatic for your happy ending." They sat at a table near the stage. "When Chief Coltraine attended Saturday's dance he had to be interested in something or someone. Then last night when he showed again I worried about you."

"We could've made great chain gang buddies."

"I'm serious." Emily clamped two hands on her glass. "And you don't have to act funny like Jacob."

"Know you're serious. Can I ask about Jacob?"

"You can ask, but I may not answer." Emily drank a sip.

"Learning about the others, even if it's slow, except for Jacob. Know he attends B&B dances and works in Paradise. Can you tell me where?" Jake bit his lower lip while he waited.

"Jacob has for years worked at the 3N Refrigerator Plant on the outskirts of Paradise."

"Okay, now I remember a Saturday conversation tidbit where Jacob said something about an assembly line."

"Forget Jacob. What's next for you?"

"Have to stay hopeful. Making light of a situation, like when I teased you about joining the chain gang, helps me keep my sanity." He suspected Emily understood. "It's true the charges have been dropped. The coin's unmentioned other side is that the prosecutor could, at any time, re-file them or add new ones. Hearing the jailer's key turn gave me a heavy dose of reality on what can happen even when you do nothing wrong. Fear I'm not out of the woods yet."

Emily frowned, then stared at him.

"That was unintentional. I grasped an old saying not realizing that with my new circumstances I'm actually living in real, honest-to-goodness woods." Her frown disappeared. "Honestly, none of my good fortune could have happened without your help. Won't ever be able to repay you. Just . . . just won't." The return of Jake's throat lump stifled his words.

Emily trembled. "You can start by giving me a hug."

Jake squeaked the legs of his chair and stood, as did Emily. They embraced. He envisioned their sideways hug was how a father embraced his child. Their arms expressed love without the engagement of the rest of the body. Emily released her grip first. Jake realized too late he should have opened his eyes to determine if Emily really had a sunflower tattoo on her neck. *Why?* If he jettisoned the past, shouldn't he allow Emily?

"Thanks, Jake." Emily squeezed his right hand before she departed.

"Clem," Jake called out as he walked to the bar. "Please add two beers to my tab and take them home with you. You're part of this celebration too." Jake sat on a barstool. "Can I ask a question?" Clem nodded while he washed a last glass. "Has Patricia's friend Sarah been coming to dances long?"

"For the last year or so I'd say."

"You remember her dancing with a guy named Robert?"

"Can't help you there."

The imprint of sparkling stars, their light sprinkled on the B&B sidewalk and his psyche, encouraged Jake more than the dull plangent rumble of his new/old blue pickup engine. He continued to mull Patricia's laundromat comments. As he had discovered first-hand, she could be both vulnerable and possess a reserve of inner strength. While she had passed on the good news of his job to increase his stature with others, she remained standoffish. Her expression of strong family values didn't necessarily reveal her deep, emotional scar guarded with a ferocity parallel to a Hercules thunderbolt.

Jake paused before he inserted his kitchen door key. The far flung diamond-shaped leaves glistened in his real and imagined heaven. He inhaled deep to capture the bucolic woodsy fragrance to refresh the morning sunshine's invigoration of his spirit. No truck stop offered the cadre of good friends that surrounded him in Paradise.

Caught in the moment, he savored his cocoon of joy. He listened to the distance cricket thrum, a nearby owl's hoot and the faint clatter of either man or beast messing around in a garbage receptacle. He smothered the urge to investigate.

"Good night, raccoon. Tonight, I love you, too."

Chapter Seven

Jake jabbed a spoon at his oat bits afloat in milk. Ordinary and mundane, they were his staple breakfast now eaten from a bowl on his kitchen counter. His laundered shirts hung on simple wire hangers in his bedroom closet. *They'd never be that neat in my truck. Have I found peace, stability?*

In high spirits, he attacked freedom's second day. "Life is better with choices," Jake said aloud to the cottonwoods and life's rustle hidden by brush and weeds as he strode to Ranger Headquarters.

"You're prompt," Jon said. "I like that." The lodge blueprint still lay spread wide on the ranger's small office desk. "Have a seat. Be with you shortly."

Jake fiddled with the blueprint edges until he summoned the courage to sit and inspect the main schematic. The outside dimensions of each level an identical thirty-by-fifty foot rectangle. He flipped to the basement blueprint. Drafting notations indicated forty-five feet from the south entrance doors to a concrete block wall. East-to-west this wall measured thirty feet, the entire basement's width. Jake's finger traced past the drawn arc, six feet east of the west wall, that marked a planned door. The narrow space to the door's right ended with a second door, this one steel-plated.

Jake leaned closer to read the small print: "six-by-five foot closet" with an asterisk. Jake gasped when his retina registered the legend's asterisk preceded: "dynamite storage."

He stared at the words until he heard Jon's footfalls approach. "Did you know there's dynamite stored in the lodge's northeast corner?"

Jon nodded as he stood opposite a seated Jake. "Not since 2002 when a visiting dignitary complained it wasn't safe to stack dynamite crates a floor beneath people meeting. The dynamite we blast stumps with is now stored in a concrete vault beneath a shed, three hundred yards off a deep woods trail."

When the headquarters telephone rang, Jon picked up the handset as he maneuvered to sit behind his desk. He motioned for Jake to lift the small desk's extension.

"Ranger Scott, this is Janet Guthrie in accounting. There's no record of any lodge masonry work approval since the building was set on its new foundation in 1999."

"What about a work expense claim?"

"Couldn't find one. I asked the clerk who records expense authorizations. Her excellent memory didn't remember any."

Jon lowered his right elbow to his desk. "To double check me, would there be any other agency for such records?"

Jake didn't finish a breath before Janet said "Simply, no."

"That's what I thought," Jon responded. "Appreciate your hard work, Janet. As it stands, we've had an unauthorized lodge basement modification. Bye now. Thanks."

"So what do we do?" Jake asked. "Leave it be?"

"We'll get a sledgehammer."

"Think that's wise?" While Jake didn't wish to contradict his boss, his breaking the law could activate his dropped charges. Jake massaged his temples. "Busting . . . busting through concrete block doesn't seem usual."

"Don't you worry any. It'll be my decision, not yours. You wouldn't know about this, but back in 2007 a major bank robbery happened in Paradise. The loot was never recovered."

Jon sat up straighter. When, after five silent seconds, he

spoke, Jake sensed Jon chose his words with care, an indication he withheld something. "Authorities captured only one of four gang members, and he's in Stillwater Prison. I suspect he waits to claim his share of the cash, on-demand bond certificates and two bags of gold coins. Treasure fever reached a frenzy until the ground froze. Whispered rumors all but died by Christmas."

Jake couldn't initially fathom why he needed to know this. Then a hint of inspiration struck. "Are you saying you think it might all be in the lodge basement?"

"As good a place as any, better than most." Jon's smile grew into a self-satisfied grin. "The lodge, inside a state park, is isolated, but still accessible. The old, specially-built, dynamite storage area would keep the loot dry, protected from rain and/or snow. No one except you would feel it necessary to pace off the basement and the floor above to note a length discrepancy."

Whether complimented or criticized, Jake decided to let Jon lead. "Never been a gold rush prospector before."

Jon arose. A muscle in his jaw steeled. "You go find a sledgehammer in the barn-shed. I forget if we have one or two. I'll get my goggles and gloves from my truck and meet you at the lodge's basement doors."

Jake handed Jon a twenty-pound sledge when they rendezvoused and then maintained an eight-foot separation as he traipsed into the basement after him.

Leery he should be there, Jake watched Jon land a sledge blow a foot beneath the ceiling. The only damage was a hairline crack in one block. After two additional swings, Jon explained that any blocked-in door would have started at the bottom. Thus, the top row or two might have less joint mortar.

Jake bought into the theory. However, it required Jon nine swings to knock out a hole the size of one sixteen-inch block. No light emanated from the dark hole.

"You want to join the block party?" Jon quipped.

"Yes, sir." Jake cast off his misgivings and targeted the block next to the one Jon had pulverized. After five swings, Jake equaled Jon's one block and kicked debris off his boots.

Jon shone a flashlight beam through the opening. "No

surprise. Just another brick wall."

Jake lifted the sledge head off the floor and whacked at a third top row block. His four solid swings completed the demolition of one block row between what Jon had suspected were once vertical doorjambs.

Jon reached for the sledge, and Jake gave it up without a protest. When sweat beads dripped from Jon's brow, Jake volunteered to alternate after each had multiple swings. With their coordinated pounding, they attacked the blocks until no row except the bottom two remained.

Jake coughed twice after he inhaled and swallowed a mouthful of airborne dust and fine cement particles that danced before his face. He wiped two left-hand fingers across his right cheek. The grit dug into his pores. When he handed Jon the sledge, he noticed a grayish-white powder cover Jon's exposed skin and his uniform.

Now I'm getting my arms in shape to match what Saturday's dance did to my legs. If only I'm able to lift my arms tomorrow.

"Let's take a break," Jon suggested. "We need to let this dust settle. I could use a drink of water from upstairs."

Jake nodded. As he passed the tarps and paint cans, he dismissed his gung-ho attitude to straightened them up. The fresh air helped clear his nostrils. As he stood on the grass, he slapped dust from his jeans and brushed specks from his shirt.

He sipped water from a paper cup Jon gave him until Jon crushed his cup and pointed his flashlight into the basement. Jake's march after him stopped when Jon stepped through the hammered-out opening.

Jon yelled: "Whoa. Whoa, Nelly!"

A startled Jake called out, "What? What's going on?"

"You won't believe this."

"You found gold, discovered the stolen treasure?"

"Not gold. No bank loot. Just bones. There's a skeleton on the floor."

Jake braced his right hand on a jagged block and leaned forward into the narrow space where Jon stood. The ranger's flashlight beam exposed an adult-sized skeleton, prone, shoeless and clothed in decayed trousers. "Shouldn't we be careful? The bones might be booby trapped like I saw on TV reruns with our soldiers in Vietnam."

"You're absolutely right. We're no experts and also might destroy evidence. Stand clear. I'm backing out. I'll call the state police from headquarters."

Jake, as requested by Jon in what resonated as an order, waited by the park entrance for a state police trooper. While his handkerchief wiped sweat off his brow, Jake let the beads sliding down his spine evaporate. A dispatcher had said the closest trooper patrolled either thirty miles or minutes away. Jon had told Jake to expect Trooper James Kessen in a maroon highway patrol car.

After he raised and lowered the park's entrance barrier, Jake, in his pickup, led Trooper Kessen to the stone lodge building where a showered Jon paced, his uniform clean.

"What's going on, Jon?" Kessen asked in cheerful tones. "My dispatcher gave me the code for injury, but I don't see any ambulance." Kessen smoothed his shirt.

"Once you lay eyes on what I saw, you'll agree that the time for an ambulance has long since passed." Jon led Trooper Kessen to the hole in the basement wall. Jake lingered in the background, his senses alerted for the unexpected.

Jon handed Kessen a flashlight. "Take a look to your right."

A stooped Kessen tiptoed into the darkness. "What the—"

Jon, his hands braced against the hole's cement block sides, leaned his head and shoulders forward. "You see it?"

"Yes indee-dee. We'll need the investigative team. Can we secure this area? We need to safeguard the scene?"

"We can lock the basement entrance doors."

Kessen exited the confined quarters backwards and completed a one-eighty turn. "Let's do that." He slapped a grayish powdery dust from his right pant leg and coughed. "Who found the bones?"

Jon gazed straight at Kessen and in a monotone said, "I made the decision to bust down a suspiciously blocked-in door. Jake here uncovered the disparity of a basement length shorter than the floors above when the blueprints showed them equal."

Kessen brushed his left pant leg. "I need you both to vacate this scene while I go outside to my car and call this in."

Jake, confident Kessen harbored no intent to arrest him, stood with Jon on the grass, five feet from the basement doors.

Jon pulled a notepad sheet from his front pocket. "I've got a list of three families we must ask to vacate the park as soon as possible. Their vehicle license plate numbers are on this list." He handed it to Jake. "We'll do it when the trooper leaves."

When the trooper walked toward him, Jake marveled at how, in body build, Kessen could be Jon's twin. What distinguished Kessen was a crew cut, short sideburns and a broad-brimmed hat that camouflaged the gray sprinkled behind his ears.

"The state crime guys are on their way," Kessen announced.

"We've already locked the basement doors. All early visitors will be cleared from the park grounds within the hour."

"What about the Paradise Police?" Jake asked.

"No jurisdiction on state park land," Kessen said. "We'll put them in the loop to the extent necessary, but I don't see their involvement." He gazed at Jake. "For now, if anybody asks you a question, refer them to me. Otherwise say nothing."

"Yes, sir."

Jake twisted three lodge keys off his park key set for Trooper Kessen. The trooper pocketed the keys and returned to his car. Jake gave Jon a ride to headquarters.

At 2:19 p.m., Len and Bob's white state crime lab van rolled to a halt behind the state trooper cruiser parked next to the lodge. They hopped out. "Trooper Kessen, nice to see you," Len said. "We were at the Mayflower in Paradise. Chief Coltraine was anxious for us to recheck a trailer and vacuum a motel room. Understand you radioed in a request for us to examine a body."

"Sure did." He pointed. "It's in the lodge basement."

"Let us grab our kits."

Len and Bob, kits in hand, waited for Kessen to pluck a key from his pocket and click open a padlock.

After their stair descent, Kessen pointed to the far wall. Len requested Kessen and Bob to step aside to allow his digital camera to document the basement and the wall hollow. Without a step past the busted cement block, Len instructed Bob to retrieve an ultraviolet light from their van.

Bob extended his left arm with the portable ultraviolet light through the wall's hole and steadied it in a horizontal position. Len squeezed up against Bob's side to view the scene through his viewfinder. After Len released a sigh of relief, he shouted, "We're clear."

Len let Bob ease away from the opening before he stepped into the cavity to squat behind the skeleton's feet. Warm breaths on his nape told him his partner stretched to obtain a better view. His glance confirmed Kessen gawked at them both.

Len delegated the note-taking to Bob as he snapped close-ups. His gloved left hand traced an inch scar on the concrete floor. Within two feet of it was what Len judged to be a .38 caliber bullet fragment. He nudged Bob and pointed. Bob shined his flashlight at fragments in two other locations.

After ten minutes, Len requested Bob get one body bag for the remains. Outside the confines of the narrow passage, Len stretched his tightened thigh muscles. He updated Kessen with the skeleton basics: male, estimated height six-feet, body weight 190 to 200 pounds. In response to Kessen's ethnicity question, Len replied that all further facts would have to await a forensic pathologist's detailed laboratory exam.

A persistent Kessen asked, "How long has he been t here?"

"Hard to say," Len replied. "A lot of factors can affect the decomposition rate. Temperature, humidity and insects are the major factors. In our cold winters, subzero temperatures can suspend the decomposition process. Corner cobwebs suggest that flies, the most important factor, were present. Maybe even wasps helped."

"Do you have a guess, considering all you just rattled off?"

"Two years."

"Doesn't make solving this case easy." Kessen slapped his trousers to dislodge the dust. The miniature swirls settled to join the concrete fragments that littered the floor. "What can I do?"

"Nothing now. Bob and I will put these remains in a body bag, carefully re-examine the scene and collect what we find. We saw at least three bullet fragments. It should take us two to three hours."

"I'll be at park headquarters." Kessen's departure added footprints in the dust.

Len refrained from dipping his right forefinger into a suspected bullet hole in the skull's occipital bone. If he couldn't breathe life into an execution victim, he sure as hell wouldn't contaminate the crime scene. He bagged a deteriorated pair of Wrangler blue jeans, noted a bloodstain near the waist and scanned the floor a second time to find no ropes or other restraints present. Based upon his experience, he estimated that less than a hundred milliliters of gravity-pooled blood discolored the floor beneath the body's upper torso.

He watched Bob seal one reasonably intact .38 caliber bullet and three partial fragments into separate evidence envelopes. They discovered no gun, club or other potential lethal weapon before Bob's key, given to him by Ranger Scott, failed to fit into the closet's steel door lock.

Len scribbled a note to ask the park ranger about the availability of an alternate deadbolt key.

Trooper Kessen joined Ranger Scott and Jake in Jon's office.

Jon leaned back in his chair. "What do we do now?"

"At this stage, we wait for the crime technicians," Kessen replied. "Let's hope we get a quick identification."

"Jon, what do we do about the lodge party scheduled for noon tomorrow?" Jake asked.

"Good question. I have no problem with the luncheon proceeding as planned. The only difference between past luncheons and tomorrow's will be our lack of ignorance a skeleton had been cemented into a basement corner."

The doorbell chime clanged. Jon left to answer the door while Kessen debated Twins baseball with Jake. Kessen handed Jake a business card with his telephone number. Jon returned with reporter Josh Miles.

"Hey, Josh. What brings you to the park?" Kessen asked.

"I was at Sadie's when I learned campers had been told to leave the park. Then I saw your trooper car after I bypassed the entrance's lowered gate bar. I sensed a story. You're the one who should tell me why you're here?"

"Really can't. It's too early . . . we're still investigating. Suspect, oh, that's not a proper word to use." Miles lifted a curious brow. "Come back tomorrow, three p.m., and we'll likely have something for public release."

Kessen observed that Miles had eyeballed Jake every few seconds since the reporter's arrival.

"You can bet I'll be here tomorrow, three p.m. sharp." Miles flipped his notebook closed.

Jon, who hadn't returned to his chair, offered to see Miles out. He returned within a minute. "Jake, are you going into town for your practice?"

Kessen interjected a question. "What practice?"

"Theater practice. Jake here joined the Paradise acting group at the Spring Daisy Theatre."

"Never would've guessed in a million years."

"Well, I'm doing it," Jake said. "It's been fun so far. Don't expect it to be a career or that my name will be spelled out on a marquee. I've met very nice, exceptionally generous people. They're one reason I've been given a chance to work here."

"Wasn't that your semi the police found the body in?"

Jake rubbed his wrist. "Yes, sir. If I hadn't decided to stick around for the theater, I could've avoided everything. Instead, I'm arrested. Lucky for me all the charges have been dropped." Kessen glanced at Ranger Scott.

"Jake, do me a favor," Jon said. "On your way out, drive very slow and make sure the reporter left. Would you do that?" Ranger Scott dropped a set of keys into his desk's top drawer.

"Sure. Nice meeting you, Trooper Kessen." Jake departed.

Kessen swiveled in his chair. "Can we trust him."

"Everyone I've talked to has offered positive comments."

"It's just that he's involved with a homicide and now a

skeleton." His right hand smoothed his crew cut.

"I'll agree it doesn't look good." Jon slid into his desk chair. "But Jake would have had to have been here years ago."

"You've scored a point. To ease my mind, I'll run a criminal check. Can you give me specific background information?"

Jon nodded. "Be right back."

Kessen tapped his fingers on his knees.

"Here's a copy of his caretaker application."

Kessen stood. "I'll be in touch."

He tossed Jake's application on his cruiser's front seat and walked to the lodge basement where he interrupted Len packing. "What more can you tell me?"

"Not much," Len replied. "This skeleton met his maker via a .38 caliber gunshot to the back of his head. Healed and calcified right leg tibia bone indicates an old fracture. Lack of blood residue suggests the victim's fatal wound wasn't inflicted in this basement. Although he may have been shot at where he collapsed or was pitched."

"What about that closet?"

"It's locked. Didn't mess with it."

Bob wiped dust from his crime kit's closed top.

"Would one of these keys work?" Kessen displayed the lodge keys Jake had given him.

"We could try." Len exchanged his camera for the keys.

"What about it being booby-trapped?" Kessen asked, his voice low, even though he knew it was just the three of them.

"Don't think so." A troubled expression belied Len's reply. "No signs point that way. I'd guess it was locked at the time Person X was entombed or else it would've been natural for him to have been tossed into it. If the park keyed the dynamite closet to the lodge master, the body's discovery would have been delayed only by sealing the first entrance door."

"Seems like a helluva lot of work. Only thing that makes sense to me is that whoever did this was extremely vengeful or didn't plan to leave Paradise in a hurry."

Len nodded. "Let me try those keys."

Kessen didn't stand too close. In fact, he placed Len's

camera on a step and faced the basement doors with a support pillar at his back. Bob's kit jangled as he and it found a step to sit on. With a wink, he asked, "You scared of a blast? Me, too."

Len's right hand inserted the lodge's front door key into the dynamite storage door's deadbolt. Metal scraped metal before he jiggled the key. His right thumbnail grazed the lock's outside cylinder. He held his breath. This was the third key he tried and the one easiest to insert.

Ever so gentle, he began to transmit left-to-right pressure from his thumb to the key. The lock tumblers resisted. He tried not to snap his wrist. His forearm flexors began to ache, yet he didn't want to rush. When he heard a click, not imagined, he began to let restricted lung air escape through his nostrils.

His left hand twisted the doorknob. Door hinges creaked as he eased the closet door toward him. He released his grip with the door six inches ajar. Len completed his exhale.

His gaze searched the door's perimeter for an explosive or its trip wire. He slumped to the floor and called out: "All clear." He patted the concrete at his left side for his flashlight and grasped the door's handle. A twist and a tug exposed the closet's interior.

"What's there?" Bob asked from a four-foot distance.

"Not much. One fiber and one push broom. And a dusty one hundred dollar bill."

"A C-note, wow!" Bob exclaimed. "Let's see."

"Wait. Don't grab it. I haven't taken any pictures yet."

Len shouted for Kessen to return his camera. After several photos, Len directed Bob to slip on a clean pair of latex gloves. He utilized tweezers to grip the C-note before he slipped it into an evidence envelope that Bob held, then labeled. Len pointed his flashlight beam at the floor beneath the push broom. When he lifted the broom, his eyes caught a shiny reflection.

"Don't crowd me." Len reined in his irritation before Bob could offer a retort. A gold coin's edge protruded from between the second broom's corn fibers. Len snapped photos before his tweezers pinched the solitary coin and he carefully extracted it for closer admiration.

"Bob, put this gold coin into a new envelope."

"How much more money or gold?"

"Don't see other coins or paper. We need to dust this door for latent fingerprints and spray for blood splatter, even if there doesn't appear to be any. It's all very similar to that woman's body in the trailer—blood under the corpse, but nowhere else."

Len allowed Bob to exit the closet first.

Jake, on the lookout for any double-backing reporter, drove his pickup at five mph along the park's main road. He saw neither hide nor hair of Josh Miles in the park or on his trip to the B&B.

He chitchatted with the assembled *Cowboy* cast until their tardy director arrived.

"Let's start in the Second Act, saloon scene," Emily announced. "This should include everyone."

Jake criss-crossed Jacob's path as both hustled to their imaginary stage blocking-marks with Pastor John in the wings to await his later entrance. Happy for the diversion that play rehearsal brought, Jake fought his impulse to disclose the finding of a skeleton in the state park. While he didn't have all the gory details, he didn't doubt his revelation would be big, big news in Paradise. For the second time in a week, he'd be caught in the public limelight. He cringed at being a bulls-eye for gossipy accusations.

After two hours, play rehearsal ended. Jake bade good night to Emily and the men and rued the fact that Patricia had slipped out the George Street exit without his chance for a private word.

Moonless darkness teased his nerves until he garaged his pickup. A security light's glow attracted Jake to the yellow crime tape laid across the lodge's locked basement doors. The deserted park's peaceful soft buzz contrasted with his stomach's occasional gurgle. Sadie's and the Sunrise Restaurant had no doubt closed. He strolled to his residence.

He lolled in his kitchen doorway while a stove burner heated canned vegetable soup. A flash of outside light streaked across his living room window. Jake bypassed the window to retract his front door's deadbolt.

Through a three-inch crack, he squinted into the darkness that began at his front steps. Crickets chirped, unaccompanied by snapped twigs or footsteps.

Puzzled that the only light on the front steps streaked in from the kitchen, Jake stepped outside and unloosened the porch light globe to find no bulb. He carried the dusty sphere inside as a reminder to get a replacement bulb.

After he filled a bowl with cooled vegetable soup, he killed his kitchen light and stood in his darkened living room. He spooned soup into his mouth while expecting to identify lights he never saw and sounds he never heard.

Chapter Eight

With his keys retrieved from Jon, Jake met the luncheon co-chair and the caterer at nine a.m. Friday in a lodge that sparkled. When the caterer eased Jake's anxiety by saying he'd used the kitchen for a dozen prior functions, Jake excused himself.

Ten minutes later, Jake angled his pickup into a visitor parking space in front of the Paradise Police Station. As promised by the clerk of court, the police dispatcher had his bail money ready. Check in hand, Jake drove to Paradise First Bank, although he could have easily walked. He expected no difficulty and the new accounts clerk, noting the check issuer, didn't balk at handing Jake a new savings account receipt and the $200.00 cash withdrawal he requested.

By ten-thirty, Jake, en route to the lodge, clamped the park's entrance bar into its upright position. He met Jon outside the stone lodge's front entrance. "I hope the Rotarians aren't disappointed."

"Don't worry. I saw it last night, and it never looked better."

"Yesterday, when you talked about busting through the block wall, you mentioned bank robbery loot." Jake glanced sideways to verify privacy. "Has the skeleton been identified?"

Jon waved an arriving car to the left. "It's too soon."

"Did you know my porch light had no bulb?"

"I had planned to fix that. Add two one-hundred-watt bulbs to the lodge's next supply request. This afternoon, when the lodge guests are gone, check the barn-shed for metal stakes and snow fencing. Better we disguise the crime scene tape with a fake construction site barrier."

Jake nodded. "No problem. If you don't need me to help direct traffic, I'll walk the trails to clear small branches and mark snowmobile track damage to flower beds."

"Glad to know you've read the duty list. See you later."

Jake skipped lunch to make up for his personal time in Paradise. As he tramped a new trail, he noticed his first cooper hawk. He estimated its height at fifteen inches with its speckled feathers colored by various shades of brown. Not blending in with the park's tree branches were its yellowish claws tipped with sharp talons. Jake gazed in awe as its compact wings, large head with a short beak and a proportionally large, rounded tail maneuvered gracefully around and through tree branches.

The Chief smoked in the solitude of his office. He rearranged his half-eaten cold-cut sandwich and slid the orange slices to his desk's left corner to receive Trooper Kessen.

"Chief, it's subject to crime lab verification, but I'm certain we've uncovered a 2007 Paradise bank robbery link."

"The jailed robber ratted out his companions?"

"Guess again. James 'Slim Jim' DiCecca's a tough cookie. Since his Stillwater imprisonment, he's kept his mouth shut. FBI says his confident air shows he believes that his loot share is safe somewhere. He had no visitors until seven months ago. Since then a Joseph DeCamp lieutenant visits once a month.

FBI calculates DeCamp wants to befriend him to fence whatever loot still exists."

With all prior leads dried up, The Chief's imagination salivated for new details. "So what's the bank robbery news?" Without any finger lifting the cover, his left hand slid his 2007 robbery folder to his desk's center.

"We found stolen bank loot at Cottonwood State Park along with a skeleton." Kessen tossed his hat onto the sofa and slumped into a visitor chair. "We believe it's a bank robber."

"Tell me more."

"State crime office e-mailed my office an update last night on the one hundred dollar bill and the gold coin found in the state park's lodge basement. The bill's serial number matched one stolen in 2007 from the Paradise State Bank. The coin, a 1931-D twenty-dollar gold piece, is a one-of-a-kind design with its female Liberty figure in flowing robes and a large torch in her right hand. Secretly, your Paradise Bank had two bags."

"Why wasn't I informed in 2007?" The Chief glanced and reached right for his e-cigarette to hide a glare he knew would irritate Kessen.

"Sorry, don't know." The Chief interpreted Kessen's sentiment as sincere. "The coins were a private investment of a wealthy Minneapolis industrialist, a Krump family friend. He desired to keep the coins close to, but outside, the Twin Cities. The gold coin's rarity activated a special alert. That the C-note and coin were together solidified the Paradise heist connection. While C-notes are easily laundered, investor-grade gold coins require underworld expertise."

The Chief nodded but once so as not to distract Kessen.

"The coin tells me the skeleton is either Robert Case or Jake Braun. Both identified with the original Paradise gang."

"Recall Case's name. Wouldn't both have vamoosed?"

"Case, with Paradise friends and employment, was considered the most likely to return, yet, never reported."

The Chief heard Kessen's portable radio buzz and held his tongue. When the trooper pressed a button without removing it from his hip, The Chief spoke. "I've thought a lot about this

2007 robbery ever since this office discovered Kathie Krump's corpse." He lifted his file folder and opened it. "FBI suspected her as the gang's lookout. After the fact, an FBI confidential informant, unknown to me, fingered her. Dark sunglasses, a scarf and a swirling multi-colored fluffy skirt created a skimpy informant composite. She wasn't picked up because no witness or bank employee could identify her in a photo lineup."

"I remember those vague interviews."

"Halloween costumes muddled many recollections. Persons confused scarf colors and no two individuals could identify the style of shoes the woman wore. And then her brother swore she had been working at the family store before, during and after the parade. After the 2007 bank customer pumped us up by stating he saw a woman wearing a white wedding dress and veil similar in stature to Kathie, he contradicted himself later by admitting to me he only saw the woman inside the bank. Thus, if Kathie stood guard outside, then that meant the gang had two women when reliable sources counted only one."

"Two brides? Multiple swirling skirts? Who knows? The FBI had Kathie under surveillance for the last six months."

"They did! No one gave me the courtesy."

"You'll understand if I don't respond." Kessen winked. "They, the FBI, this past February tailed her car round-trip to South Dakota. It stopped twice for gas and at one business about ten miles past the state border. Without a reason to question, they laid low. I shadowed her car along I-90 ready to intercept for any infraction, which didn't occur. Two days later, DeCamp hosted a big drug/gambling party. The Bureau expected she would again journey west. She never did."

"While I'd like vindication for my actions in 2007, I'm more concerned today with bringing her killer to justice."

"I agree." Kessen stood and retrieved his hat. "I'd like to help you nail your murderer and clear my Cottonwood cold case. Between you and me, I'd lay odds there's a Joseph DeCamp connection. For starters, there's Krump and her trip right before a DeCamp party and his interest in Slim Jim."

"I'm reading my 2007 notes. You may recall the robbers

used a semi in the bank robbery. It's highly coincidental that Krump is found dead in a trailer with confirmed information DeCamp had paced near it the night of Krump's death?"

"Well, 2007's hazy. Unless the state crime guys provide irrefutable physical evidence, I've got to be officially skeptical of any 2007 connection. My radio vibrations are giving my hip a massage. Let's keep in touch."

After Trooper Kessen left, Chief Coltraine hiked to Herman Krump's tailor shop without the courtesy of an appointment.

"I don't care if he's busy," The Chief insisted. He lowered his voice. "I need five minutes now."

A perturbed Herman Krump escorted The Chief into his office. "I thought your previous visit had been sufficient."

The Chief remained standing and surveyed the office he had visited Monday until Herman sat behind his desk. "I'll get to the point. I don't appreciate being buffaloed."

"I don't understand."

"In 2007, when the Paradise Bank was robbed, I talked to several Krump family members. And this week I spoke with you. At no time was I informed that your family had a connection to the gold coin bags stolen from the bank." The Chief constricted his throat to throttle his rage.

Herman arched his back. "That wasn't a family investment. We deal with important people in our suit-making business and don't have anything to do with their other transactions. . ."

"Let's hope so for your sake." The Chief stared. "I thought we agreed to be honest. I've protected your sister, but don't push me. Did Kathie have friends or relatives in South Dakota?"

"Not that I know of. I've been aboveboard with you. I'll ask what others know to show my good faith."

"I believe my five minutes are up. Have a good day."

At three p.m., Josh Miles arrived at Ranger Scott's office.

"You're prompt. Must be a slow news day?" Kessen teased.

"Not really. However, I don't like to keep important people waiting." He smiled as Kessen glanced sideways toward Jon.

"There's not much I can say. State crime lab investigators

have been called in, and I'm waiting for findings. I can say park employees found a deceased person in the lodge basement."

"You mean Jake Brown found a body?" Miles's eyes widened.

"You should only say park employees," Kessen cautioned.

"But Jake Brown is the park's only employee, right?"

"Wrong. There's Ranger Scott and his deputy." The skin between Kessen's eyebrows contracted into deep vertical lines. His hands fisted. "Look, it makes no difference who found what. Other than a person was found, we're not releasing investigation details on who found what."

Miles, for several seconds, kept writing in his notebook. "Okay. Don't get testy. I'm assuming the person was dead?"

Kessen relaxed his shoulders. "I said that."

Miles allowed a small smile to emerge. "Male or female?"

"Male is our present assumption."

"Then I guess I won't have to stifle any great fantasy for seeing the crime scene photos, once released, now will I?"

"Probably not. A male bone probably doesn't look all that different than a female one."

Jon's chair wheel creaked as he moved his chair sideways.

"What else will you say?" Miles asked.

When Miles flipped a notebook page without a pointed question, Kessen believed Miles had missed his slip. "Nothing until the crime lab completes its tests."

Miles jerked his attention left. "Jon, what about campers? I saw the park entrance bar raised."

"We're open for normal off-season activities."

"Are the remains still in the basement?"

Kessen shot a glance at Jon and jumped in to answer Miles's question. "All evidence has been removed, per normal procedure, to safeguard it. If the lab guys have any human remains, I'd suspect it's in Minneapolis at the lab. However, it's not for us to speculate in private or in print."

"Any problem with me snapping a picture of the lodge's basement doors? I heard there's a barrier."

"No, not really. You should know the park had a scheduled

mid-day luncheon at the lodge today. There's no danger to any park visitor." Kessen stood.

Jon did likewise and escorted Miles out.

True to his estimate, Trooper Kessen drove out of Cottonwood at 3:29 p.m., ready to resume his highway duties.

At four-thirty p.m., Jake knocked on Jon's office door to inform him he'd be driving into Paradise for play rehearsal.

His enthusiasm for a welcomed distraction blunted by Rev. Olson's rehearsal absence. Emily said he'd called to say the hospital summoned him for a church member's illness. When Emily skipped a scene that excluded he and Patricia, Jake's chagrin intensified he might miss a second rehearsal opportunity to apologize to Patricia.

Not in a scene Emily rehearsed, he sat in a chair off to the side to review the dialogue he had flubbed earlier.

"You'll make us all look bad, studying like that," Jacob teased. He twirled a chair and sat on it backwards to face Jake. "Say, what was so funny about Patricia's red costume? You couldn't stop laughing."

"Oh, nothing really." Jake wished not to further anger Patricia by adding her lingerie catalog embarrassment to community gossip. "Your ladybug quip was clever, perhaps cute. But I don't think Patricia, deep down, appreciated it."

Jacob rubbed his cheek. "Sure she did. She told me later she never envisioned her top resembled a bug, but, on second thought, she agreed it did. She worried about how a real audience would react. I told her it would be great, especially with the crinoline in the dance number."

"What dance number? There's no dance in *Cowboy*."

"You're quick. I hope Patricia chuckled later."

"Coming to the dance tomorrow night?"

"You betcha. And you better, too. If you disappoint the ladies by not showing up for two dances in a row, you're headed for trouble. Three or four years ago a fellow employee at the plant, and a dancer the ladies adored, missed three Saturdays in a row without explanation. For the first half of the fourth Saturday, no lady would dance with him. Then one lady said to heck with this. She danced two foxtrots with him to break the boycott. I've always remembered."

"Plan to be here." He added a lilt to his words. "Even washed clothes."

When Bob said Rita expected him for supper and bid good night, Jacob excused himself. Emily and Patricia approached and both sat at Jake's table.

"What's up?" Emily asked. "You've been quiet tonight, like earlier this week."

"He wasn't quiet last night," Patricia interjected. "I seem to recall he laughed awful loud at my costume."

Emily whispered, "That was Wednesday, not last night."

Jake closed his script and gazed at Patricia. "Like to apologize for laughing so loud and long. When you glided that dress out of the bag at rehearsal, I couldn't stop myself. It was such a surprise."

"Accepted."

Jake appreciated Emily's silence, an enclave of friendship where integrity protected confidences promised. "Want you to know I agree with Emily that the audience will love your creation. Fits your stage character and it's a wonderful idea to feature the high school's red color."

"Great idea," Patricia declared. "I'll snip off the sewn on black polka dots, add white dots, and everyone will think high school red and white, not ladybugs."

With Emily giving no departure indication, Jake assumed he'd have no private opportunity to expand his apology to Patricia to include his laundromat statements.

He excused himself.

"Hi, Jake."

Kate's frilly white waist apron indicated to him she wasn't today's cook. His quick scan showed Sadie's tables, especially his No. 12, occupied, even past six p.m., supper's peak.

He followed her instruction to grab a menu and sit at the one open counter seat. The menu's paper insert listed Friday specials he'd seen before. He chose the German plate.

"Good choice," Kate said, not writing out his order. "Will get you to come back." Her hazel eyes twinkled. "No pie?"

"Maybe later with coffee. Lemon meringue if you have it."

Kate made a note and twirled toward the kitchen in response to a cry of "Order up."

Jake had finished his last wurst when Kate tapped his shoulder and whispered into his left ear. "Coffee, black, being served at Table 12. Reserved the last piece of meringue pie."

Jake, remembering his laughing for no apparent reason begot apologies, raised his left hand to suffocate a chuckle. With a nod to the last counter patron, he migrated to Table 12. After a coffee sip, unseen fingers tapped his right shoulder.

"This seat taken?" Emily asked.

"No. And if it was, I'd toss the person out."

"Thanks." Emily pulled out a chair and sat opposite Jake. "Clem said you might be here."

Jake's cup rattled his saucer. "Didn't know he kept tabs."

"Oh, he doesn't." Emily's right forefinger pointed out a front window. "But it's a small town and Ranger Scott wouldn't be parking his pickup in front of Sadie's on a Friday night. He'd be home with his family."

"Hi, Emily," Kate said. "I'll have your tuna fish sandwich with the German potato salad in a minute."

"Will you join us if we dilly-dally over coffee?" Jake asked, his gaze on Kate. "Offer to share this meringue pie."

Kate wiped her hands on her apron. "I'll be back. My server can handle the diner after I satisfy the counter customer."

Jake sipped his coffee and nibbled at his pie.

"You've been awful somber these last two days at play rehearsal." Bread crust crumbs and a bacon bit remained the last morsels on Emily's plate. "I can realize your extreme stress with the arrest, however, I thought you'd escape the gloom once the charges disappeared. I saw a fleeting glimpse of your former joy in your reaction to Patricia's, ah, play costume Wednesday."

"Had two stressful days at work that's all. Thankful you didn't let on to Patricia that I had blabbed to you about my library encounter with her and the lingerie catalog."

"I figured we spoke in confidence." Her lips formed into a straight line. "I couldn't own the B&B without confidences."

Jake clasped his hands around his empty coffee cup.

"Say, you two." Kate carried cream and a to-the-brim second carafe steaming hot coffee. "You look serious."

Kate seated herself between Jake and Emily. He broke the silence before it dragged on. "So how's it been?"

"Been great." Jake didn't read anything into Kate's sideways glance at Emily. "What's new at the state park?"

"Not much. Learning the ropes of my job."

"You're kidding, right?"

Jake struggled to tame his vocal chords. Perhaps the invisible forces that tied him to a rack were why Ranger Scott avoided Sadie's for the cocoon of family life.

Kate lifted her downcast eyes. "I've had people in here this week complaining that you, I mean park authorities, closed the park. One claimed the ranger escorted him out. My antennae sensed a disaster happened that would scare us. Correct?"

Jake created a steeple with his fingers. "Park was open today with a lodge luncheon. Won't lie. Park closed Wednesday and Thursday." Emily's eyes widened. "Can't say more."

"I spoke with a caterer earlier," Kate continued. "He said the lodge basement doors had been wrapped with ribbons of yellow crime scene tape."

Emily's eyeballs strained their socket boundaries.

"Kate, you're putting me on the spot." Jake couldn't dive under the cover of a lie to shatter the confidence he'd built with Emily. "Only began working there this week after Emily helped me get the job. Can't be talking out of place and lose my job. That would be an insult to Emily."

"I certainly don't want to hurt my good friend Emily." Kate's eyes roamed left and right. "You can trust me to keep my lips sealed. If my customers gossip, I don't participate." Kate let her eyes plead with Emily. "Ask Emily."

"Please don't put me in the middle," Emily said. "I didn't realize the park closed. I'm hopelessly out of touch." Emily, joined by Jake, stared at Kate. Emily sighed.

With resignation in her voice, Kate said, "Okay, you win."

Jake decided to say good night.

Before he could utter the words, Kate asked, "Will you be attending tomorrow's dance?"

"Was told by Jacob that I had better show up or you ladies will scribble my name on your no-dance card." Emily riveted her eyes on him. "So yes, I'll be there."

Kate refilled her coffee cup. "Jacob must have been telling you about his co-worker Robert who, for a reason unknown, didn't show up to the Saturday dance for a month. We single ladies made a pact to teach him it wasn't polite to ignore us. Remember that, Emily?"

"Not really, might be before I owned the B&B. I've heard Jacob mention it. He claims it motivates him not to be sick."

"It almost backfired on us ladies. The guy tried to organize a men's no-show for the next week. Everybody finally settled down. There's been an informal understanding ever since."

"Glad to hear that I can be absent," Jake replied.

"Don't be so confident. We could restore the old ways next month just for you." Kate chuckled.

Emily's right hand lost its cup grip. Her left hand caught the cup before it bounced off the table. "You wouldn't, would you?" Emily pleaded. "I don't want any trouble at the B&B. We've been trying hard to make it pleasant."

"I wouldn't do that to you. I'm teasing Jake."

Jake stood. "Do you have meringue pie for takeout?"

"You ate the last piece. Apple maybe?" Kate rose.

Jake shook his head. "Unless Emily wants me to arrive earlier for her offered dance lesson, expect me at seven."

A coy smile emerged on Emily's face. "I'll think about it."

"Have a good evening," Kate said. She directed a whisper to Jake before he left: "Remember, the first waltz is mine."

Emily and Kate dallied to gather cups and saucers.

Emily approached Kate at the counter. "Tell me more about the park closing. Jake appeared very nervous when you mentioned crime scene tape."

"I've catered at the park lodge, but never explored its basement. Could be a dungeon. Heard prior rangers stored dynamite in it. One camper speculated to the cook that a dead body bigger than a raccoon caused the evacuation."

Emily's stomach flip-flopped. "Not another."

"Well, if human, we have proof it wasn't Jake."

Emily sucked in a shaky breath, unprepared to assume the future. "Only this time."

Chapter Nine

Leonardo swerved his blue 1999 Lincoln Continental onto the rural Paradise County township gravel road shoulder to park next to a mailbox and a homestead entry road. He hated mid-afternoons. Blurry in the shadows, his black suit, crimson tie, white shirt and white Panama hat threatened mayhem, not while speckled with sun rays. Night or day, a loaded revolver tucked into his pants waistband completed his ensemble.

He retrieved a double-barrel, buckshot-loaded shotgun from the trunk. With the care of a mother cradling a newborn, he laid the shotgun on blades of ditch grass growing wild below the Lincoln's front passenger door.

Two cars approached from the east, slowed and turned left onto the entry road. They, and their gravel-dust cloud, proceeded the three hundred yards to a rustic farmhouse framed on the north and west by five rows of hardwoods and evergreens. Across the farmyard from the clapboard two-story loomed a large, two-story, rectangular Dutch provincial-style barn with four stonewalls topped by wood-framed construction.

Leonardo expected the cars to stop outside his view behind the north-side trees where they would be next to the house and safe from detection by township road vehicles. Ten minutes later, also from the east, a white three-quarter-ton box truck with a plumbing company logo approached Leonardo. He waved his Panama hat overhead to okay the truck's left turn into the farmstead.

Joseph DeCamp observed his truck drive past a living room window. He adjusted his white tie. He'd picked it from a GQ catalog when purchasing his tailored-silk pale-blue shirt and the fitted dark-blue imported Italian suit. He stroked his Vandyke beard and ordered the four who had arrived by car to guard the front door.

Expecting the evening to be as profitable as the day beautiful, DeCamp strolled to the kitchen's rear door to meet the truck driver and his helper. "How many poker or gaming tables did you bring?"

"Three regular-sized poker tables, one craps table and one roulette wheel," replied Joseph 'Little Joe' Amos, one of Big Joey's lieutenants. Two fingers of his right hand labored to stretch a tight, starched blue-patterned shirt collar visible behind his gray suit.

"Push all of the living room's stupid furniture aside and set two poker tables and the craps table there. Create space in that other first floor room for the third poker table and the roulette wheel. We'll use the kitchen for the bar. This butcher-block table blocks the flow so toss it outside. Angle our bar away from the refrigerator, which we can use."

"We gonna put anything upstairs?" Little Joe rubbed his neck where he'd tried to stretch the collar.

"And, stop with that collar. Rip off the shirt if you don't like it. We'll let the ladies reserve the three bedrooms. I want the high rollers where I can see their money."

"Anything else?" Little Joe motioned to a setup worker.

"Yeah. Leave three or four chairs on the back lawn. I want

170

no pot haze in my face while I escort our guests to the cleaners. Assume you stashed the party drugs."

"Yes, sir. Special delivery package hidden with care."

"Good. Leonardo's shotgun will give us plenty of warning. In Paradise, the sergeant's on duty tonight so I don't expect any police harassment. Besides, they have no jurisdiction out here." Big Joey straightened his tie.

Amos hollered at two guys to haul in the roulette wheel.

Pleased they would ready when the chips and cash arrived at eight p.m., Big Joey winked at Amos.

Little Joe hustled to meet his boss at the front porch. Big Joey pointed a pudgy right forefinger toward the barn. Each circled the barn's interior from different directions to flush undesired visitors. They reconvened inside the milk house.

"Say, boss, since Kathie burned us with a light package from South Dakota, we must replenish our Lucy Star Diamonds. You have a plan?"

"Talk straight. This old barn isn't wired; I had it checked. You can say LSD. We're on target to receive a shipment in Des Moines. I'm thinking of having A.C. pick it up."

"You think we can trust him?" Little Joe leaned his right shoulder on an evaporation tank.

"He passed my test. I had him solve our Kathie problem. At the party everyone watched her get high and prance across the sofa and coffee table. I gave her pills on the house to create her stupor." Big Joey reached into his rear pocket for a handkerchief. "A.C. tossed her onto his shoulder and carried her out of the party. He knew what I expected and I even suggested that he could play with Kathie first. Tickle her in her most sensuous places. I doubt he did, but he did a good job on the major task, except for calling me to the Mayflower's rear parking lot in the middle of the night."

"What!" Little Joe regained his cool to pick a lint speck off his sleeve. "I'd kick his butt out of this farmhouse until he learned better manners."

Big Joey folded and laid a cow sheet across a trunk lid and plopped onto it. "I've known A.C. almost four years. In

November 2007 he said he had business in Mississippi, and he didn't return until this March."

"You think he's planning something solo?"

"Not if he knows what's good for him." Big Joey waved at a barn swallow that flew above his head. "I made that clear."

"Why would A.C. drag you to the Mayflower? That makes little make sense." Little Joe offered Big Joey a cigarette.

"He asked for a place to meet. Nobody hangs out there at three in the morning. A.C. had planned to dump Kathie's body in the river at the state park, but he found off-season campers holding an all-night let's-stay-up-to-get-drunk-and-holler party. A.C. didn't know what to do with Kathie's body."

Little Joe shared a lit match. "That's easy. Drive to a public ramp downstream and heave ho."

"A.C. didn't see it that way. Scared stiff if he did something without my explicit approval, he didn't want me thinking he contrived a fake death scenario to let Kathie live. Maybe he spotted Leonardo's tail."

Big Joey blew two smoke rings.

"Thus, A.C. in his van met me minutes after three with Kathie's dead body wrapped in a tarp. The big rig trailer had no padlock and, with gloves on, I unlatched the tailgate door for A.C. He dumped Kathie. Then we split."

"But the police found the body right away."

"Who knew if that dumb truck driver had the notion to leave town or to inspect his trailer? Besides, the body would smell. A.C. borrowed one of my throwaway cell phones to give Sgt. Smyth an anonymous call at six p.m. I stood next to him when he did it. We expected Roger would jump to the conclusion that the truck driver did it and arrest him. Worked like a charm. A.C. said this trucker, Jake, had double-crossed him and hightailed it to Mississippi. His being framed for murder was poetic justice."

"But I've seen that truck driver on Main Street, near the library and at the B&B." Little Joe stomped out his cigarette.

"Yeah, he's out. If the dumb cops had any smarts, they'd have towed that bloody trailer to the sheriff's impound lot."

"Last Monday, I saw the trucker and the bitch that runs

Sadie's having a picnic at the river overlook."

"Thought you said it was a wasted trip."

Big Joey loved the way his subordinates cringed when he caught them in even the smallest of lies.

"It was. I got bad vibes from the new buyer and left. He fidgeted too much with his camera. But you should've seen the trucker dude's nice clothes. Probably tried to put dancer moves on that bitch. I should tell him she'll never uncross her legs."

"Sour grapes?" Big Joey chided. "Like you flamed, huh?"

"Never. I heard stories she put out for married sailors until one died, shot by an angry wife. The guys at Jack's report she rebukes them all. Under that frilly, fluffy skirt she swirls around the diner in must be a locked girdle—the key lost."

"I think you're a bitter ex-Army guy." Big Joey inhaled a last puff. "Let's go inside. Be ready for our paying guests."

Big Joey enjoyed his laugh. He'd heard street rumors that behind his back punks claimed he giggled. He put out the word that, if said to his face, the mouth would be closed—permanent.

Amos preceded and stood guard next to Big Joey in the overcrowded, shabby poker room that had been the farmhouse's living room.

"How are you gorgeous ladies doing?" Big Joey asked.

"Great, sir. We're ready to show the party's big winners a really grand time here tonight," said Shirley, a petite redhead.

"W-h-a-t!" Big Joey drew out the word for emphasis. "You want a no-name fop to take my money and then show him a good time?" Shirley and a second lady cowered, unable to utter a word. "Amos, you better straighten out these two fine ladies."

Big Joey handed Amos his white tie.

After Big Joey nodded, Little Joe poured him an Old Bushmills Black double shot on the rocks. He promised, whether sipped or not, to replace the drink when the ice melted.

Little Joe counted twenty-three gamblers, all male, in the farmhouse at ten-fifteen p.m. Four specially selected women mingled near the gaming tables. When Little Joe overheard Shirley and another talking, he tried to be inconspicuous.

"Victoria, what's so interesting?" Shirley asked. "You're staring, not circulating. It's too early to pick a target. They won't leave the table until the chips pile up or disappear."

"See the guy over there in the pinstriped suit? Does he strike you as British?" Victoria didn't wait for an answer. "He's not."

"How do you know?"

Victoria undid a top blouse button. "See his intense eyes, dark, near brooding, the hint of an erupting volcano. I recognize him from three months ago."

"You still didn't tell me how you know he's not British."

"Quiet. I want to concentrate on his eyes. I have to tell you it was those eyes I saw up close as his veined skin pressed my hips and shoulders to a backroom table, my skirt up, and his pants down, his rigid torso thrilling me with naked pushups."

Little Joe arced six shuffling steps around the two women. A time or two he looked away, but his ears never closed.

"When was that? Big Joey's last party?"

"No. Minneapolis," Victoria said. "I wondered if I'd ever see him again. No first time kisses. No thank you. And since, no regrets and no problems. He touched my heart, and I don't mean that literally. Now my dreams can be fulfilled."

"What's to say he'll remember you?"

Little Joe crouched to retie a black oxford shoelace.

"Oh, I think my special tattoo will do the honors. And, I can be moist in all the right places." Victoria's cunning smile didn't alert Little Joe that she'd made his eavesdropping. When she lifted her all-to-short black skirt to clean her eyeglasses, Little Joe swallowed hard.

Shirley's sidestep blocked Little Joe's view of Victoria, but not his ability to hear. "Not that sunflower again. I'm thinking you've joined a secret society with that tattoo. I hate to shatter your dreams, but we're here working, not taking pleasure in teasing a losing sad sack or posing for Mr. Right."

"Excuse me. Intense eyes with an empty glass beckons."

Little Joe seized on Victoria's leaving to continue his rounds. He smiled when Big Joey's bluff stole a generous pot. His associates also stacked chips into piles ready to collapse. He interceded to restrain one intoxicated guest who threatened a fight after inhaling "weed" at the backyard kitchen table.

With the help of the guy's friend, Little Joe guided the staggering guest to the barn. There Little Joe tied him up in a stall and confiscated a hidden cell phone. He enforced Big Joey's rule that no guest left the premises or used a phone until the party's official end. Big Joey abhorred guests who tried to salve their frustration by ratting out his party to any lawman.

Little Joe dusted barn-stall straw from his pant leg to continue his monitoring of everyone's whereabouts. He encountered A.C. at the kitchen bar pouring scotch into soda. "You had better dump that drink. We're not allowed alcohol while a party's in progress, just cola or Shirley Temples."

"It's my first and I've not had one sip," A.C. scolded. "A guest accosted me that my not drinking showed a rigged game. I've asked Gloria to slip him double shots. I'll stand here a few minutes until the guy stumbles by and then ditch this drink."

"Did the boss ask you to make a trip to Des Moines?"

"Why?" A.C. toasted a passing gambler.

"I dislike long car trips." A visor-wearing dealer interrupted to whisper into Little Joe's ear and then leave. "A dude asked me other day if your first initial, A, stood for Amos, like my last name. I didn't answer because I know your first name's Austin. Does your C represent a middle or a last name?"

"Stands for Cohen, my last name. Austin Cohen."

"You Jewish?"

"Yeah, what's it to you?" A. C.'s jaw stiffened.

"Oh nothing. I overhead two ladies tonight discuss searching for a Jewish guy. Must be the money."

"Not all Jewish guys are rich." A.C. straightened his lips into a line, and then added, "I'm not."

"Hey, none of us are. I hail from Pennsylvania. Went to school in Michigan. You a Minnesota native?"

"Not Paradise, but south of here. Personal business, and that I owe Big Joey, led me to return ten weeks ago."

"Do you know Kathie? Heard she worked in a Paradise men's store. She partied with us, but haven't seen her?"

A.C. scowled. "Why all the questions?" He plunked his drink glass on the bar. "Satisfied. You witnessed I didn't drink."

"That's fine. You can trust me. I'm no rat. All I was doing was protecting myself. You know, CYA."

A.C. tugged his right suit sleeve. "Okay. See you later. I should win a few big poker hands so the ladies you overheard will at least be impressed that I'm rich and Jewish, even if I'm not a Rockefeller." He lit a Camel.

Little Joe knew A.C. talked out of his head. Big Joey expected A.C. to win, and all money stayed in house. If his winnings were exceptional, A.C. could expect a winning percentage bonus if Big Joey, at daybreak, felt generous.

Big Joey's lieutenant grabbed Shirley's waist from behind. His hand to her mouth prevented the gamblers from hearing any scream. "Shirley," he whispered. "I won't bite. Shake your head as your promise not to scream and I'll release you."

The redhead did and he did.

"What was that for? You scared me."

"Follow me outside. It'll only take a minute or two." He led them out the kitchen door to stand on the lawn. "What can you tell me about A.C.?"

"Not much. A.C. values his privacy and lies to maintain it."

Little Joe remembered Victoria when Shirley readjusted her skirt. He struggled to say, "How so?"

"His well-to-do family lived south of Paradise. When Austin's father went bankrupt, he'd started his junior year in college and never graduated. Like his father, Austin's always blamed the crooked bankers who sunk his family's business."

"Thanks. Let's go back in before we're missed." He opened the kitchen door and stood in front of Shirley until he surveyed the kitchen. When satisfied, he announced, "The coast's clear."

"I heard A.C. grew up a spoiled brat and he still is. Call me sometime." She squeezed his hand.

By daybreak, Victoria's pinstriped guest counted twenty-five thousand dollars in poker winnings. She had stroked his left shoulder when he raked in thousand dollar pots. Big Joey once confided in Victoria that at least one guest should boast about shaking his money tree because a reputation that no player tapped Big Joey's bankroll didn't attract new money.

Victoria plotted to attract her target. While Big Joey would invite the hunk again, Big Joey's goal was to recoup his losses with interest. Pleasure and money configured Victoria's goal.

She pressed her curved physical assets against the pinstripes and whispered she and he should celebrate upstairs.

In the warm 600-count satin sheets, she lay naked with her black hair fanned across a dented pillow. While bent elbows braced his body, the dark intensity of his eyes stared at her.

By her peek into the dark recesses of his visible soul, she ascended to new pleasure plateaus as he drank in her sweet curves and experienced each slow gyration she initiated. He seethed with anticipation as her quivering femininity pulsed their journey to nirvana and the exploding erotic streams flowing from deep within her.

Chapter Ten

Beach bonfire ashes swirled off Jake's lifted spade. Ranger Scott had scribbled Jake's Saturday morning chore on the lodge's cleanup note left after the Rotarians departed. In crude fashion, revelers had ignited dead branches with store-purchased firewood bundles. Jake tried to save as much beach sand as possible by raking the six-inch to one-foot embers into a pile he could dump into an ash receptacle. Then he dug beneath the flaky ashes to mix and blend the ashes with sand. A final raking muted or hid the telltale fire debris.

"Hey, sonny, you're new aren't you?"

Jake spotted a lanky senior gentleman, dressed out in marbled, green hunter camouflage, complete with a brilliant orange cap that matched a deer hunter's vest.

"Yes. Started this week. I'm Jake. What's your name?"

"Oscar, Oscar Jenkins. Me and the missus been coming here since I retired. My being here two weeks before Memorial Day is unusual, but come summer you'll run across me often."

"Nice to meet you, Oscar." Jake leaned on his shovel.

"I see them kids have been at it again, building a fire on the beach. You'd think they'd learn to follow the rules."

"Why, does it happen often?"

Oscar removed his cap to display thin, white hair. "No, not really. Holiday weekends, yeah, or when a group brings a keg. Us regulars expect it. We're only upset if the music blasts loud or the hollering continues after midnight like a past Wednesday night. Wasn't kids either. They were older, scary people."

"How so?" Jake slid his shovel under a rake to lift its handle. His left hand then grabbed the rake.

"About two a.m., this green van comes driving through real slow. Real muddy it was. From behind my window curtain, I couldn't read its mud-covered license plate. Wife said I should try to sleep, not call attention to myself or our camper."

"When something similar happens, you come and get me at the caretaker's residence. Will you do that?"

"You betcha." Oscar ran a finger inside his cap. "I was beginning my morning walk. Walk early and late. Not one trail I haven't traipsed over a hundred times. I love the trillium."

"Nice meeting you." Jake watched Oscar stride toward the trail he'd walked the day before. He stowed his rake and dumped his bucket of collected cold embers into a red fifty-five-gallon drum stenciled: Hot Coals.

In Paradise, Chief Coltraine hung up his public line receiver after he promised Roberta he'd be home by noon this Saturday.

When his private line Caller ID said Agent Redburn, The Chief set his mind to be polite, nothing more.

"Need your help," Agent Redburn said.

The Chief's disposition softened.

Redburn continued, "Trooper Kessen yesterday told me he's investigating a skeleton at Cottonwood State Park. Based on the money found, I believe the skeleton is one Robert Case, a Paradise bank robbery fugitive and a former employee of 3N Refrigerator in Paradise."

The Chief grabbed a sheet of paper and wrote a few notes. "Do you have that identity confirmed?"

"Not yet. State crime lab's working on it. Strong circumstantial though. If you could visit the plant where Case worked and use your fresh eyes to dig up what you can, it would be helpful."

"Will do. Have you any evidence that connects Kathie Krump to the Paradise bank robbery. Fingerprints from an arrest five years ago confirmed her identity as the Mayflower victim."

"I didn't understand that the FBI arrested her."

"FBI didn't. Silverton Police arrested her on a prostitution misdemeanor. The charges died after the john refused to testify. An old sergeant there, and you know I use the word 'old' out of respect, told me on the telephone that the john worked as a Silverton Bank loan officer. This john refused to cooperate. He feared he'd lose his job and fiancé if he testified." The Chief coughed. "One question. Is this robbery and Kathie's death why you had me back off Jake Brown?" The Chief waved Bell away from his office door.

"Joseph DeCamp, alias Big Joey, is our person of interest. Reliable information had Krump as his drug courier."

The Chief peeked at his notes. "One more question. How many did the FBI consider were in the Paradise bank gang?"

"Five total. Four guys and Kathie. One, James DiCecca, alias Slim Jim, is locked up in Stillwater. Other male suspects were Robert Case, now dead in my mind; Jake Braun, not the color brown; and one Austin Cohen."

"What was Kathie's role?"

"She cased the bank and then served as a lookout. Will admit there's confusion on whether she wore a bride's dress at all times. If the bride's dress was a costume, she could've easily zipped it on or striped it off. Since she's dead, doesn't matter."

The Chief hung up on Agent Redburn and telephoned the 3N plant to secure an afternoon manager appointment. He underlined his investigative findings with a sense of pride. His instinct to contact the Silverton Police had helped.

Jake deposited a rinsed soup can in a pavilion receptacle and began Saturday's second stroll through the state park grounds. On the far side of the pavilion, he ran into a recognized face.

Josh Miles's right hand pushed a baseball-cap visor off his forehead, but not his head. "Remember me?"

"You're the reporter." Jake cautioned his mind to be wary.

Miles put his left hand and its notebook behind his back. "Saw the barricade obscuring the lodge's basement doors. Did you find the body?"

"Can't answer. You must talk with Trooper Kessen." When Miles stared at him, Jake's distress level rose to register uncomfortable. To break their silence, he posed a question. "Have you been a Paradise reporter long?"

"About thirteen years. First job right out of college. After two kids, found it hard to move. Wife has family here."

Jake nodded. "You must know all the city officials." Jake didn't wish to divulge he zoned in on Sgt. Smyth.

"You could say so. Why?" Miles groped for a pocket object.

Jake rotated his eyes up past Miles's square chin to his blue eyes. "You must talk to the police often?"

"Yeah. Four, five times a week."

Jake, on the cusp of trusting Miles, couldn't decide. If Miles had repeated his pushy motel self, Jake would've clammed up. Instead, Jake had to probe whether the reporter spilled his guts to the police. "How can you be so chummy with the police without them learning everything you know?"

"It can be a concern. But I've found that if I keep asking questions, and get none in return, what I know never escapes."

"Never thought of that. You act very circumspect, like with Trooper Kessen at the headquarters. You didn't let on we'd met at the motel." Jake wiped a right shoe toe on the denim that covered his left calf. He swiveled his gaze. "If I show you something, would that be kept in confidence or is that different from what a person says?"

"It's kept confidential."

Jake glanced to his shoes. "Stay here." His split-second gaze at Miles's chin left no time to reconsider. "I'll be right back."

When Jake returned, Miles hadn't strayed from the pavilion. "Let me show you this Gideon Bible I found at the Mayflower."

As Jake's hands mimicked a lectern stand, Miles leaned forward to read the Jeremiah 48 passages Jake displayed.

Miles, a pen in his right hand, asked, "Why are these words circled?"

"Don't know. I've tried, heaven knows I've tried, to make sense out of them, but I can't."

Miles's forehead furrowed. "Let's see what we have. 'Bethel,' 'men,' 'brick,' 'wall,' 'waters,' 'beard,' 'shaven,' 'hands,' and 'tied.' All are common words except Bethel, which may indicate it has special significance."

"What significance?"

"Let me look through this Bible." Miles leafed through several pages. "Can't find it. Remember from Sunday School that when Elisha went up to Bethel, youths jeered at him because his head was bald."

Jake squeezed his elbows to his sides. "Bald could mean shaven." This insight added one promising note to Jake's otherwise blank musical staff.

"I guess it could. Don't see a mention of Elisha and I can't keep track of what Jeremiah refers to with his rapid reference to different places. Jeremiah 48 does say: 'found him among thieves.' Who, I can't determine. Maybe if I read it slower?" Miles glanced around. "Can I take your Bible with me?"

Jake shook his head. "You can copy the words into your notebook." Jake feared disclosure of his twice-written name, located on the Bible's inside cover.

While Miles scribbled the words, Jake wondered how long the reporter had been in the park. He speculated the reporter must have been trying to interview Wednesday campers told to leave the park.

Jake's memory cells morphed into strands of worry when he realized that Oscar could have been out and about. Animal sounds traveled miles within the park. Oscar or another camper may have heard he and Jon pound. He was positive he and Jon were alone in the lodge's basement.

"You have something else to say?" Miles asked.

"Waiting for you. My arms are tired."

"I'm done."

"If you discover a link, I'll be around."

Jake resisted the temptation to scout who Miles encountered at the RV campground. He meandered west to a park trail and dismissed worrisome thoughts that he and Jon had been observed. Although there were no windows, he'd double-back to stare into a lodge basement vent to see what he could see.

Jake shook his head in disbelief. He'd been so careful not to mar his newly-shined black slip-ons in the grocery store. *Next time there'll be no shopping before a Saturday dance.* After he parked on George Street, a block from the B&B, he locked his pickup with his bread and canned goods inside.

Six steps past the Main Street entrance, Jake spotted Emily's pearl necklace, luxurious in front of a black turtleneck blouse. She stood aside her table cashbox. A v-neck kaleidoscopic tunic layered her blouse and flowed to black flare-leg slacks that ended above stylish black sandals, each with a white fabric rose. Four dancers occupied Emily's attention. Jake absorbed her radiated, socially-acceptable sex appeal.

He scrambled to close the line's gap in front of him. "Hi, Emily. Don't you think sandals will hamper your dancing?"

The ice crystals in her eyes didn't sparkle like her pearls.

"Sorry. Who's the band tonight?"

"A trio that has been here before. They call themselves 'The Saturday Night Band.' Appropriate isn't it?" Jake handed her five singles. "Give me your hand. I must stamp it."

"Wow, a J. Thank you."

Emily smiled. "Next."

Jake espied Jacob's wave from across the dance floor. Mary, who he had almost pancaked last week, and Patricia's friend Sarah were present, but no Patricia or Kate. Jake, as he strode to Jacob's table, wiggled his right hand fingers at Clem.

"Hey, Jake, looks like my name Jacob inspired the letter of the evening. That's what I'm telling everybody."

"I'll not challenge your honors. If I agree to the conditions attached to the chair in front of me, you'll let me sit, right?"

"Correct. Did you invite Chief Coltraine to join us?"

"Indeed I did." Jake added a wink to his lie. Although early, he estimated a repeat proportion of couples and singles. "Save my seat. I'll return in a minute."

Jake sipped a diet cola in a beer glass delivered by Clem. He alternated his glances between entrance doors. He spied Patricia enter. If the band was a trio, Patricia's clean-silhouetted black slacks and Emily's flares with his non-designer black trousers would make them a trio. While his blue shirt was no match for Patricia's multi-colored silk blouse and tailored black jacket, he still favored her last week's pink chiffon dress. Although her slacks hid any sexy ankle straps, Jake thought he saw the toe of her once-seen, low-heeled dancing shoes.

Patricia waved in his direction as multiple pearl strands gleamed to accent her neck. He saluted her with a hoist of his beer glass.

Jake maintained his entrance door stare. No Kate. When the bandleader shouted out a five-minute warning for dancers to lace up their waltz shoes, Jake slumped onto a bar stool. *What happened to the traditional foxtrot start?* What happened if she didn't show to claim his first waltz promise?

The band tuned up and he stood to face Emily. No Kate.

Jake felt a tap on his right shoulder. Ready to say he wasn't dancing yet, he turned to a radiant Kate.

He couldn't slow the uptick in his blood's warmth. Her cap sleeves emphasized the scooped neck of a blushing-pink blouse matched to a graceful, flowing, below-the-knee white skirt, silky nylons and pink pumps. An amazonite necklace adorned her supple neck.

Without words, Jake pivoted Kate into closed dance position and their progressive waltz steps cleared the advancing crowd. Two promenade steps, the second with a lady's underarm turn, kept them in the flow of dancing couples and in step with the music's rise and fall. Neither spoke. They elegantly ended the song with four—front, back, side—waltz hesitation steps.

Patricia, without a partner, asked, "May I cut in?"

"Yes, you may," Kate replied. "Jake, I'll catch you later."

He listened to Kate's nylons swish without a swivel of his gaze or allowing it to drop below Patricia's chin. "You really look great."

"Thanks. Last week we only danced foxtrots so I thought maybe we could try a waltz. I expect the band will play a waltz double set." And right she was.

Jake rotated three basic box steps in one-two-three waltz rhythm before he lifted his left arm to lead an underarm turn. As was his custom, he asked Patricia before he switched to the waltz progressive step. Compared to his and Patricia's foxtrot, his waltz dance frame pressured a hesitant Patricia. He tried to adjust and complimented her jasmine perfume scent.

She said thanks twice as he walked Patricia to her table. Jake asked a smiling Sarah to dance the expected foxtrot. A swing with Mary kept him on the dance floor.

The band slowed the tempo with a rumba. As a woman he didn't know asked him to dance, Jake agreed, but associated the Latin rhythm with Kate. His energy ebbing, he stayed on the floor thirty minutes until the band's break. While he'd rotated past Patricia and Kate, he had no second dance with either.

Jacob greeted him at their table. "Boy, you still have last week's magic. Remember, don't tire out the ladies."

"I enjoy this." Jake's left foot hooked a chair leg and dragged it closer. He sat opposite Jacob. "Life is good."

"Do you think we'll be ready for *Cowboy's* opening night in two weeks? You buy a costume?"

"Not yet. Can you recommend a western wear store?"

"Try Needles and Pins men's store. While it specializes in suits, it sells western shirts and bandanas. Not a big selection. If you beat Pastor John and me, you might luck out." Jacob laughed. "You get your truck back?"

"It just collects dust, dressed in undisturbed yellow crime tape. Can't even rescue my cell phone from the cab."

"Something must be happening. Chief Coltraine came to the 3N plant this afternoon." Jake's heart skipped a beat. "After he left, the boss asked three of us if we recalled a Robert Case. Remember when I told you about the guy who missed three B&B dances and the ladies shunned him?"

Jake laid his right wrist across his left. "Yes."

"Well, that guy was Robert. A terrific dancer, he loved the foxtrot and would change the rhythm from slow, slow, quick, quick to slow, quick, quick within different routines. He always said he danced at the bronze level, but others told me his routines equaled silver, if not gold, dance patterns. He frequently traveled to out-of-town dance competitions."

"So you said he's not around anymore?"

"No. I mean, yes, he's not around anymore. Last saw him, oh, two years ago. He'd shaved his beard and I almost didn't recognize him. Co-workers assumed he had money problems and disappeared to avoid creditors."

Jacob raised his right hand and waved. Jake twisted his neck, only to gaze at Patricia's back move away from him. He faced Jacob. "Why'd The Chief ask about him at the plant?"

"He worked there on my refrigeration assembly line. We weren't close at work, but he was very friendly at dances. Dancers stopped to watch him. He was damn good."

"Did the boss say why the police had an interest in Robert?"

"The boss made it sound important, but he avoided a direct answer. When he overheard me whisper to a buddy that Chief Coltraine was interested in dance lessons, he frowned and left."

"What was Robert like?"

"If you met him on the street, he would impress you as shy and reserved. Like me." Jacob chuckled. "On the dance floor he was debonair, confidant and fully in control. Never witnessed him bump another dancer. Any couple collides a time or two. It's natural. Not Robert. He danced like he had rear-view eyes."

Jake rose when a keyboard note pierced the room's commotion. "Later." He asked Kate if she'd dance a foxtrot.

"Always willing to give it a try."

Jake discovered in two basic steps she could foxtrot and waltz. His dance whirlwind began anew. Jacob, on the floor himself, twice flashed a broad smile at Jake.

Jake made sure he asked Patricia to foxtrot and waltzed with Kate. He hated keeping score. The band announced a foxtrot mixer. What was he to do? No score could be kept in a mixer. He sighed and danced.

At the mixer's conclusion, Jake spied Emily pulling out a chair at an unused rear table. For the first time that night, he refused a lady's dance request.

"Hey, Emily." Uninvited to sit, he did anyway. "Good crowd. You look nice."

"Thanks."

Jake didn't require a college degree to sense the gloom in her voice. "There's one problem, real serious." Jake forced his voice to sound somber. "Requires that you solve it."

Emily hesitated. "I'll do my best." Concern etched the edges of her eyes and her cheek muscles tightened. "What is it?"

Jake extended his right hand. "You see this J?"

"You know I put it there. It's tonight's dance letter to keep track of who paid and who didn't."

"Well, Jacob tells me the J stands for Jacob, not for Jake. And I thought you were highlighting my name, treating me as a special guest rather than just listing my name under the band."

Emily hesitated. "I'm sorry to disappoint. The J stands for what you're now trying to do."

While Jake had a donkey-family idea of what Emily referred to, he didn't want to say it out loud.

Emily smiled. "The J stands for Joker."

Jake busted a gut. He gazed toward the dance floor and Jacob returned a there-he-goes-again expression.

186

"Emily, that's classic. I can tell you hire better writers." Jake wiped his right hand across his chin. "If it's late afternoon, you can schedule me with your sixth grade class next week."

"That's great." Emily jumped out of her chair and hugged Jake's shoulders from behind. With her left cheek close to his right ear, she said, "I'll check Monday. I'm not a full-time sub next week. Maybe Thursday or Friday will work."

"Remember," he whispered, "I earn a big IOU."

She released her grip on his shoulders. "I have a feeling what that IOU will be for."

Jake rotated his buttocks on his chair's seat. "Bob Hunter's wife could be talked into a dance lesson if it wasn't at the B&B. At Pastor John's church last Sunday, the room we ate in had a part-wood floor. It would make a great practice room." Emily tilted her head and Jake lost sight of her uplifted mouth corners. "With your help, we can talk Pastor John into it."

"You're a conniver. That's what you are." She lifted her chin to meet Jake's gaze.

Jacob's voice interrupted their solitude.

"Jake, the women appointed me to head their dancer-retrieval committee. Their vote requires you on the dance floor—right now." Jacob smiled, his back to two dozen ladies who lined the dance floor.

"I'll be right there." Jake rose and grasped Emily's hands. "We'll finish this after play rehearsal Monday."

A silent Emily pressed a stray blonde tendril into place.

On the dance floor, Jake's left foot grazed Sarah's right toe when he glimpsed Patricia dancing with Roger Smyth. *Can't be.* Jake twirled Sarah on his next floor rotation to confirm his vision. And poof, the sergeant had vanished.

The bandleader prepped dancers for a foxtrot followed by a polka. Jake, thinking Patricia, like last week, requested the polka, asked Kate to dance the foxtrot. He yearned for it never to end as her hazel eyes glinted with enthusiasm. To his chagrin, it did and Jake walked Kate to a table.

He pivoted to be entrapped by Patricia's come-hither saloon belle stare that penetrated his psyche on and off stage.

With the first oompah sound, Jake and Patricia led the counter-clockwise triple step. After the last musical bar, Patricia excused herself. He ventured to guess restroom, but Patricia weaved through tables between her and the George Street exit.

Near Jacob's table, pairs of feminine eyes avoided Jacob to dance their rapt attention his way. Jake believed the dance wizard had cast a spell. He failed to enlist Jacob's help and the remainder of Jake's night became a whirling flash of fast and slow steps, pivots and turns and an endless partner exchange.

Exhausted when the band's drum roll signaled the end, he said good night to a line of dancers, especially Kate, Jacob and Emily. Sarah gushed compliments. At the bar, he ordered two light beers with caps on.

"Two?" Clem teased. "Must have been a rough night, huh,"

With the beers between left hand fingers and two plastic grocery bags clasped in his right, Jake expected no raccoon to impede his twenty paces from his garage to his park residence's rear entry. The soles of Jake's slip-ons crumpled twigs scattered on the concrete pathway to alert park animals he was home.

Ready to juggle either the beer or his groceries to find his door key, he froze. Two large red lipstick eyes, pupils and eyebrows, stared at him from his rear door windowpanes.

Jake shuddered. He reached his right forefinger to the left eye and couldn't smear it. A beer bottle that slipped from his fingers, startled him when it shattered on the concrete path.

He fixed his flitting eyes on the lipstick ones. He could swear he had locked the door when he left.

Like the motel eyes, the eyes he stared at were . . . were painted on the . . . painted on the door's inside!

Chapter Eleven

Rapid knocks on Jake's front door forced him to roll off his bed and kick aside a shirt on the floor to find his jeans. Sunray slivers circumventing the blind verified the world this Sunday had awoken. He struggled to match its energy.

"Sonny, you home."

If he could hear words propelled across his living room and into his bedroom, whoever it was had to be shouting. *Who was Sonny?* He peeked through his front door window and pulled open the door, careful not to strike his bare left foot toes.

Stalled for a second, he asked, "It's Oscar, right?" Oscar's flushed face and shallow pants extended Jake's inability to speak until his voice creaked. "Another bonfire?"

"There's a big ruckus." Oscar struggled to enunciate his words. "Down at the campsite . . . near the river . . . shovels . . . people. They're digging . . . digging holes everywhere."

"What for? How many?"

"Dozens. You have to help. One lady already tripped. There's buried electrical cables. They'll close the park to us campers." Oscar's rapid breathing slowed. "It's not right."

"Will get my shoes and Ranger Scott. Wait here or I'll meet you at the pavilion."

Jake jogged past a locked headquarters to find Deputy Ranger Joel Coleman at the park's entrance shack issuing entry permits to vehicles lined twelve deep. He showed his badge to the deputy he'd never met.

Car horns blared while Jake lowered the entrance bar and Deputy Coleman telephoned Ranger Scott. The deputy drove Jake to the RV campsite where Oscar, in his orange hunter's vest, pointed his fingers frantically in every direction.

Coleman grabbed a bullhorn and called out: "Attention, stop digging now. There's no digging allowed on park property. Violators will be arrested and prosecuted."

Whatever Coleman's power, his message sunk in at once.

Lifted shovels loaded with dirt halted in midair.

Jake approached the individual nearest him. He asked the tank-topped man in beige shorts sporting a ponytail why he'd started digging. The man replied that a *Herald-Gazette* story that morning indicated buried bank loot at the park.

A middle-aged woman with owlish eyes dressed in a blue peasant dress showed Jake that Sunday's front page with a three-column picture of lodge basement doors wrapped with crime scene tape. Below the picture, a one-half-inch boldfaced headline screamed: "Skeleton Found At State Park." Reporter Josh Miles, in a by-lined story, quoted Trooper James Kessen's disclosure of an unidentified, presumably male, skeleton discovered in the lodge's basement. Miles also reported complaints by irritated park campers escorted off state park land Wednesday under claimed mysterious circumstances.

A sidebar story, headlined: "Missing Loot Still Out There," referenced a 2007 unsolved Paradise bank robbery. It repeated man-on-the-street speculation James "Slim Jim" DiCecca buried the bank haul in the park where he had been arrested.

Coleman directed Jake to command people to fill in holes already dug alongside the pavilion, beach and RV camping area. Jake then watched Coleman disappear into the woods near where Jake knew a trail existed. The deputy's bullhorn boomed and echoed stop-digging commands. Jake encountered visitor resistance until he mentioned the ranger would be present within minutes, accompanied by police.

"Thank you, Sonny," Oscar said. "I forget your name."

"Name's Jake, Jake Brown. People are crazy stupid."

"Like the summer after the robbery." Oscar unzipped his vest. "When a weekend RV camper spied two bank C-note band wrappers in a cottonwood cavity, the bank offered a reward and the frenzy started. Day and night treasure hunters searched ravines and rock formations. Gunfire warned hikers that wild men blasted squirrel nests. Ranger Scott told me the wrappers had no serial numbers or bank ID. When I said, 'Could have come from anywhere. He nodded.'"

Jake shook Oscar's hand. "Thanks, you really saved me

days of work."

"Missus says I need to rest. See you later."

Jake diverted his attention to three cars parked by the pavilion that didn't display windshield park permits. From the barn-shed he retrieved a pad of park notices telling the driver to stop at headquarters. As he lifted each wiper blade, a tinge of law-enforcement pride swelled his ego.

Jon approached him. "What's happening?"

"People here have stopped digging. Last I saw, Ranger Coleman went out on a trail with his bullhorn cautioning people not to dig. Have placed notices on cars without permits."

"Good. There's a permit line I must attend to. If you see Deputy Coleman, ask him to report to the park entrance."

"Okay if I leave for church?"

"No problem. Joel and I will handle this. If not, I'll call the state police. Again, thanks. Good job."

While Jake had planned to visit Pastor John for ten-thirty services, his desire ebbed. He fretted about not having told Jon about the eyes. Awakened a third time by nightmarish dancing lipstick eyes at three a.m., his bathroom-mirror reflection showed a haggard visage he didn't recognize.

Even if he ran away scared, he'd never again subject his nerves to the trepidation of entering a vandalized house. Finding no intruder didn't calm or prepare his stomach to digest oatmeal. Any loud or unexpected noise had awakened him. He caught one man on his home's lawn with a flashlight at three forty-five a.m. Rising from his hands and knees, the man, claiming he searched for night crawler worms, apologized profusely. Now, six hours later, Jake's memory failed to remember if the man's hair had been tied in a ponytail.

Relieved to hear a bullhorn, he scampered to a trail terminus to relay Jon's message to Ranger Coleman. As he marched to the residence, noisy mufflers alerted him to cars before they passed. Two middle-aged men in headbands scurried toward the park exit and tugged empty kid's wagons. The wheel rumble meant Jake didn't have to look to learn they found no treasure.

When his kitchen drawer had no coffee can opener to attack

his caffeine-induced headache, Jake reversed his decision to close his eyes. If Pastor John offered no coffee, he'd belly up to the counter at Sadie's.

Driving into Paradise, Jake turned left off Main Street onto Hancock Blvd. He hadn't anticipated the skeleton story impact. On the Presbyterian Church's ascending steps, two ladies, front and back, sandwiched him and peppered him with questions. He achieved the sanctuary entrance when Pastor John intervened.

Several churchgoers addressed him after services, but he kept repeating he had nothing he could say. When the reverend interceded a second time, Jake asked to borrow a can opener and drove past Sadie's without stopping.

He waved to Deputy Coleman as his pickup skirted past the vehicle line waiting to enter into the park. He circled through a full pavilion/beach parking lot. Picnickers speckled the adjacent grounds, their busy hands without shovels.

Jake parked outside his residence garage, entered through the front door and paced the kitchen until he sipped his brewed caffeine. A front door knock interrupted his second cup. When he answered, Jake's eyes widened.

Patricia blossomed like a peacock's fanned tail feathers. He gulped a mouthful of coffee. His brain cells twirled with the multi-colored print, charmeuse dress with its handkerchief hemline and a brown polyester satin ribbon belt. His caffeine-enhanced mind absorbed every flowing line from the adjustable bodice straps to the dressy, brown, high ankle boots.

"Hi, Jake. I've exhausted my *Cowboy* lines. Sorry to disturb you. I would've telephoned, but didn't know your number."

"Did the *Herald-Gazette* lure you to the park?"

She shook her head slow. "Last night gave me concern."

"Huh, what concern? Did I mash and injure your toes?"

"Of course not." Patricia clasped her hands together. "I perceived your expression changed when you saw me last night dancing with Roger."

When his expectation that Patricia would blurt out something didn't come true, he asked, "Roger who?"

"Paradise Police Sgt. Roger Smyth," she whispered.

"Oh, that Roger." Jake's voice soft. *How could I be so scatterbrained?* "Would invite you in but I don't have any furniture. My outdoor dining room table is, I think, quite full with paying park guests." Jake trusted Patricia understood he alluded to the park pavilion. Hindsight told him not to use the word "picnic."

"That's no problem. We can sit here on the front steps."

Jake gazed at the three steps. "Just a minute. Don't sit." He rushed to a kitchen drawer and returned. "Here, sit on this bath towel. Your dress is too pretty to be stained by dirty concrete."

"I'll share." Patricia's finger point invited Jake to sit next to her. Their knees accidentally bumped without comment.

Jake situated himself on the top step. "Don't understand your concern. We both danced with different partners. That's dance etiquette. Never occurred I had a funny face."

She laid her clasped hands on her lap. "About etiquette, I agree. That's why I said yes to one dance with Roger. I knew you saw us dancing. That was why, I thought, we didn't dance more, except for the one polka."

Jake fidgeted, interlacing his fingers. "No, not at all."

"I remember you called him a jerk at the laundromat."

"Yes, but . . ." Jake wouldn't explain trying to keep track of how many times he danced with each lady. Nor would he revisit laundromat topics. "Did you read the paper this morning?"

"If you mean the skeleton, it jumped right out at me. At the dance last night, Jacob asked me if you had said anything about the park closing." Patricia squirmed on the towel. "He said you were . . . were evasive. That's my polite word, not his."

"Guess I can tell you I knew about the skeleton." Jake sighed. "Police gave me strict orders to keep my mouth shut." Jake ran two right hand fingers and his thumb past his mouth to imitate a zipper close. "Obeyed because I wasn't ready to be fired in, or after, my first week on the job."

"That's understandable. I saw you surrounded at the Presbyterian Church this morning."

Jake adored her infrequent smile. "Are you Presbyterian?"

"No. I live nearby. Was headed across town to meet a friend for the eleven a.m. Mass at Our Lady of Lourdes and crossed onto Hancock from Chestnut. First, I recognized a blue pickup and then, when I drove by, you were visible for seconds near the top of the front steps before I lost you in a sea of hair and hats. I guessed you were being asked about the skeleton."

"People went bonkers. They dug holes everywhere."

Patricia raised her eyebrows. "People did what?"

"Brought spades, garden forks and started digging holes."

"Oh, story mentioned that happened two years ago." Patricia lifted her skirt at the knees and let it float and settle. "How silly."

"You mentioned Jacob. He told me last night about a Robert somebody or other who was a champion foxtrot dancer. Is that true? Jacob oftentimes tries to pull my leg."

"It's true. Robert Case was employed at the plant where Jacob works. He danced and exhibited great skill."

"Did you dance with him?" Jake's gaze met Patricia's.

"For a while." Patricia hesitated. "But then he far outpaced my ability to keep up with his dance choreography."

"Find that hard to believe." Jake stood. Patricia didn't.

"Thank you. It's true. Robert was a fanatic. I believe he danced foxtrot in his dreams." Patricia cleared her throat. "At least he said he did. I practiced the foxtrot with him for about two years." She blushed. "Not in his dreams mind you."

"Wasn't thinking that. Why did you stop?"

"He wanted to excel, win trophies. Social dancers, like at the B&B, want to execute maybe a few steps, be it swing, foxtrot, waltz or maybe polka. Robert's goal was one-dimensional. He sought to be the best in one dance and chose the foxtrot. Why? I don't know. He became too intense. I couldn't keep up." Patricia placed her hands at her sides.

Jake believed she intended to push herself to a standing position, but didn't. "What did he do?" Jake sensed a hesitation in Patricia's face as if her dancing with Robert had been layered. "It's not important." Jake didn't want to pressure her as he had at the laundromat.

"He changed partners. You've met Sarah at the B&B?"

"If you ask me, Sarah dances the foxtrot really well."

"Sarah practiced foxtrot with Robert four, five times a week for a year. They once placed second at a state event and then he disappeared."

"What do you mean disappeared?"

"Just that. One day he vanished. As Sarah tells it, Robert had told her he expected money that would pay their expenses to a New York City USA Dance Ballroom competition."

"Was Sarah ever more specific?" Jake ran his right hand forefinger across the rim of his ear.

"She said Robert wasn't either. She thought him secretive because he wanted to avoid paying taxes."

"That's plausible, although hard to do. Now I realize why you and Sarah dance a tremendous foxtrot. Better ask you two for lessons."

Jake sat and shifted closer to Patricia.

"Oh, I don't know. I'm happy with dancing once a week in a relaxed way at the B&B." Patricia struggled to stand.

"Maybe Robert got his money, and he's on a Caribbean island sipping fancy, fruity drinks with umbrellas."

"Doubt it." Patricia's skirt swayed without a flounce. "A decent, if not sophisticated, man, he never requested help to learn a complicated gold-level foxtrot routine or for home repair. In other areas, Robert requested tons of help, well, maybe not tons, but more than most."

"What do you mean?"

"Fix a car or fill out paperwork."

Jake skipped expanding their discussion to the one-dimensional truckers he had met. He stood. While he appreciated learning about Robert, he desired to coax Patricia into sharing more about herself. "Want to take a walk? We have lovely trails that start at the pavilion or the lodge." Jake pointed his right hand forefinger south.

"We could visit the lodge. My boots aren't fit for hiking trails. Isn't there a paved road?"

Jake rotated his gaze to all directions. "Let me show you

something else first."

Patricia arched her eyebrows. "What?"

"Follow me." He picked up his towel and led Patricia to his rear door. "See those eyes?"

"Eerie." Patricia bent forward to inspect. "Who did this?"

"Have no idea. Showed up last night when I arrived home from the dance." Patricia's gaze froze on the eyes. "Scary in that the eyes were painted on the inside and I'm positive that all the doors and windows were locked." Jake dropped the towel.

"I'd be terrified if someone left that for me."

"It's happened before."

Patricia stretched her shoulders upward and executed a foxtrot leader's quarter-turn. "Where?" Her voice pitch rose. "When?"

"At the Mayflower."

Her eyes flickered with interest. "Is that red lipstick?"

While Jake sensed Patricia's desire to learn, he couldn't guess a reason other than curiosity. "Think so. Haven't touched them. I'll let the state police examine them the next time they're in the park."

"Good idea. Which way is the lodge?"

Jake led their single-file stroll. They avoided the shoulder gravel and stayed on the paved park entrance road. He dared approaching vehicle traffic to swerve to avoid them.

Jake was happy to note no holes damaged the lodge's west side grass. At the kitchen entrance, they discovered a trampled snow fence. Jake's inspection uncovered no apparent damage to the locked and yellow-taped basement doors.

"This building seems everyday normal," Patricia said.

"Everything occurred in the basement." Jake broke their extended silence with a question. "See these garden flowerbeds? The caretaker, that's me, is supposed to tend them and I don't have the foggiest. Would you?"

Patricia squatted. Jake didn't.

"You could fill bare spots with annuals, plants that flower and die in the same year. Critical is the plant's sun toleration. Hostas are shade plants. Petunias crave sun. Most nursery plant pots have information on a tag or stake."

"Don't have the luxury of using a garden store."

Patricia stood. "My idea then would be to find flowers already growing in the park and transplant. If they are in the shade, plant them on the lodge's shady side. Vice versa for plants in the sun. Add a handful of fertilizer, water every now and then, and your problem's solved."

"Great idea. I'll scout around." Jake stuffed his right hand into his front jeans pocket. "You have any family in Paradise?"

"I think I mentioned caring for my mother." Jake winced. "My father died a decade ago. He transferred to Paradise to be a 3N account manager in the mid '90s when I was in college. I've got an older brother and a younger sister living in California."

While Jake didn't know if any existed, he asked, "Must be hard to see your nieces and nephews?"

"Mom and dad always made my brother and sister feel special. I ended up overlooked when the grandchildren were born. The five kids haven't been here since Mom's funeral."

Jake squashed his inquiry into her attitude toward children. He feared it could be as explosive as the picnic word. "Bet you excelled in college. Did you attend the college in Paradise?"

"A university in the Twin Cities. For me, I liked to read and library science made an easy major. What I learned in college has little application to today's library operations."

Jake picked up a twig and snapped it before he explained his deceased parents and the brother he wasn't close to. He ended with: "I'm impressed you graduated college."

"Education's overrated." She affixed her gaze on Jake. "To be an adult isn't to pile up academic credits but to develop the discipline to care about other people and to sacrifice for them, over and over."

Jake reached out to enfold Patricia's right hand in his. She clamped her right elbow tight to her side and angled her eyes past his left shoulder.

Jake turned to catch sight of Bob striding toward them.

"I didn't know we had play rehearsal today," Bob called out. "You look very, very nice Patricia."

She blushed. Jake's left hand smoothed his windblown hair.

"Oh, we don't," Patricia replied. "I had a curiosity about what could be seen at the lodge based on the *Herald-Gazette* story. There's not much to see. And Jake doesn't talk much about anything." She smiled. "You might twist his arm."

"Didn't think there'd be much."

Jake hadn't seen a butterfly net like Bob carried in the barn-shed. "Does that net indicate you're capturing park bugs before they eat your picnic lunch?"

Patricia shuddered. Jake cringed, appalled at himself for his clumsy attempt to be witty.

"Merely trying to catch new insects for my collection."

Determined to exclude the word "picnic" from his vocabulary, Jake asked, "You find any strange bugs?"

Patricia squinted her stilled eyes and twisted her head left.

"Not ones that'll kill you in your sleep." He smiled at Patricia. "Have collected park bugs for years, even at night." He shrugged. "When might we be told who the person was?"

"Don't really know," Jake replied.

"See, Bob, he's not telling us anything," Patricia chimed in.

"Had to ask." Bob gazed at Patricia. "Wouldn't expect him to, at least, not until later." Bob jammed his net pole into his right rear pocket. "See you two tomorrow at rehearsal."

Jake and Patricia uttered good-byes.

Bob strode toward the pavilion area and its parking lot.

When a silent Patricia edged toward the lodge's south end, Jake completed three rock steps until her return.

"Anything new?"

"Said a blessing. That's all."

As Jake and Patricia set out for the caretaker's residence, Jake stuffed his hands into two front pockets. Jake circled wide around Patricia's car and his garage to avoid the rear door.

"What's the best way to discover sales of used furniture," he asked. "For example, a kitchen set?"

"Check the newspaper. You could've asked Bob. He often has advance knowledge of client household sales. I'll try to remember to bring today's ad section to rehearsal tomorrow."

Patricia's eyes twinkled. "Or-r-r-r, at lunch, you could read the library's newspaper copy."

"You deserve a hug."

Jake didn't wait for Patricia's answer, nor feel her object. Was she acting? Her body warmth indicated no. He'd bask in the knowledge she knocked on his door without an invitation. While she couldn't garner parental love, perhaps she might wish to have more in common with her brother and sister.

Chapter Twelve

Late morning Monday, Trooper Kessen ignored his e-mail program to telephone Chief Coltraine. "State crime guys called. Dental records confirm skeleton is one Robert Case. Cause of death ruled gunshot to the skull's occipital, perimortem, likely .38 caliber" When static filled the line, Kessen figured The Chief scribbled this information into his file.

"Plant manager here told me Case AWOL two years ago."

Kessen read his own notes. "That corroborates forensic bone analysis, which estimated 2007 death. Skeleton's broken and healed right tibia linked to older trauma."

"FBI has Case as a Paradise bank robbery suspect."

"Let's discuss. Does two p.m. work?"

"I'll be here. Also like to bring my officers up to speed."

Kessen added a note to his day planner and telephoned Jon Scott to inform the ranger to expect him about two-thirty.

The Chief, with the skeleton's identity determined, called Len.

"Any Mayflower trailer tarp news?" The Chief heard a

sharp noise from the hall outside his closed door. It didn't repeat before he could stand so he let it go.

"The tarp has enough paint spots to have been a day care drop cloth. However, one side had splotches of a powdered pigment, zinc oxide, and traces of concrete residue. Tested bloodstains, side opposite the zinc oxide, matched Ms. Krump. We got lucky on the trailer's male blood residue."

The Chief's pulse quickened.

"Traced it to a West Virginia dockworker who's never traveled outside the state. Records show Brown earlier this year had picked up a load at the worker's terminal. No need to pursue further. All non-smudged fingerprints lifted from the cab and the cell phone match Mr. Brown."

Isabella buzzed him on the intercom. He ignored it.

"Thanks Len. Keep me updated."

A knock rattled his office door. "Come in."

Isabelle appeared. "A Larry Hutton is holding."

The Chief nodded and pressed the blinking line-two button. "Is this Larry of Larry's Tattoos?"

"Yes. It's neither here nor there, but Bill's payment hadn't arrived in here in Clearwater, so I called him. He mentioned you pestered him, my word, for old sunflower tattoo records."

"I did." The Chief hoped his admission created empathy.

"There was a note in a box of old tax records. Before I retired in '07, I did half a dozen, both men and women. Recall nape of the neck, but can't be positive. Note says tattoos inked on Emily Hutchins, Kathie Krump, a Victoria somebody, can't read the last name, maybe Jessup, Robert Case, the initials A.C., James DiCecca, and a Jake, first name followed by a capital B and a line."

"Were the tattoos permanent?"

"I'd say permanent, however, tattoo removal technology's improving, especially for smaller ones. That fits the sunflower tattoos. All were the size of a half dollar."

Pleased to the hilt, The Chief hung up. He reread his tattoo notes. All but Emily Hutchins and this Victoria fell into the bank robber camp. He searched for Jake Brown's jail records.

The space after identifying marks had the word "none."

He rued two ambiguities that spawned a dead-end. The jail intake form contained no checkbox for a "had-but-removed" tattoo. Larry's reported illegible or undecipherable: Jake B____.

He interrupted Bell at the dispatcher's desk. "Reach me on my portable radio. I'm headed to the flourmill to talk with Robert Brand."

The manager met Chief Coltraine in the mill's meager reception. "Your call surprised me." He faced away from the receptionist. "What's so important?"

"Retracing my 2007 Paradise Bank robbery investigation."

Brand ushered The Chief into his private office and closed the door. The Chief wriggled on the uncomfortable wood chair. "I expect the FBI talked to you back then."

"They did. But I'll help you if I can."

"Interrupt me if anything strikes you as wrong." Manager Brand nodded. "The Saturday robbery occurred on the Paradise Halloween Parade's tenth anniversary. Its ninety-minute, one and one-half mile route, kicked off on time at two p.m. A witness reported a late model Cadillac Sedan de Ville with a rear bumper 'just married' sign. With crepe streamers dragging, it drove into your mill's parking lot minutes before three p.m. and stopped behind a parked Mack tractor-trailer. My note says the white painted trailer had no advertising and its white cab only DOT license numbers."

"That's my recollection and we checked our afternoon dock shipment records and nothing moved in or out." While he listened, The Chief slid his butt side-to-side. "That happened because parade floats filled the mill parking lot."

"The Cadillac, reported stolen in Silverton, ended up abandoned there within a week. A Mack semi, identical to one seen in your parking lot, found bombed and burned at a highway rest between Paradise and Silverton two days later."

Brand ignored lighted buttons on his desk phone. "You probably know about the skid marks. I told the FBI."

"What skid marks?" The Chief's pulse quickened.

"Fresh black skid-type marks on the parking lot asphalt

indicated that a car's rear wheels spun. The marks were suspicious. They were not near a spot where a vehicle's forward progress would be impeded."

"Let me add a note. My gut tells me the marks show the Cadillac, aiming for the trailer, had trouble shooting up a ramp."

"Although it happens in the movies, I never thought of that." Brand's left hand rubbed his chin. "That could explain the two parallel gouges near the skid marks."

The Chief interrupted, "Made by the ramps' edge under the car's weight." His pride swelled. Facts were beginning to come together. DiCecca arrested in a Cottonwood State Park camper. A gold coin and C-note cemented into the lodge basement. The nearby disposal of car and truck tied into The Chief's past speculation the stolen bank money hadn't gone far. He referred to his 2007 notes. "Does Francine Kellogg still work for you?"

"In accounting, two offices down the hall. Let me buzz her."

The Chief rose when Brand ushered a white-haired, stooped lady into his office. Her cane struck a chair arm as she sat.

"Miss Kellogg, I'm Chief Coltraine. I understand that on the day of the 2007 Halloween Parade you witnessed what you considered to be unauthorized flourmill parking lot visitors."

"My mind's lazy of late, but my eyesight, then and now, exceptional." The Chief tried to smile and encourage her on. "There was this big, dark-blue car. Cadillac. I recognized its hood ornament. My late husband loved his Cadillac."

"How many people?"

"Two. Young man, late-twenties, and this beautiful young lady dressed in all white. Wouldn't say it was a real fancy wedding dress, but she had a veil. From the office window where I was, I could see her best. I had offered to stay late while the younger women took their kids to the parade."

"Could the woman have been Kathie Krump?"

"Absolutely not." Francine's vigorous head shake didn't disturb her curls. "Woman walked different. I've met Kathie at the grocery store, several times in fact. Positive it wasn't her."

The Chief, distracted by Brand's telephone button press, returned his attention to Mrs. Kellogg. "What about the guy?"

"Black business suit. From a second story window, he appeared to be average height, weight. Like the woman, he wore a mask, only his went to his chin. They looked like others lining up for the parade. Minutes later, they weren't there."

"Did you see the Cadillac drive out of the parking lot?"

"I left the window to get a tonnage report off another desk. When I returned, the car and the two people were gone."

"Did you see a semi?"

"Oh, yes, a white one. It appeared parked without a driver."

"Did you hear the truck start?"

"Heard tires squeal when I walked to get that tonnage update. When next at the window, the truck started to back up."

His questions answered, The Chief rose and excused himself. In his squad car, he sat satisfied he now knew how the gang escaped. The 'just married' car, seen across the street from the bank, had blended in. At the flourmill, the semi trailer, like Jonah's whale, swallowed it and the wedding couple.

His notes detailed the bank's antiquated security. Each lens of three cameras, visible to customers, sprayed with paint. The robbers had passed three teller windows to avoid marked money and dyes. Their target had been the vault with its gold. The parade outside provided a great diversion. In costumes, the gang's nucleus hadn't aroused a security guard's suspicion.

The bridal couple at two-thirty-five distracted the employees and their one customer. A third robber overpowered the security guard, bagged his head and immobilized his hands with his own handcuffs. The gang left by two-fifty, ten minutes before the bank's automatic vault timer locked it to safeguard the vault's violated air and hamper all investigation for fifteen hours.

The Chief chose to bypass a fired bank manager interview.

His excited neurons, fired by Larry's tattoo lead, longed to find a woman named Victoria. If Kathie Krump hadn't been the bride, at least he had a witness who confirmed two women.

He stopped his cruiser at the B&B to find Emily. He hated to be skeptical of one of Paradise's up and coming business leaders, but he had to be thorough. Her receipt verified her attendance at a state liquor control training session in Faribault the day of the 2007 Halloween parade. She exhibited true embarrassment about the sunflower tattoo and blamed it a wild fling with Kathie. When he considered no stolen bill or coin had circulated, he augmented his 2007 notes with the updated results that the B&B hadn't engaged in money laundering.

Around eleven a.m., Ranger Scott surprised Jake and a barn-shed spade at a tree line near the caretaker residence.

"I see you've joined the stolen treasure hunters," Jon joked. "Will you split with me?" His loud voice quieted into a smile.

"No, no, no," stammered Jake. "Let me explain. The caretaker duty sheet says I'm supposed to take care of or tend the lodge gardens. I'm seeking to move these plants, two, maybe three, to fill in a shady spot between the prickly bushes."

Jon expanded his smile. "Great idea. Trust me, those wild Swedish turnips or rutabaga plants aren't flowers." Jake dropped his shovel. "Better you cannibalize the hostas a garden club planted three years ago under the large cottonwoods near the boat landing. However, I'd wait. We don't want yesterday's treasure-hunt shovel-brigade regrouped."

"What if I dig out a plant growing close to a meadow trail and replant it? The lodge lacks south side flowers."

"No problem. I've a meeting with Trooper Kessen this afternoon. I'll fill you in. Be careful of that lurking reporter."

Jake picked up his shovel. "Fixed the lodge's trampled fence section and could you point out the residence's lipstick eyes if Trooper Kessen has time?"

Jon's smile transformed into a quizzical stare. "What?"

"Saturday night. In the turmoil yesterday, I failed to mention the rear door's drawn eyes. It's a long story, but I found a similar pair behind a Mayflower bathroom mirror. Paradise Police were informed, but I never heard anything. What rattles me is that the eyes are on the windowpanes's inner side and I'm positive I locked up before I drove into Paradise."

"I'll mention it to Trooper Kessen. I hate park vandalism—I just do. Initials shouldn't be carved into our wood picnic tables nor the barn-shed sprayed or brushed with paint. If you catch anyone vandalizing anything, I want a report. Later, Jake."

Prior to surveying the park's longest trail for debris, and now flowers, Jake exchanged his barn-shed shovel for a hand spade and a plastic bag.

Jake couldn't wait to tell Patricia she had a great idea. He'd withhold mention of his digging wild Swedes for he didn't wish to be perceived as . . . What was the old saying about the last turnip to fall off the truck?

As for the lipstick artist, Jake guessed the color red wasn't chosen because the high school band matched under it.

Trooper Kessen squared his boots on Chief Coltraine's office threshold. He ignored mentioning the tobacco smoke scent and the observed raised window sash. Unacknowledged, the trooper tried not to sound sarcastic. "How's Paradise's finest today?"

"Doing fine. Mind if we meet in the conference room next door, away from the telephones?" The Chief's chair rollers squeaked as he grabbed a folder. "I've asked Lt. Sigourney and Sgt. Smyth to wait there."

Kessen stepped into the hall and followed The Chief. "This'll be short and to the point."

As no introductions were necessary, Kessen began, "Gentlemen, we've a positive ID on the Cottonwood skeleton. Male named Robert Case, age thirty-two at last birthday." Kessen's fingers tapped his closed day planner.

"I knew him," Lt. Sigourney said. "He mysteriously disappeared two years ago. He was seeing Sarah Kleinschmidt, then just divorced. You knew him, too, didn't you, Roger?"

"At the B&B." Roger intensified his scowl. "He'd come to the dances. Embarrass us men in front of the ladies."

Kessen thought he saw The Chief feel his pocket for a pipe. The Chief gazed at Roger. "How's that?"

"He'd mesmerize the ladies with his foxtrot footwork . . . his floating hands. They'd only want to watch him dance, not dance themselves. He'd offer two or three of them a dance, but usually he just danced with his competition partner."

"That it?" Sigourney winked at Kessen. "He cut you out of

dancing with Patricia?" Roger's scowl deepened. "Explains why you're so uptight."

The Chief interjected, "Gentlemen, we're wandering off course. Let's not waste Trooper Kessen's time if waits to add critical information."

Kessen nodded. "Forensics estimated Mr. Case's death as late 2007. Since Lt. Sigourney mentioned Case disappeared two years ago, we must assume he's been dead that long. Cause of death ruled a homicide. There was a bullet hole in his skull with .38 slugs on the floor nearby."

"The body or skeleton was in the lodge basement, right?" The Chief asked. Smyth lowered his gaze.

"Correct. Behind a blocked-in storage room. This isn't for public release but the storage area contained a $100.00 bill and a gold coin, both identified from the Paradise bank robbery."

"Who found the body?" Lt. Sigourney asked.

While Kessen pondered who he should name, the lieutenant captivated him by the ease with which he twirled a pen in his right hand. "Seems the new park caretaker started it all."

Sgt. Smyth bolted upright. "I knew it!" His chair bounced off the floor. "That's Jake Brown. Bet there was only a hundred dollar bill found because he's returned to dig up the rest when the heat's off. And, he killed Kathie Krump because she wouldn't cooperate to stiff the gang, like that guy in Stillwater."

"Hold on, sergeant," Kessen warned. "The park ranger was with Brown when Case was found, so unless you're accusing the ranger of being in on this, you'd better hold your tongue."

"Well, well I . . ." The sergeant's voice trailed off as he slumped into his uprighted chair.

"Chief, can you report any local background on Mr. Case?"

"Confirmed with the 3N Refrigerator manager Saturday that Case worked there eight years. As Roger said, Case was a ballroom dancer of high local stature. Foxtrot was his forte. He had a decent reputation as an employee, although a co-worker said he wasn't the most intelligent." Smyth bobbed his head. "His personnel jacket showed he missed a Friday or Saturday four times that fall. Not serious enough to warrant discipline.

He was paid vacation days for the Friday before and week after the Paradise bank heist."

"Ever injure his right leg, perhaps dancing?" Kessen asked.

"He once broke his lower leg, think right," Lt. Sigourney said. "He played on a town softball team, third base, say '94 or '95. Recall he hobbled on crutches for six weeks."

"Good," Kessen replied. "Matches the skeleton's bone info given us by the crime guys. Any questions?"

"Two," Sgt. Smyth said. "Do we have a suspect?"

"No, not at this time. If you think about it, there's the robbery connection. It's not outside reason a gang member shot him. Also, don't rule out someone else who thought Case had the stolen loot, found out he didn't and then still killed him. Possible, but not probable, the fatal shot was accidental." Kessen glanced from The Chief to Sgt. Smyth. "You had a second question?"

"Was he killed where found?"

"Evidence suggests no. Scene blood quantity and lack of splatter indicates Case was shot elsewhere and hidden in the lodge basement." Sigourney wrote himself a note.

"See, Chief, just like Kathie in the trailer." Sgt. Smyth's face flushed. "Method matches. That Brown fella is the killer."

"Roger," intoned The Chief, "you're missing a major point. Mr. Brown arrived two weeks ago, not two years."

Sgt. Smyth again stood. "One, a killer doesn't have to live here two years to have murdered someone two years ago. Second, the flourmill's Robert Brand says Brown's been trucking loads to the flourmill at least three years. He could've easily been here two years ago, killed Case at the state park and then skedaddled. Back to collect his share, Kathie tells him it's gone and he strangles her."

Kessen, stiffening under Sgt. Smyth's glare, refused to debate conjecture nor lose a staring contest.

"Did you tell the trooper, Chief, that Kathie was witnessed alive at the Mayflower parking lot a night or two before with Brown's truck there and she prancing or parading?"

"Okay, Roger, that's enough. Sit down."

Kessen clenched his fists. Held his tongue and endured a ten second silence. He would've ordered Sgt. Smyth out, not to sit.

The Chief continued, "Even if I agree, she may have been trying to score a hit or sell her charms. Who knows? There's little, if anything, to connect her with Mr. Brown, contrary to what you would suggest."

"You're wrong," Sgt. Smyth said, his volume a third of his rant. "Brown knew Case was dead so he, quote, discovered him, unquote, before someone else did. He knew no treasure was buried with Case's body." Sigourney stopped writing. "Doesn't hurt him in the least to look innocent. Takes away suspicion that he killed Kathie, too. You'll have a hard time to convince me otherwise." Sgt. Smyth folded his arms across his chest.

The Chief ignored his sergeant's smug face and gazed at Kessen. "You have anything else?"

"Nothing." Kessen pushed himself from the table. "Keep your eyes and ears open. Two original bank gang members are unaccounted for."

"Can you refresh my memory?" Lt. Sigourney asked.

"Not for release, but FBI says there's a Jake Braun, not spelled like the color, but b-r-a-u-n; and one Austin Cohen. Whereabouts of both gentlemen elusive since the robbery."

Kessen joined The Chief in standing.

"I'll see myself out," Kessen said. "Have a good day."

Trooper Kessen, at two forty-five, arrived later than expected, but early for his scheduled meeting at the Cottonwood State Park Headquarters. In Ranger Scott's office, he hadn't finished his hello to Reporter Josh Miles when Jon lit into Miles for Sunday's park damage. Miles offered no apology and challenged Ranger Scott to prove he wrote an untruth.

Kessen interrupted, "Gentlemen, let's all be calm." He waited to be the last to sit. "Victim found in the lodge basement identified as Robert Case." He related the identical public-releasable facts he'd given the Paradise Police.

"Have you located any weapon used?" Miles asked.

"Not yet," Kessen replied. He tossed his hat on a chair.

"Any relatives in the area?"

Kessen readied himself for an inquisition as he observed Miles read from a notepad page. A quiet Jon, a disinterested outsider to the reporter's questions, leaned back in his chair.

"Mother lived in Paradise. Told she died three years ago."

"Do you know where in Paradise?"

"Chestnut Street. Didn't get the address."

"You mentioned the skull's occipital area. Right or left?"

"Left, I think. I'll have to reaffirm."

Miles flipped a page. "Will you describe the gold coin?"

"We're not releasing those details. We don't want glory-seeking media confessors to inundate us."

Jon yawned.

"Any reward out there?"

Jon's eyes perked up.

"Not that comes to mind. Wait a minute, the bank originally offered $25,000.00 for conviction and the stolen money's return. You should contact the Paradise Bank to verify if their reward offer remains valid. That's all I have."

"When will I have basement access?"

"Don't have a fix on that. State crime guys are still investigating." Miles raised his right hand to indicate a question, then dropped it as Kessen continued. "As far as we can tell, there's no bank loot in the lodge or elsewhere in the state park. If people dig, we'll arrest. Mention that."

"My story didn't encourage people to dig."

Kessen lowered his voice when he noticed Miles arch his back. "That's a fine line. We don't want a repeat. That's all."

"I'd like to be told when I can view the lodge basement."

"We'll do that. Can you find your way out? I need to speak with Ranger Scott before I resume my regular patrol."

Miles smirked. "Tell me you haven't found another body?"

"We haven't. You're on your toes though."

Miles left Scott's office and Kessen listened for, and heard, a vehicle engine start.

Ranger Scott straightened up in his chair.

"What else did you want to talk about?" Kessen asked.

"Jake told me today that strange caretaker residence graffiti scared him Saturday night."

Jon escorted Kessen out of headquarters by a rear door. They marched along a dirt path, and across grass, to the rear of Jake's residence. "Here it is: two windowpane eyes."

Kessen bent forward to scrutinize and to measure the left eyeball span with two fingers. "Was the door left unlocked?"

"Jake said no." Jon then detailed Jake's story.

Kessen stood erect. "Can we see them from the inside?"

"Sure." Jon reached for his keys. "When the park re-keyed the lodge three years ago, the old lodge locks replaced those in the caretaker's residence." He unlocked the door.

Kessen flexed his knees to inspect. "Looks like red lipstick. I'll have Len tell us more." The two stepped outside.

Jon locked the door. "Good. Jake said he had similar eyes appear ten days ago at the Mayflower and he told the police."

"Anybody issued house keys other than Jake?"

"Joel and I have a master. A spare set's locked in a supply cabinet. I'm sure they're still there. If not, I'll notify you."

"Tell Jake not to disturb. Since I can't justify a special trip, I'll ask Len to examine them when he returns for the lodge. Give me a heads up if you find anything else like this."

"Will do."

Kessen, anxious to leave, double-timed it to his cruiser.

"Jake, how's it going?" greeted the baritone voice.

Jake seized upon the unexpected early play rehearsal presence of Pastor John to say, "Thanks for yesterday." He closed the Spring Daisy Theatre partition after the two entered on their walk to the stage. "Never been a gossip celebrity."

"Please accept my apology for the zealous Presbyterians. A person shouldn't have to shove. clash elbows or be denied entry on his way in to praise the Lord."

"Or battle his way out." Jake laughed. "Didn't even have a chance to grab a bulletin. Is there another feast coming up?"

"Next month we're doing Swedish."

"Serving turnips?" Jake hid his knowledge source.

"Oh, I think of Swede turnips as Scottish. No. Envision plates of meatballs, pea soup, knäckebröd, biskvi and lutefisk."

"Enticing." Jake couldn't pump enthusiasm into his word. He let footfalls pass behind him without disengaging his attention from Pastor John.

"Patricia," Pastor John called out. "Jake wants Swedes." When Jake turned, her puzzled expression surprised him.

"Mashed with seasoning or simply boiled?" she asked.

Neither Jake nor Pastor John replied.

Emily's voice boomed. "All right, cast, time to put on your acting masks. We'll start with the campfire scene."

Halfway around the stage perimeter, Jake, out of the corner of his left eye, caught Pastor John grin at Patricia, flash a thumbs up and mimic one eating with a fork. Jake didn't pursue what it meant when neither said a word about anything related to the turnip family.

When Emily didn't ask Jake to repeat lines, his acting confidence soared. During a lull before the troupe's dismissal, Jake asked Pastor John for a private word.

"I'm working on securing a place for dance lessons that would be less public than the B&B. Is there a possibility to use the room where you served the Greek food?"

"With notice, sure. What do you have in mind?"

"Partner ballroom dance lessons. Need to convince Emily and Bob's wife Rita to attend. If two or three couples from your church could join us that would be a nice group, not too big, not to small. Bob owns a Sinatra CD."

"Fantastic. Let me think of who would be good church candidates. What type of commitment do you expect?"

"Once a week for six weeks."

"How will you convince Emily? She offers dances here and I understand she still doesn't dance."

Jake placed his cupped right hand two inches from his mouth. "There's a little bribe. I'll not say more."

Emily approached and Pastor John said, "Good night, all. Hope to see you in church." He winked at Jake before he split.

"How's Thursday afternoon at three?" Emily asked.

"Will be there. If I get my truck, can I bring it? Kids love to blast the horn."

Their feet sidled to a stage-right table.

"Fine. I planned inside, but outside will work. Only you must restrict the horn blowing. I'm glad your upbeat."

"Life's positive again." *Yes, indeed.*

Emily reached into her director materials and pulled out a newspaper section. "Patricia said you planned to buy furniture. She didn't wish to interrupt you and Pastor John."

Jake's clasped hands pinned the folded newspaper to the table. "Thanks. Met Bob and Patricia at the state park yesterday. We talked and I asked for hints where I could buy used furniture. Patricia offered to bring me a copy of sales ads."

Emily smiled. "You act ready to stay in Paradise."

"Jury's still out. Sorry, Emily, poor choice of words."

"I know what you mean." And Jake believed her for she didn't appear upset. "You driving to Sadie's for supper?"

"Not tonight. I'll study my script and turn in early. Today's fresh air and hiking has tired me out. And then there's this early morning bird chirping that wakes me earlier and earlier." Jake's right hand reached into his chest shirt pocket. "Write down this telephone number. Ranger Scott told me that with a dial tone tomorrow I'll be connected to the world."

"Thanks. The kids will love the truck."

Chapter Thirteen

The driver cursed when a right foot brake stomp fishtailed the sedan and whizzed gravel pebbles into the early a.m. country darkness. Whirled dust blanketed the hood and limited rear-view visibility to the trunk's lid.

The driver, hankering to locate the missed right turn, rocked the gear shift into reverse and hit the accelerator. The front tires spun in the loose gravel until the driver's right foot eased its pressure. After a twenty-foot challenge into an obscured fate, the driver clocked the steering wheel ninety degrees and shifted into drive. The car lurched into a copse.

The edgy driver remembered the typed instructions left in the Paradise Library's copy of *A Body To Bones:*

One half mile north out of town, turn left for two and one-half miles. After the train crossing, about 200 yards, turn right into the copse, an oasis amid cornfields. Unlock all car doors, sit looking straight ahead, and do not turn around when the rear door behind the driver seat is opened.

The driver squeezed the steering wheel. *How long?* A solitary stare through oak and linden tree branches at twinkling stars accented by a first quarter moon failed to tranquilize the ire of being treated as an untrustworthy simpleton.

The driver swallowed a snarl when a door lock clicked.

"Good evening, Roger," said a throaty-voiced male. "Glad you made it."

While Roger expected the alcohol and nicotine stench, he bristled at everything else. "Why all this rigmarole."

"Security. You're stupid if you think I've worn this disguise for the couple of months I've been back because I like it. We're both taking a risk. Big Joey would have me diving into the river with concrete trunks if he doped out I was buddy-buddy with a police sergeant. Why couldn't you keep Jake in jail?"

Roger blew an exhale at the windshield to divert from his lungs the fetid cigarette smoke that streamed past his shoulders.

"I gave you the perfect setup. Had Kathie meet me at the Mayflower. He had no alibi. It was his truck trailer."

"I've tried."

"Obviously not hard enough. So far it's no skin off my nose. Leonardo, not me, paid off the motel clerk for the three-hour hot sheets rate. By my not opening my room door right away, she could be seen loitering when the clerk took his usual smoke break. Have the feds narrowed or disclosed the loot location?"

"Give me a break. They're clueless."

"That's what Kathie swore. She kept muttering she didn't know, she didn't know, she didn't know. She wouldn't stop crying, and I hate crying women." A smoke ring floated past Roger's face. "That's all my mother did after the bank swindled my father and the bankruptcy devoured the last family dime."

When an owl hooted, Roger didn't dare ask or swivel his eyes to see if a live bird existed.

"No matter. I earned points with Big Joey by solving his Kathie problem with a bottle to her head."

Roger flinched when a cigarette-lighter flash, reflected off his rear-view mirror, hit his eyes. Unwilling to choke on secondhand smoke, he cracked his driver's window. "Chief's not convinced Jake's guilty."

"No way I cozen up to Big Joey and then let him get his mitts on any gold, bearer bonds or cash. It's mine. I've taken all the risk. Damn scavengers camped out near the park tool shed stopped me from stealing a bolt cutter to search the lodge."

"State trooper claims but one gold coin and a C-note discovered with Case's skeleton. Nothing else there."

"Big Joey's dispatched a guy to Stillwater to befriend Slim Jim. However, it'll be a cold day in Hell before Slim Jim trusts anybody. He'll die in prison first. He and Case were to hide the money until the heat cooled. Now Jake's back to pocket it all. And you let him wiggle off the hook."

A blow rocked the driver's seat and jostled Roger.

"You sure this Jake Brown helped knock over the bank?"

"Hell, yes. He may have changed his last name's spelling, but his chin's still creased. Two years hasn't changed his double-crossing face. At first glance, Case fooled others when he shaved his heist beard. Jake bought an easily trashed ski mask and hunter's outfit. I figured he wouldn't stay secluded in a backwoods Mississippi cabin forever."

Roger heard a cough, glad it wasn't his.

"Did you put the Gideon I gave you in his hotel room and

paint those eyes behind the bathroom mirror with Kathie's red lipstick tube?" A muffled chuckle died in the backseat.

"Nobody's linked Kathie to Brown's motel room or the lipstick." *Should've tossed the tube under the bed.* "Switched the Bible without understanding why?"

"We all watched Slim Jim in a Hutchinson motel doodle in a Gideon when we planned to hide the loot for six months in the lodge's basement. I wanted Jake to believe he'd stumbled across Slim Jim's Jeremiah code and then notice the repent admonition written in Psalm 23, Jake's favorite. If he doesn't figure his life depends on divulging the money's location, then I hope he thinks a crazed sicko is gunning to kill him."

"Why dead?" Roger squeezed the steering wheel until his fingers cramped. "Why all the anger?"

"Visited Slim Jim before his trial. He told me Jake snatched our haul and ratted on him."

"So why tell me all this?" He flexed his fingers.

"Quit being wimpy. I have an old Cottonwood Lodge key duplicate Case pilfered. Saturday night, Victoria drove me to the park and Case's key opened Jake's back door. I drew another pair of eyes to tell Jake he couldn't hide." Roger stifled a cough. "He didn't even recognize me the other day when I wore a theatrical beard and asked him for a light on Paradise's main drag."

"Don't get all high and mighty. Buying a new tarp would've left a trail. Even after you gave me a lodge key that didn't fit, I got you the untraceable tarp no one will ever miss."

A muffled chuckle behind Roger preceded smoke that swirled past his right ear. "You must have concocted a damn good story to convince the deputy ranger to use his lodge key."

"So what's in it for me?"

"Another envelope with cash. It's on the backseat. I also hear that Jake's acting cocky with that woman you have the hots for. What's her name? Patrice?"

"Patricia, Patricia Swanson."

"Right, the librarian. Stick with me and your romantic competition will be history." Roger couldn't decipher the words muffled by repeated coughs. "If you'd like to play house with another woman, I can assist by removing this Patricia like I did Kathie. Just give me the word. No charge."

"Wait a minute. I'm . . ." Roger labored to breathe— lengthen his short gasps. "I'm not asking you to kill anyone. Help you a little. Be a source of police information. That I'll do. Order a hit? No way. That's going too far."

"Don't go soft. Contact me the normal way if you learn the feds are sniffing around Big Joey. He's planning a Paradise high roller party next month on the twenty-fifth. You should be on duty. We'd like a calm and peaceful free enterprise night to glorify the American way."

"Okay, the twenty-fifth. I'll make sure I'm on night patrol."

"You want Victoria to meet you in the city park like last fall? I can make it happen."

"I'll pass. Who would've thought morning joggers start that early and run with flashlights? Barely escaped being caught butt naked in my car's backseat." Roger choked. *Damn smoke.*

"I've been here too long. You continue looking forward for five minutes after my door closes. Then hightail it outta here."

Chapter Fourteen

Amid Sadie's crowded diner tables, Kate stared at and then called out to Patricia: "Wasn't the skeleton your dance partner?"

Patricia shuddered. She despised all connection to Paradise gossip. She nodded at Kate and prayed this deafening Tuesday chatter beckoned Kate elsewhere.

It didn't. Kate's right hip bumped Patricia's left shoulder.

"Shouldn't have shouted. You danced with Robert, right?"

"Way back. Then he moved on to Sarah. She was Robert's partner when he disappeared."

Kate twirled to her next diner table customer.

Patricia debated if she should she leave? She didn't see herself as one to engage in cafe gossip. Sunday at Mass, Patricia had said a prayer for Robert's soul. The morbid skeleton tales and the gallows humor that floated around her irritated her sensibilities on the value of human life.

She dipped a toast point into an over-easy egg and let it soak. For the third time, she scanned the diner for Jake and didn't see him. A blue, park pickup outside Sadie's had encouraged her to enter. Once inside, she recognized Deputy Ranger Coleman with a carry-out bag and couldn't slink out after Kate's wave to an empty chair.

Patricia fussed with her silverware. If others recited stories of how decent a man Robert was, she couldn't tell hers. Her lips reacted as if she had "locked-in-syndrome" where a fully awake person thinks within a paralyzed body.

Three years ago, after a high school fund-raising picnic on the football field, Roger amused Robert with his teasing her about being a spinster. When Roger tried and failed to kiss her, Robert laughed. He taunted Roger to pucker up a second time.

When the extinguished lights left the field dark and abandoned by Paradise residents, they caught her off-guard. Robert swept his arms under her arms while Roger locked his right arm around her knees and lifted her legs. She struggled the entire carry into the stadium's storage room. Her pleas to be set free unheeded.

Roger assumed control. He stripped off her black slacks and panties before he unbuttoned her white blouse to remove her bra. It wasn't until Roger reached his right hand between her unclad thighs that Robert, his hands clasped beneath her exposed breasts, voiced objection. While Patricia trembled in his arms, Robert's conscience and his threat to punch Roger limited Roger's major thrill to a leering ogle.

Thirty-six months and a desire to erase all attack memories

had dulled Patricia's remembrance. One remained vivid. Robert's yelling at Roger: "She's not a sunflower girl." Robert never explained what his sunflower girl reference meant. That night she pledged to never attend another picnic.

Patricia's right hand jiggled her half-full glass of orange juice. Roger had threatened her that if she ever squealed he'd make her a varsity football team comfort girl, or worse. To ensure she obeyed, Roger attended an occasional B&B Saturday dance where he'd softly sing the first chorus of the high school's fight song into her ear. Last year when she dared to refuse his dance request, he caught her outside her detached garage. He shook her until she feared he'd sexually assault her. He didn't back off until she promised she'd never embarrass him again.

Kate's voice shattered Patricia's tortured-memory trance. Kate with Chief Coltraine at the register delayed Patricia's exit.

"Chief, that's a gorgeous calabash pipe," praised Kate. "You're not staying for breakfast?"

Patricia guessed not as he grabbed a white pastry bag. When she spied reporter Josh Miles twist sideways through the front door, she bowed her head and strained to listen.

"What happened?" The Chief asked Miles. "I didn't see your name under any on-the-scene crime photos."

"Told you law honchos sealed the basement."

"Not me. Well, enjoy your breakfast in this zoo."

Patricia pushed her chair into an aisle to follow The Chief outside. Her rotated head stared at a notebook before her elevated gaze bumped Miles's chin to pause at his eyes.

He lowered his gaze to her. "I heard that you were a dance partner of Robert Case. Is that true?"

"For a time." Two cups and the silverware of Patricia's tablemates rattled against saucers and plates. "He and I weren't partners when he disappeared. I'd rather not talk about him, become involved or be quoted in the paper. It's ancient history. Forgotten as far as I'm concerned."

She hoped her expression didn't belie that Robert had dominated her thoughts since word of his death. Why had she told Jake about her foxtrots with Robert? Why? She knew why. Dancing with Jake invigorated her. Similar to how Robert first enthralled her, but he had become compulsive and demanding. The ugly incident with Roger reined as the final straw.

Jake spoke of substituting the past with a new future. He revealed, didn't bottle up, the tragedy of his wife's illness and his two-year reaction to her death. She doubted she could release her mental gag. She divined no answer whether her secrets handicapped a future with Jake.

"What motivated you to dance with Robert?" Miles asked.

"Without understanding that the required practice entailed hard work, I thought it would be fun. The thrill evaporated after two years. That was twelve to fourteen months before someone told me he'd left town. That's the sum total."

"Who partnered with him after you?"

"Sarah, Sarah Kleinschmidt." Patricia yearned to leave.

"Thanks. Sorry if I bothered you."

Patricia watched Miles zigzag across the room. Her tablemates resumed eating their breakfasts.

Kate's twirl obstructed a risen Patricia's step away from her table. "What did Josh want?"

Patricia reached for her purse. "Asked about Robert. Not much to tell."

"Yeah, Robert never talked about anything except foxtrot dancing. I only danced with him twice at the B&B. He nagged me I had to point my foot right . . . or was it left? Heck, who cares. I went there to enjoy myself. As long as I wasn't stepping on anyone, my foot could go any which way." Kate retied her apron. "That's why I like Jake. He's a good dancer, and he hasn't ever said one word of criticism. You must like him. I see you dancing with him more than he dances with others."

"Well, ah . . . yes, he's a good dancer . . . Jacob, too,"

"Isn't he also in Emily's play with you?"

Patricia shuffled her feet. "Yes, . . . Along with others."

"You going to the B&B dance tonight?"

"Hadn't given it a thought. It's not my type of music."

"As work starts before dawn on Wednesdays, I've never

danced Tuesday nights. However, was toying with the idea to experience it once and not stay the entire night. Emily told me I need to get out of my rut."

Kate grinned. "Sorry, time for customers. That skeleton story is making people stay longer. Cost of my bottomless coffee cup with its unlimited free refills will deplete the extra breakfast revenue. You can be glad you don't have to add extra pages to a book if more people read it."

Patricia's doldrums exploded into an old-fashioned belly laugh. "Kate, you create the funniest comparisons. I hope that no matter what happens we'll forever be friends."

"So do I." Kate initiated her departure with a twirl.

Without a twirl, Patricia set out for the library.

Jake's feet broke into a kitchen quick-quick rock step when the dial tone buzz filled his left ear. Gloom descended as he stared at the lipstick eyes and twisted his rear doorknob to leave.

His early morning frustration mushroomed with each mower lap when the park's bedewed grass clogged his riding mower's chute. Wet clumps of mowed grass dotted every campsites. With the sun nothing more than a brighter cloud, he offered Oscar a noontime lift to Paradise's hardware store. He bypassed Sadie's and the Sunrise in favor of a thirty minute library visit.

"Jake, what are you doing here?"

He straightened his legs from a head-to-the-shelf-one-knee-on-the-floor aisle position. "You look real nice."

Patricia blushed. She wore her black suit-type outfit from Saturday's dance with a change to a ruffled white silk blouse. "Thank you." Their gazes held. "What brings you here?"

"Came to sign up for my library card now that I have an address the library accepts. Also, need to find a flower book. You had a great idea for the lodge and the idea impressed Ranger Scott. I should've given you credit. However, I'm glad I didn't for my wild rutabaga would've embarrassed you."

"No problem. Many mistake wild Swede turnips."

Jake released a shaky breath. "I guess." Her eyes hinted at depths unfamiliar to him. If they were on a dance floor, he'd sway holding her. But they weren't, and the moment evaporated. "Where can I find an illustrated flower book I can check out."

"That's easy." When Patricia angled right at the end of the aisle, she exaggerated her head turn into a glance over her right shoulder. "I ran into that *Herald-Gazette* skeleton reporter this morning at Sadie's. He questioned me about Robert."

"Did you explain what you told me Sunday?"

She responded with downcast eyes. "Sort of, no detail."

Best not to, thought Jake. His trust in the reporter not repaid.

"Please follow me." She entered a new aisle. "The garden club sponsors magazines and donates flower books."

"Did Robert have any kids, brothers or sisters?"

"Not that I know of. His mother lived in Paradise and passed away three years ago. I've been living in her house."

Gravity jerked at Jake's jaw. "You live in Robert's mother's house!" A woman library patron glared at him while he pressed his right hand to his mouth.

Patricia waved her right hand at the lady Jake believed he'd upset. The woman arched her shoulders and left. "That's also where Robert lived when I knew him."

"What a coincidence," Jake whispered, the act of a student who had learned his lesson. "Any other family?"

"When his mother died, the newspaper obituary listed Robert as her sole survivor. It said her husband, a veteran and Robert's father, predeceased her."

Jake fumbled for a question to break the budding silence. "Did you do all your practice foxtrots at the B&B?"

"And at Robert's mother's house."

Jake sensed he and Patricia sought a distance greater than physical. His floated into the future. While he feared Patricia stood before him locked into the past, one way out for her was for him to encourage her to speak and he to be a good listener. "One learns to be agile when practicing next to furniture in confined and irregular spaces."

"Robert had fixed up the basement while his mother lived there. He laid a wall-to-wall hardwood maple floor, covered the ceiling in large, suspended tile squares to hide whatever you call them, the thick wood planks for the floor above, and painted the block walls a pale green. While I didn't favor the green, I visited often enough to fall in love with the house, its porch and the neighborhood."

"Having a private dance floor is terrific." Jake rubbed his right hand fingers to soothe his nape's ache.

"It would be if I needed a place to practice. Wait here." After two steps into an aisle, Patricia pulled a shelved book and handed it to Jake. "Do you remember I told you I saw you at Pastor John's church Sunday?"

"Is this a puzzle? Twenty questions?"

Patricia's lips parted into a grin. "No."

"Let's see. The Presbyterian Church is near the corner of Hancock Boulevard and Chestnut Street. More likely the latter."

"You're learning. Leaf through this flower book and ask at the circulation desk for a new patron form." Patricia buttoned her jacket. "I'll enjoy seeing you and rest of your posse at the B&B later."

"And me, yours." Jake stifled his curiosity about where Patricia lived. His hands cradled the desired flower book with his nostrils sweetened by her citrus perfume.

When Oscar strode toward him carrying a brown bag, he hustled to get them both home beneath the cottonwoods.

Reporter Josh Miles squinted to read a Chestnut Street house number distracted by four elementary-aged kids on next door Dutch colonial's front yard. They chased each other in fits and starts with frequent whoops and stumbles. When a sandbox clump flung by the biggest boy landed at his feet, he leaped a tricycle and quick-stepped to the adjacent two-story bungalow.

Red and white tulip petals littered the bungalow's walk. His left hand forefinger traced the lacquered porch swing finish as he reached to twist an old-fashioned key which mechanically activated the raspy doorbell. With no answer, he waited and duplicated its summons. He didn't doubt this had been the house where Robert's mother had lived. He trusted her obituary's address and hoped the new owners might augment his Case family information. His tax record research listed the house as owned by a trust—the ABCs Trust. Stymied by the legal fiction, he struck out when he tried to tie the initial C into being a reference to the Case family, its former owner.

He doubled the speed of his third bell-key twist to release his mid-afternoon disappointment. He scribbled a request for a return telephone call on the reverse side of his business card and stuck it in the door's mail slot.

As he strode to his car, two boys with cap guns ran by him, pointing their pistols at his chest. When he shouted "bang," they scampered into the Dutch colonial.

Jake, at the pavilion, refused a second piece of Oscar's eighty-first birthday party cake. A beaming Oscar unwrapped a new orange vest and kissed his wife on the cheek.

Jake waved good-bye to the six campers before he bounced to the lodge atop his riding mower. While he mowed around the lodge, Jake amused himself with a crazy idea about a second floor missing-bank-money hiding place.

With the mower key in his pocket, he bounded up the lodge vestibule stairs to test his theory. He unlocked a second floor glass case that displayed stuffed birds to lift a stuffed cooper hawk he'd seen live. Its weight told him the probability was it contained no gold coins. Without a taxidermist's knowledge, his untrained eye failed to detect where a scalpel cut might have slit the hawk's skin to insert currency. Undeterred, his right forefinger smoothed a stuffed owl until his enthusiasm fizzled. When his eyes registered the chickadee he held was smaller than his hand, the case glass reflected his emerging smile.

He locked the case and the lodge to trim perimeter weeds. Oscar's party continued as Jake stored the mower and Deputy Ranger Coleman caught up with him to say he'd dropped four uniform sets on his residence's front steps.

Jake tossed the uniforms on his bed and headed out for play rehearsal. On his drive to the B&B, Jake congratulated himself for not having been foolhardy enough to tell anyone about his bank loot idea.

"**H**ey, Jake," Jacob called out from the Spring Daisy Theatre stage apron. "You want to join my vocal group with our newest hit single, 'These Bones Are Made for Dancing'?"

Jake withhold his answer until he reached Jacob. "Joking has its place, but please don't disrespect a mourning family."

"At the plant today, we couldn't recall any family still living. He was an only child and nobody remembered Robert talking about having kids. His mother always helped with the Memorial Day celebration. We should ask Kate?"

Jake pivoted to see Kate carrying a garment bag.

Jacob asked, "Kate, what are you doing here?"

"I'm taking a shortcut to Emily's apartment with a change of clothes for the dance tonight. I overhead mention of Robert."

"Co-worker recalled his father as a veteran, although not a Legion member. You know his father?"

Jake stood silent.

"Not personally. A Desert Storm veteran this morning pointed out a memorial room picture of four sailors. The reverse side identified a CPO James Case. He said James's wife lived on Chestnut Street and they had one son named Robert, born during the 70s. That seemed to match Robert Case." Kate glanced left. "Hi, Patricia."

"Hey, Kate. You auditioning to be our audience?" Jake steadied his eyes so as not to resemble a badminton shuttlecock.

"Funny." Kate's reply curt. "Ask Jacob about Robert's father. I gotta go."

Jacob waited for the cast and its director to assemble to repeat Kate's information.

Pastor John invited everyone to a Presbyterian Church memorial service for Robert at eleven a.m. Saturday.

"Reverend, that's a nice thing you're doing," Patricia said.

"Amen," Jake added.

Emily requested all to bring in their play costume Thursday. Jacob winked at Jake and he shook his head before he ignored Patricia's lifted eyelids. Emily's coy smile extinguished as she announced the saloon gambling scene.

When Jake picked himself off the floor, he did so with an air of achievement. His expert fall to his side spared his knee a bump. He said good-bye to Bob and Pastor John and gravitated to Patricia conversing with Jacob at a side table.

"Hope I'm not intruding," he said. "If not, I'm buying."

He passed Jacob a beer and handed Patricia her requested diet cola. "The book you handed me at the library earlier today helped me identify a real flower."

Jacob's eyebrows arched at Jake's praise of Patricia, yet. Jacob didn't stretch the interest Jake assumed existed in Jacob's mind into a question.

"You all staying to dance?" Emily asked from Patricia's side. "Bet Jacob is. If you are, I'll collect your admission now."

Jacob grinned. "Going to stamp a J again?"

Emily gazed at Jake, "No repeat. Tonight's letter is a Z, which should be no one's name."

"Wrong," piped up Jacob. "You've chosen my middle name, Zechariah. You're the best, Emily. I oughta kiss you."

Emily retreated and her Z stamp bounced on the floor. Jacob's front chair legs hit the floor as he scrambled to retrieve the stamp. Jake couldn't help but feel amused.

"And here I thought it was for Zipadeedodah, the Oscar movie song. I've hummed that tune many a cross-country driving night to fight off the sandman."

Unseen cowboy-boot-heel thuds confused Jake. Jacob was the sole cast members still present who wore them on occasion. If Clem had left the bar, he didn't circle the stage.

"Is this band any good?" Kate asked.

Jake couldn't believe his eyes. *Annie Oakley in the flesh.* Kate's twirl flung the leather fringe that adorned her blouse and knee-length skirt to forty-five degrees.

"You're about an hour late," Jacob said through his grin. "Play rehearsal ended fifteen minutes ago. The saloon's closed. Cowboys have ridden beyond the sunset."

Patricia leaped to Kate's side. "Don't listen to him. He's jealous he doesn't have an outfit as gorgeous and charming."

"That's right, Jacob's jealous," Jake added. "You look great, Kate. I'm treating so if either you or Emily would like a drink please tell me, and I'll go get it."

"Diet cola, straight up, no ice, please, and thank you."

At the bar, Clem, with a twinkle in his eyes, gazed at Jake. "Appears you have a full house tonight. Emily won't want to see you leave town."

Jake tried to will a chill into the blood that warmed his cheeks. "Flattery will get you everything."

Jake returned to the table to find his spell broken. Emily guarded her cashbox at the Main Street entrance and Patricia sat with her friend Sarah. Jake delivered the diet cola to Kate chatting with lady friends on the ballroom's opposite side. He retreated to Jacob at his regular table.

"Boy," Jacob said. "Kate's never danced on a Tuesday. Patricia rarely. Did you mention you were coming?"

"Don't think so. Last week I did laundry. Were they here?"

"Both peeked in at different times. Neither stayed."

Jake counted the crowd to be half the prior Saturday and rated the band so-so. He divided early swing and foxtrot dances between Kate and Patricia and, after an hour, bought two capped beers from Clem and left to go home.

Jake, his ears on alert beneath the cottonwoods, paused ten steps from his rear door.

Chapter Fifteen

Jake let a bedroom shade flutter to expose windowpane rain streaks fed by dripping cottonwood leaves. For the first time, he tucked his official khaki uniform shirt with its state park patch into creased khaki pants. When he stood next to his kitchen counter savoring his morning coffee, his telephone rang.

"Mr. Brown, Trooper Kessen. I failed to catch Ranger Scott before he left home. Are the eyes still there?"

"Yes, sir." Jake rapped the phone cord around his fingers.

"The state crime guys will check them about ten a.m."

"Will be here, sir." Jake untangled the cord, pressed the phone's connection buttons and kept the receiver in his hand. The trooper's crime guys reference gave Jake an idea. He retrieved an old phone book from a kitchen drawer and telephoned the Paradise Police.

"Chief Coltraine, this is Jake Brown. The judge told me I could get my truck back. Oh, I see. That would be fine. Tomorrow noon? Will pick up the keys at the police station's front lobby. Thank you, Chief."

Ecstatic he would have his truck, Jake punched in his dispatcher's 800-number. No, he told himself, hitting the road would abandon Kate, Emily and her play plus Patricia. His brain's flip side argued he should skip town before he's jailed again. His conscience's retort asked him to cast an eye at his new uniform and remember his promise to Ranger Scott. You keep your promises, his conscience reminded him. His brain's flip side countered with three words: *red lipstick eyes.*

When his dispatcher answered, Jake gave him his new telephone number and reaffirmed his status: off-road until further notice.

Not everyone could squeeze into Jake's rear entry for a close inspection of the red lipstick eyes. Upfront were Len and Bob, the state crime guys, and behind them were Trooper Kessen, Ranger Scott, Jake and Chief R.P. Coltraine.

Len twisted toward Jake. "Tell me again when these eyes first appeared."

"Saturday," Jake said. "Left at five p.m. and they were there when I returned at ten-thirty. Saw pair at the Mayflower."

Jon inadvertently bumped Jake's leg.

"We did test. Mayflower lipstick type matched the type the coroner found on trailer victim Ms. Krump."

Chief Coltraine's eyebrows rose. "It was? I wasn't told."

"Sorry, Chief. I received the results yesterday afternoon and didn't read until riding with Bob this morning." Len gazed at Bob. "We need a comparison sample." He then turned to Trooper Kessen. "First impression, two different artists."

"Don't follow," Kessen replied.

"See these pupil swirls. They circle counterclockwise. The motel dots went to the right, or clockwise. That's unusual. A person drawing the same dot would be consistent." Len's right forefinger circled a dot, not smudging the lipstick. "That the eyes have surfaced twice indicates a warning symbol and being watched. The red color intensifies the danger."

Jon edged forward to lead the law enforcement officials to the lodge. Jake stayed behind. "Chief, do I still get my truck?"

"I gave my word. However, do me a favor. Park it where it will be safe, lock the trailer and stay in town."

"Thanks. Will talk to Ranger Scott."

"Have the eyes followed you from another town?"

Jake rubbed his forehead. "No. First time here."

"What about Sgt. Smyth? You two ever step on each other's toes?" The Chief smiled. "And I don't mean dancing."

"First time our paths crossed was the day he arrested me."

The Chief scratched his chin. "Any problem with anyone related to the sergeant?"

"No, no. Haven't met his family." Jake gazed at his shoes. "Have the lab guys examined the tarp found in my truck? The lodge basement is missing a tarp. Could be important."

"Well . . . thanks. I don't have an answer. I'd better catch up. They'll think I went off someplace to light my pipe."

Chief Coltraine walked up to Scott and Kessen chatting next to the lodge's flung back basement doors.

"Crime guys told us to wait outside," Jon said. "As there's time, I can complete a lodge check for an upcoming function. I'll be back in a minute." He entered the lodge's kitchen door.

"What's the lipstick's significance?" The Chief asked.

A metal container clang emanating from the basement forestalled Kessen's answer. The Chief assumed a paint can and said, "Everyone must be okay, I hear no profanity."

Kessen smiled and his right hand removed his hat. "As to the lipstick, can't figure. If someone is to be framed, I would expect a victim's personal item to be left in the suspect's possession. Your report said nothing of Ms. Krump's was uncovered in Brown's motel room. Or, flipping the coin, the person being framed has his item left with the victim. I'm told that didn't happen either."

"We still have a major hurdle in that there's no Krump murder weapon. Analysis confirmed that the glass fragments embedded in her head wound compare favorably to a Hofensteger Beer bottle. However, my motel property search for glass pieces with bloodstains or discarded bottles resulted in a dead end. The bottle in Brown's room tested clean and the room lacked Krump's blood type."

"As an observation, even with prints or blood on it, a killer wouldn't have toted a broken beer bottle very far."

"Right, and Len's room vacuuming after Brown checked out disclosed no glass shards. Didn't surprise me since the maid had vacuumed. The scraps of trace evidence in the trailer itself added up to unidentifiable trash. The tarp may tell us more."

The Chief continued to sketch out for Kessen his latest tattoo information and his updated flourmill witness details relevant to the 2007 Paradise Bank robbery. He nodded to acknowledge Jon's return. When Kessen paced, The Chief noted Jon's in-sync eyeballs.

"I keep coming back to the same thought," The Chief said. "In this day and age it's still the motivation."

"What's that?" Jon asked.

"Sex, money and/or revenge," Kessen replied.

"Add drugs," The Chief interjected.

Kessen sighed. "Sorry to say you're right. I'm finding even run-of-the-mill drunk-driving accidents have pipes, syringes and pills scattered within demolished vehicles."

Jon's boot toe scattered a stone with his kick.

"What's your take on Mr. Brown?" Kessen asked.

The Chief replied, "While I don't think he killed Ms. Krump, everything doesn't add."

"On first blush, I'd agree," Kessen said. "But he could've had help. A drug dealer, or an unaccounted for bank robbery gang member." He donned his hat and adjusted a shirt cuff.

The Chief's words uttered slow. "I've concluded the Kathie Krump's killer isn't Mr. Brown. Doesn't make sense he carried a dead body across town. However, as I said earlier, puzzle pieces don't fit. Can't put my finger on it. It's like we're dealing with two different spirits. I lack a long history in Paradise, but the Jake Brown we met this morning has made a favorable quick impression on many townspeople. I've always been advised it takes quite a while for a small town newcomer to be accepted, unless there are family connections."

Jon's body stiffened.

"Sorry, if that offends, Jon. The truth remains that what's been related to me indicates that Brown's connection to this area is Paradise flourmill hauls. And no trip corresponds to the robbery or any gang activity."

"You're right, Chief," Jon said. "I'm out on a limb to have hired him as the caretaker. But people vouched for him. So far he's been a good employee. Spoke to Oscar, an old-timer who's been coming here forever, and he said Jake impressed him."

"When I went to the B&B the other Saturday night, he wasn't a typical newcomer, ignored or allowed to sit off to the side. He had a line of women waiting to dance with him."

"We have to be careful," Kessen said. "Robert Case was a good dancer, and he joined the Paradise robbers. Or, a person under the influence of drugs can act like a different person."

"Good point. However, Jake tested clean on his arrest and I tried to say that the people at the B&B treated him as a friend who dances rather than merely a good dancer. All in all, it probably won't help us to focus on the ability to dance, or its lack." Kessen nodded. "I'll retreat to what I said a couple of minutes ago, which was my instinct that there's a critical fact not evident on the surface. To repeat, it's like there could be two different Jake Browns."

"I'll trust your instincts," Kessen stated. "I wonder when these crime guys will be done. It seems like it's taken forever."

Jon switched his gaze between The Chief and Kessen. "If I'm not needed, I'll be at headquarters."

"Leave me the keys," Kessen replied.

Jon did and strode away.

The Chief pulled a pipe from his shirt pocket. "I'll wait to see the basement. Mind if I smoke?"

"No. Mighty fancy pipe you have there."

After ten minutes, Len emerged. He picked a basement cobweb off his left sleeve. "We checked everywhere. Expect no usable fingerprints. No gold or C-notes."

The Chief extinguished his pipe and moved closer. "Were there any tarps in the basement?"

"Yes, two," Len said. "Saw no blood stains."

"Mr. Brown told me that the lodge missed one tarp."

"Can we trust him?" Kessen asked. "Where would his information come from?"

Len cut in, "Hey, guys, don't fight." He then smiled. "Since both tarps are of the same type as the truck tarp, I'll take both to the lab. There should be cross-contamination if the three had been near each other, that is, if the wall destruction concrete dust doesn't ruin everything."

"Good idea," Kessen said. "Now can you bring me up-to-date on any findings since we last talked?"

The Chief hurried to dump spent pipe tobacco behind an evergreen, fifteen feet from the lodge's basement doors.

"Spoke to the forensic pathologist," Len began. "It'll be in the final report, but what we've found collectively would indicate the following: Three bullets total. Since one projectile nicked a rib, its trajectory says it ripped through the heart. That shot powerful enough to have killed him. Since we lack organs and flesh, it's hard to confirm. We don't have any upper torso clothing, shell casings or presumably the fatal slug. Lack of blood tells us the body was carried into the cavity. Blood Type matched Mr. Case."

Len cleared his throat.

"Two bullets were fired in the basement. Striations were sufficient on bullet most intact to indicate Smith and Weston handgun. Slug weight matched a .38 caliber. Negative search through the ATF database. One into the skull, mentioned before, can't be ruled out as cause of death. The second may have missed or entered and exited a fleshy part of the body, such as a thigh, without striking any bone. This last bullet, probably a ricochet, broke into at least two fragments and caused separate floor and wall marks. The shooter should consider him or herself lucky he or she wasn't wounded."

"Any clue tell us Case's last activity?" Kessen asked.

"The lab checked the skeleton's pants. Usual dirt and grime indigenous to this area. Out-of-place traces consisted of minute quantities of cellulose and asbestos fibers. Not a large deposit, but basically on the leg fronts at or above the knee. You should understand that the U.S. in the 1970s banned this asbestos."

"Wouldn't it be on construction workers?" The Chief asked.

"Not new construction, but old buildings not renovated can contain floor tile and linoleum that most often contains asbestos. On occasion, up to forty percent chrysotile asbestos. It's frequently called serpentine asbestos. Old joint and wall compounds can have measurable concentrations that are only released when drilling a hole or sanding a rough wall. Pipe or other types of insulation have it. But as older commercial buildings undergo mitigation its presence has diminished."

"What about the cellulose?" Kessen asked.

"Can be found in multiple products, for example, wallboard and ceiling tiles. Ceiling tiles may be the best example of cellulose usage."

The Chief condensed what Len said and closed his notepad.

"I can't repeat those specific asbestos types," Kessen said, "but how would a person get that on their clothing?"

"The asbestos or cellulose would be airborne, especially the asbestos fibers. Tile motion, for example, releases fibers from suspended ceiling tile when the tiles are removed to allow access to hidden piping and wires." Bob dropped his tool kit behind Len. "Cleaning the powder from tiles or other sources can transfer the asbestos fibers to a sponge. From the sponge, the fibers can migrate to one's clothing, either on purpose or by accident. Or, hands collect residue and fibers are deposited when hands get wiped on pants."

"Any clue pinpoint who blocked in the door?" Kessen inquired.

"No," Len replied. "Old stain indicated the mortar was mixed on the floor. Demolition corrupted our ability today to find more telltale evidence."

"Thanks," Kessen said. "We'd like to look. I can lock up."

Len and Bob hauled their equipment and two sealed paper evidence bags to their van. The Chief stood with Kessen in the basement when the lab guys returned for the tarps. He shied away from the cavity except for a brief gaze to be impressed by the steel closet door before Kessen tiptoed to it.

When Kessen exited the cavity, The Chief accepted Kessen's invitation to ascend the basement steps first. They left Cottonwood State Park in separate vehicles.

FBI Agent Harris Redburn, invited with Chief Coltraine to the state park, declined without offering a reason. As he drove his unmarked car, he tried to recall the directions he had followed in his first trip to the meeting place. He remained doubtful of his country road choices until he bumped across the railroad tracks and spied the copse ahead on his right.

At three-forty p.m., a punctual Agent Redburn sat within the small trees, his driver window cracked and his car doors locked. When he heard the crunch of twigs, he confirmed his visitor in the rear-view mirror and unlocked his driver's door.

He slid off his vehicle's leather to await Joe Amos.

"Sorry I'm late," Amos said, veering along the vehicle's passenger side. Redburn ambled to the front of his car. "Saw a farmer disking and doubled back." Amos joined Redburn.

"Well, what's new with Big Joey?" Redburn asked.

"He's looking for a new shipment of LSD for pick up in Des

Moines, location unknown. Sizeable quantity. DeCamp's playing it close to the vest. Don't know when except soon."

"What about DiCecca?"

Amos's forehead tightened into vertical creases. "Slim Jim's happy to wait. Wouldn't agree to meet me two months ago until I bribed a guard to explain to him I represented DeCamp. Even then, DiCecca kept speaking in annoying biblical riddles. He showed me his Gideon Bible with words circled. I tried to tell him he'd be able to fence his share or invest it with Big Joey and make a killing. He would only smile. You just wanted to punch the guy."

"We'd better split before we're seen."

"You should know. One of Big Joey's men killed that Krump woman for shorting Big Joey on a Dakota LSD shipment. Guy's nicknamed A.C. I recently pressed him for a name—Austin Cohen."

Thrilled as a five-year-old opening his first gift from Santa, Redburn asked: "Austin Cohen, C-o-h-e-n, is that right?"

"Yeah. Real vicious. Has a mean streak a mile long. Real paranoia about banks hurting people. While I sensed an earlier history, he but joined DeCamp a couple of months ago."

"What's he look like?"

"Six feet, one hundred seventy pounds, chisel chin, dark hair, has this delicate sunflower tattoo on the back of his neck. Moves as if he took karate. Dominant left hand."

"How old? And, who killed Krump?"

Amos fidgeted with a cuff button. "Guess mid-thirties. Big Joey said A.C. killed the Krump woman on his command and then failed to dispose of the body at the state park. Eventually, A.C. dumped her in a truck trailer parked at the Mayflower. That's not our bailiwick, is it?"

"You keep tabs on this Cohen fellow. If he comes into your focus, I want to know everything he does and where he goes. Don't blow your cover to stalk or run him down. Play it cool."

"Yes, sir." Amos scuffled left.

Redburn waved his left hand for Amos to stop. "Cohen say anything about lipstick eyes?"

"Haven't heard anything about lipstick. Don't know if you'd be interested, but Cohen's been uptight about a fellow new in Paradise that he believes changed his name and was, it seems, his partner in a bank robbery. He refers to him as a low-down, good-for-nothing weasel who would sell out friends for gold."

"Did he mention the guy's name?" Redburn pressed his right palm to his car's hood.

"No, and I held back on asking. Didn't seem to involve drugs or drug money. Maybe Cohen confused a rival distributor? He'd been drinking, and he's an ornery drunk."

"You keep your eyes and ears open about that fellow Cohen's upset about. We're at loggerheads on the Paradise Bank robbery and any new lead could burst the dam."

"Heard one of the gang was dead at the state park. Maybe the jerk Cohen seeks?" Amos ran his right hand over his hair.

"Doubt it. Robert Case died two years ago. Keep in mind it's secondary to the discovery of Big Joey's supplier. We've invested too much time, effort and your skin to blow it now. Has that police sergeant been nosing around?"

Amos shook his head no.

"Good. Now be gone," Redburn ordered.

In the wet aftermath of a morning rain, Jake's spirits plummeted when the dreary task of cleaning the mower chute and shed tools caked with dirt lasted an hour. He dropped a kneepad to keep his park uniform dry and unstained as he transplanted two yellow daisy clumps eighteen inches apart on the lodge's sunny south side.

His pride swelled when Jon praised his work as he handed Jake his first paycheck. He remained animated when Oscar introduced him to two regular campers, now ensconced in second row spaces. Jake then hid his merriment to ease a toddler's fears that just because he wore a uniform he wouldn't throw the four-year-old into jail, even if his mother asked.

Repetition bored Emily's Spring Daisy cast members. Minor

rehearsal slipups generated snippy retorts.

In a mood reversal, Jake's heart swelled when Patricia asked him after Emily had ended rehearsal if he'd found plants to transplant. Until Patricia cut him off, he rhapsodized his daisy achievement as if he were a New World explorer fertilizing barren territory. He chased after her to scribble his park residence number on a bar napkin.

"Don't leave, Jake," Pastor John called out.

From the George Street exit, Jake strode the bar's entire length to meet Pastor John at the Main Street door.

"Church fellowship hall is available Tuesday or Thursday."

"Thursday's best," Jake replied. "Tuesday nights conflict with B&B dance and I don't want to give Emily an easy excuse not to participate."

Pastor John nodded. "Thursday night it is. Two young church couples are excited about the opportunity."

Patricia's energy ebbed from the moment she parked her car in her detached garage. She entered her Chestnut Street residence through the rear kitchen door and collapsed into a kitchen chair.

Her front door bell clanged.

I'm not home.

The bell's echo softened until a second clang refurbished it.

Okay, okay. Hope you're gone when I get there.

Patricia cracked her front door and stretched its safety chain taut. "May I help you?" She toggled her porch light on.

"I'm Josh Miles with the *Herald-Gazette*. Could I speak with you about the Case family? I left my card."

Her right hand fingered the safety chain without releasing it. "Why? I'm not related."

"You're the town librarian. My information is that Robert Case and his mother lived here. At Sadie's, you said you danced with him."

"That's true. And that was all." Even if she had to cast off her natural instincts and act rude, she wanted him to go away. "You should go."

Miles persisted. "Do you own this house?"

Patricia concentrated all the energy she possessed to mimic the brusque authority of her least-favored college professor. "This doesn't have anything to do with me. It's tragic what happened to Robert." Patricia readied her right hand to force the door closed. "It's over."

"Mind if I come in and take a picture or two?"

"Yes. I'm saying good night."

"One last question. Do you know a Jake Brown or Braun?"

"Yes, now good night." Patricia pressed her left shoulder to the door to noisily shut it before the reporter challenged her with another question. She locked the door, switched on a lamp and retreated to the kitchen to collapse into her warmed chair.

Patricia listened to her telephone try to connect. She bit at the skin beneath her left thumb's nail. After five rings she counted six, seven, eight, nine, ten. Jake answered.

"Reporter Josh Miles knocked on my door sixty minutes ago. He's been here before. This time he mentioned Robert and your name." Patricia's right hand twitched. "It's like he's stalking me."

"If it's any comfort, he knocked on my motel door." Patricia heard a familiar, repetitive line click. "Took his card, never called him and he hasn't bothered me since."

"That helps. He asked if I knew a Jake Brown or Braun. That confuses me. Don't know if he meant two men or if he corrected his pronunciation. Do you know any Jake Braun?"

"It's close to mine, but not any name that's familiar."

"He was also curious as to who owns my house. When Robert wanted to sell and get out quick in 2007, I promised to let him return for two boxes he left in the basement." Patricia tossed a pillow from her sofa to the floor. "When they got mold spots on the outside, I struggled, but threw them out."

"Say that again. Threw what out?"

"Robert's junk, whatever it was. Main thing was—being single—didn't want my name on the public record. My lawyer suggested a trust. Now people will gossip there's something underhanded."

237

"Wouldn't worry. Many properties are put into trusts. Told the main reason is that it avoids expensive probate."

"Thanks, Jake. I'm pleased you now have a telephone, and apologize for taking advantage so quickly."

"It dawns on me I've never followed up on my comment that first night in the library about having a conversation." Patricia's fingers and toes grew chilly. "Envision a quiet restaurant outside Paradise. Sometime . . . if you're willing."

"Yes." Caution kicked in after her impulsive response. "I'd suggest after the play performances. Tonight I'll be rushed to finish the sewing on my costume to keep Emily happy."

"Not saying anything about anyone's costume, especially not yours." She heard him laugh. "Good night."

Patricia sighed, comforted to know it was easier to reach Jake. She hadn't translated his library conversation comment into a requested date. If she had, her answer would've been a definite no. Tonight, without a second thought, she'd said yes, and then hedged.

Patricia couldn't crystallize her exact doubt. Jake, in bits and pieces, had begun to convince her he cared for others, and that met her definition of a responsible adult. She shrugged aside the future to retrieve the purchased white fabric from her spare upstairs bedroom. She set about cutting and sewing the seven white bodice polka dots required to replace the black.

For a second time, Jake witnessed a horizontal beam of light streak across his living room window. With the ten p.m. radio news an hour away, Jake, from a forty-five degree angle, stared at his front lawn. He expected no raccoon carried a flashlight, and the dark hour too early for the worm hunter. At irregular intervals, he left his post for the kitchen to refill his water glass.

No moon outlined the shadows nor brightened the sky.

Jake challenged his willpower to wait.

Chapter Sixteen

Chief Coltraine's private line rang. "Hi, Len. What's new since we bumped knees in the park residence yesterday?"

"Cashed in a favor and had a chemical expert lab buddy do a preliminary inspection of those two lodge tarps."

The Chief kept his mouth closed. Since the tarps came from the lodge, any information should rightly go to Trooper Kessen.

"No bloodstains amongst the paint splatters, but a trace quantity of zinc oxide powder appeared on a side uncontaminated by the concrete demolition dust. Similar zinc oxide traces surfaced on the trailer tarp. Because zinc oxide is a pigment in wide use, commonality may raise its ugly head. I won't digress, but your dentist knows plenty about zinc oxide."

"You said what about splatters?"

"A scanning electron microscopic examination identified similar physical and chemical paint splatter characteristics on all three tarps. A confirmation test is yet to be run."

"Good work. I've made a note." The Chief hung up and sat back. He needed to be prepared for Kessen's anger and plan his next investigative move before Jake and his truck drove off.

"Chief, Chief," blared Bell's excited intercom voice.

"Take it easy, Bell. What's going on?"

"Blue, state park pickup reported in the ditch, edge of city limits, on the road to Cottonwood State Park. Witness reported driver to be unconscious."

"I'm on it, Bell. Where's Lt. Sigourney?"

"He and the fire department ambulance are responding."

The Chief tossed and locked his folder into his middle desk drawer. His squad's harsh siren ordered vehicles to the curb.

When he arrived at the scene, emergency medics had strapped a person to a backboard and placed him or her atop a portable gurney for lifting into the awaiting ambulance.

A state park pickup lay on its right side in the ditch. The caved-in cab roof convinced The Chief it had rolled once, if not twice, before coming to rest. A rut, eight to ten inches deep, six inches wide, ran for four feet along the paved road's edge. Skid marks, which began in the shoulder gravel at the rut's end, extended to where the pickup compressed overgrown ditch weeds. The Chief surmised the pickup had been eastbound.

The uniformed Chief stepped forward. An exposed muscular left arm identified the victim as male. One medic stood aside him to pressure an inserted needle and adjust an I.V. fluid bag's flow. A second medic recorded vital signs. The Chief recognized Deputy Park Ranger Joel Coleman.

Onlookers crowded the road's shoulder. The Chief edged away from the medics to help Lt. Sigourney clear a departure lane for the ambulance. Task accomplished, he left the lieutenant in charge to shoot accident scene photos, arrange for a tow truck and to canvas the gawkers for any witness.

"Good morning, Chief." Ranger Scott answered his office telephone. "You forget your pipe near the lodge?" When met with silence, Jon regretted his jab.

"Deputy Coleman's been hurt in an accident."

Jon dropped his pen. "When? How bad?"

"Happened minutes ago. Appears his pickup, traveling east on the Main Street extension, hit a shoulder rut and careened into the ditch. The pickup rolled. Ambulance took him to Loretto Hospital. Can you contact his wife?"

"Sure. I'll do that right away." Jon grabbed a set of keys on his desk. "If you need me, I'll be at the hospital."

Jon punched in the number for Joel's wife. Busy. He abandoned further attempts, drove through the pavilion area, found Jake and told him he was in charge, and why.

The campers's persistent questions about Joel's health that Jake had no answer to intensified his worry. When he saw Jon's pickup at the pavilion at eleven-thirty, Jake rushed over. "How is he?"

"When I left, he was awake, talking. May have a broken

240

wrist. Doc Beck plans to x-ray once the swelling goes down."

"That's good news, I guess. He tell you what happened?"

"Joel said he was driving to the park. A large blue car from the opposite direction, he thinks a Lincoln, swerved toward him. He swung right to avoid a collision. Joel believes the gravel, or a culvert, caused him to roll. He didn't know. I didn't stop at the accident scene."

Jake noted Jon's somber expression. "Anything I can do?"

"Follow your duty list and I'll cover Joel's park entrance duties. Even if his wrist sports a cast, I estimate he'll be back within a week."

"As mentioned yesterday, I'm picking up my truck at noon. I'll park it where we agreed, but probably not until after I show it off this afternoon to Paradise sixth graders."

Minutes later, Jake bypassed Joel's pickup with its fluttering yellow tape. He admonished himself for thoughts that only his skill, not Joel's, kept a state pickup out of the ditch. He filled an empty Paradise Police visitor parking space. With his truck keys in hand, he drove to the tailor shop.

A clean-shaven young man approached Jake at a shirt display. "Can I help you, sir?"

"Looking for a western shirt and bandana."

As Jake expected, his choices were less than six. He chose a long-sleeve, mixed-color, line-patterned, predominately brown shirt and a red bandana. A large belt buckle with a Bar X brand logo caught his fancy.

"Can I interest you in a pair of chaps?"

"No thank you. Surprised you have them."

"We only have one pair. Special order. Guy left town."

Jake paid the clerk.

At the Mayflower, he stomped twice on his truck's accelerator pedal to coax its diesel engine to belch smoke. When it roared to life, he let it idle and balled up the yellow crime tape. He unlatched the tailgate and tossed the tape into the trailer before he affixed his own lock. To guarantee it locked, he yanked it hard enough to pain his biceps.

Jake, reunited with his past life within its steel cocoon, subdued his interstate urge, switched off the ignition. He locked the cab and steered his pickup to Hunter Realty.

The entry door bell tinkled and Rita greeted him. "Bob's not in until later. I can take a message."

"Not here exactly to see Bob." Her eyes widened. "There's permission from the Presbyterian Church to use their lower level for ballroom dance lessons. If you and Bob attend, there'll be eight, no gawking bystanders."

"I don't know what Bob will say."

Jake crossed his right-hand fingers. "Tell Bob he'll find it easier than acting and never as messy as bug collecting. Will be Thursdays. Details next week. Know you'll be persuasive."

The doorbell tinkle signaled Jake's exit. Next stop: Sadie's.

"Hi, Jake. You need a table?" Kate asked.

Jake, becoming accustomed to the noon bustle, ignored the stares, sat on a stool and leaned across the counter to be nearer Kate. "No time. Need your lunch sandwich special."

"Heard about the accident this morning. Deluxe ham okay?" Jake nodded. "A regular speculated that since the state park has multiple blue pickup trucks the hit-and-run target may have been someone other than Deputy Coleman. Maybe Ranger Scott . . . or perhaps you."

"That's farfetched."

"If you ask me, someone's jealous of dancers. Patricia or Emily told me you've had lipstick eyes watching you."

Jake sucked in his gut. "Shouldn't have."

"Well, don't blame either. We're all a little nervous. We're not used to two dead bodies in two weeks. I desire fun things. Like another lookout picnic? I've a basket, food and a fancy red-and-white tablecloth. We could take tennis rackets and swat those flying cottonwood puffs. First one to a thousand wins."

"Love picnics, but I suspect that after two or three eighteen-hour days Ranger Scott will request my help. Let's talk next week about a picnic, okay?"

Kate frowned. "I'll hold you to it, partner. Would that be that how they say it out West?"

Jake felt the warmth building in his abs radiate to his cheeks. "You're learning the trail lingo."

"Here's your grub. I'll saddle up with you later."

Jake left, his spirits bolstered by Kate's smile. The bag registered heavy. He peeked—pie.

Miles proofread Robert Case's profile he'd written for the next day's edition. An only child, born in Leeville, Minnesota, Case had been thirty-five when he died. He had spent his teen years in juvenile detention facilities. Thereafter, he lived on the fringe of criminal activity. Arrested for car theft, he wasn't convicted.

In Paradise, Miles uncovered no recorded incidents of trouble, especially during the years Case lived with his mother. Based on interviews with co-workers, Miles concluded Case definitely wasn't the brain behind the Paradise gang. He speculated either Kathie or the allure of quick and big money had seduced him into gang participation.

Miles's failed efforts to pierce the mystery shroud that hid Case's ballroom dancing motivation upset him. Sarah Kleinschmidt had avoided Miles entirely and Patricia Swanson did little than confirm the obvious.

As to Case's death, Miles longed for additional lodge basement information. He needed to interview Jake Brown again. Brown's nine Gideon Bible words, despite their tantalizing Paradise robbery connection, aligned into no word sequence that made sense to Miles.

He tried to summarize. Money and gold had been hidden in the lodge basement. Its cement block possibly confused with "brick," and "walls." While the river harmonized with "waters," the words "shaven," and/or "beard" brought forth a reference to a disguise or the guard responsible for the gold of "Bethel." "Men" left out Kathie unless it was used as a universal word for mankind.

Miles grappled with the two words, "hands" and "tied." The easiest to visualize, they were the hardest to integrate. If figurative, in the sense the bonds would be hard to fence, that is, the gang's hands were tied, clicked with Miles. That the gold coins required smelting, although not necessarily into idols reminiscent of the biblical Bethel, struck Miles as feasible. Then again, perhaps, the loot's location had discovered and those person's hands had been the ones tied before the body weighted with a brick and tossed into the nearest body of water.

His mind entertained the plausible conclusion there might be no cognizable key to fit all the circled words if a crazed individual had selected them.

Miles sighed. No Pulitzer Prize awaited.

Trooper Kessen dumped his cold coffee. He required inspiration and facts, not caffeine, to identify Robert Case's killer. Case's assembly-line employment at 3N Refrigerator tied him to no known robber.

Case hadn't ventured far from Paradise, even for dance competitions. His most recent had been a one-day trip to Minneapolis. Only once had Case entered a two-day competition. While he returned home each night, Kessen didn't consider this behavior odd. Others, especially farmers with dairy herds, had a similar habit.

He connected Case with no safety deposit box rental or large wire transfer.

Given Jake Brown's employment application by Ranger Scott, Kessen considered it unenlightening. By utilizing a false name, Jake could cache anything in any visited city. A sleeper cab generated no hotel or motel records and his official DOT log, if like most, wouldn't be close to the truth. Side trips, Kessen mused, could be hidden by driving past the mandatory rest times to allow unrecorded detours before a facility supervisor recorded his on-time arrival.

A death certificate notarized Athena Brown's death. A newspaper obituary in her New Jersey hometown said Jake attended the funeral. The funeral director confirmed. Kessen uncovered no connection between trucker Jake and any known Paradise gang member.

Kessen had no ready answer for the fibers found on Case's pants. A message on his desk from Chief Coltraine stated Case worked the day shift. Asbestos fibers, if encountered, limited to 3N's third-shift maintenance, which Case never worked. Moreover, cellulose fibers didn't exist in 3N's steel building. The Chief had pronounced 3N a dead-end.

Kessen flipped through Jake's phone records. Midcom Telephone reports listed several unanswered rings to the park caretaker residence within the past week. All calls originated by a blocked wireless number. The Chief reported the Mayflower, on Jake's last day, forwarded several unconnected calls to Jake's room. Len reported no unexplained same-number calls to Brown's cell or suspicious numbers saved in its SIM card.

At two twenty-five p.m., Jake, in his bedroom, changed from his park uniform to a blue shirt and blue jeans to become a big rig jockey for Emily's elementary school class. He parked his pickup in the Mayflower's rear lot and, exhilarated, hopped up into his old world. His mind visualized miles of converging telephone poles, no worries except the ever-present loneliness.

He angled his dusty red Kenworth cab and its fifty-three-foot steel trailer into six parallel parking spots alongside the school. Twenty excited sixth graders startled Jake when they burst from the school's front door and abruptly sat on the lawn. Their enthusiasm thrilled Jake.

Emily, in a flowered spring dress, also wore a big smile. "Children say hello to Mr. Jake Brown. He's the truck's driver."

A pigtailed girl in the front row frantically waved her hand. "Mr. Brown, can we blow your horn?"

"If your teacher says it's okay." Twenty pairs of pleading eyes bombarded Emily with one intent—say yes, please yes.

"Later. First, we'll listen while Mr. Brown tells us what it's like to work as an over-the-road truck driver."

Jake tried to keep it simple by explaining how he'd be hired to pick up or deliver specific cargo. When the time arrived to have the students sit in the cab, infectious glee gripped the class. Giggles abounded and startled kids ran after each cord pull activated his truck's air horn.

Emily averted potential disaster when her student count

totaled nineteen, not twenty. Jake discovered Edward hiding in his sleeper compartment. The boy, while his parents fretted, could've spent a scary night listening to raccoons rattle trash receptacles at Cottonwood State Park. In front of Emily's stern expression, Jake's arms released the boy.

Jake tried to smile. Emily now owed him big, real big.

"Chief, Chief!" Bell's intercom voice echoed her morning's panic.

The Chief, excited by constant high-activity police work, pressed reply. "Bell, I'm here in my office. Believe I heard you through the walls without the intercom. What's up?"

"Call Lt. Sigourney on his car's radio. He . . . he needs backup on Hancock Boulevard, near the Presbyterian Church."

"Tell him I'm on my way." In Ohio, The Chief never made patrol officer response calls. He'd add this to his documented support for adding an officer.

The Chief killed his flashing Mars lights and braked to slow his car when he perceived the pulsing red and blue of Lt. Sigourney's squad. When The Chief approached, he observed that Sigourney stood in front of a green van, not recommended academy training procedure. A woman sat behind the van's steering wheel, glaring straight ahead at his officer.

"What's going on lieutenant?" The Chief halted his advance aside the van's front left fender.

"I pulled over this van for speeding along Chestnut. Sgt. Smyth had targeted this area for special enforcement. When I approached the driver door, she acted belligerent. She shouted, threw a partially eaten apple and swore profanities. I feared she'd make up all sorts of accusations if I didn't have a witness." Sigourney's flushed face gave The Chief an indication anger brewed deep within.

The Chief retraced three steps to the driver's window and tapped twice on the glass. "Ma'am, I'd like to speak with you if I might. We can get through this without unnecessary conflict. I'm willing if you are."

The driver's window slid into the door. A woman he

guessed to be in her late thirties glared at him. "He's a pig. You should lock him up for demanding sex to tear up a bogus ticket. I know my rights."

From what he could observe, her clinging white blouse and tight blue jeans hid no weapon. "Ma'am, could I please see your driver's license and registration? That will help me sort this."

The woman's left arm reached for her feet.

"Hold on. Please step out of the van."

"Need my purse. It's got my license."

"Do it slow. Keep your right hand on the steering wheel."

The woman complied, and The Chief appreciated that the traffic stop's tension appeared to be de-escalating. Out of the corner of his left eye, he saw that Lt. Sigourney hadn't moved.

When handed a state driver's license, he read the name— Victoria Jessup. "Thank you. We have a slight problem. This license is expired."

"Pig. Jerk."

The driver's door slammed into The Chief's right forearm. By instinct and training, his left hand swung the van door wide and he jerked the woman's right arm until her feet landed on the pavement. Lt. Sigourney raced to him. With both hands on her shoulders, The Chief spun her to face the van's side. "You're under arrest for assaulting a police officer."

She mumbled a profanity that he ignored.

The Chief detached his handcuffs and cuffed Victoria's wrists behind her back. It wasn't official arrest protocol, but he stretched her blouse collar from her neck's nape—a sunflower tattoo. He, with his lieutenant as a witness, gently pushed his arrestee's head lower than his car's backseat door frame and guided her to have a seat. He confiscated her purse, removed the van keys and locked it before radioing Bell to have the van towed to the impound lot.

Lt. Sigourney followed The Chief to the police station where they escorted Ms. Jessup to the city's remodeled jail. He stood outside as Bell completed the mandatory pre-lockup search. Once Victoria had been locked into the city's modern cell designed to detain one female, he went upstairs to his office to telephone Len. Unable to reach him, he left a state crime lab voicemail to notify Len of the impounded van.

Thirty minutes early for rehearsal, Jake approached Clem at the bar and asked if the bar sold scotch smaller than fifths. Jake bought a half-pint and then rushed out of the B&B.

The antiseptic hospital corridor tingled Jake's nose. At the nurses's station he asked for Joel Coleman's room number. The nurse balked until Jake showed his official park identification.

Jake peeked around a half-open door. "You okay, Joel?"

"Been better. It's kind of you to visit."

"Recall you said you liked scotch. Since I have no card, there's a 'get well' written on the label. Hope you'll enjoy."

Coleman pointed with his uninjured left hand. "Put it in the lower drawer and I'll have a nightcap after lights out. Can you stay and meet my wife? She left to run an errand."

"Sorry, can't. Play rehearsal." Jake waved good-bye as Joel stretched his white top sheet.

Jake tried not to visualize himself in a hospital bed.

Chapter Seventeen

Emily's theater survey counted one actor missing when Jake, a western-styled shirt and bandana draped over his right arm, double-timed it toward her at the stage.

"Isn't Patricia with you?" Jacob asked. "I told everyone we should expect you and her to show up together."

"No, she isn't, and my apology for being late. Thought I had enough time to visit the deputy ranger in the hospital."

Restive to move beyond costumes, Emily didn't comment on Bob's whisper to Pastor John how unusual it was for Patricia to be late. The reverend nodded. "Okay, guys. Although Patricia isn't here, we've seen her dress. Jake, as the last here, you can go first."

Jake spread his shirt and bandana on the stage and pointed to the branded belt buckle he wore. Bob stepped forward with his vest and string tie ensemble. Jake quashed a laugh when Pastor John displayed a pair of chaps to go with a reddish, western-styled shirt. Jacob displayed a western-styled shirt paired with a fancy, tan cowboy hat that appeared to be felt.

"Since you all had different outfits, our audience will be able to distinguish roles. I'll be back."

Emily asked Clem to lift the telephone to the bar and punched in Patricia's home number. Her efforts were rewarded with a busy signal. "Clem, please try redial in five minutes." Emily hustled to the stage. "Patricia's line was busy. Let's start at the cemetery scene."

Emily's praise failed to enliven the stilted rehearsal. Clem twice reported Patricia's home phone rang busy and his library operator try connected him to Patricia's voicemail.

After a show of hands, Emily abided by the consensus to end rehearsal. Emily's stomach churned. Jacob and Bob volunteered to visit the library to determine if Thursday's later hours had delayed Patricia's departure. Jake and Emily chose to visit Patricia's home. Pastor John said he'd meet them there after a stop at the parsonage.

Jake rapped on the Chestnut Street house door Emily pointed out to him. Patricia didn't appear. He twisted the mechanical door bell's key and banged again. No answer.

"Walked by this house one Sunday." Emily didn't ask why. "Recognize the red tulips. Long story. Fantasized Dennis the Menace lived in the corner house."

Emily asked Jake to try and glimpse into a front window while she darted toward the home's rear. She returned to find Jake pacing the front walk.

"There's a car in the locked garage." Emily wheezed. "I'm assuming it's Patricia's. Nothing's disturbed."

"There's no sign of life in the house."

Emily gasped. When a door banged, she dashed to knee in front of a young boy she believed exited the neighboring Dutch colonial. "Hello. Do you go to Roosevelt School?"

"I'm in third grade."

"That's great. After school did you see the lady that lives in this brick house?"

Emily didn't rush the boy's answer.

His eyes filled with fear as they fixed on Jake stepping to Emily's right side. She flashed her right palm for Jake to halt.

"Did you see the lady who lives here?" Emily pointed to the bungalow.

The boy nodded. "The policeman had a badge."

"You saw a badge?" Emily, her right hand behind her back, crossed two fingers. "Are you sure?"

Jake dropped to his knees.

The boy nodded. "Me and my brother play cops and robbers. Policeman had a gun, too." Jake wiped a left hand on his jeans-clad thigh. "I ran to get my brother. But he didn't see the man and said I lied."

"What about the neighbor lady?"

Emily's heart bounced from rib to rib.

"Don't know." The boy glanced at Jake, then Emily.

"Was there a police car with flashing lights?"

The boy shook his head. "The man had a big blue car."

"Do you remember what time you saw the policeman?"

Emily tried hard to listen, but the echo of her rapid heartbeats filled her ear canals. She doubted the boy answered for she didn't see his thin lips part.

"Hi, Timmy," called out Pastor John.

Emily rotated her head to see the reverend approach from the Presbyterian Church's direction.

Jake's right hand on the grass helped push him to his feet. "Pastor John, do you know this boy?"

"Sure do." Pastor John stopped between the boy and Emily.

"Don't I know you, Timmy?" Timmy nodded. "Where's your mother?" Timmy pointed a finger. "Would you go get her?"

Timmy ran and let the Dutch colonial screen door bang.

"Pastor John, the boy said he saw Patricia with a policeman and a big blue car," Jake said. "Could that be a tall story?"

Emily's shoulders trembled.

"Probably not. Timmy's intelligent. As with most boys his age, he loves make-believe games like cops and robbers. But he can tell you what he sees."

Emily shuddered and hugged herself.

A woman dressed in white sneakers, blue jeans, a man's shirt with the sleeves rolled up and a scarf tied beneath her chin emerged from the same door the boy had disappeared into.

"Jane, nice to see you," Pastor John began. Jane halted her approach six feet from Emily and stood motionless. "These are friends of mine, Emily and Jake." Jake bowed. "We're looking for Patricia Swanson. My friends believe Timmy saw her with a policeman. Have you seen your neighbor this afternoon?"

"Sorry, not today. Only heard a car and a garage door about the time she usually comes home. For the last hour I've been inside preparing supper."

"Thanks. Tell Timmy he did good."

Jane went inside.

After a brief discussion, the three cast members set off to visit the Paradise Police Station with plans to regroup with Bob and Jacob. Emily's call to Bob's cell rang to voicemail.

Patricia clenched her jaw. Pain still radiated from her wrists to her shoulders. She held her breath. Little comfort. Behind the blindfold one dull light spot didn't focus either retina on any object. She closed her eyes to lessen her physical pain. Worse. A nightmarish skeleton danced on her inner eyelid. She gasped as it lifted a bony hand for her foxtrot's underarm turn.

Unseen handcuffs pinned her arms behind her back. She pressed her palms to a chair back, unable to poke her hands between vertical slats or spindles. When she twisted a hand, the cuff abraded her skin as if the cuffs were lined with sandpaper.

She tried to raise or lower her hands without success. Rope under her armpits, around her waist and below her knees kept her body tied tight to a straight-backed chair.

She agonized over and over why she had been so trusting. After she had parked her car in her garage, the suited man appeared out of nowhere. Her numbed brain recalled he used her first name, flashed a badge and said he needed her help. Two youths arrested at the library seen stuffing illegal drugs in garden books.

When she had turned her back to him to close the garage door, he jerked her right arm into a hammerlock and clicked a handcuff on its wrist. Her struggle to no avail as he pressed her against the garage sidewall, grabbed her left arm and clicked the second handcuff on her left wrist.

He then said softly into her left ear. "Do what I say and you won't be hurt. Walk with me to the car, don't motion or say anything to anybody. Lean into the backseat."

Patricia tried to veer left to catch a glimpse of the license plate. He pushed her body right and then her face into the rear seat cushion. A cloth gag choked her before her raised eyes saw a red bandana on the seat. A man's rough hand grabbed it, rolled it and blindfolded her with it. Before the blackness, she forced her memory to forget the hand and recall her assailant's facial features last seen near the garage. All she could concentrate on were his piercing eyes—deep, dark, menacing pools of wickedness. He had no facial expression.

Righted into a seated position, her captor shoved her further into the car. She sensed the seat cushion to her right being depressed. Her world rolled forward. She hadn't glimpsed a second person, but a new fear thread unraveled to wrap her tight when she grasped the car required more than a backseat driver.

When she wiggled, a strong hand pressed her right knee. Fingers squeezed it three times. Her thigh and calf muscles contracted. The fingers on her knee patted her inner thigh on their creep toward her stomach. The gag in her mouth muffled Patricia's scream. Muscular fingertips indented her inner thigh. She swallowed hard before every muscle in her body tensed.

She braced to be groped. The flashback of a football stadium storage room and Robert's hand reactivated her tremors.

Patricia's heart skipped a beat. She'd never been able to kick forward with force, much less sideways. She waited for the four fingers to double their distance from her knee.

"Later," the raspy voice whispered. "There'll be fewer clothes to worry about." The fingers released their grip.

Patricia prayed a silent Our Father.

Her mind didn't register her route or expected destination. A breeze chilled her cheeks. The sensation lingered. She jettisoned her attempt to count minutes on her fingers. The warmer breeze indicated a slower speed. A stone ping and the crunch of wheels on gravel preceded the dust that filled her nostrils. They weren't in the City of Paradise. But where in Paradise County?

She feared the hours until she failed to report for work would be an eternity. When, for an extended time, the soles of her shoes no longer vibrated, she believed the car had reached its destination. The creak of one rear door and the click of an opposite latch confused her. What didn't were hands that squeezed her left arm and ankle. The ankle hand first swung her left leg at least ninety degrees, and then her right. With her feet on ground, a hand atop her head pressed her chin to her neck while a second tugged her left arm. As she stood, she heard neither city sounds nor farm animal cries. Lilac and faint lavender overpowered the prior dust. A male voice not heard before pierced the stillness. She guessed the car's driver.

Fingers jabbed into the small of her back directed her forward. She stumbled when her left toe struck an immoveable object. Strong arms squeezed her elbows to her sides. Splayed fingers clasped each breast. She squelched a scream. Each hand, not content to elevate her shoulders, fondled a breast.

"It's a door. Lift your feet," directed the male voice. The fingers inched across her chest in opposite directions to grasp the front of her shoulders. Once he had steadied her after a step up, his hands, shifted to her shoulder blades, shoved her ahead.

Muffled footsteps she cataloged as her walking on carpet. A slide of her left shoe confirmed. Within her nostrils, a new smell of cheap perfume mingled with prior scents. She sensed a rather large room based on how her captor's voice carried.

The finger jabbing stopped and two hands on her shoulders twisted her torso one hundred and eighty degrees, and she plopped onto a chair. Palms on her knees pressed her handcuffed hands against a chair back. She felt ropes constrict her chest, arms and legs. When the sound she associated with rope fibers being rubbed against each other stopped simultaneous to a tighter constraint, Patricia believed knots had been cinched. Whatever he did, she couldn't move except to slouch her shoulders.

A calloused finger, its tip floating atop her skin's moist foundation, inched across her right cheek. Her captor's raspy voice rekindled Patricia's trembles first experienced at her home. "That's a good girl. Do what I say and you won't feel pain." A hand squeezed her right knee. "I can see why someone on the Paradise Police force would want to have you."

Her fast and weak breaths failed to slow her racing heart. Each beat pulsed epinephrine to her extremities. Unable to fathom his exact meaning from either his tone or the memory of his eyes, she shuddered thinking the worse—picnic. Skeletons and groping hands, with and without skin, galloped through her brain. When she flexed her ankles, no toes tapped.

Was she paralyzed? Had the pain she experienced in her neck been an injection site? Fear of an imminent attack, or left to die, evaporated when her abductor spoke in the distance.

"Leonardo, you make sure the broad doesn't run. As long as she's here and not dead when I return, you can do anything you want." Patricia shuddered. "I'm ready to personally renew my acquaintances with my old friend Jake. I'll be back after dark. Give me the keys. I'll take your car."

Ever-advancing footsteps chilled her. Then they stopped. Patricia's heart pounded. Shallow and rapid breaths soaked her gag with spit.

"Be still, bitch, while I start with your shoes. You're all mine now and you ain't going nowhere . . ."

At the police station, Jake, Emily and Pastor John learned the one lone officer on duty, a patrolman, had responded to a citizen's barking dog complaint. Since the one dispatcher couldn't leave the entire headquarters unmanned, they decided to return to the B&B.

"Emily," Clem called out, "Mr. Hunter telephoned to tell you Patricia left the library, normal time, headed home."

"What do we do now?" Jake asked.

"We should contact Chief Coltraine," Pastor John suggested. "He should know what's going on, especially since it may involve someone on the police force. I'll stop by The Chief's house on my way home."

Worry lines etched Emily's forehead. Jake waved good-bye to Pastor John and asked Emily. "Can you follow me to the state park in my pickup? I must move my truck from the Mayflower parking lot."

"Sure. Let me tell Clem he's in charge."

Jake left his pickup engine idle and the driver door ajar for Emily to become its driver. He experienced no problem in getting his big rig to roar out of the Mayflower lot, headed east on Main Street. In his side mirror, he viewed Emily following.

Jake bypassed headquarters without a park permit and, near the pavilion, hopped out long enough to instruct Emily to wait for him there. After two back-up maneuvers, Jake eased his trailer past the camping spaces onto a gravel service road and cut the engine. He failed to spot his cell phone in the cab before he double-checked the trailer padlock and the cab lock, patted the fender for luck and jogged to where Emily waited.

Jake succumbed to his feeling of inadequacy and a gurgling stomach. "How about we stop at Sadie's for a bite?"

"**H**ello, guys," Kate welcomed. "What's new tonight?"

"We're eager for supper," Jake said. "Table 12 available?"

"It's yours." Kate handed him a menu. "Forget the spaghetti special. Only early birds eat that one."

While Jake enjoyed Kate's coffee, he tried to figure out why a quiet Emily broke her habit and read the menu insert. Her cola lost its fizz without her tasting one sip.

"Emily, I thought you had all the specials memorized."

"Kate sometimes surprises with an unusual one based on day-before leftovers. Since it's Thursday, I can't have my favorite German plate combo. Guess a plain ol' tuna sandwich will be it."

"Don't look up," Jake whispered. "Sgt. Smyth's in uniform. Didn't the police dispatcher say he wasn't on duty tonight?" Jake ducked his head to avoid Smyth's gaze.

"You're right." Emily flattened the menu to her face. "What do you think he's up to?"

"Beats me. Can you see if his squad car is outside?"

"Can't. I'm visiting the ladies room. That'll let me answer your question. Won't be long." Emily darted for the restroom.

"Have you two decided what it will be?" Kate inquired.

"Not yet. Emily left. What's Sgt. Smyth doing here?"

"He said duty called. Needed to have his coffee thermos filled. That's all."

Jake observed Smyth speak with a counter customer. "We might have to skip eating."

"What's going on with you two? How does Roger fit in?"

"Trust me. Can't explain, not now." Kate frowned. "Think Emily and I will be leaving shortly." Kate, in her departure from the table, screened a returning Emily from Sgt. Smyth.

"Well?" Jake asked.

Emily sat next to him before speaking in a darkened theater voice. "Squad car sits out front." Emily's hands trembled: first on the tabletop and then lowered to her lap. "What do we do?"

"Told Kate we might leave. We should follow the good sergeant, that is, if we won't be discovered."

Jake barely heard Emily. "Is that wise?"

"What else can we do?" Jake considered his question a statement. "His being in uniform, when the dispatcher says he's off-duty, is suspicious."

"What about getting the police chief?" Her voice quivered.

"I'm not proposing we do anything other than follow to see

if he goes anyplace unusual. We're not doing much to find Patricia by sitting here eating supper. Get ready to leave. His conversation is ending."

When Smyth surveyed the diner, Jake lifted his coffee carafe in front of his face. Smyth spun on his heels and left.

Jake and Emily arose from their chairs. His hip bump to an empty table spoiled their attempt to make an unobtrusive beeline to the street. Outside the diner door, they discerned the squad car's taillights a block ahead on Main Street. Jake seized Emily's elbow and urged her jog to his pickup.

They tailed Smyth's fifteen mph cruise west toward the B&B where he turned left onto George Street. Jake executed a Main Street u-turn and parked before crossing Hancock Boulevard. Smyth's appearance confirmed Jake's guess that Smyth had used George to reach Chestnut and reverse directions. In front of he and Emily, Smyth followed his right blinker to continue east on Main to Paradise's city limits. Good visibility allowed Jake to maintain a quarter mile interval.

"Where's he going?" Emily gripped a passenger door handle.

"Have no idea. While there's little likelihood of police business outside the city, gravel makes our tracking easier."

"Why would he need a full coffee thermos?"

"Suggests he plans on staying up late. Do you see the dust now drift to the right, none straight ahead?" Emily nodded. Jake slowed. "He entered this farm's driveway. We're staying here." Jake switched off his headlights. "Can you see anything?"

"It's a farmhouse, barn and another building. The yard light creates shadows. It doesn't show any cars."

"We must choose. Stay or get help." Jake had no remedy for Emily's trembling hand except to let it rest on his right hand as he clenched the steering wheel. "Have your cell phone?"

"Yes, but I vote to go for help. To call 9-1-1 would be a huge risk with a police officer involved." Emily's breaths were shallow. "You said the thermos indicated he would be staying up. Let's hope it's here." Jake sandwiched Emily's steering wheel hand. "And, he has one revolver against our none."

"Okay. First, let me see if I can find a name or number to identify this place." The cab's dome light flicker signaled Jake's exit and his return.

"Did you find any name?"

"No. But I did locate a fire department rural locator number on the mailbox post. Authorities will recognize RFD 137."

Heels elevated on a chair, a startled Leonardo sprang erect when Sgt. Smyth, his revolver drawn, entered the farmhouse kitchen unannounced. Smyth banged his thermos on the cabinet counter and braced his shoulders against the closed living room door to protect his rear and give him a clear shot at Leonardo.

Smyth's words jumped from his lips. "What's up, Leonardo? I put on my uniform after I received a garbled call alerting me to a Big Joey party. Thought it was the twenty-fifth, not tonight."

"Hey, slow down." Leonardo righted his upended chair, sat and stretched his legs horizontal, shoes on an adjacent chair. "You got wrong information. I'm out here to baby-sit some bitch for A.C." An empty Hofensteger rolled towards Smyth.

Smyth holstered his revolver and kicked the bottle into a corner. "A.C.? Where's Big Joey? What's A.C. doing?"

"He's hell-bent to recover the bank loot heisted two years ago. He thinks either that trucker or the bitch from the dancer's house holds the key." He patted his right rear pants pocket. "I'm happy to be paid for helping out, although this bitch spits. Not your TV's quiet, mousy librarian."

Smyth paced in front of Leonardo. "You kidnapped the Paradise librarian?" Smyth bolted forward, his nose within an inch of Leonardo's face. He wanted an immediate answer.

"Yeah, in the living room." Leonardo pointed to the closed kitchen door. "She's not going anywhere."

"If she's hurt, you're going to the hospital." Sgt. Smyth yanked the doorknob Leonardo pointed to. *Damn*. Patricia appeared comatose, bound upright in a chair, blindfolded, one foot shoeless, her blouse unbuttoned and the top button to her slacks undone. He pivoted into the kitchen and slammed the living room door shut.

"What in the hell did you do to her?" Smyth's two hands seized handfuls of Leonardo's shirt and pulled him to his feet. "She looks dead."

"Relax, chill." Smyth released his right hand—his shooting hand. "A.C. tied her to the living room chair before he left. He said I should, without killing her, make sure she didn't leave."

"I think you did, or are damn close." Smyth's right hand fingered his revolver's grip. "She didn't move."

"She must be asleep," Leonardo suggested. "I told her if she promised not to scream I would undo the gag, and did. Then I tried to unlace her shoes so she'd have a hard time running if she slipped free. I knelt on one knee to undo the second shoe. When I placed my hand on top of her leg, she spit on me. With an open palm, I slapped her hard across the face. She spit at me a second time, but missed."

"That's not all you did, was it?" Smyth asked. He dug his right hand fingernails into his palm.

"Say, how 'bout letting go of my shirt?" Smyth did and backpedaled two paces for arm clearance to draw and shoot. "After she spat at me the second time, I told her that she'd pay. I unbuttoned her blouse, counting to ten between each one. When I came to the last button, she spit on me. That was three times and I could have killed her."

"You sure you didn't? You force her to swallow LSD?"

"Hell no. I'm not afraid of you, but A.C.'s different. I yelled she really made me angry. Stepped behind her so she couldn't spit at me and, with my lips next to her right ear, whispered, 'I hope you're a virgin.' My left hand reached around to undo her slack's top button. My right hand groped for the zipper. She then started crying and pleading: 'Don't hurt me. I won't spit. I promise. I promise. Please don't hurt me.' So I quit."

"C'mon, you did something?" Smyth's face felt flush. He clenched his hands. Perspiration trickles chilled his spine. Vivid memories flooded his mind of how he'd planned to be Patricia's first lover after the picnic until Robert chickened out and foiled everything. He knew of no other man in her life.

Smyth fantasized that if he were to rescue Patricia, she would be forever grateful and willing in bed. If he shot both Leonardo and A.C. and claimed line-of-duty self-defense, he'd lose his extra income. Plus, there was no guarantee of Big Joey's passive acceptance of his killing Leonardo. He had to think. Leonardo's voice brought him back to the moment.

"I spit on her face, twice. Then I noticed a lacy red and black bra she wore that reminded me of a ladybug. I warned her I'd return to discover if she's hiding any other insect." Leonardo laughed. "You want to help me check her pants?"

Smyth sidestepped to the living room door. He opened it a crack and saw Patricia's chin rise to stretch her neck. He closed the door. "You did enough. You'd better not come within ten feet of her while I wait to speak with A.C." Smyth screwed the top off his thermos and stared at Leonardo.

Leonardo smirked, sat, raised his heels onto a chair and his lean forced his first chair to tilt rearward.

Thankful for no gravel road speed traps, Jake's hands twice jounced his pickup's steering wheel to avoid a fishtail into the right-hand ditch. Color washed life into Emily's face when he dropped her at the B&B with advice to contact Pastor John and Chief Coltraine in person.

"We'll need Trooper Kessen since The Chief lacks arrest authority outside the City of Paradise. I have his telephone number on a card in my kitchen drawer."

"I'll expect you back in half-an-hour," Emily said.

Jake parked his pickup outside his garage to save time. His subconscious counted thirteen of Emily's thirty minutes as he quick-stepped to his dark house. He unlocked the rear door and bumped his right hand along the wall until it flicked on the kitchen's overhead light with its two sixty-watt bulbs. With his back to his bedroom, he flipped socks from a drawer next to his refrigerator without finding Kessen's card.

His step straddled six sock pairs, and he left them scattered on the kitchen floor to check his bedroom's closet floor where yesterday he had tossed his blue jeans.

Two steps into his bedroom, he gazed straight into a revolver's barrel opening, the weapon's hammer cocked.

"Hello, Jake. Long time no see."

Jake froze. "What the—" He faced a suited man, a badge hung from his left breast pocket. A sudden cold fear congealed in Jake's stomach.

"Step back into the kitchen light so I can see you better." Jake didn't argue with the gun pointed at his face. He reasoned little Timmy could have seen this badge and gun. If so, where was Patricia? Bile soured a taste bud closest to his throat. He craved a peek into his unlit living room, but feared even the slightest twitch would test his skull's hardness against that of a bullet fired at close range.

"You need to be more hospitable." The intruder edged closer, blocked Jake's limited living room view. "It's one thing not to buy chairs, but dreadful not to recognize an old friend. On the street you didn't remember the beard when I asked for a light. You never cared I called the motel and here several times. Never answered my shined light signal into your window."

"Honest. Don't know who you are." Jake kept his arms pinned to his side. "Never seen you before in my life."

The intruder laughed. "You're good, Jake. I heard you act at that Paradise bar. As you don't fool me none, you need to get your lesson money refunded. With Slim Jim in prison and Robert dead, I bet you planned on not splitting the loot with anyone. Well, think again." The intruder re-gripped the wrist of his left hand, which held his revolver. "You'll split my way. I'll take our shares plus Slim Jim's and Robert's. You'll bunk with Slim Jim until your execution."

"You have the wrong Jake." His stomach twisted. The blood behind his eyes fixated on the trigger finger circulated at the speed of sound. "Don't have nothing to split with anybody. Anything I've received in life came from hard, honest work."

The intruder faked a cigarette pack toss at Jake.

On instinct, Jake raised his hands to catch it.

"Good, now catch these." The intruder's right hand flick propelled a cigarette pack and matches at Jake. He caught both.

"Now light me a cigarette. And do it slow."

Jake did and the man's right hand snatched it.

"Remember the initials A.C.? Surely you enjoyed our eating crawfish in Moss Point?"

"You're a complete stranger. Never shared a meal with you." Jake tried to memorize the intruder's features, always returning to the black swamp of his eyes.

"Time to stop this charade and tell me the loot's location. We had a weather-protected hiding place in the lodge basement, didn't we?"

Jake's eyebrows arched. His involuntary squint didn't allow him any greater vision into the living room.

"Nobody ever went into that basement. Signs warning of explosives kept the curious away. A part-time farmer who worked at 3N had lamented to Robert about overestimating the number of cement block needed to repair a barn wall. Robert latched onto the brilliant idea to block in that wall door."

Jake didn't dare scratch his itchy nose.

"He and I, the week before the Halloween Parade, bought enough concrete blocks, cement and sand to close off the door. Robert lied he wanted to build an outdoor fireplace. Handy Robert had previously added a suspended-ceiling grid and wood floor in his mother's basement for his dancing. When we loaded the concrete block, Robert asked the 3N worker about a package of unused ceiling tile and purchased it. Lark happy we were."

The man waggled the revolver as if he lacked Jake's undivided attention. "We delivered the ceiling tile to Robert's home and hauled the concrete materials into the state park two weekend's later at midnight. Robert somehow had a lodge key. Then you showed with your selfish greed."

Jake hankered to scratch his nose.

"You buffaloed Robert into a new hiding place. Robert spoke of leaving Paradise. Kathie argued she had family in Paradise that, along with his job, would create a cover for both. She convinced Robert it would be easier to hide in the light than run in the darkness."

"Know nothing . . . not any of this." Jake stuttered. "Didn't .

. . didn't participate in any of this. Don't . . . don't know. . . ."

"Damn it, you do." A foot tapped and it wasn't Jake's. "You witnessed the truck's and the Cadillac's destruction. The only part you didn't participate in was when Slim Jim and I returned to his park camper to ensure the loot's safe hiding. We met Robert, and he claimed you double-crossed him and were on the lam. Both Slim Jim and I believed Robert lied."

The intruder's right foot crushed his cigarette into the floor. "Even if you hid it, Robert knew where. He drove us after midnight to a deserted Minnesota River scenic overlook. Robert said he needed a beer and reached into his car trunk. Instead, he threatened Slim Jim and I with a .38. He hollered at us to lay off him. You and he weren't going to shaft us. Slim Jim distracted him; I lunged for Robert's gun. As I struggled to disarm him by twisting his wrist, it discharged a bullet straight into his heart. He collapsed. We removed his upper clothing and pressed both his flannel shirt and undershirt against the bleeding chest wound. While he stopped bleeding, so did his breathing after one choking gasp. We figured he died."

"You could have taken him to a hospital," Jake said softly.

"S-u-r-e." The man shook his head side-to-side. "There was no way we were going to alert every lawman, or have every Tom, Dick and Harry with a metal detector roaming the state park. I agreed with Slim Jim the money hadn't traveled far. We took off Robert's clothes, laid him into his car's trunk and parked it near the park. His key unlocked the lodge and we found the basement empty. Since we required time to find the loot, we blocked in the basement wall door as originally planned with Robert's body behind it."

Jake gasped.

"After the first three rows, we lugged Robert to his tomb. Why Slim Jim put his jeans on, I didn't ask. A week later I ditched Robert's car in a Mississippi lake."

Jake felt vomit rise to the back of his throat.

"At the lodge, Slim Jim fired a bullet into Robert's skull for his pointing a gun at him. He had to try twice for he could never shoot straight. If I couldn't find you in Mississippi, we were ready to wait until you returned to claim the loot. You were one step ahead, ratting out Slim Jim's park camper. I figure you stayed out of jail as a snitch's reward while Slim Jim stares through a twelve-inch portal with iron bars embedded in concrete to watch life pass."

"You've gone to much trouble for nothing. While my first name's Jake, my last name's spelled like the color: B-r-o-w-n. Wasn't with you two years ago."

Sweat ran down Jake's neck.

"You keep saying that. I don't believe you. Turn around slow. Hands on your head. Walk under the light."

Jake complied.

"Face the sink. Take off your shirt."

Jake's shirt dropped from his left hand. "You gonna shoot me in the back of the head, like Robert?"

"If you run." Jake felt his T-shirt's neck hem stretched. "Pick up your shirt. I've made a mistake, a big mistake."

Jake swallowed hard. "What do you mean?"

"You've got no tattoo. We all had sunflower tattoos. Now you know too much. I need to think. We'll take a ride to the country."

Jake kept his hands on his head. Horror rose within him.

"Put on your shirt and walk in front of me. No funny stuff if you know what's good for you."

Jake buttoned his untucked shirt. "Need my keys from the drawer."

"Hold on. If it's the drawer above the socks, stand still." The intruder poked his left hand into the drawer.

With the intruder's attention distracted, Jake dashed for his rear door. He jumped the steps to the landing and bent low to rotate the doorknob. A bullet crashed through the lipstick eyes before he kicked the door wide. No voices or other noise emanated from the camper area. He dismissed racing there for fear he'd put others in mortal danger. Darkness shielded his run toward the lodge.

His leap cleared the lodge barrier he'd built to hid the crime tape. He gasped for breath. *Athena, what do I do now?* To avoid discovery, he laid prone on the basement doors. Each twig break or leaf rustle doubled his efforts to hold his breath. He feared the worst.

"Jake. Show yourself or this gentleman in orange will have walked his last trail. I'll count to three. One."

Jake shuddered, horrified. He knew only one person who walked trails at night and wore orange—Oscar. He squirmed sideways to tempt fate and press his face against the snow fence. The lodge security light profiled two figures. One eerie in an orange vest.

"Two."

"Leave him be." Jake stood. "It's me you want."

The intruder barked instructions for Jake to step out. He did. Jake requested Oscar to lead them to the caretaker's residence and tried to retard his pace to allow Oscar an opportunity to run. It didn't work. The intruder prodded Jake with repeated revolver pokes into the small of his back.

When they reached Jake's pickup, the intruder produced Jake's spare-key set. Jake hadn't lied about his keys being in the kitchen drawer. Still, his gamble had fizzled.

"Everyone stand still," the intruder ordered. He smacked Oscar's skull with his revolver's handle. Oscar crumpled to the ground. Jake bent forward. Oscar didn't wheeze or cough.

"Leave him. We'll take your pickup. I'll tell you where."

Jake's worry refocused on Patricia. If a misidentification explained what had been happening to him, it did him no good to have it written on a tombstone—his or Patricia's. What about the Bible words? Sgt. Smyth? Dare he ask? Would he stay alive longer if he led this thug on a bogus treasure hunt?

"Where we going?" Jake asked while driving. He had to forget about himself. Patricia came first.

"Don't ask," snarled the intruder.

Jake drove, turned and slowed when told to and entered a farmer's yard. He recognized a Paradise squad car next to the farmhouse. Was it the shadowy house he and Emily had seen earlier? Maybe.

With a gun in his back, Jake opened the farmhouse door as

instructed to find Sgt. Smyth and a muscular man in a kitchen playing two-handed solitaire.

"Howdy, gentlemen. We now have two visitors."

Jake calculated his escape odds doubled if there was a second visitor able to help.

Sgt. Smyth leapt up and growled. "Why did you bring him in here without a blindfold? Don't appreciate that at all."

"Then you'll have to dispose of him when we're done."

Jake steeled his emotions against the threat. If this home intruder would strike an old man, he had to gather his wits. He tried to size up the disinterested muscular second man without reaching a satisfactory conclusion.

"He looks like he is," A.C. continued, "but he's not the Jake I thought he was. I botched the sunflower tattoo. Now he knows too much." A.C. smirked. "Bet he'll tell me what I need to know to save his pretty co-star."

Jake's heart raced faster than when he had faced the Paradise judge. An irrational spasm squeezed his lungs. He began to feel lightheaded. If he wasn't going to be driven to his residence, Patricia had to be somewhere in the farmhouse. What would they do to her and would it be in front of him? If authorities failed to find the loot, how would he? Had Robert let his secret slip to Patricia?

He should've hit his big rig's accelerator when he had the chance. His mind reminded him, yes, he'd be alive in the sense that his lungs breathed air and his heart pumped blood. Only his soul would be dead. His mind imaged the veteran memorial walls at Sadie's Friendly Home Town Diner. Fallen veterans he hadn't met had faced horrific challenges with a bravery buoyed by honor and a belief in principles of a better life. He'd taken a sailor's oath, yet, in the USS Midway galley, there were no personal decisions with unknown or dangerous consequences.

He'd been right to stay. He'd sworn a never-ending allegiance to uphold his fellow veterans and he wouldn't be living a deserter's life of regrets. If he were to die, it wouldn't be because he didn't try to stay alive. First, he had to help Patricia. He had comforted Athena until her last breath and he'd stand shoulder-to-shoulder with the heroes of Paradise.

Jake stared straight into the piercing eyes of A.C. "Told you. Can't tell you anything not known. You lost the golden calves when you shot and let your fellow robber die. His blood is on your hands."

"Shut up. Slim Jim irritated me when he tried to find Bible quotations to explain things. His constant doodling ruined every Gideon Bible he stole. Robert's shooting was an accident. I may want to rescue what greedy bankers scam from hardworking people, but I ain't no cold-blooded killer."

Jake prayed A.C. hadn't lied. He needed to find Patricia. Although a clammy chill coursed his veins, he strove to appear unruffled. "What about the real Jake you're looking for?" Jake tried not to make quick arm movements. "He'll check, I'm sure, to see if it's safe before he returns, that is, if he hasn't already fenced the loot. If he finds out you're killing gang members, odds are he won't show his face anywhere near here, ever. And, think about Slim Jim. He's comfortable behind bars knowing you can't shoot him. Bettcha he's relishing the day he'll be paroled to begin a carefree life with the entire treasure."

From between his shoulder blades, Jake felt new sweat droplets slip and slide to his butt crack. "After you cemented Robert into the lodge basement, bet you weren't with Slim Jim every day. You said your Jake had left town. What if Robert trusted Slim Jim and brought out the pistol to shoot only you at the overlook?"

Sgt. Smyth edged away from the muscular man.

"Slim Jim could have easily buried the loot before authorities caught him. Now only he knows where it's stashed."

"Don't confuse me. Slim Jim would never do that." A.C.'s eyes darted to Smyth's right as it glided upward to the snap of his leather police holster. A.C. glared at Smyth. "Nobody get any fancy ideas to be a hero."

Smyth hastened to sit at the kitchen table next to his card partner.

"Slim Jim trusts me. I saw it in his face when we met prior to his trial. We go way back."

Jake added volume to his voice. He hoped Patricia, if near, would recognize his voice. "Maybe he doesn't feel he should share, since he, not you, has spent these last two years behind bars." Jake tried to think of *Cowboy* dialogue recognizable to Patricia. He grew frustrated when his mind froze on the words he couldn't shout: "Put that gun down."

Sgt. Smyth stood, but didn't approach.

"What has Slim Jim had? No freedom. No dinner parties with free flowing alcohol. Not one conjugal visit. Bet he's not the type who believes the parable that the biblical vineyard owner acted justly to pay the same wage to those who worked the last hour while others had worked the whole day."

"Shut up about the Bible." A.C. waved his revolver in front of Jake's face, cocked the hammer. "Now open that door and walk straight ahead. Remember, this loaded Smith & Wesson is aimed to blow a hole through your brain."

Jake gasped when he saw her blindfolded, bound with rope, her clothes unbuttoned and tear streaks moist on her lovely face, his hands clenched into fists. He trembled. What had Patricia been forced to endure? An unyielding rage gripped and overpowered his emotions. Logic told him he needed to act with reason. "Patricia, can you hear, speak?"

"Jake, Jake is that you?"

He struggled to pinpoint her plaintive voice.

"Everybody shut up," A.C. ordered. "I'll do all the talking."

Jake glanced to see Sgt. Smyth in the kitchen doorway, his right hand patted his holstered revolver. The second man stood back-to-back with A.C.

"Okay, little lady. I see someone has peeked at your charms. Hope you enjoyed it as much as he or they did."

Jake's blood boiled at A.C.'s teasing, although he appreciated the lull A.C.'s banter allowed to let his eyes focus in the room's dim light.

"We now have serious business. Little lady, you need to tell me where the money, bonds and gold coins are that Robert, your dancing partner, had."

"I don't know . . . don't know." Patricia sobbed. Her

shoulders slumped. Her right heel rubbed against her left foot.

"Well, let's start over. In your mind, little lady, picture I have a loaded pistol at the back of your friend Jake's head. My finger's ready to squeeze the trigger if I don't hear the answer I want." Jake's heart missed a beat. "Again, tell me, and tell me now, where's the money, the bonds, and the two bags of gold coins Robert had?"

"Jake, I'm sorry. I swear on a Bible I don't know."

"Shut up!" A.C. shouted. Jake heard an animal or someone outside the room rattling a loose piece of metal.

Jake slid each foot a baby step toward Patricia. Footfalls behind him faded, but he dared not swivel his head to verify if the second man had vacated the room. Closer muffled footfalls proved his guess correct that A.C. shifted his position. Jake tensed his calf muscles and halted a sliding right foot step toward Patricia when A.C. called out, "Jake, don't you move." His voice creaked a chilling menace and resonated deathly cold. "This gun still points at you."

Jake mustered his courage and peeked over his left shoulder. He spied A.C. closer to the kitchen door. Sgt. Smyth appeared after A.C.'s left hand motioned into the kitchen. A.C. whispered words Jake couldn't hear into the sergeant's left ear. Smyth disappeared from Jake's view. With measured movements, A.C. slid his soles across the carpet. Jake estimated he stopped six feet behind him. *Why?*

A.C. fired a bullet into the living room ceiling, above and slightly to the rear of Patricia's head. Jake jumped, in part because he felt the percussion of the revolver's hammer.

Patricia shouted, "Jake! Jake, what have they done to you?"

Jake pressed his elbows parallel to his sides fearing his slightest movement invited a shot aimed at him. He remained quiet and motionless, his thighs together. The thin reed that A.C. believed he stashed the bank loot kept him alive. Without head movement, his eyes stretched the limits of his peripheral vision. He didn't know where all doors led or if Sgt. Smyth waited beyond one of them. The out-of-sight second man hadn't said one word since Jake's arrival.

If the goon returned to torture Patricia, Jake planned to dive at A.C.'s revolver.

The entire room registered surreal to Jake's conscious mind. He and Patricia floated in suspended animation until he heard Patricia sob.

Tear gas canisters crashed through two living room windows and landed near Patricia. They spun and spewed forth nauseous gas. Additional window glass broke.

Jake revived his military training and dropped to the floor to begin his elbow-and-stomach crawl toward Patricia. His eyes burned. Aside Patricia, he rose to a kneeling position and his arms encircled her waist. His yank of her and chair crashed both to the floor. Patricia screamed.

Two gunshots rang out behind him. He clamped his left hand to Patricia's mouth and cradled her head in the crook of his right arm. A trickle of a sticky, warm substance gummed his left hand fingers. His tongue verified it was blood. Two new gunshots echoed farther away.

Strange voices yelled: "Give up." The loudest voice bellowed a *Cowboy* line: "Put that gun down." Rapid-fire gunshots convinced Jake not all heeded the command. Masks with canisters and padded vests bobbed in the billowing and circulating smoke.

The sting in Jake's eyes forced him to close his eyelids. He held tight to Patricia until stronger hands pried his away.

Tears evoked by the painful grief in his heart, not the tear gas, flowed. He had buried Athena, the one woman who had been his life. Evil now ruled. His courage insufficient to save the woman who represented his hope for the future.

Chapter Eighteen

"**H**ow many hand fingers am I holding up?" asked the woman in scrubs standing next to his hospital bed. "C'mon now."

"Six," Jake replied. He had to joke to stave off his deepening depression. The nurse had earlier asserted state and federal privacy laws prevented her from divulging information on Patricia.

His tears throughout the night had required the nurse to change his pillow cover twice. Jake rolled onto his stomach. He'd not eaten the first two meals. He'd wait for what Loretto Hospital had on the dinner menu.

His room's door's hydraulic piston groaned. "Okay, nurse, my best side's up. You can give me another shot in the butt."

"Say, cowboy, can you buy this lady a drink?"

Jake tore a top sheet in his haste to turn over. "Patricia! You're alive!" Tears rolled soft and wet on his cheeks.

"You really know how to impress a woman. I'd give you a hug if the doctor hadn't ordered me to be strapped into this wheelchair." Patricia set the brake with her right hand.

"Don't care about any wheelchair," Jake whispered. "My greatest hope revolved around whether you'd accept me. You have a college education and me without. You have a well-respected community position and me not so glamorously employed. You're different than the other women I've met in Paradise. The thought had flickered that you and I had the makings to become a family. Sort of like the Dutch colonial household that lives next door to you. It was hell riding in that ambulance convinced I'd not only let you down but delivered you into the evil clutches of a killer."

"It wasn't you. I'd have been in jeopardy because of Robert. His greed did him in. I never told anyone, but he always shared with me his dream of striking it rich. Other than dancing, he never involved me in his life. If I don't feel sorry for myself, neither should you."

271

"Dancing . . . the wheelchair." Jake buried his head in a pillow.

"Only temporary. Your yanking me to the floor caught my left foot under the chair. My ankle's severely twisted. Doc Beck doesn't want me to step on it until he has an MRI done."

He gazed at Patricia. "Blood . . . I tasted blood."

"Bit my tongue. No big deal."

"Had hoped all the kindness I'd received could be repaid."

"You've done that. You might not realize it, but others have been blessed by meeting you, especially me." Jake glanced toward the ceiling. "You've been honest even when it hurt. I've never been married so I can only imagine the closeness that develops between a husband and wife. I fulfilled my duty to care for my ill mother. You had to have added a greater love for your wife. If it had been a chore, you would've repressed the experience, not been as open as you have been."

Jake stretched the bed sheet with his toes. "Didn't do anything special. You said it best when you said being an adult is having the discipline to care about other people and to keep doing it. Paradise welcomed me when I strove to find out if I could live outside my cab." He gazed at Patricia. "Are we still on for dinner?"

"Never off. I'm learning to like having you around." Jake absorbed each ray of her radiant smile.

"Great. We'll survive this together. I'd like that. We can go visit your nieces and nephews."

"That would be wonderful. I like children."

Joy blossomed within Jake. She'd answered his unasked question. His gaze at Patricia eyes noticed an emerging gloominess. "Do you feel all right?"

Patricia wiped two fingers of her right hand across her forehead. "You should know this about Robert. He may have been misguided in many ways, but on one occasion." Jake eyed a tear teeter at the corner of her right eye. "When Roger grabbed me after a high school picnic and forced me to strip, Robert stepped in and prevented Roger from raping me." Jake couldn't believe it. "You're the only person I've told. And Roger threatened that the entire football team would have me if I told. Every now and then he'd sing the high school fight song to me at a B&B dance to reinforce his terror."

"The bastard. I'll kill him."

"No need. His terror hold doesn't exist anymore." When the tear escaped, she wiped it off her cheek. "I'm physically safe and you've made me mentally free."

After a silent two minutes, there came a knock on the door. "Is there room for another?"

"Trooper Kessen, you're always welcome," Jake replied. "Do you know Patricia Swanson, the prettiest librarian in the entire state? She's practicing for a role on Broadway."

Patricia blushed and pressed both hands to her cheeks.

"Met her at the Sunrise." Kessen smiled at Patricia. "I stopped by to see how you both were doing. If you've read the paper, Chief Coltraine killed A.C. after he refused to surrender. Sgt. Smyth and the other thug, Leonardo, are in custody. Victoria Jessup, shown the morning paper in jail, admitted Robert Case recruited Kathie Krump to be a lookout for the bank robbery."

Patricia asked, "Why was she left in Jake's truck?"

"Let me explain later," Jake urged. "Trooper Kessen has more to tell us, don't you?"

"Yes. Victoria posed as the bride to A.C.'s groom. From what we can tell, DiCecca masterminded the concept to take advantage of the Halloween celebration. While he could copycat ideas, like cars driven into a big rig, he's done for the future. His attempt to destroy or ditch all the physical evidence succeeded except for two things: a piece of untraceable bridal veil and the tattoo on all their necks. The second done him in."

Patricia, in her wheelchair, squirmed her body toward the trooper. "What about the bank robbery money?"

"It's still missing. We're sort of at a dead-end. Victoria claims she fled to Minneapolis to await her share, which never came. Then Big Joey lured her back. Slim Jim won't talk. And three robbers are dead with your look-alike, Jake, still on the run and hunted in Mississippi."

Patricia asked, "Did Robert hide the money?"

"There's no facts he did. All we can determine is his skeleton blue jeans held traces of his blood, asbestos and cellulose. Our 3N speculation didn't pan out."

"He also remodeled the house I live in."

"What do you mean?" Kessen asked.

Jake gazed at Patricia.

"He redid his mother's basement. Isn't there asbestos in old ceiling tile?" Patricia ran her hand along her wheelchair's arm rest. "He often complained about stained ceiling tile when we practiced the foxtrot. The tiles had been replaced when I purchased the home. If he did all the rehab, maybe he hid something in the ceiling?"

Kessen's eyes widened. "Can we check your basement?"

"Jane next door has a key. I'll telephone her to let you in."

"Trooper Kessen," Jake asked, "what about Oscar at the park and Emily? She had a sunshine tattoo."

"Oscar, one floor up, is resting comfortably. He's nursing a terrific head bump. He told me he's walking to the park later today if the hospital won't call him a cab."

"He'll do it, too," Jake interjected.

Kessen nodded. "As for Emily, except for experimenting with LSD on two occasions, we're convinced she had no role in any criminal activity." Patricia gazed at Jake. "Victoria has admitted Emily didn't get her tattoo at the same time as the others. Emily says she had the tattoo inked one weekend when Ms. Krump supplied the drugs. I doubt charges will be filed."

A second knock announced the arrival of Chief Coltraine. He tipped his hat to Trooper Kessen.

"Would you believe I was in the neighborhood?"

"Only if you pass a lie detector," Jake teased. "But you're welcome in my neighborhood any day."

"Mine too," Patricia said.

Jake perceived the expended emotion and multiple visitors were taking a toll on Patricia, although she hadn't complained.

"You'll be happy to know that there's physical evidence linking A.C. to the murder of Ms. Krump thanks to your tip about a missing tarp," The Chief said. "Briefly, the tarp that A.C. transported Kathie in had zinc oxide on it. A lodge basement tarp had the same powder. And then, when we arrested Victoria Jessup driving the van registered to him, an examination discovered zinc oxide powder traces on the cargo floor. Also, common paint types tie the two tarps together. We expect the .38 A.C. died with will be shown to have killed Robert Case. Leonardo, facing serious jail time and expected to take a plea, has cooperated to collaborate A.C.'s actions the night Ms. Krump was killed."

"How did A.C. get the lodge tarp? Steal it?" Patricia asked.

"It proved difficult to unravel, but Deputy Ranger Coleman admitted that he allowed Sgt. Smyth access to the lodge basement. Roger had said something about needing to protect a Boy Scout painting project. It's clear Roger duped Joel."

"What about Big Joey?" Jake asked.

"We're working on him. Leonardo and Sgt. Smyth have willingly and unwillingly given us leads to convict him. And before I forget, A.C.'s van had glass shards from a Hofensteger bottle. That may not prove he killed Ms. Krump, but it's helpful. Wherever she died, we're convinced A.C. struck the fatal blow. Regardless, the evidence proves she wasn't killed in Jake's trailer."

The chorus of "For He's a Jolly Good Fellow" filtered faint into Jake's room. Jake stared at Patricia.

"Not my doing," she pleaded.

The repetitious chorus high and low notes resonated louder and louder until the melodious song reverberated within Jake's room. Leading the songsters were Pastor John, Bob, Jacob and Emily. As they filed in, Jake waved to Trooper Kessen and Chief Coltraine as they slipped into the corridor.

Beneath his top sheet, Jake crossed left and right hand fingers Patricia's stash idea would pan out.

Chapter Nineteen

Thunderous applause rolled in waves onto Main Street. The wildly cheering audience stood. While an infant cried in reaction to the deafening crescendo, joyful hollering emanated from the back row. Revelry and rejoicing spiced the Spring Daisy Theatre's *Cowboy Boots Right Side Up* opening night.

After the final curtain, Jake's facial muscles ached from grinning. Adoring friends and families engulfed him and his fellow stars. Reverend John Olson, in chaps, stood amidst the Presbyterian Church delegation. Bob Hunter hugged wife Rita and shook all hands not sticky with gooey treats from the Lutheran Women's fund-raising dessert table. Co-workers from the 3N Refrigerator Plant ringed Jacob Z. Cummings. Patricia Swanson, surrounded by members of the Paradise Library Board, autographed their playbills.

Director Emily Hutchins stood tall, head and shoulders above her entire sixth grade class. Her head swiveled in response to raised student hands. The flash of Josh Miles's camera captured candid theatre crowd photographs, although the dizzying hubbub in the room drowned out the cast quotes the reporter scribbled on a notepad.

"Say, sonny, you did a super job." Oscar Jenkins, aside Rangers Scott and Coleman, carried a folded orange vest. An eagerness to live life pranced in Oscar's eyes. Coleman's ruddy complexion not dulled by the autographed cast on his wrist.

Jon bent forward to speak to Jake. "State approved new lodge and residence locks. I'm honored to attend tonight." He shook Jake's right hand. "And you needn't worry about any job probation."

"Thanks Jon, Joel, Oscar. Your friendship means a lot."

The ballroom audience thinned as townspeople offered each other good-byes and good wishes. Near the bar, a stationary man fiddled with a pipe in his shirt pocket. With slow rhythmic steps, he approached Jake.

"May I have a minute?"

"Certainly. Let's find an empty table away from all this noise." Three paces from the George Street exit, Jake righted a tumbled chair for Chief Coltraine and sat across from him.

"I received a call today from the Paradise Bank and their $25,000.00 reward announced two years ago remains claimable," said The Chief. "They wanted to know whom I would recommend. I thought of you first because you alerted me to the tarp and stood tall in the face of real danger."

Jake rubbed his thumb and forefinger. "Please recommend Patricia. She deserves it more. Her deduction that Robert hid the money in the ceiling of her home's basement proved accurate." The Chief nodded. "Still don't quite understand how you rescued us that evening at the farmhouse."

"You need to thank Emily and Reverend Olson. They tracked me down. Emily frantically explained you didn't come back in the thirty minutes she expected. She told me about RFD 137, and why, with Sgt. Smyth's involvement, there was no call to 9-1-1. That also alerted us not to use the police radio. With her information, I knew we needed sheriff and state police manpower. When Ranger Scott reported the park residence empty, your big rig parked and your pickup not in the park, we gave greater urgency to Emily's fears."

The Chief's right hand cradled his unlit pipe.

"Bob, Kate and Jacob all contributed." The Chief removed matches from a shirt pocket.

"We couldn't make out all of what you said to Cohen. However, at times your voice projected as if you were trying to reach the theatre's last row. When we no longer heard your voice, we had to act. Tear gas is never pleasant, and we hoped the military had given you training."

Jake nodded.

"We're in contact with Mississippi authorities to locate Jake Braun and FBI Agent Redburn volunteered to inform Slim Jim he no longer has a share to collect."

Jake caught a flutter of red and white dots draw near. Since their last rehearsal before opening night, no limp impeded

Patricia's graceful stride. The tension he perceived in Patricia's lower eyelids prompted him to stand.

She stared at Chief Coltraine. "You're not arresting Jake again, are you?"

"It's okay," Jake said. "We're plotting a good surprise." He scrambled to locate a third chair and Patricia joined them.

The Chief laid his pipe on the table. "I have the honor, after talking with Jake, to tell you that I'll be recommending you for the Paradise Bank reward."

"That's fantastic." She leaned sideways to wrap her arms about Jake's shoulders. "What about Jake?"

"Maybe he'll help you spend the money." The Chief arose and gazed at Jake, still embraced by Patricia. "Good night to you both."

Before Chief Coltraine reached the Main Street door, he struck a match.

Jake squirmed to hug Patricia, their knees touching. In the hospital, both had gained emotional strength from the other. After Patricia's horrific picnic tale, he promised he'd marshal the posse that would substitute Roger Smyth for their play's mannequin if the legal system failed. He visualized the good use of a local cottonwood tree's height.

"You dazzle everyone. The applause gusto for your costume drowned out half my line, but I'm happy." Jake hid his face from Patricia. "Your fantastic dance routine sizzled."

"Jacob had me once with his comment about a play dance routine. I'll not be had twice." She rested her hands on the table. "You know, I can't thank you enough." Her gaze met his. "I'm still having nightmares. Sarah has slept over several nights. Timmy now runs every time he sees me to avoid my giving him another hug. I'm thankful this play has helped keep my mind off being kidnapped and . . . "

Patricia sobbed. Jake released his hug and enfolded her nearest shaking hand into his. Their gazes radiated warmth and kindness—until interrupted.

"Howdy, sorry I missed opening night," apologized Kate.

For Patricia's blurry eyes and tear-streaked cheeks, Jake

offered her his handkerchief.

Kate continued, "From what I see it had to be a success. I'm looking forward to seeing it live tomorrow night. Jake, I hope I don't embarrass you, but at Sadie's you'll discover your picture, clipped from the *Herald-Gazette*, in a frame on the wall above Table 12."

"Couldn't be more honored. You put me in great company. Can't explain why my mind remembered your tribute to Hans and all the heroic Paradise veterans. It provided a source of strength when faced with a real loaded gun, not a play prop."

Clem advanced toward them with a tray full of drinks, pretzels and chips. "Help yourself. Drinks are courtesy of Emily."

"Say, where is Emily anyway?" Jake asked.

"She had three or four sixth graders who wouldn't have been able to attend the play tonight unless they had a ride home," Clem explained. "Emily guaranteed parents every student would make it home safe. She'll be here later." He set the tray on the table and asked Kate if he could ask her a personal question. They stepped away, out of earshot.

Jake jerked his gaze from Clem when Patricia spoke.

"So . . . I remember what you said in the hospital. However, now with the play performances about to end, and your big rig fueled, will you see life differently?"

"You surprise me." Jake cleared his throat. "Never found it easy to make life decisions. Yet, when I add up my Paradise promises, they total excellent choices.

"There's my commitment to Ranger Scott, which I'll honor.

"Emily will stage, if not write, another play and this time I can offer her experience.

"The Presbyterians will repeat their Greek dinner and there'll be tables cleared for dance lessons.

"Bob has given me a lead on furniture.

"Table 12 at Sadie's shouldn't be abandoned.

"Can't not use my new library card."

Patricia kissed his cheek.

"And most important, was hoping to be invited to practice

the foxtrot on a private, wooden, dance floor on Chestnut."

Jake hesitated. While he respected Kate and cherished her friendship, he wasn't willing to abandon his goal of having a family that included children. He also adored Emily and relished his future role as Emily's unofficial uncle.

Jake lifted his eyes to the ceiling. He cherished, and would never forget, Athena's advice to keep an expanding love in his heart. And he realized that love included children of his own.

Patricia's lips parted as if she contemplated speaking. Jake pressed his right forefinger to them.

"On a gloomy day in my life I read the sign outside Paradise. I can quote it. It says: 'Where Fulfilled Dreams Begin.' You're my fulfilled dream. I'm not going anywhere."

The End

Experience the gift of Donan Berg's writing
with a sneak peek of

"ADOLPH'S GOLD"

Available now in e-book and trade paperback
at your favorite book retailer.

Donan Berg loves to hear from readers.
Contact him c/o
DOTDON Books
514 17th Street
PO Box 1302
Moline IL 61266-1302
or via email at
mystery@abodytobones.com

Excerpt from Donan Berg's "Adolph's Gold,"
which is available today at your favorite bookseller.

Chapter One

Sonja Maria Sanchez's apartment-ceiling fan blades swirled a gagging, greasy-bacon aroma that settled like a loose noose on Detective Second Class Adolph Anderson's shirt-covered collarbones. He'd carried beads of August perspiration inside with him, leaving his blue blazer on the front seat of his yellow Monte Carlo. Listening to Sonja Maria's squeaky and faltering alto, Adolph failed to conjure up how he'd earn the shiny gold first class shield he craved. Rather than ask her to repeat her undecipherable English pronunciations, he pressed his sweaty left elbow into her living room recliner's cracked vinyl armrest and rotated his cocked left ear toward her in faked rapt attention. Behind his well-practiced facial facade, his distracted mind wandered to the yet to be interviewed bar homicide witness he'd stumbled upon yesterday. Solving homicides, he knew from eight years of being a detective, generated accolades and earned gold shields. He couldn't pin sentiment to his chest.

Sonja Maria hesitated twice without his prompting or encouraging her to continue. The seething, curdling waste-of-time anger clawing his innards was intensified by his remembering that Bridgetown, Iowa, Police Chief Ronald Howard had dropped this wild goose chase on him. Adolph damn well suspected that, with Yancey out, The Chief would try to appease the League of Women Voters by giving the one gold shield up for grabs to Luann.

His left hand clamped closed his notepad as Sonja Maria described the explicit deportation threat, her physical damsel-in-distress cowering, and her feared sexual assault. For Adolph, her details too vivid for a real-life assault victim, even if her droopy lower eyelids glistened. He chomped-at-the-bit for an exit strategy that wouldn't rile her to file a citizen's complaint. After ten years on the beat before being promoted to detective, Adolph had promised himself he'd never again wear oxfords whose soles had been scraped holey. He'd paid his dues and his numbing brain had heard Ms. Sanchez's fuzzy TV-drama scenario countless times.

He'd already scribbled notes detailing the absence of visible bruises on her forehead, chin, arm, and the below-the-knee skin of her rail-thin frame. "So, you didn't go to the hospital?" Why he delayed his departure with an objectively answered question, Adolph couldn't fathom. He'd called the hospital to learn no admission record existed for Sonja Maria Sanchez, the name she'd given him and, thus, no traceable rape kit evidence. Wouldn't take an armchair genius, he thought, to determine that any effort he spent trying to nail this gossamer suspect wouldn't enhance his jury-verified reputation for jailing criminals. With his chance for a gold shield needing a higher percentage of cases closed, he planned to administratively deep-six this investigation as fast as he could without risking charges of insubordination or dereliction of duty.

Adolph's mounting disgust for this colossal waste of time splashed in his stomach like a limestone brick plunging into the surface of a nearby backwater river pool. If he abandoned logical reality and believed the story behind the streaking tears, choked words, and pregnant pauses, Sonja Maria, a hard-featured woman who'd celebrated her thirty-fifth birthday the previous month, had been overpowered and/or drugged by an unknown attacker and raped at St. Mary's, a local college populated by scores of comely co-eds.

While it was true he strove day and night to keep his town, his high school daughter, and his arthritis-disabled wife safe, he had no qualms to shun fakers or bend a legal rule or two. He dismissed each transgression as a necessity to remove another scumbag from Bridgetown streets and to earn his longed for gold shield.

He finally said to Sonja Maria he needed to go and would

call her if additional info were needed. Sonja's eyes, obscured by a new moisture drizzle, stared at him across the diamond-pattern of threadbare carpet and pleaded that he believe her and shelve all doubt.

If, gold shield or not, he forgot the jailing-the-bad-guys end result, did swearing to uphold the law and serve the public justify emotionally trampling a reeling, weakened fellow human being? His eyes scanned the shabby brown-fabric sofa that almost swallowed Sonja Maria whole, the faded emerald green living room wall paint, the hung picture of Jesus, and that face, hers, smiling at him from a family eight-by-ten photo enlargement set on an end table beneath the lampshade's tattered fringe. This apartment in which he sat, like her, without excess adornment and scrubbed clean. Especially prominent were the back of her hands—purplish, popping veins from calloused fingers that dived to be submerged and invisible under wrist skin en route to a heart in a small muscular body. Five-foot-two, he estimated, tipping scales between ninety and one hundred pounds. Straight, neck-length black hair framed unmoving dark eyes, surrounded by a caramel complexion.

"When were you grabbed?" He angled forward. His interrogation tape recorder pointed at them from atop a stack of People magazines on the glass-topped coffee table. He stopped short of asking her not to drink for that would've been heartless. By the observed halting sips, he fathomed that alcohol had never been Sonja Maria's painkiller; especially the straight undiluted 1800 Tequila she poured into a scratched, clear plastic tumbler.

"Don't want to feel bad again. Dishonor beloved husband Philippe."

"Need you to explain everything to have any chance of putting this guy behind bars where he belongs." *If the scumbag exists?* "Tell me again. Yesterday, where were you?"

With a head bowed, her eyes gazed into a vacant lap. "Third floor janitor closet."

"That's your job. Cleaning, right?" Adolph re-opened his notepad.

"Si."

"You working?" Adolph tried to distill his questions for he lacked strong Spanish skills.

She waggled her head sideways. "On break, spit out tequila when see bottle worm."

He'd misjudged her capacity for alcohol. "Go on."

"Not wanna be sent back to Guatemala."

Adolph envisioned a defense attorney's field day. Assault cases were hard enough to win, even with a stellar witness. Prosecution attorneys ran the opposite direction on learning alcohol clouded a complainant's judgment and memory. "And, then?" At this rate he'd never finish. Bridgetown's St. Mary's College hired mostly Hispanic janitorial/cleaning staff, forged immigration papers common. He always looked the other way if the illegal didn't evidence gang affiliation and Sonja Maria lacked visible tattoos.

"No hear. Lift head from sink; bag cover face. Can't see."

He remained silent. She raised her head to stare, this time above and beyond his right ear.

"Voice say be quiet. Say police outside."

"Man, woman?"

"Man. He say don't try escape. Squeeze my arms. March me into another room. Feel cold on left ankle. Heard noise, what be English word . . . clinking."

"Any other noises?"

"Un poco pop. Man jerks my head; hand press bag to face and my tongue feels hole. Sweet cola drops wet my tongue. He tell me 'drink,' and cola fills my mouth. Something, I don't know, move along my right arm to back of hand."

"How'd you know it was cola you drank?"

"Fizz makes me almost spit it out. Hand, not mine, cover my mouth. He tell me 'swallow, stand still, drink more.'"

Pad full, Adolph quit scribbling notes. When, not if, she jumbled her story, the tape would be more reliable than his notes. "How long you stand there?"

"Think long time. Piano play. Not Latin. Danced salsa before married. Hear students play music late at night, what they call classical. Don't know. Wild thoughts go through my brain. Me have to do work. Not get fired."

"In the room, what else did you hear?"

"Not hear nothing until tap, tap on car window."

Adolph didn't think he'd heard right. "You were in a car?"

"Si. Man with badge tell me I can't park in Music Department faculty lot. Move pronto. My head aches. Clothes torn. Naked below dress." Her veined hand briefly covered her mouth. "Sun makes me close eyes." Sonja Maria bent forward to lower her left ankle's white sock.

Adolph observed the inch and half wide red mark with faint bluish edge tint that circled her ankle. He passed on further documenting any higher injuries. "You make security report?"

"No. Have to get home to make breakfast. Philippe shout at me saying he be late to drive truck at six. Rosano cry when Philippe slam door. She and Joshua still in their beds."

Above the clanging living room window air conditioner, Adolph thought he heard a small boy in the next room. "Are they your children?"

"Si. Rosano's thirteen. She's at school. Joshua, five, is in my bedroom."

"At St. Mary's, how'd you get from your building work area to your car?"

"Not know." Fresh tears slid onto and moistened both cheeks.

Adolph handed her a folded white handkerchief; he shook his head no when, after use, she extended the floppy cloth forward to offer it back to him. "If you remember the trip to the car or anything else, please call me." He handed Sonja Maria his card, pocketed the tape recorder, and offered a quick good-bye.

Stepping into the mid-morning sunlight, he strode to his Monte Carlo. Road dust dulled its bright yellow color but not the sparkling broken glass sprinkled onto the narrow strip of boulevard grass outside 409 Tinley Street. The unseasonable heat and humidity perspired Adolph's wiped forehead. His investigative experience convinced him that, if distraught women remembered anything at all, the narrative would be distorted by memory trauma half-truths and the forced sobs a ruse to disguise lies. Adolph deplored the thirty-five minutes wasted with Sonja Maria. He reached for his handkerchief, only to remember its loan to Sonja Maria.

A bright graffiti gang tag sprayed on the apartment building's brick wall visually announced that the Dragons street gang claimed this turf. Eighteen years ago, he, as a rookie police officer, walked this Bridgetown neighborhood beat and residents were safe and the building wall brick crevices, not filled by canned spray paint, collected wind-blown dust to be displayed as rain-streaked dirt. He wouldn't apologize one iota for his hardnosed, boot-to-the-throat tactics that propelled his promotion to sergeant, then detective.

Years ago, Sonja Maria's Tinley apartment building, framed in his rearview mirror, was known for marijuana dealers. Judging by the latest reports, cocaine was now the drug of choice. He suspected she had little economic choice. And, while she could've just as easily have been attacked in her small two-bedroom apartment by outsiders or forced to submit to an angry drunk husband, that would've meant there'd be no professor, no college, or no trustees to sue.

(End of Excerpt)

Read Adolph's full story in "Adolph's Gold." From DOTDON Books at your book retailer.

About the Author

Donan Berg believes that imagination, personal or shared, accents positive desires and fulfilled dreams living in all of us.

His life's journey has been as a journalist, corporate executive and lawyer. A native of Ireland, he now endures Midwest winters in America's heartland. A U.S. Army veteran, his military experience and civilian travels have never involved driving an eighteen-wheeler or a stagecoach.

He'll never volunteer he danced a hole in a ballroom dancing shoe sole or that he owns four other pairs.